Limbo

Andy Secombe acquired his love of fantasy at an early age, but he had to overcome a natural talent for prevarication, and an acting bug that lasted thirty years (including appearances in two of the Star Wars films) before he was able to settle down to the writing of this, his first novel. He now lives with his wife, two sons and five chickens (at the last count) on a farm in rural Devon.

Andy Secombe

Limbo

TOR

First published 2003 by Tor
an imprint of Pan Macmillan Ltd
Pan Macmillan, 20 New Wharf Road, London N1 9RR
Basingstoke and Oxford
Associated companies throughout the world
www.panmacmillan.com

ISBN 1 405 00484 3

3 5 7 9 8 6 4 2

A CIP catalogue record for this book is available from
the British Library.

Typeset by Intype London Ltd.
Printed and bound in Great Britain by
Mackays of Chatham plc, Chatham, Kent

To Caroline

Acknowledgements

I'd like to thank Robert Kirby for saving my life and then giving me lunch; everyone at Macmillan, especially Peter Lavery, for his great enthusiasm and support; and the greatly missed H. S., for teaching me to read in the first place.

I'd also like to thank my wife, Caroline, for her selfless support, unfailing insight and great beauty, and not least for looking after the boys and allowing me to escape upstairs.

And my two sons: Matthew, for his insistence on excellence in all things; and Charles, for his fairy kisses.

The Great Golden Hoop of Eternity hung in the darkness, spinning silently. The impassive river of destiny flowed forever on, forever moving, forever staying the same, and all the while the glittering, laughing strand of fantasy danced and weaved playfully around it . . .

Part I

Chapter 1

The castle lookout heard the pounding of the horse's hooves long before he saw it. Indeed, normally there would have been nothing to see. The land of Limbo had been in darkness for over a thousand years, so why the lookout was posted at all was a mystery that, through the long, dark hours, kept the soldier chosen for this thankless task preoccupied. It was about the only thing that kept him awake – apart from the desperate need he felt to be useful. He couldn't allow himself to think that he had no real purpose, that would have been too depressing. Life was bad enough already in this endless night.

He listened as the distant thumping of the hooves grew closer. He'd years ago ceased to strain his eyes into the distance, only to have them met by blackness on all sides. These days he used his ears. 'Now shush,' he said to himself, 'listen. From which direction does the horse come?' He turned until he faced the approaching sound. Feeling for the incised figure cut into the stones of his cramped and lonely turret, he traced the letter E with his fingers. 'East,' he said. 'The rider comes from the east.' There was something in the phrase so familiar that it took him a moment to realize what he'd just said; like the name of a lover uttered so often one is no longer aware of its beauty. Then he gasped and looked up. Using his eyes for the first time in twenty years, he peered towards the horizon. The sun was rising, there was no mistaking it. Thin fingers of light were reaching across the sky, pushing aside the everlasting gloom.

'The Prophecy,' he whispered. 'And I'm the first one to see it . . .'

Looking out over a landscape previously only imagined, there in the distance, beyond the dead, grey forest, whose branches reached skywards like the arms of drowning men, he could see a dot on the horizon trailing a great cloud of dust. The lookout held his breath and wiped a tear from his eye. That he should witness this moment, it was almost too much to bear. The speeding animal grew ever larger as it raced towards Castle Limbo. Closer and closer it came, the thunder of its hooves echoing off the grey, mildewed battlements of the huge, misshapen edifice. Now he could make out the figure of a man, swathed in black, astride a white horse. Its mane, backlit by the rising sun, was streaked with red, as if on fire. *"The rider comes from the east . . ."* He searched his memory for the exact words. *'"The rider comes from the east – a dark man on a white horse, its mane on fire . . ."* The Prophecy. The Prophecy!' he yelled over the rooftops.

The lookout ran in trembling haste down the spiral staircase from his turret, the soft leather soles of his boots slipping on the well-worn stones and nearly sending him flying. 'The Prophecy!' he shouted as he raced across the castle courtyard. 'The Prophecy!'

One of the windows in the otherwise blank wall of the castle was thrown open. 'What's all the bleedin' noise?'

The lookout stopped and looked up. 'He's coming! The Rider! He's coming! It's happening – the sun is rising!' he said, jumping up and down on the cobblestones. 'Wake your children. There ought to be children at a time like this – and a great rejoicing! Wake up!' he sang, banging on the great doors of the keep. 'It's over! The night is over! The Dawn has come!'

By the time the strange rider and his horse clattered into the courtyard through the great castle arch, the palace guard and the entire household staff, some still in their sleeping attire, had assembled to greet him. Throwing back his cowl and shaking the dust out of his black locks, he looked down his long, aristocratic nose at the assembled throng, his dark eyes blazing with portent. 'Hail to the dawn! I come to see the King!' he intoned, and was startled to find the entire company joining in with his every word, like a Greek chorus.

Limbo

They carried him off his horse and into the dark, damp fortress of Castle Limbo as someone in an over-optimistically high tenor launched into the first verse of 'There Will a Rider Come!' The moment the small, rotund singer had opened his mouth he'd realized his mistake, but he was committed now – there was no going back. He gritted his teeth and went for it – his high, strangled tones bouncing off the walls of the keep and echoing down the long, winding corridors of the ancient castle.

Castle Limbo was old and rather sad and had been the home of the Royal House of Yardley for as long as anyone could remember. A great many additions had been made over the centuries – turrets, wings, flying buttresses – and all at strange angles and different heights because of the simple fact that they had been built in the dark. Only with the coming of daylight could the full extent of the castle's architectural incoherence be appreciated.

What made the castle all the more confusing was that it seemed to have a mind of its own. Stairs would suddenly appear where before there had been none; doors that had once led somewhere would open onto solid brick; corridors that for years had stayed comfortingly level would of a sudden slope precipitously down-wards, sending any that were not familiar with the castle's ways to certain death. There was even rumoured to be a banqueting hall, complete with chef, maître d'hôtel and an army of servants, that hadn't been seen since the fifth dynasty. But most puzzling of all was the room, perpetually illuminated, high up in the west wing, which could not be reached by any known means. So brightly and so steadily shone its light through the never-ending gloom of Limbo's night, that travellers used it as a beacon.

There was a legend that, during the building of the west wing, one unfortunate stonemason had bricked himself in, and it was his torch, still burning after all these years, that lit this strange and inaccessible room.

The Rider was carried down the damp, green corridors of the castle, the way ahead lit by foul-smelling torches belching soot.

'. . . *And with him will come not sa-ah-ah-ad-ness!*

'*But joy and a very nice time!*'

The tenor shrieked on, his voice cracking on the top F of '*-ness*' and forcing him to drop an octave for the last line, which he thought rather spoilt the effect. But nobody seemed to mind, and the company cheered with gusto as they lowered the Rider onto the slimy floor at the very entrance to the King's bedchamber.

The King had endured a troubled night. For some time now he'd been having a recurring dream about a man called Beasely who boarded a great and strange, red and white machine at a place called Hove. The man enquired of the pilot, sitting high up behind a huge wheel, whether he went to a place called St James's. Then the man called Beasely broke out in a cold sweat, as the ground seemed to dissolve beneath his feet. The King could feel his panic and always awoke at that point with a start. What did it mean?

Rheumy-eyed and dry-mouthed, the King sat up in the vast, curtained four-poster bed, set at one end of the huge room, and looked at his alarm clock, ticking on the bedside table. It was a gift from the Wizard after one of his 'trips'. The King had never actually seen the point of owning a clock – after all, night was night, whichever way you looked at it – but he kept it to please his Wizard, and he had to admit, he did find its ticking immensely comforting.

The King yawned and scratched his sunken cheeks, smoothing the tangles out of his snow-white beard, and wondering whether or not he should get up. He hadn't risen for a decade now and saw no reason why today should be any different, but he had to address the question all the same. After all, he was the King, such issues had to be pondered, weighed, and once a conclusion had been drawn, such conclusion acted upon.

He went through all the usual procedures – asking himself how he was; how he had slept; and did he need to go to the little boy's room? He had already decided that the answer to each enquiry was no, but thought he'd better seek a second opinion – what's the point in having an advisor if you never use him? 'Smeil!' he said, kicking the diminutive, mouse-haired figure that lay across the foot of the bed.

The small man was instantly awake. 'Sire?' he said, blinking his big, owl-like eyes.

'Should we rise?' enquired his lord.

It was the same question. Every morning for the last ten years he'd asked him the same question. 'Rise?' replied the tiny advisor, pushing back the hair that fringed his face like the curtains of a theatre. 'Is your majesty feeling unwell?'

'No, right as rain.'

'Does your majesty have need of the usual offices?'

'No. Pissed out of the window about an hour ago. At least I think it was the window, you can never tell in this bloody castle.'

Smeil wished his lord and master had a little more finesse. He was, after all, supposed to set an example to his people. One good thing about the darkness was that at least nobody would have been able to witness his habitual and very public nocturnal micturition. 'And how did your majesty sleep?'

'Like a log – woke up in the fireplace!' The King dissolved in a fit of giggles.

Like the initial question, Smeil had endured the same joke for a decade.

'In view of that fact, my lord, why should you rise?'

'Quite right, just what I was thinking myself.' The King was just about to pull the sheets back over his head when he heard a strange sound: a sound he hadn't heard since his youth. Somebody was singing. He remembered his nurse. Whatever had happened to Nursey? He closed his eyes and once again he was tucked up on her soft, expansive bosom, wrapped in clean, sweet-smelling sheets, as she rocked and soothed him to sleep with a gentle lullaby.

The tenor's strangled and broken high F on '... *sadness!*' brought the King, wincing, back to the present. Joyous shouts and cheers were now echoing down the dark and winding corridors of Castle Limbo.

The Rider knocked at the massive door. 'Sire! I bring good news!' he exclaimed, and much to his chagrin, the chorus at his back joined in.

'Sire,' said Smeil, his large eyes ablaze with destiny's reflected fire, 'your presence is requested.'

The King, sitting up in bed, listened to the din at the door with a sinking heart. He knew the phrase well; had known it from childhood, and had sincerely hoped never to hear it in his lifetime. 'The Prophecy!' he whispered, and gathered the bedclothes around him. A low, piteous moan escaped his lips. 'Oh no!' He groaned. 'Why me? Couldn't the fates have waited a little longer? Surely they can see I'm not up to this? Nursey, Nursey where are you when I need you?' He got up unsteadily, and massaging the blood back into his withered legs, slowly paced the room while in his mind's eye he watched the whole terrible chain of events unfold. He had a pretty good idea of what was to come. His future had been foretold, albeit cryptically, in The Prophecy, and it seemed there was no escaping his fate. How well he remembered his lessons in the dampness of the castle cellar. There he had spent many a grey hour, getting splinters in his knees from his old wooden desk, trying desperately to stay awake while the Wizard paced the room reciting the mysterious phrases of the Forbidden Codex over and over again.

The heir to the throne of Limbo was often brought back from the edge of sleep by the Wizard's cane slamming onto his desk. 'Highness!' the Wizard would shout. 'Complete the following sentence: *"Black crow on black beast ..."*'

'Er ... er ...' The young prince would search his sleep-fuddled mind in desperation. 'Brings joy for almost everyone?'

'No, boy! If you think I am here for the benefit of my health you are sadly mistaken. I am here to teach, you are here to learn –

and learn you will, if we have to stay here all day. Remember, forewarned is forearmed. Now, from the beginning, once again ...'

The King shivered at the memory. 'Smeil – throw another brick on the fire, and help me on with my robe.' The mousy little man picked up a peat brick almost as big as his head, and chucked it onto the endlessly burning fire in the great open fireplace. The King watched as small tongues of blue flame began to lick around the dried fuel brick, and for a second he considered following it onto the glowing embers, but cowardice and a very low pain threshold put the thought quickly out of his mind.

Smeil ran to the wardrobe and pulled out the King's robe. Grunting with the effort, he draped the heavy, maroon velvet cloak around his master's stooped and narrow shoulders. The King sank even lower under its weight. Then, smoothing back his long, yellow-streaked hair, the King bowed low to let Smeil place the Limbo crown on his head.

Smeil stood back to admire the effect. 'Sire, you look so ... kingly,' the little man beamed, his eyes brimming.

'Hunh,' the King grunted. 'Oh well, there's no sense in putting off the inevitable. Open the door, Smeil.' He certainly didn't feel like one, but reasoned that if he couldn't be the genuine thing, he would at least try to look like a king. He drew himself up to his full height and took a deep breath. His intention had been to intone 'Enter!' in a booming, kingly fashion. Unfortunately, the fresh peat brick on the fire was throwing up thick clouds of acrid smoke, which caught in his throat and started a violent coughing fit. When the Rider and chorus burst into the room, they found their King doubled up on the floor, hacking his guts up.

Smeil and sundry attendants gently helped the King to his feet and walked him to the edge of the bed, where he perched, his crown half over his eyes and his white beard glistening with gobs of oozing, black phlegm. Recovering his composure, and after a cautious and rasping in-breath, he whispered to the Rider, 'Speak your news!'

' ... *your news*!' The crowd whispered with him.

'Sire, the sun rises!'

' . . . *sun rises!*'

'The sky to the east is aflame,' the man continued, 'and soon the creeping fingers of dawn will reach into your kingdom and banish the gloom!'

' . . . *banish the gloom!*' went the echo.

'The Prophecy,' breathed the King.

'*The Prophecy*,' breathed the crowd.

'Aye sir . . .' the Rider began.

'*Aye sir . . .*' went the echo.

The Rider turned angrily on the crowd gathered eagerly around him. 'Do you mind!' he barked. There were a few raised eyebrows and pursed lips, but not another word did they utter. The Rider continued, 'It is The Prophecy.'

'From which direction do you ride, sir?' enquired the King.

'The east, sire.'

'On a white charger?'

'The same, sire.'

'The Prophecy, there can be no doubt,' said the King sadly.

'And the Queen, sire?'

'With child, sir. With child, as it is written.'

The King couldn't actually remember the last time he'd slept with the Queen. He'd taken to his bed ten years ago and in all that time didn't recall any conjugal visits from her. Indeed he had no recollection of her visiting him at all. But that didn't mean that she hadn't, even though he remembered all the other details of his too-long life with aching clarity. He was the King and she was the Queen, and if she was pregnant, then it must be his child; the King's rigid grasp of logic admitted no other possibility. 'You must bathe, sir, then join us to break your fast.'

'As it is written.'

The tenor couldn't resist. 'Alleluia!' he piped.

The Rider narrowed his eyes and peered menacingly at him.

The tenor looked up and smiled. His small, strangled 'Sorry' was pitched somewhere near top B♭.

*

The Prophecy of which they spoke was contained in a book called 'The Book'. No one knew who wrote it or whence it came. It was found accidentally, many years ago by a young girl called Alcahoona while she was busy collecting blind shrimp from Castle Creek – a deep, dank pool under the waterfall that flowed out of the rock beneath the huge bulk of the castle. The story goes that in the dark, with her skirts full of wriggling shrimp, she had tripped over something. Cursing whatever it was that had caused her to lose her whole evening's catch, she had picked up a rock and hurled it to the ground. Hearing the sound of shattering pottery, she had investigated on her hands and knees. When her fingers touched what could only have been a broken terracotta jar, she had thrust her hand into it and felt a large number of tightly bound papyrus leaves. Filling her skirts with the leaves, she took them home to examine them by torchlight.

Carefully unwrapping one, she discovered that it was covered with strange markings. Being illiterate, she could have no idea that these markings were writing. Neither could she have guessed at the importance of her find. At least half of the contents of the broken jar, or the 'incomplete Codex 47', as it came to be known, fuelled her family's cooking stove for several weeks. If it hadn't been for the death of her father, the discovery might never have come to light.

He was on his way home from the local tavern when he had fallen into a cesspit. He knew the way home like the back of his hand – he'd done it often enough in the pitch darkness – but Limbo was like that. Things would suddenly appear or disappear at random. It was as if the land got bored with lying so long in the same place and decided to up and change itself. It was fairly common for husbands or wives to come home to what they thought was their house, only to wake up later to find they'd slept in someone else's bed. Sometimes the mistake wasn't realized for years; though sometimes it was, with all parties tacitly agreeing that things were perhaps better this way. Limbo ebbed and flowed like the sea. Sometimes great chunks of the countryside would go missing, then, some time later, reappear miles away.

There was a legend that the Great Dragon of Phnell –

'*Worm, worm, worm, sleeping in the mud,*
Coals she has for eyes and black oil for blood . . .'

– as the nursery rhyme went, was flying around in the dark, spitting fire and terrorizing simple village folk, when she'd flown into the side of Castle Limbo, knocking herself cold. While she'd lain there unconscious, the land had moved and covered her like a duvet, and she'd been there ever since. Most of the time she slumbered peacefully and, if you listened carefully, from time to time you could hear the Great Dragon grinding her teeth in her sleep. But occasionally she would wake and try to break free of her tomb, and the land would move and split and great plumes of fire would rise from the earth. Children who made too much noise were warned that if they didn't pipe down they would rouse the dragon, with dire consequences.

But back to Alcahoona's unfortunate, half-drowned father. The terrified yells of the poor man as he thrashed about, out of his depth in excrement, brought his family running. As they crowded helplessly around the lip of the foetid hole, their shouts attracted the attention of Dr Ohthyrhis Perch MD – humanitarian, philanthropist and also, by happy chance, scholar of ancient languages. Dr Perch was feeling rather pleased with himself. He was on his way back from the annual Limbo Gyratory Club dinner where he had delivered a speech on the ancient peoples of the Salient shoreline. His theories about their evolution and migratory patterns had been extraordinarily well received, and his joke about the mating habits of the giant clam had gone down particularly well. He was still basking in the warmth of the applause – and several large glasses of fine old Tawny – when he heard the clamour round the pit.

Approaching the hole and enquiring if he could be of assistance, he called for a torch. Alcahoona thrust a bundle of flaming papyrus into his hand, and he was about to peer down into the foul-smelling depths of the stinking pit when something caught his eye. There, on the papyrus, was a fragment of a sentence:

'*... shall land and bow the knee,*
On cobbles hard at Brighthelm by the Sea ...'

It was written in an ancient script: Franklin Gothic Lucida 2. Having only recently been decoded, very few people – of whom the doctor was one – could read it. The only other previously known example of this language had been found in a cave halfway up the cliff that rose sheer out of the dark and forbidding Salient Sea, and seemed to be a recipe for fruit scones. Immediately the doctor dropped the makeshift torch and stamped the flames out. Asking the girl where she had found it, he demanded to be taken to her house immediately to view the remaining bundles of her 'fuel'.

'What about my father?' Alcahoona had asked as he'd led her away.

'Throw a rope down to him and drag him out,' the doctor had instructed the rest of the family gathered around the hole. Without the guidance of the doctor, those simple people, untutored in the behaviour of inflammable, heavier-than-air gases in confined spaces, lowered a rope down to the drowning man and, so that he'd be able to see it, tied the end around a bundle of flaming birch twigs. When the bundle reached the blanket of methane floating above the surface of the liquid contents of the cesspit, it ignited. The *Whump!* was heard twenty miles away, and a tongue of flame half a mile high leaped into the night sky. All over the land, people thought the Great Dragon of Phnell had awoken. Alcahoona's father was burned to a crisp in the explosion.

Only when all the remaining terracotta vessels were opened and the texts therein deciphered and transcribed was it clear what an immense and important work had been discovered. It ran to forty-seven volumes of fifteen books each (apart, of course, from the last volume, transcribed from the incomplete Codex 47, which ran to only seven and a half books and a few loose leaves) and covered a vast amount of time, from just before the beginning of the dark age right up to the present day, and beyond. Strictly speaking the whole book was one long prophecy, and because, by the time it had been discovered, most of what was in it was verifiable history, its authority as an almanac of prediction was never in any doubt.

Written in a variety of styles, from blank verse to deathless prose, as a work of literature it left a lot to be desired. But its literary merit was not its main attraction. What excited scholars and laymen alike was the fact that the extant fragments of the last book of the last volume foretold the future. This was the book that came to be known as 'The Prophecy'. In it are many strange and wonderful predictions. Opening with the phrase *'What will be will be'*, the first chapter goes on to describe Alcahoona's discovery, the death of her father, and the publication of the first edition of 'The Book', embossed and leather-bound. It then goes on to catalogue a series of events, culminating in the coming of the dark rider foretelling the dawn: *'The rider comes from the east, a dark man on a white horse, its mane on fire...'* The next chapter continues with a detailed account of the rider's meeting with the King, which every schoolchild in Limbo was made to learn by heart. Then follows the account of the birth of a prince:

'... and at that time, from his mother's womb,
A child shall spring; a light, the one whom
Every daughter and every son shall call The One,
That brings from high great joy and eke great happiness for almost everyone!'

Here though, there is a gap, since only fragments remained of the papyrus bundles that fuelled Alcahoona's family's bread oven. The work of piecing together the half-charred scrolls had been immensely difficult, and the resulting text was open to various interpretations. This had caused great conflict, splitting the community into two camps: the *Substantialists* and the *Conceptualists*, who had even gone to war over the meaning of such verses as:

> *'A fishy smell inside a shell*
> *Doth rain on man and beast as well.*
> *Look up, look right up in ye sky,*
> *Not a cloud will you espy.'*

The Substantialists said that it meant exactly what it said – a fall of shellfish out of a clear blue sky. But the Conceptualists believed that it was an oblique reference to a time of plenty, with abundance flowing from the skies. Another prediction which divided opinion went:

> *'By [?]umbles man will realize his destiny,*
> *Inside the door he'll find eternity.'*

The first letter of the second word of this couplet was indistinct and was to prove yet another bone of contention between Conceptualists and Substantialists. The Substantialists believed it referred to somebody's house – a Mr or Mrs Bumble – wherein one may find eternity, or death. They took this to be a reference to a funeral parlour. The Conceptualists, on the other hand, believed the disputed word was 'humbles', and interpreted the phrase as an instruction to find oneself through humility.

Other phrases, though not as contentious, were frankly puzzling:

> *'The wages of sin is not as much as it used to be.'*

> *'. . . and the number of the . . . [missing] . . . is 176.'*

> *'The skirted ones shall land and bow the knee,*
> *On cobbles hard at Brighthelm by the Sea . . .'*

> *'The wise one will lose his heart and home . . .*
> *. . . [illegible] . . . foreign shores but not alone . . .'*

But there could be no mistaking the underlying message of other fragments:

'Black crow on black beast rides unhindered through castle gate.
Darkness and death is Yardley's fate . . .'

' . . . four hands grasp the sword as the point is driven home.
The King meets his maker unshriven, alone.'

'The land will run with rivulets of blood,
Children will lose mothers, fathers, all.
Upon the King the slaughter and the blame thereof will fall,
While innocence lies broken in the mud.'

'The earth will shake before the Dawn,
The herald of a dreadful doom . . .'

'The monster with two heads will rise,
Dawn awakens old blood ties,
He alone can cut him down to size.'

'Behold four horsemen in a blink,
One black, one white, one pale, one pink,
And Hell and darkness follow in their stink . . .'

'The end, the end of everything you see:
Life, Happiness, Destiny,
Suns and moons and galaxies.
The end of Time; end of Hope.
Silence and darkness. Silence and darkness.
Nothing, nothing, nothing . . .'

Scholars had concluded, from the complete disintegration of the
rhyme scheme, the dating of the ink, and the fact that it was
followed by the phrase 'THE END' that this was the last stanza in
the book. Beneath this, someone had scrawled in a desperate hand:

'Well, thank goodness that's over.'

It was these phrases and others like them which formed the so-called 'Forbidden Codex', a collation of verses thought 'too downbeat' for public consumption and so left out of subsequent publications of The Book, lest they have a negative impact on sales. Only certain scholars, most of them now dead, and members of the royal family knew about the 'FC', and it was the contents of this dreadful book that made the King less than eager to join in the general celebrations. One of these verses ran:

'*Happy sovereign, gladsome be,*
A son is born, be ay merry.
Yet should the child reach one year old,
Then king, take heed of what's foretold:
Darkness, despair and death I see,
Secession, accession and rivalry.
But foolish king, let be, let be.
You cannot flout your destiny.'

This faced the King with a terrible dilemma. The obvious solution was to kill the Prince before his first birthday. But to kill his infant son to spare his own life? Then there was that phrase, '*you cannot flout your destiny.*' He was trapped, and it seemed that whatever he did he could not escape his fate.

Of course, everybody knew the bit about the dawn coming and everyone having a nice time, but the general population were as ignorant of the dark message of the Forbidden Codex as they were about sunscreen. Not so the King, who had studied every word of every last remnant, and knew every depressing phrase by heart.

As the King rose sadly to see the Rider out, down through the winding corridors of Castle Limbo echoed the cry of a newborn baby. The nightmare had begun.

Chapter 2

The rage from the exhausts of the twin-pot Harley careened off the houses of the narrow street and echoed down the hill. The distancing effect of Malcom's open-faced helmet stripped the gut-churning roar of its naked aggression, so it reached his ears as a comforting low rumble. It made him feel a lot better.

That morning he'd woken from a horrible dream: he was being carried aloft through the corridors of a rancid old castle, with someone singing loudly in his left ear. Outside a big wooden door, he had been lowered to the ground. But as he touched the floor, he slipped. Scrambling to his feet, he noticed in the dim light that his hands were covered with blood, and as the door creaked open he could see a man being disembowelled by a hideous creature. He shuddered at the memory of it and blipped the throttle. The answering roar of the engine was soothing balm to his troubled mind.

Reaching the bottom of the hill, Malcom paused. From a distance he looked like an American motorcycle cop. He wore a buff-coloured shirt stretched taut across his big belly, and American police-issue motorcycle pants, which were tucked neatly into high, glossy-black boots. But closer inspection would have revealed that at least two things were wrong here. One being the 'Millwall' tattoo on his left forearm, and the other that this was Brighton.

Malcom looked left and right with his small, deep-set eyes, and with one stubby finger pushed the American police-issue Ray-Bans back up the bridge of his nose. His over-large nostrils, set between the pink, fleshy mounds of his cheeks, twitched as he sniffed the morning air. Nobody about. He loved this time, with the sun barely risen in the sky and just his Harley and the empty road for company. He wasn't due at the station for another three-quarters of an hour, so he could enjoy himself. Anyway, he had to do something to dispel the memory of that horrible dream.

Snicking the big Harley into gear, he turned left towards the sea. Reaching Marine Parade, he turned right and headed west. Steppenwolf's 'Born to be Wild' ran through his head and he smiled. In his mind's eye it wasn't Hove he was heading for, but Malibu – up the Pacific Coast Highway from Santa Monica, with the great wide Pacific to his left. He screwed open the throttle, and by the time he reached The Grand Hotel he was doing ninety. The obscene blare of the exhausts shattered the early-morning calm and caused at least one ancient resident to suffer a heart attack, believing it to be the Luftwaffe thundering back for a rematch.

Slowing as he approached the Hove Street traffic lights, Malcom saw an old but immaculately kept blue Rover turn out of the King Alfred car park. The Rover passed him, heading back towards Brighton. Years of experience told Malcom something. 'He's speeding,' he said to himself. Slipping down a gear, he wheeled the Harley round in a wide circle and set off in pursuit.

He trailed the Rover for about half a mile. His instinct was right; the car was doing thirty-five miles an hour in a thirty-mile-an-hour zone. When the car stopped at the Grand Avenue traffic lights, Malcom threw the bike across its path and killed the engine. The driver of the car, Councillor Michael Daniels, the sixty-six-year-old president of the Brighton and Hove Bowls Association, with a previously unblemished licence, watched in amazement as Malcom slowly removed his gloves and, heaving his bulk out of the saddle, strode casually towards him. Malcom opened his warrant card and held it flat against the windscreen, like he'd seen Karl Malden do in *The Streets of San Francisco* on Sky Television.

'Is this your car, sir?' Malcom enquired.

'Yes, is something wrong?'

'Yes sir, something is very wrong. Can I see your driver's

documents please?' Much to Malcom's chagrin, the relevant pieces of paper were duly produced. 'Dear oh dear, Mr Daniels,' said Malcom as he scrutinized the man's licence. 'We've been a bit of a naughty pensioner haven't we?' The uniform may well have been *Electroglide in Blue*, but the language was straight out of *The Sweeney*.

'Now then,' Malcom continued, 'I know it's easy to get confused at your age, but can you tell me the speed limit along this stretch of road? Don't strain yourself.'

Councillor Daniels was a contending mixture of anger and apprehension. He was not used to being spoken to in this fashion, but this man was a policeman, a guardian of the law, and as such required respect from every right-minded citizen, even if he was in fancy dress. 'Er . . . thirty, I believe,' he replied.

'Correct! You're doing well. Have a look at the next question – you don't have to answer it, but you might as well have a go. Remember you've still got "50-50" and "phone a friend". What speed were you doing? Take your time now.'

'Thirty?' Councillor Daniels replied hopefully.

'Final answer?'

Councillor Daniels nodded. Malcom looked at him inscrutably, his head to one side. Suddenly he blurted out, 'You've just won yourself a speeding ticket! Aw, now if you'd said thirty-five' – he paused – 'I would still have given you a ticket!' He thrust the ticket in Daniels's face and saluted. 'Have a nice day now.'

Whistling, Malcom sauntered back to the Harley, fired it up and blasted away.

Once the red rage had subsided and his palpitations evened out into something resembling a regular heartbeat, Councillor Daniels looked at the crumpled piece of paper in his fist. 'DI Collins,' he muttered between clenched teeth, deciphering the barely legible scrawl across the bottom of the ticket, 'you've just made a big mistake. You picked the wrong pensioner, and he's going to have your balls for bowls practice.' Pulling out his mobile phone, he keyed in a number. 'Hello? Can I speak to Superintendent Gerrold, please?'

Chapter 3

Limbo was flourishing. The fields, which had so long been dark and barren, now sprang into verdant riot. Animals that had spent their lives cooped up in cramped winter quarters roamed the strange new land and feasted on the lush grazing. People went about their business singing, and their usual greeting, 'All hail the dawn!' was uttered with renewed vigour. A new spirit was abroad: alongside the green shoots that pushed their way out of the earth sprang hope. The darkness was gone, the long night banished.

The King felt feverish. What was it that Nursey used to give him as a boy when he had the collywobbles? It was soothing and sweet, and he badly needed a draught of it now. What had he been thinking? He knew that this moment was going to arrive sooner or later, so why hadn't he prepared for it? But what could he have done? 'O foolish King, let be, let be. You cannot flout your destiny.' There it was, the simultaneous cause of his greatest anxiety and his excuse to do absolutely nothing.

He had hoped, oh how he'd hoped that The Prophecy would fall on some other, far distant sovereign's head. But in his heart of hearts, he knew – had always known – that he was the chosen one.

He shook his head and paced the carpet. 'If I should kill the child, then there is a fair chance that I shall live, remain King, and things will carry on as before. If I don't, then there is every possibility I shall be deposed and suffer a very painful death. But kill my own child? What sort of a monster would that make me?'

'An infanticide, sire,' said his Wizard appearing at his elbow. The King leapt several feet off the floor.

'I wish you wouldn't keep doing that!' The Wizard had a habit of turning up unannounced, and usually inside locked rooms. The King had long lost his curiosity as to how he managed it, and he probably wouldn't have understood the explanation anyway. 'So, what do I do, O wise one?'

The Wizard, tall and elegant, with fine pointed features, stroked his immaculately trimmed black beard and, staring off into the middle distance, lowered his lanky frame slowly to the floor, his long robe spread out in a circle around him. He always did this when pondering a particularly difficult question and sometimes remained thus for several days. People would often come to him asking for his advice, wanting to know, for instance, if their spouse was cheating on them, or the possible outcome of a chancy business opportunity. They assumed that during these trances he left his body and travelled to the nether realms, seeking advice from the ancient ones. But in reality, the Wizard had learned the marginally more mundane trick of projecting his mind above the endless ribbon of time, to squint at the distant and hazy images of the future. This usually took but a few minutes – he only adopted his 'trance' pose for effect.

'The future is now,' he would say whenever the outlook was grim. 'What we sow today, tomorrow we will reap. The moving finger has writ – and that's it,' he would add with sad eyes, leaving the expectant seeker none the wiser.

'He's off again,' said the King, raising his eyes to heaven. This time the Wizard didn't need to ponder long, he already knew the answer. But of course, he couldn't let on to the King that his fate was already sealed.

'Let's just wait and see,' said the Wizard.

'Wait and see? Wait and see what?' said the King. 'Wait and see the colour of my insides? Because if I don't do something soon, my friend, that is exactly what we're all going to discover.'

'Have you seen your son yet, sire?'

The King stopped his pacing and in an instant great wet tears were pouring down his sunken cheeks. Up to that moment, he hadn't allowed himself to think about anything but the awful mess he was in. But suddenly it hit him like a tidal wave of sweet-smelling talcum powder. He looked up at the Wizard, a stupid smile on his great, wet face.

'I'm a daddy,' said the King.

The Queen's beauty was famed throughout the land. Her dark brown eyes blazed with life, and the untamed black curls which framed her heart-shaped face, and cascaded down over her shoulders, set off the delicate pink of her cheeks, and her full red mouth.

She was the daughter of the last Lord Chancellor, and when only nineteen had caused a sensation by posing naked for the famous Limbo painter Giacomo Unguente. The painting still hung in the Limbo Gallery and was to this day the cause of sleepless nights for countless young men. But now, propped up in bed, her infant son lying asleep and gently gurgling in the crook of her arm, she was the perfect picture of motherhood.

She had been married to the King when barely twenty. The King, already well into middle age, couldn't believe his luck. She may only have been a child when she was joined to the King but, unlike him, she wasn't stupid and had insisted on separate rooms from the word go.

She'd made few friends at court, and had a reputation for being vain and arrogant. But even her severest critics had noticed the change that had recently come over her. She'd softened noticeably, and it had little to do with the coming of the dawn.

She nuzzled her baby's tiny head and kissed his ear, taking in his strange, animal scent.

The nurse came in. 'It's time for his feed, ma'am.'

The Queen looked down at the small bundle in her arms, serene in his deep sleep. 'But he's so comfortable, it would be a shame to wake him.'

'He needs feeding, ma'am, if he is to thrive,' the nurse persisted.

'Oh, very well,' said the Queen, reluctantly sitting up and loosening the neck of her nightgown. The boy woke and looked up at his mother with his remarkable eyes – blue like the morning sky, as deep and as placid as a mountain lake, with here and there a fleck of white, like swans taking flight. The child yelled briefly as she manoeuvred his tiny head onto her nipple. Then, realizing he was being treated to a warmly comforting milky meal, settled into a gentle rhythm of sucking and moaning.

In the tranquil air of the bedchamber, the sunlight poured in over the bare stone flags and fell obliquely across the bottom corner of the bed. 'Shall I close the curtains, ma'am?'

'No, bless you, the light is like a miracle. Let's enjoy it while we may. And open the window.'

'But ma'am . . .' The nurse came from the school of thinking that too much fresh air was deleterious to the constitution, especially that of a newborn infant.

The Queen was of a more modern, liberal opinion. 'Open the window, I want to smell the morning,' she insisted.

'Very well, ma'am.' Tight-lipped now, the girl did as asked, and the room was immediately flooded with the chirrup of cicadas and the musky smell of damp, sun-kissed earth wafting up from the plain far below. 'Will that be all, ma'am?' The nurse waited at the foot of the bed.

'Festrina, come and sit by me.' The Queen patted the quilt beside her. The nurse hesitated, then stiffly complied. 'How long have we known each other?'

Festrina looked down at her hands, clasped in her lap. 'I first came into your service when I was thirteen, ma'am.'

'Thirteen? So young. And how old are you now?'

'Twenty-two, ma'am.'

'Nine years. Can it really have been so long?'

Festrina kept her head down, eyes fixed on the tips of her fingers. 'Can I go now, ma'am?'

The Queen bowed her head and tried to look up into Festrina's face, but the nurse looked away. 'Do you like me, Festrina?'

The girl shifted uneasily. 'I'm your servant, ma'am,' she replied.

'Festrina, if I've ever done anything to hurt or upset you, I'm sorry. I know at times I must have appeared spoilt and selfish, but

I want to put all that behind us. Over the course of the last year I've found something it seems I have been searching for all my life. With the birth of my child I've found true contentment.' The Queen took Festrina's hand. 'I want us to be friends. The dawn has come, and with it the hope of a better world.' As the Queen leant forward to squeeze Festrina's hand, her breast, heavy with milk, fell from the infant's mouth with a gentle *thwup*. The baby sucked the air frantically, wondering where his source of delight and comfort had gone. The Queen relaxed back and, holding the nipple between her two fingers, guided it gently between his lips. Soon he was feeding contentedly again. 'Look at my son, how beautiful, how innocent he is.'

The nurse looked down at the happily suckling child. 'He's got his father's eyes,' she said. The Queen looked up sharply, her eyes filled with confusion and horror. Festrina met her gaze unflinchingly. In that moment, all barriers of class, rank and privilege fell away; everything that in the course of normal, daily life kept them at a respectful distance disappeared; they were just two women who shared a dangerous secret.

'The King approaches!' No sooner had the doorkeeper uttered his warning than the King marched into the Queen's bedchamber, followed closely by the Wizard. At first all the King could see was his wife's exposed, alabaster-white breast, which seemed to fill the room. God she was beautiful, surely he would have remembered spending a night with her? The Queen, guessing his thoughts, removed the infant from her breast and, hurriedly adjusting her décolletage, held the child out towards him.

'My lord, behold your son.' The King manoeuvred himself around the bed and gazed down at the infant. Looking into his small, crumpled face, he was once again moved to tears.

'He looks like me,' he sniffed. Festrina caught her mistress's eye.

'You may leave us, Festrina.'

'As you wish, ma'am.' The nurse bobbed a curtsey and left, a small, secret smile on her lips.

The King took his tiny heir in his arms. The child, used to the gentle twilight of its mother's breast, screwed up its eyes in the brightness of the room. 'He's got my chin,' the King chuckled. 'Choochy-coo-coo!' he cooed, tickling the baby's face with the end of his beard. The heir to the throne of Limbo peered cautiously up at the strange, hairy thing that floated above him and suddenly yearned for the comforting warmth of his mother's breast. He burst into tears. The King handed the wriggling bundle back to its mother. 'Over to you, my dear. More your department, I think.' Almost immediately the child calmed, and fell fast asleep. 'So, all well?'

'Perfect, sire. He is all I could wish for.'

'How was the birth? Everything go according to plan?'

'His birth was easy – like him.'

'Good, good . . . good.' The King wandered aimlessly around the room, picking things up and putting them down. He stopped in front of the open window. 'Shouldn't this be closed? Too much fresh air, you know . . . ?'

'I like it open. We've all been shut up here for so long.'

'Very well, very well. Well then, nice to see you my dear. Glad you're in such good spirits, and very good to see little, er . . . what's his name? Have we decided on a name yet?'

The Queen and the Wizard spoke together. 'Harmony,' they said.

'Harmony? Isn't that rather girly? Don't want him getting picked on at school, you know,' said the King.

'Harmony should prove the perfect name for turning away anger, sire,' the Wizard replied.

'Is that the name you've chosen, my dear?'

'You only have to spend some time with him to realize how apt it is.'

The King stopped in the doorway, looking from the Queen to the child to the Wizard, then back to the Queen again. Then he looked out of the window at the clear, bright day, with the great greening plateau stretching to the horizon, and suddenly felt wonderfully magnanimous.

'Very well, Harmony it is. Come, Wizard, we have work to do.'

The King swept out of the chamber. The Wizard, bending over the child, touched its cheek and it smiled up at him. 'Come along, Wizard!' the King called from the corridor.

The Queen reached out and took the Wizard's hand. He raised it tenderly to his lips and looked at her with his remarkable morning-blue eyes, as deep and as placid as a mountain lake, with here and there a fleck of white, like swans taking flight. 'We shall be together, my love,' he said.

'Wizard!' yelled the King. The Wizard smiled at his mistress, and followed his sovereign out of the bedchamber.

Chapter 4

It was their first holiday abroad. It was their first holiday anywhere apart from their honeymoon in Skegness and that little weekend break on the Isle of Wight that Iris had won in *Woman's Realm*. But that had been back in 1966 – twelve long years ago. Bernard and Iris Boggs held hands as they stepped into the departure lounge at Gatwick airport.

'Well, I've never seen anything like it!' exclaimed Bernard at the rows and rows of glossy magazines and bestsellers, the gleaming shelves full of exotic liquor, the yards of cashmere, the gallons of expensive French perfume.

'Ooh, Bernard, it's like an Aladdin's cave. Hold me back, I could spend a fortune in here!'

'Steady on now, Iris. Remember we've only got our £100 allowance to play with.' Bernard pulled out a small notebook. 'I've worked it all out – breakfast and an evening meal are included in the price of the room, so our only extra expense will be lunch. Now, allowing £5 a day for a meal out, and another £1 for a couple of drinks before dinner, that leaves us with £16. I suggest that we spend our surplus cash on excursions to the various and interesting bird sanctuaries that Lanzarote is justly famous for.'

'Oh, lovely,' said Iris, patting her perm and trying to sound enthusiastic.

'Or,' said Bernard, 'we can blow the lot on booze and fags!' Iris's round face crinkled and she dissolved into fits of giggles.

'Ooh, Bernard, I thought you were being serious for a moment, there.'

'Let's go and find a place by the window where we can watch the planes take off.' Bernard wrapped an arm around Iris and led her over to the big plate-glass windows that ran down one side of the lounge. They were a comical sight – his six and a half feet escorting her small and compact five foot two. As he sat her down at a table overlooking the runway, a VC-10 screamed noisily down the strip and hurled itself at the sky.

'How do they manage to lift all that metal into the air?' asked Iris. 'And once they've got it up there, how do they keep it there?'

'Anti-gravity pills,' said Bernard.

'Eh?'

'The stewardess comes round with them before you take off. You pop one in your mouth and you become weightless.'

Iris looked up at him with her big moon eyes. 'Really?' Bernard's long face burst into a grin. 'Ooh, Bernard, what am I going to do with you?' Then her smile vanished and she looked thoughtful. She gripped his arm and pulled him close. 'But seriously, though, Bernard, I am a little nervous. What if we crash?'

Bernard crouched down in front of her and took both her hands. Then, looking up into the face of the woman he adored more than life itself, he said, 'Then we'll go together, my love. You've given me more happiness than a man could wish for, and if I die this minute, I could honestly say, hand on heart, my life has been totally fulfilled. As long as I have you, I want for nothing, and if our number's up, we'll walk into heaven hand in hand – together forever.'

Iris wiped a tear from her eye and bent and kissed his shiny bald pate. 'You big soft thing,' she said. Bernard took both her hands. They looked so small and delicate on the great expanse of his huge palms. 'Little hands,' he said tenderly, kissing them. 'Now then, what's it to be? Tea – or tea?' he said, heaving his large frame up from the floor.

'You know how to show a girl a good time. I'll have a coffee,' she smiled.

'You're right cheeky, you are!' Bernard checked his pockets for change and strolled over to the café.

Iris looked out of the window at the big planes trundling down the runway. She followed one as it rose up on its haunches and lifted off, parting the thin, greasy drizzle and disappearing through the blanket of grey cloud that hung over the airport. What was it like up there? Did the sun really shine forever? And Lanzarote, what was that like? She'd heard it was hot, hotter than the hottest British summer. Sitting in damp, cold England, she found it hard to imagine that somewhere out there, there was a place where it was always warm; where thermals were optional. Was it really possible? Abroad – she was going *abroad*. But what did that mean? They spoke a different language, yes, and ate different food, but they did that in Southall. This was *abroad*: foreign, overseas. What would it be like? Would they understand English? She'd never manage if they didn't, and would she be able to eat anything? What did they eat? Snails and frogs like the French? Oh, please no, she couldn't stand that. Would they have beer? Bernard wouldn't be able to do without his beer. Cornflakes! She'd forgotten to pack the cornflakes. Oh, no! What would they have for breakfast? Everything was sure to be smothered in garlic. Eggs, they're bound to have eggs. She'd eat eggs, they were safe – she'd eat nothing but eggs. But if they had eggs that meant they'd have chickens. She liked chicken. So, that was all right, eggs and chicken. She was quite sure she could survive on those for a fortnight. Feeling a little happier now that the food question, at least, was sorted, Iris sat back and tried to get into the holiday spirit.

Bernard came back with two cups of coffee and a big smile on his face.

'What have you been up to?' asked Iris. Bernard sat down and placed one of the steaming cups in front of her.

'The holiday starts here. Cheers!' He chinked cups with his wife, and drank. Iris sipped the hot coffee and detected a warm, throat-tingling sensation, strangely reminiscent of . . .

'Brandy! You naughty man, you're trying to get me drunk.'

'Of course I am.' Bernard leant forward conspiratorially. 'How about starting an over-fifties branch of the Mile-High Club?'

'Ooh! You wicked, wicked man, you're trying to corrupt me.'

'Better late than never.'

'You started the moment we got married. I'd never touched liquor before our reception. You got me blind drunk on that Asti Spumante.'

'I had to carry you out to the car,' laughed Bernard. 'On the train down to Skegness you could hardly keep your hands off me.'

'Shh! Bernard, keep your voice down.' Iris blushed.

'What a honeymoon night that was, eh? A scent of roses and the gentle sighing of the sea, a serene backdrop to our lovemaking.'

Iris looked off into the middle distance, misty eyed. Then she remembered something else. 'And the next morning we had to apologize to the manager for making so much noise. Nobody would talk to us at breakfast.'

'They were all jealous. There wasn't a woman to hold a candle to you then, and there still isn't now, my little sex dumpling.' As he reached across the table and took her hand, Iris was all confusion; she glowed like a furnace.

'Bernard, there are people . . .' she whispered.

'They don't care about us. They're on holiday too.' Iris looked round the lounge, and saw he was right. Everywhere there were couples, or families, all talking excitedly together; all focused on just one thing – getting away.

It had been years since they'd had any time together, without the distraction of running the shop. At first she'd been worried they might have forgotten how to be alone with each other – what would they find to talk about? But, of course, Bernard soon put her mind to rest on that count – he was as good company as ever, full of laughs, full of love. Even after all these years, he could still make her feel like a woman who was desired; desirable.

Wonderful, adorable, daft old Bernard, she'd loved him the moment she'd set eyes on him. It was during the war, and the streets were filled with rubble. He was outside his father's newsagent's, helping an old lady who'd just tripped over a pile of bricks that had once been a butcher's shop. He'd looked up as Iris had walked by. 'Hello,' he'd said. 'Any time you need picking up, just let me know.' She'd giggled, and that night he'd taken her to the pictures. He proposed a month later, and they were married the following spring.

Soon after the war his father died, and he'd taken over the running of the shop. Up at five every morning and never in bed before ten, seven days a week, three hundred and sixty-four days a year. Christmas was their only day off. It wasn't much, just a newsagent's in Lancing, but they'd given their lives to it. For a time Iris had run a sub-post office in the back, and she'd enjoyed the responsibility; but when the new main post office had opened two doors down, it was pointless carrying on, so she'd let it go. Then, when the shoe shop across the street closed down, Bernard had thought about opening a small off-licence; he'd even been to the bank to enquire about a loan. But it would have meant taking on extra staff and starting from scratch in a business they knew little about. In the end, like so many of their schemes and dreams, they had decided it would be too much work, and satisfied themselves with their small but busy life as it was.

Iris would have called herself a fortunate woman. She'd had a full life with a wonderful man who was devoted to her, her only regret being that they hadn't been able to have children. She knew that Bernard felt it too; he would have dearly loved to have had a son to pass the business on to. They'd put so much into that shop, they couldn't just let it go to a stranger, could they? They weren't getting any younger, and the question would have to be faced sooner or later. But it was the one subject he flatly refused to discuss.

'Bernard . . .'

He knew what she was thinking. 'Now don't you worry about the shop, it's only a couple of weeks, and George and Betty are quite capable of looking after it.'

'No, it's not that . . .'

'If people want to start buying their papers elsewhere, then let them.' Bernard picked up a discarded magazine from the chair next to him and started flicking through it. Iris gave up and took a sip of her alcoholic coffee.

'Hey, look at this,' Bernard said. ' "The Coffee Revolution".' He turned the magazine round so Iris could see. Underneath a picture of a smiling woman drinking out of an oversized cup was an article about the resurgence of 'coffee culture' in America. 'Listen to this: "Café Library is the first of a new breed of coffee shops. Set inside a bookshop, it threatens to start a trend – after you've bought your book, you can sit down and peruse your purchase with a coffee and freshly baked muffin. A café in a bookshop? Only in America, I hear you say, but traditionally where America leads, Europe follows, so it probably won't be too long before you'll be able to order a cappuccino along with Margaret Drabble's latest at W.H. Smith."'

'Ridiculous idea,' snorted Iris.

'No, I think it's very clever.' Bernard half-closed his eyes and looked up at the ceiling. Iris knew that look.

'Now don't go getting ideas, Bernard.'

'But it's not as if we haven't got the room. Ever since we closed the post office, there's all that wasted space at the back.'

'It's a useful storeroom.'

'All we'd have to do is pull that plasterboard down – stick up a few bookshelves. We could extend the counter into a bar; add a few tables and chairs . . .'

'How many people do you know that read books in Lancing? And cappuccinos? Most people I know drink instant.'

'It's 1978, Iris, times are changing. Who knows, maybe café society is just what Lancing's been missing? We'll talk about it when we get back home. In the meantime, care for a top-up?' Bernard smiled and pulled out his silver hip flask.

'Ooh, what am I going to do with you?'

Chapter 5

The King strode into his private chamber – or what should have been his private chamber. It turned out to be the broom cupboard. 'Bloody castle!' he yelled. 'Smeil! Smeil! Help me out of this mess.' His small servant was instantly at his side.

'I think you'll find it's in here, sire,' said the Wizard from across the hall, indicating the large oak door in front of which he was standing.

'How the bloody hell do you ever find your way around this place?' growled the King, as Smeil helped disentangle him from a small armoury of mops, brushes and buckets.

'I follow a simple rule, sire,' said the Wizard. 'If I am searching for a room I believe is in the west wing, I look in the east. If last time I turned left, this time I turn right; if before I went up, now I go down. It seems to work.'

'Bloody ridiculous! Why can't rooms stay where they are put?'

'And where would be the mystery in that?'

'I don't want mystery. I just want to be able to find my bedroom!' The King pushed open the door and to his relief, found himself in his own private chamber. 'Ah, here we are, except . . .' The King could have sworn that the last time he'd vacated it, the bed was over on the right, near the window. Now it was on the left, and the window seemed to have disappeared entirely. The King shook his head; he'd never been able to come to terms with the fluidity of this building, but that was Limbo for you. He collapsed in a chair near the fire, which was now over by the bookcase.

'Your son grows big and strong, sire.'

The King looked up at the Wizard and sighed. The Prince's first birthday was fast approaching. 'What can I do, Wiz? He grows more beautiful every day. Each time I see him, for a moment I forget . . . But then that bloody Prophecy rears its ugly head and I'm back in the thorns again, with devils screaming around my head, and it makes absolute sense to take my dagger and . . . Then he looks up at me with his innocent little face and I feel wretched that I could even consider putting an end to one so . . .'

'Perfect?' offered the Wizard.

'Aye, so perfect.'

The Wizard put his hand tenderly on the King's shoulder and the King reached up and patted it. Was the Wizard trembling? No, he couldn't; he mustn't falter now – the King was relying on him. If it was at all possible to find a way out of this mess, the Wizard was the only person who could do it. The King looked up into the face of his mentor and friend. He'd never worked out how it was that his erstwhile tutor remained as youthful as ever, while he himself grew daily more old and decrepit. The King put it down to the man being a wizard, and left it at that. He didn't like to delve – wizards were strange, unpredictable beings who were likely to take offence at the most innocent of enquiries. What the King didn't know – and what he would never have understood, even if he had known – was that the Wizard *was* history. To look into the Wizard's face was to peer into past, present and future – into destiny itself. 'We've come through a lot, Wiz. Help me now, I'm at my wits' end.' For a second the King thought he detected a look of anguish flicker across the Wizard's face. But in an instant it was gone, and he looked his old sanguine self again.

'Fear not, sire.' The Wizard sat down on the floor, his cloak spread out around him.

'Oh, don't go into all that nonsense now,' said the King. 'Talk to me!'

The Wizard pursed his lips and rose. When he had drawn himself up to his full height, he suddenly froze, regarding the King with an odd, unblinking stare. He seemed to be looking not at him, but through him. The King watched in amazement as tears began to roll down the Wizard's cheeks.

'Are you all right, Wizard?' the King asked.

'Sorry?' the Wizard replied, as if returning from far away.

The King shifted uneasily in his chair. 'Anything you want to tell me, Wiz?'

The Wizard's face crumpled. He pulled out a handkerchief and buried his face in it. 'Oh lord, lord, what have I done?' he muttered.

The King cleared his throat and jerked his head in the direction of Smeil, standing obediently by the door. '*Pas devant les domestiques, eh?*' he said, *sotto voce*. The Wizard wiped his eyes and noisily blew his nose. 'Courage, Wiz. I'm depending on you.'

'Very well,' said the Wizard, stuffing the handkerchief back in his pocket. A look of manic intensity came into his eye. 'As it happens, sire, I do have a plan.'

The King leant forward in his chair. 'You do?'

'It's a little extreme,' the Wizard said, 'but I think we could make it work without too much bloodshed.'

'No, no, no.' The King collapsed again. 'No bloodshed.'

The Wizard, looking somewhat relieved, bowed low and was about to take his leave when the King stopped him. 'Whose blood?' he asked.

The Wizard looked up. 'Not yours, sire.'

The King thought for a moment, stroking his beard. 'Very well, we may as well hear it.'

The Wizard glanced over at Smeil, still waiting patiently by the door. 'Do you think, sire, we might speak in private?'

'Eh? Oh, yes of course,' said the King. 'Smeil – go and make yourself useful somewhere else.' The little man didn't altogether trust the Wizard, and was loath to leave them alone together. But what could he do? He had sworn to serve and obey his master to the death. With deep misgivings, he slipped soundlessly out of the door. The King turned back to the Wizard. 'Quite right,' he said. 'Can't have the servants earwigging matters of state.'

The Wizard closed his eyes and raised his face to heaven. Then, throwing his arms wide and declaiming like an actor, he began: 'Imagine if you will, a time where there is no Prophecy; no record of time past nor of time yet to come. A land ignorant of the death of kings and the succession of princes; a land where, save the coming of the dawn, life has gone on, unchanged and unchanging, for a thousand years!' He finished with a flourish and stood, eyes blazing, waiting for a reaction.

The King scratched his head. 'Is that it?' he said.

'Sire, don't you see? If the Prophecy had never existed, then how could it affect you?'

'But it does exist and it does affect me!'

'But remove the record of it and what is left?'

The King gradually began to catch on. 'You mean destroy The Book?'

'Yes!' the Wizard hissed.

'But there are thousands of them out there.'

'A joyous book-burning. You could say that since the dawn is now here, what need does anyone have of The Book? It is no longer necessary – the end of history has arrived.'

'But most people know nothing about the horrible bits, the . . . what's it called?'

'The Forbidden Codex, sire,' the Wizard spat venomously.

'Yes, that's the feller. Couldn't we just destroy that?'

'If only it were that simple!' the Wizard shouted to no one in particular, and for a moment, the King thought he was going to break down again. But, gathering himself together, the Wizard continued with renewed vigour, hopping around the room like a psychotic stick insect. 'It's all of a piece, sire. The Prophecy is the future. It is, if you like, the framework within which the Forbidden Codex exists. If you are to survive, all trace of The Book must be destroyed. As long as any part of it remains, you will be doomed to follow the grisly path it has laid out for you.'

The King got up and began to pace. 'Hmm . . .' Suddenly he stopped. 'I see a flaw. The Book has been taught in school for many years now, everybody knows great chunks of it by heart, how are we going to make them forget?'

'That's where the bloodshed comes in,' the Wizard said darkly.

'I was afraid of that.'

'Listen carefully now. We make it illegal, on pain of death, to quote from or allude to The Book or anything contained therein.' The Wizard said it slowly, as if reciting something committed to memory a very long time ago.

'But bits of it have passed into everyday language. Are you going to have me hang people for saying *"All hail the Dawn!"* to one another?'

'I never said it was going to be easy!' the Wizard suddenly exclaimed. 'If the plan is going to work, all memory of The Book must be expunged, it must be as if it had never existed. To give people time to get used to the idea, you could operate a "three strikes and you're out" scheme.'

' "Three strikes and you're out"? Very good, very good. What does it mean?'

The Wizard spoke quickly, his words tumbling out in a rush. 'If a citizen quotes from The Book *once*, nothing shall be done to him. Likewise, the *second* time. But should a phrase from The Book escape his lips a *third* time, his property and lands shall be confiscated and he shall suffer death by hanging, drawing and quartering. The population will very soon get the idea. In this way the bloodshed can be kept to a minimum and your future secured.' The Wizard turned to the King expectantly.

The King stopped his pacing and looked out of the window, which had suddenly reappeared behind the bed. 'But will it work?' he said, gazing out at the cheerful sunshine that poured down on his ever-greening land. 'The Prophecy seems to suggest that whatever I do I'm in the shit.'

The Wizard grabbed the King by the shoulders. His eyes were bulging, and his chest heaved as if it were about to burst. 'Will it work?' he gasped, as if in pain. 'Will it work?' he repeated, looking heavenwards as if for divine inspiration.

'Wizard, you're hurting.'

The Wizard's fingers were excavating deep holes in the King's shoulders. 'Sorry, sire,' he said, letting go. Then continued, looking deep into the King's eyes. 'Remove The Prophecy and you remove the danger. It is the only way.'

The King stroked his beard. It was a difficult decision and once set in motion, this plan must be seen through to the bitter end – there would be no going back. It would be tough, but history turned on such hard choices. The King, decisive for the first time in his long and indolent life, turned to face the Wizard. 'Let it be done,' he said, and with this simple phrase set in motion one of the bloodiest episodes in the entire history of Limbo. With a cry, the Wizard slumped, exhausted, into a chair, and far off, just above the horizon, at the very edge of vision, a thin black cloud suddenly came into being. The Great Terror had begun.

Chapter 6

Prince Nostrum strode across the desert plain that would one day become Nebraska. There, in the distance, thrown into sharp relief by the rising moon, was the huge central plateau of Laurasia. He prayed his calculations were correct. It was hard enough guessing the location across half a billion years of shifting continents, let alone arriving at the precise year, day, hour, second. But if he was right, he would find the hideously disfigured Orvis McKiel at the western edge of the plateau, putting the final touches to his device.

The Prince looked at his watch. The seven dials showed second, hour, day, date, month, year and the rate of decay of the time portal through which he'd arrived. Only the last two of these dials were illuminated. One read '-500,000,000' and the other '36 hours, 7 minutes, 25 seconds'. He had just over a day and a half to save the world . . .

The tinkling of the bell above the door interrupted Rex's reading. He turned down the corner of the page and closed the book. The tall man approached the counter. 'Have you got a copy of' – but Rex already had the latest edition of *Gramophone* in his hand – '*Gramophone*?' said the man redundantly. Rex handed him the magazine, and the tall and now rather confused man paid and left.

Rex was like that. He had a knack of knowing what a customer wanted the moment they came through the door. He didn't know how – he just did. It was one of the many puzzling aspects of life that Rex pondered in his spare and empty hours.

Rex Boggs was an unprepossessing character – tall, ungainly and with a big, round face. Half an hour in his company would reinforce one's first impression that here was a simple soul with no knowledge of politics, polite society or the films of Jean-Luc Godard. He had no conversation, save the exploits of Prince Nostrum – the creation of his favourite author, F. Don Wizzard – but the simple fact of his presence was immensely calming. On the late train, it was always him that the loud drunk would choose to sit next to. People wanted to be around him. They'd come into his shop not just to buy a newspaper, but to be near him – he made them feel good.

Although people felt at home around him, Rex didn't feel at home anywhere. He understood the worlds in which his hero Nostrum existed much better than he did planet Earth and the people who visited his Lancing newsagent's shop. To him life – this life – was a never-ending puzzle, a secret that no one else would share. What was it that drove so many men to pull on shorts and football boots on a freezing cold Saturday and go and get covered in mud and bruises? And cricket? Did anyone actually understand cricket? No, the whole point of sport, which for a large chunk of the population was as necessary as breathing, had passed him by.

He sighed and picked up the *Evening Argus*. After catching up on the local news – 'Vicar's Headless Corpse Found in Wheelie-Bin' – he turned to the small ads section. He was always amazed at the sort of junk people would try to buy and sell. There was one ad for a second-hand truss: 'barely used, slight staining – £10'. And another for a five-hundred-piece jigsaw: 'few pieces missing – best offer'. Scanning down the page, another ad caught his eye: 'Wanted, large carpet-bag. Collector will pay best price.' He remembered finding a dusty old carpet-bag among his parents' things, but couldn't sell it – no, that would be like breaking a sacred trust. He didn't like to think of any of his parents' possessions ending up in the hands of some sad old collector.

Collectors – that was another branch of the human family that was beyond Rex's understanding. In their shop, his parents had stocked a wealth of weird and wonderful periodicals; there weren't many places where you could find *Cheese Label Collector* or *Flower Pot Fancier's Compendium* next to *Computer Shopper*, if at all. As a boy, Rex had been intrigued by them, and had found that there were hundreds of these small, independent publications devoted to the collecting of the detritus of modern society; many of them published by elderly people out of their garages or garden sheds. It was altogether fascinating, but the deeper Rex delved the more perplexed he became. Why would anybody want to collect used tea stirrers? Who knows – but they did.

It wasn't as if it only affected one particular sort of person. Such a desire, it seemed, could land on anyone at any time. He'd come to the conclusion that you were better off not getting started on it in the first place. One unfortunate he'd happened upon during his research had been a happily married, successful businessman. One day he'd been passing an antique shop and seen a Victorian trivet in the window. He'd liked the look of it, so had gone in and bought it. When he awoke the next morning he was a Victorian trivet obsessive – it was that quick; he just had to have more. He started neglecting his business, only travelling to meetings in places he knew he'd find more trivets. His wife couldn't stand it, he was spending more time with his trivets than with her. Eventually she and the kids moved out. Three years after the collecting bug had struck, he'd lost his business, his family, and he was flat broke, but he did have the biggest collection of Victorian trivets in Europe. So what? What's he going to do with them? He can't sell them, as he doesn't want to break up the collection. And he wasn't the only collecting obsessive. Rex had uncovered similar stories relating to all sorts of everyday objects, from golf balls to drain covers.

Rex sighed and put down the *Argus*. 'At least Prince Nostrum hasn't been struck by the collecting bug,' he said, picking up F. Don Wizzard's *Beast on Top of The World*. 'Now where was I . . .?' He licked his finger and flicked through the pages. 'Ah, here we are.'

. . . just over a day and a half to save the world.

It was the yapping of Sparkie, his android dog, that first alerted the Prince's attention. 'Shush, Sparkie, shush! I thought I told you to wait in the ship!' But Sparkie wouldn't shush; she kept on barking until the Prince saw what she was trying to point out to him – a tripwire, just centimetres from his left boot. The Prince crouched and tickled Sparkie behind her ears. 'Good girl. You've earned yourself double doggie-chows tonight.' Standing, the Prince followed the wire as it ran, knee-high, for several metres before disappearing into a small thicket of low-growing tree ferns. Gingerly parting the prehistoric plants, the Prince saw what he had dreaded. The tripwire was attached to the detonation mechanism of a five-billion-megaton bomb, primed and ready to blow.

'That's right, Prince! That's how close you came!'

The Prince looked up. There, on the edge of the plateau far above, stood the ghastly, misshapen figure of Orvis McKiel. 'It's not too late, Orvis!' said the Prince. 'Defuse the bomb and I'm sure we can sort this thing out.'

'You'll never take me alive, Prince. I've come too far to give up now. Now mankind will pay for laughing at me, for calling me deformed, a Frankenstein's monster!' Orvis held up a small rectangular box with one big red button on it. 'I was hoping that you'd spare me the business of actually using this. Imagine – Prince Nostrum destroying the world – what a great story that would have made!'

'But it doesn't make any sense, Orvis. Explode this bomb and mankind will never exist – so they'll never know. Where's your revenge? Where's the satisfaction in that?'

Orvis smiled down at him – a ghastly leer. 'I take my satisfaction from the fact that no one will ever suffer as I have suffered. That the little guy with buck teeth and glasses will never be laughed at, or have his glasses trampled in the dirt. That the fat girl at the school prom will never have to wait in vain all night to be asked to dance. That those with yellow, black or brown skin need never suffer the indignities piled upon them by our colour-coded society!'

'Orvis, you're right. I agree with a lot of what you say. But just think – that little guy with the buck teeth and glasses just might turn out to be the next Woody Allen. The fat girl could have the voice of Mamma Cass. And what about the Dalai Lama? And think of Gandhi and Nelson Mandela – two of the finest statesmen that ever lived. How impoverished the universe would be if they had never existed!'

'Time's up, Prince.' Orvis raised the black box high above his head. 'Nice talking to you, but it's time to call it a day.' Savouring the moment, Orvis rested his thumb lightly on the button. He was about to wipe out five hundred million years of evolution before it had even begun, and he smiled at the irony. 'Goodbye, cruel world!' he called and began to squeeze . . .

Chapter 7

Malcom Collins parked the Harley in the bay marked 'Solo M/C's', and retrieved the panatella from his boot. Narrowing his eyes, he bit the end off it and stuck it between his teeth. He inhaled involuntarily and a bit of dry tobacco broke off and stuck in his throat. Coughing violently he managed to dislodge the offending shard, then leaned against his bike, eyes streaming, while he caught his breath. Easing himself back into the world of The Man With No Name, he put the cigar back in his mouth. Pulling out a match, he flicked it with his thumb, an action he had seen Clint perform many times. A lump of flaring sulphur stuck underneath his nail, and burned deep into the delicate tissues of the nail bed.

'Ow! Ow, ow, ow!' Malcom leapt around in agony. He stuck his thumb in his mouth to try and stop the stinging – it tasted horribly bitter. 'Shit!' he said, and spat. Removing his Ray-Bans, he inspected the damage. There was a white-ringed scorch mark on the nail, and a small black cavity in the end of his thumb. It was throbbing violently. He looked round to make sure nobody had seen, but the car park was empty. 'Fuck it, I'm buying a lighter,' he scowled, as he headed into the police station.

The sergeant behind the desk whistled the opening bars of the theme from *A Fistful of Dollars* as Malcom went past.

Malcom stopped and turned slowly back towards him. 'Is that supposed to be funny, sergeant?'

The man looked up, all innocence. 'Sorry sir?'

Malcom wagged a finger at him. The sergeant waited as a series of hard-man movie clichés ran through Malcom's brain, from 'Go ahead, make my day' to 'I am the fucking Shore Patrol', but none of them seemed quite appropriate here. Eventually, defeated, Malcom let his arm drop limply to his side. 'Arsehole,' he muttered.

'The super wants to see you.' The man behind the desk beamed.

'Do you have *any* idea of the damage you may have caused by your little escapade this morning?' Malcom was standing to attention on Superintendent Gerrold's small square of carpet while the dapper, snowy-haired superintendent vented his fury. Outside, a steadily growing knot of officers listened at the door. 'Councillor Daniels is one of the few friends we have left. If we alienate him we may find the council less than eager to meet our funding targets, which could leave us with a manpower shortage. We're in the middle of a recruitment crisis as it is, and so, to comply with the government's directive to put more bloody "bobbies on the beat", if they are not extremely careful, certain underachieving detectives may find themselves back in uniform. Do I make myself clear!'

'Yes sir, sorry sir. I didn't realize who he was, sir. But, in mitigation I would like to say that he was breaking the law.'

The superintendent stood up. 'He was doing thirty-five miles an hour!'

'In a thirty-mile-an-hour zone, sir,' Malcom interjected.

'At six o'clock in the morning! The streets were empty! And purely on a point of procedure, is the speedometer on your ridiculous motorbike calibrated and regularly checked, as per police regulations?'

'Well, no sir . . .'

'Well, no sir! So technically speaking you committed an offence. You're bloody lucky Mr Daniels hasn't decided to sue!'

'Yes sir.'

'And as for the manner in which you approached Mr Daniels – since when has insulting and intimidating behaviour been part of police procedure?'

'As long as I can remember, sir.'

The superintendent went scarlet. 'Get out! Get out, you moron! And take off that ridiculous fancy-dress uniform!'

Malcom opened the door, scattering the large group of eavesdropping policemen, and walked with as much dignity as was possible down the corridor towards his office.

Gerrold, spitting with rage, yelled after him. 'Make one more mistake, Collins, just one, and I'll have you on round-the-clock seafront lavatory watch!'

Malcom pushed open his office door and slumped at his desk. 'Fuck him,' he murmured. 'And fuck that bastard Daniels too.' Unzipping his American police-issue blue serge trousers and divesting himself of his crisply ironed shirt, he called for his sergeant. 'Beasely!' A thin, red-faced man with a nose like an Indian tomahawk appeared at the open door. Malcom looked up from his chair. Without his shirt to hold it in, his white, dimpled belly slopped untidily over the top of his Y-fronts. 'Beasely, help me off with these fucking boots.'

Beasely crept into the room and knelt at Malcom's feet. 'You should get one of those wooden bootjacks, then you could take them off by yourself,' he said in his nasal whine.

'Nah, I like seeing you grovel – it's the only pleasure I get these days.'

Beasely took hold of a boot and pulled, as Malcom pushed with his other foot against Beasely's shoulder. At last, the boot came loose and the sergeant was propelled backwards against the filing cabinet.

'You push too hard! Don't push so hard next time,' the small man complained as he picked himself up and took hold of the other boot. As it came loose, Malcom gave an extra-hard shove and Beasely found himself out in the corridor.

'Ow! That hurt!' Beasely wailed.

'What do you know about Michael Daniels?' Malcom asked, trying not to smile.

Beasely got up and came back into the room, rubbing his bony backside. 'You mean Councillor Daniels, people's champion and defender of the faith?'

'That's him. Thinks he's God. Any dirt in the files?'

'Not likely. He's as clean as they come, lives like a hermit – though God knows why, as he's rolling in it.'

'Anything not right about him?'

'He plays bowls. But that's not a hanging offence, apparently.'

'What about his business interests?'

'He is Hilditch Leisure – which owns the casino in Second Avenue, and various parts of the leisure facilities on the Palace Pier. All perfectly legit.'

'See what you can find out.'

'Why? Do you want to get back at him for dumping you in the shit?'

Malcom got up and advanced on the small sergeant, his belly wobbling slightly.

'This is a police matter, so it's got nothing to do with how I feel. Are you inferring that I'd let my personal feelings get in the way of my foremost duty to the law, and to the public at large? Call it intuition, but I've got a feeling about him, that's all.'

Beasely looked up at Detective Inspector Collins's big moon face, with its over-large nostrils that made him look like a pig. He stared into the man's small eyes and strained to see if he could detect a flicker of humanity, of intellect, of anything but naked self-interest. He couldn't. 'I'll get onto it right away sir.'

Beasely disappeared and Malcom slipped out of his trousers. Going to the tall, grey locker in the corner of the room, he opened it to find, not his work suit, but a full-size cowboy outfit, complete with spurs and cap-firing guns. Hearing someone snigger, he spun round to see the doorway crowded with smiling faces. 'Bastards!' he screamed, and ran at them, chasing his giggling colleagues down the corridor, still clad only in his capacious underpants.

Chapter 8

In the guttering gloom of the cave, lit by an array of stinking ox-fat lamps, Gildroy held the terrified, squawking chicken tightly in his left hand as he slit open its belly and then drew out its innards. Only when the poor animal's intestines were lying on the floor of the cave did he break its neck and put it out of its misery.

Crouching low over the slightly steaming guts, Gildroy's black cloak and pale, sharp face with its long, pointed nose gave him the look of a malevolent heron. Picking up a stick in his thin, bony hand he poked around in the bird's slimy entrails. 'Come closer, brother.' A broad black shadow detached itself from the wall and approached. It was as if a part of the cave itself had come to life.

'What does it say, what does it say?' the shadow asked in a deep, sing-song voice.

'I see a funeral . . .'

'Oooh!'

'And a wedding . . .'

'Yes! Yes!'

'And a tiny little baby . . .'

'Ahh!'

'And fire and burning books and bloodshed and wailing and gnashing of teeth!'

'Gnash, gnash!'

Gildroy looked at his brother in the flickering light and wondered how this simple, grotesque distillation of brutality had ever slipped through the evolutionary net. Stranger still, he wondered at the vagaries of nature that had made this creature his twin.

'Can I eat the chicken now?'

'Wait until I'm out of the cave, Norval,' said Gildroy, and straightening his long, stick-like legs, he strode out into the sunlight, away from the horrifying cacophony of wet slurping and crunching bones as Norval fell upon the still-warm fowl.

'Curse this pestilent sunlight.' Gildroy narrowed his small, sunken eyes and, after running a skeletal hand through his lank, thinning hair, he drew his black cowl up over his head. His massive black stallion shook its mane and pawed the bare earth with its hoof. 'Yes, my precious, we'll be riding soon.' Stroking the mighty animal's neck, he reached into a saddlebag and pulled out the proclamation that had been pinned to every bush, every tree, every wall in Limbo:

> *By order of His Majesty,*
>
> *Anyone found in possession of, or being found guilty of quoting, alluding or referring to 'The Book' in any way, shape or form, shall, upon the third offence, all lands and chattels belonging unto such person being confiscated, suffer a most horrible and painful death, to wit – hanging (firstly) and disembowelling (secondly).*
>
> *All citizens are required by law to attend and contribute to one of the many Book-burning sessions which are now being held across the land.*
>
> *Ask at your local council office for the location of your nearest pyre.*
>
> *God save the King!*

Since the issuing of this proclamation, the happy, sunlit uplands of Limbo had become streaked with red. So ingrained was The Book in the culture that the 'three strikes and you're out' rule made little difference; it was virtually impossible to go through a day without either quoting from it or referring to it in some small way. Even a seemingly simple act such as asking for the salt (*'Blessings on him who'll give me season'*) involved a quote from the banned Book. Thus whole families had been wiped out in the King's desperate effort to reshape the future.

Now the King's loyal guard were becoming disillusioned. Idle for generations, and for the most part long being eager to do what they had been trained for – to kill – they had now seen enough bloodshed, in the months since the proclamation, to last several lifetimes, and found they no longer had the stomach for it. Dark clouds were gathering over the sunny face of Limbo, and the King was frightened. He was appalled by what he'd set in motion, and yet how could he backtrack now? If it meant depopulating the entire kingdom, he must do it. He had to stand firm and see this through to the bitter end.

From his viewpoint in the foothills of the Great South Range, Gildroy looked at the small, distant excrescence that was Castle Limbo, surrounded by tiny plumes of smoke from the many bonfires. 'We are coming, gentle brother, we are riding to your aid and if I read the signs aright, soon, very soon we may once again shelter under the gentle covering of night and end this garish day.'

As Gildroy peered at the distant turrets of Limbo, glinting in the sun, all the old loathing returned. He'd kept his hatred warm, tended it, fed it like a furnace, and soon he would see it break in a howling torrent over the head of the King.

Gildroy and Norval were the King's long-banished twin brothers. Of course, there was never any doubt that Norval was an idiot and unfit to rule, but Gildroy was bright, intelligent and, as the eldest, the throne should have passed to him. But his father, King Ulrich the Second, blamed him for Norval's unhappy state, accusing him of leeching the goodness out of him when they were still in their mother's womb. Gildroy had tried his best – he'd studied hard and, as well as being the most academically gifted student of his generation, had excelled at fencing, riding and oratory. But young Gildroy could do nothing to please his father and, on the occasion of his coming of age, King Ulrich had announced that the succession would pass over his head and fall upon his younger son.

Gildroy had, of course, been furious. He railed against the decision, even invoking 'the Blood Quest of Yardley', an unusual part of Limbo's constitution that allowed the settling of disputes of accession with a fight to the death. All that was required was for the challenger to utter 'You! Outside, now!' and the other to reply 'Suits me, sunshine!' The first half of the formula had to be spoken within earshot of the rival, but because it was a magical invocation, the reply could be delivered anywhere at any time and, once uttered, would immediately bring the combatants face to face. They were then locked into combat and, until blood was shed, no one might intervene.

In the case of Gildroy's claim, King Ulrich forbade his young son from replying to the challenge – he was under age and a weakling – thereby allowing the Blood Quest to fall on his descendants.

Gildroy, frustrated, began plotting against the throne, but his treachery was discovered when a chambermaid, new to the castle, walked unannounced into the brothers' room thinking it was the linen cupboard. She had escaped and raised the alarm and the twins had been banished 'beyond the edge of the known world' immediately and for ever.

Leaving the castle, in the company of a platoon of guards, they had soon shaken off their escorts in the darkness. Norval had then crept back and slipped into the chambermaid's room. Her brutalized body was found, days later, floating in the shrimp pool under the castle.

'I enjoyed that.' Norval now reappeared, wiping his lips on the back of his hand. He was as broad as his brother was tall. His legs and torso were as sturdy as the bole of an ancient oak, and his arms sprouted like great rippling branches from his shoulders. He had a big head, with big blunt features, and when he smiled he revealed gums studded with misshapen brown stumps. His eyes were large and uneven and watered constantly, and although from a distance this gave the impression of a sad thing worthy of charity, on closer inspection all pity evaporated when it was realized – usually too late – that one was looking into the eyes of a creature trying to decide whether or not to kill you before eating you. This was a man you wouldn't want to meet at all, in any circumstances, let alone on a dark night. To meet such a man meant instant death. There was no way to reach him: he was beyond reason, beyond fear, save in one respect – dragons. When he was a baby, so hideous and brutally uncontrollable a charge was he that his nurse was driven to terrify him with stories of what the Great Dragon of Phnell would do to him if he didn't eat his greens, or go on his potty, or put that nice man from the government down. It was a fear that haunted his dreams still. 'What do we do now, bro?'

There were three obstacles between Gildroy and the throne of Limbo – the King himself, the infant Prince, and the Wizard. Of these, the last was the most formidable. He was strong and powerful, and the main reason that the brothers had kept their distance for so long. But word was he was losing his grip, for the ongoing slaughter was not to his taste and he was weakening.

Gildroy turned to face Norval. 'We fan the fires of discontent,' he replied 'We make it nice and hot for our dear brother.'

'What about the wedding? What about the wedding? When's the wedding?' Norval jumped up and down with excitement, making the ground tremble.

'Ah, yes, the joyful nuptials. Patience, gentle brother, patience – first things first. Remember, your bride, the Queen, is still married.'

'Boo!' The great, booming sound bounced off the mountains and rolled across the plain. Gildroy waited for the echo to die down.

'We must obey the proprieties: funeral first, wedding after.' A strange, gurgling chuckle, like the sound of boiling blood, issued from the very depths of Norval's being. 'Come brother,' said Gildroy mounting his huge, black stallion. 'The time is ripe. The future is ours – destiny awaits. We ride to Limbo!'

With Gildroy in the saddle, Norval took hold of the animal's tail and they galloped swiftly off, shaking the dusty plain beneath them, and leaving thin wisps of darkness in their wake.

Chapter 9

Serena Kowalski, garbage operative, 3rd class, tapped the glass of the temperature gauge. It was the only instrument in the vast computerized display that was real, and with good reason.

Through the port window of the behemoth-sized garbage scow, the SS *St Francis Sinatra*, she could see the Earth, floating far below – blue beneath a covering of wispy white cloud. This gigantic ship was the latest in a long line of 'final solutions' to the growing problem of what to do with the waste produced by fifteen billion human beings. They'd had to stop landfill disposal back in 2030, when the average height of the land had risen by fifteen feet and most city-dwellers had found themselves living underground. Soon afterwards, dumping at sea had been halted. Apart from poisoning the oceans, garbage islands were appearing everywhere, proving extremely hazardous to navigation. Then there was the notorious 'Great Asian Plain' scheme, championed by the Chinese, which involved levelling off the Himalayas by dumping garbage in the valleys.

They'd tried filling spaceships with rubbish – sending them hurtling into the Sun. This had seemed like a good long-term solution until they discovered it was interfering with the balance of the Sun's internal nuclear reaction and making it unstable. Then, one afternoon early in 2036, a researcher at Porton Down, while trying to create a creature that could clean the inside of high-pressure steam pipes in nuclear reactors, spliced together the DNA from a deep-sea hydrothermal clam with that of a silica-digesting amoeba, adding along the way a few off-the-peg genes from seagulls, aphids and wolves. What he ended up with was a clam about the size of a dinner plate – too large for its intended use in the narrow confines of high-pressure cooling pipes, but capable of eating *any-thing*. Not only that, it thrived in a methane-rich environment, reproduced asexually and had an insatiable appetite.

Soon, great vats of these clams were being exported to countries all over the world. So efficient were they at devouring rubbish, and so much confidence did the people of the world put in them that garbage production ballooned again – the rubbish depots were over-whelmed.

An orbiting fleet of garbage scows was the answer. A never-ending stream of rubbish-bearing shuttles from Earth fed vast ships, with holds so big they could swallow a small country, which were seeded with clams that busily turned society's waste into nutrient-rich fertilizer.

The clams were almost perfect, their one flaw being that they could only operate within certain very limited temperature parameters. Below 75 degrees, they died, and above 80 degrees became so active they could eat their way through six-inch steel plate in minutes. That's why Serena's eyes were never far from the glass of the internal-hold temperature gauge. Currently, it was rising.

'Seventy-seven point five? I'd better take a look.' Serena ran her fingers over the stubble on her head – it would soon be time for another visit to the barber's. She wasn't beautiful, no, but her strong chin and wide shoulders were strangely at odds with her high cheekbones and surprisingly soft hazel eyes. Striking was an adjec-tive that came to mind, closely followed by tough – but then, in her job, she had to be.

She eased herself out from behind the big, curved virtual display. Usually she had very little to do; the computer was in charge and the ship more or less looked after itself. All systems had at least five backup circuits – so it was very unusual for anything to go wrong. There *was* a manual override, a chunky red handle right underneath the pilot's seat, but it was only there to fulfil the latest regulations and, as the manual said, was never, *ever* to be used. Serena was just a caretaker. Most of the time she hung out in the virtual bar, telling stories to her virtual friends and drinking virtual beer, the intoxicating effects of which would disappear the moment she left the place. Or she would walk through the virtual mountain landscape, or enjoy a virtual massage from her virtual masseur, then go home and make love to her virtual lover. In lots of ways, it wasn't a bad life. It was to some extent preferable to crowded, foul-smelling Earth, where every last square yard of open countryside had long ago disappeared under concrete. But she was lonely. She had the company of a whole shipful of computer-generated beings, but she longed for the touch of a human hand, the sound of a human voice, the smell of human skin.

Five years, five long years, was the length of her contract. It hadn't seemed so bad when she'd signed on. What's five years out of a life? When she got back to Earth she'd be rich – the rewards were great for those prepared to sacrifice a chunk of their existence to aimlessly circling the Earth. But the day-to-day grinding reality of spaceship life, all alone with nothing to do except play computer games, was beginning to get to her, and she still had another three years to serve.

She had plenty of time to think, therefore – mostly about how the world had got itself into this mess in the first place. It was her usual topic of conversation in the bar, and a typical exchange would go something like this:

SERENA (entering traditional Irish-themed pub): God bless all here.
BARMAN: Ah, the lovely Serena. Day by day we magnify and worship thy name.
SERENA: Cut the crap, Daniel, and pour me a Guinness.
Several pints later:
SERENA: Jesus, Daniel, what am I doing with my life? What, when it comes down to it, does my job consist of, eh? I'll tell you – disposing of other people's shit.
BARMAN: Will you have another?

SERENA: (belch) Same again. I blame the politicians. They make the mistakes and it's down to us, the little people, to sort things out.

DRUNK CUSTOMER: Little People? Have you really seen the Little People?

SERENA (pulling Daniel out from behind the bar and over to the porthole): Have you looked at the Earth lately? That little blue-green ball of life, floating in the void?

DRUNK CUSTOMER (following them): Are the Little People out there? Can you see them now?

SERENA (pushing him out of the way): Do you mind? Daniel, who's going to speak for the Earth, huh? Who's going to do that? Politicians? Hah! Don't make me laugh. The only thing the politicians are interested in is their own futures – and where's the votes in garbage?

DRUNK CUSTOMER: (shoving in between them): Aw, let me see the Little People.

SERENA: Will you get out of my face!

Smack!

DRUNK CUSTOMER: Ow!

This inevitably led to Serena being thrown out for being drunk and disorderly.

Serena walked down the three steps from the cockpit display area into the large atrium of the main control deck. 'Elevator,' she said, striding across the immaculately polished wooden floorboards. Doors slid open in the blank wall ahead of her and she entered the spotlessly clean, chromium-plated lift. A formally attired commissionaire greeted her. 'Good morning madam, and where would you like to go today? Up to the viewing deck? Orion is looking spectacular at the moment. Or down to the cinema deck and restaurant court?'

'Hold,' Serena interrupted.

'Hold it is madam, and may I compliment you on your excellent choice of deck. But, my, aren't you a little hot? I know I am.' The commissionaire removed his cap and heavy coat – he was wearing nothing underneath except a bow tie. 'Do you really have to go to that dirty old hold?' he said, moving closer.

'Oh Jesus, not again,' Serena said. The naked man was a little joke thought up by the guys who programmed the ship's computer, and regularly popped up in a variety of guises, usually at the most inopportune moments. At first, Serena had seen the funny side, but after two years the joke was wearing a little thin. 'End,' Serena barked – and the naked man faded and disappeared.

The lift doors opened and a woman's gentle disembodied voice said soothingly, 'Hold. Mind how you go.'

Serena got into a golf cart and drove down the long, long passageway towards the hold's service control panel. It looked bad: pressure was up twenty points and the temperature was creeping up to 78 degrees.

'Shit!' Over the normal creaks and groans of the living ship, she could hear little thuds and clangs as the clams hurled themselves at the confining walls of the hold. They were getting excited.

Something was seriously wrong. As Serena watched, the needle on the virtual pressure gauge rose another two points. She punched the manual pressure-release valve – nothing happened.

'External monitor – hold pressure valve.' A video screen alongside the pressure gauge blinked into life. She watched as the cold grey exterior of the ship came into view. There, in the centre of the picture, was the massive domed pressure-relief valve itself, streaked with effluent. Pressure was linked to temperature, so it was important to keep the hold at between one and two atmospheres. Any higher and the great release valve on top of the ship automatically opened and released the excess gas. But something was holding it shut. Serena thought she could see a small smudge on the lip of the valve. 'Zoom in centre right.' The picture enlarged, and now it was clear what the problem was. An ancient spacecraft lay crumpled in the jaws of the great valve. It happened from time to time – Earth's orbit was packed with space debris and occasionally satellites and bits of old spacecraft would get trapped like this in the valve. It was so massive and the motors attached to it so powerful that anything caught in there was usually pulverized the moment it closed. But this was a big spaceship, so big it had pushed the valve out of line and jammed it shut.

'Shit, shit, shit!' Serena knew she was going to have to do something about this, which meant getting inside the pressure valve – which meant going through the hold itself. She hated the idea of getting so close to those ravenous eating machines, but if she didn't act quickly, they'd soon have breached the wall of the hold and would be all over the ship.

'Earth Base, Earth Base. Kowalski, Scow 1798, SS *St Francis Sinatra* calling.' Serena sat at the main control display and tried to make contact. Regulations stated that Earth Base must be informed before any operative attempted to enter the hold. 'Earth Base, Earth Base, come in please.' At last, on the main control monitor, there appeared the face of an untidy, acne-covered young man.

'Hi, er, sorry, there's no one here to take your call at the moment, but if you'd like to leave a message, please do so at the tone.'

'Bloody computers!' A long, loud beep came over the speakers. 'I really need to speak to a human being, is there no one there I can talk to?'

The scruffy youth scratched his chin. 'Sorry, er, there's no one here to take your call at the moment . . .'

'Look, you computer-generated Herbert, I'm about to enter the hold, I need to inform—'

'May I remind you,' the youth interrupted, 'that regulation 996, paragraph 7 (b) states that any operative wishing to enter the hold must first inform Earth Base of their intention to do so.'

'That's what I'm trying to do!' Serena exploded. 'Let me speak to someone!'

The youth looked troubled. 'Hi, er, sorry, there's no one here to take your call at the moment. You can either leave a message, or, if you'd prefer to hold, a service operative will be with you shortly.'

'I'll hold.' Serena sighed. There was a click and Vivaldi's *Four Seasons* blared tinnily out of the speakers.

On screen, the youth then informed Serena, 'You are currently number 9,001 in a queue.'

'Fuck it!' said Serena, breaking the connection. She looked across at the temperature gauge – it was approaching 79 degrees.

Serena pulled on the heavy canvas pressure suit over her one-piece anti-crush chain-mail underwear and thermal regulation vest. She hated wearing all this stuff – she was already beginning to sweat, and wasn't yet in the greater warmth of the hold. Finally stepping into the bulky, acid-resistant outer covering, she zipped it up. 'I feel like a fucking stuffed olive. Boots – where are the fucking boots?' Craning uncomfortably over the steel-ringed neck of the suit, she located the heavy boots and slipped her feet into them. They were meant to be oversized, but this was ridiculous, they felt like a clown's shoes – she'd forgotten to don the anti-crush socks. 'Shit!' It was too late now, she wasn't getting undressed just for a pair of socks. She tried a few exploratory steps. The boots felt huge, but what the hell, it wasn't as if she was going to be doing anything athletic.

At last she stood at the pressure-lock entrance. Regulations stated that before entering the hold, it should be vented with 22.25 metric tonnes of freezing carbon dioxide. It was supposed to calm the clams, but as it had been worked out on the ground by a civil servant with a laptop – far from the realities of space garbage disposal – in practice it was a deeply suspect operation. In a situation like this, it merely raised the pressure, and therefore the temperature. Serena hit the gas valve and kept her eye on the pressure gauge. As the carbon dioxide flooded into the hold, she watched it rise a terrifying ten points. Taking several deep breaths, she pulled the perspex helmet over her head and secured it on the locating lugs of the suit. Twisting it clockwise she heard it lock with a satisfying *kerchink*! She was ready now. Crossing her fingers as best she could inside the sense-depriving gloves, she stepped into the lock.

The hold was vast; the very size of the place gave Serena the willies, and the pressure was enormous – she could feel it, even through the many layers of her suit. Clinging to the narrow, fragile walkway that crossed the gargantuan hold, she peered off into the far distance. On one side she could just about make out the curving rear of the ship. About two miles in the other direction, the vast form of the main bulkhead rose out of the thin mist. Beneath her were millions of tons of garbage, gradually being turned into fertilizer by the hard-working clams. She made her way carefully along the walkway in the big boots, trying not to look down.

Suddenly there was a loud clang, and out of the corner of her eye she saw a clam falling back into the sea of rubbish. Then there was another, even louder clang, and then another. Clams were leaping up all around her. Jesus, she'd never seen them so lively. One managed to clamp its valves around the edge of the metal floor of the walkway, and was edging slowly towards her boot. Seeing it just in time, she stamped on it, cracking its shell and sending it tumbling back down. If she didn't get out of there soon, she was going to end up as a clam treat. With the walkway shaking and resounding to the clangs and bangs of the excited clams, Serena ran the rest of the way, in the big, sloppy boots, and scampered up the observation ladder on the other side of the hold.

Chapter 10

The plan had started promisingly enough. The contents of the castle archive were assembled in a pyre in front of the gates, and citizens were invited to add their Books, pamphlets, hymnals – anything that pertained in any way to The Book or The Prophecy. At first people gladly obliged. The night was finally gone, the Dawn that would last for a thousand years had come – why not do as the King requested?

But soon it became clear to his subjects that it was not only The Book that the King was trying to destroy. He wanted to reach into their minds and rip out every trace of it; expunge all memory. That wasn't easy, since they'd been living with The Book for as long as they could remember. Soon the body count began to rise, as more and more people fell foul of the King's ruling and were publicly tortured and executed 'as an example to others'. What made it so awful was that these weren't criminals – they were simple, ordinary people who, for the most part, weren't even sure when they were quoting from The Book or not. The only certain means to escape the gallows was to stay dumb.

Gildroy eased gently back on the reins, and the thunder from the big black stallion's hooves diminished as its pace slowed to a walk. They were nearing Castle Limbo now, and the air was full of the sound of wailing, and heavy with the acrid smell of burning paper. Approaching the sprawling habitation that had grown up in the shadow of the castle, they entered a scene of devastation. There was a fire on every street corner. An occasional breeze would pick up a sheaf of smouldering pages and hurl them high into the air, creating burning dust devils, which whirled down the ash-strewn alleys.

Women with tear-stained faces, who had lost husbands, sons, daughters, rolled weeping on the ground. Men sat hollow-eyed in silent disbelief at what they had witnessed, while, outside the gates of the castle itself, the grim task of applying the rule of law went on. The single gibbet originally erected had proved unequal to the task, and in its place there now stood a triangular erection, whose three long beams were capable of accommodating the dangling, twitching bodies of at least twelve of Limbo's citizens. Some hardy, defiant souls, after they'd been cut down and had endured the agony of having their intestines extracted over glowing coals, would, in the moments before their hearts were cut out and thrown upon the fire, look up at the castle walls and shout quotations from The Book. Around this grisly scene, a cordon of armed soldiers kept back an angry mob.

'There's no place like home,' said Gildroy.

'That barbecue smells good,' said Norval.

'Now, now,' scolded his brother. 'It's a little early for luncheon. First we must pay our respects to the King.'

Gildroy clicked his tongue. 'Walk on,' he instructed his horse, and the nightmare threesome approached the vast gates of the castle.

Gildroy looked down at his brother. 'Shall we see if anyone's home?'

Norval nodded eagerly, and with his huge gnarled fist, knocked on the solid, three-inch planking of the colossal oak gates. On the other side, with the rest of the garrison out supervising the executions, the lone sentry watched in horror as the massive locking beam split along its entire length and iron nails shot out of the gates like bullets. Running up to the top of the tower, he expected to see an invading mob armed with a battering ram. He was faced instead with a tall, thin man on the Devil's own horse and a walking mausoleum smiling up at him.

'Hello,' said Gildroy. 'We'd like to see the King, please.'

'Er, sorry,' said the sentry. 'He's not home today. Can I take a message?'

'Yes,' said Gildroy, 'tell him we'll meet him in the drawing room. Brother?' With a splintering crash, Norval thrust his fist through the gate. The locking beam gave up the ghost and the gates swung open. 'Thank you, have a nice day,' Gildroy smiled up at the sentry.

The sentry stood open mouthed as Norval held open the gates and Gildroy rode through the great arch on the massive black stallion.

As the huge horse clip-clopped into the castle courtyard, a phrase from Gildroy's childhood came back to him. How did it go again? Oh yes:

'Black crow on black beast rides unhindered through castle gate.
Darkness and death is Yardley's fate . . .'

The King looked uncomprehendingly at the strangers standing before him.

Gildroy smiled. 'You look terrible, brother.'

The King blinked and looked from the tall one that resembled an undertaker to the squat one who bore a striking similarity to parts of the west wing, and memory stirred. 'Gildroy? Norval?' He stretched out his arms and the three brothers embraced. 'Oh, it's so good to see you. I've been so lonely, so wretched. Let me look at you.' He stepped back to view their happy expressions. 'I can't tell you how it gladdens my heart to see your smiling faces. All I've had for the last three months is scowls. No one likes me any more! They all . . .' The King could not continue. He stood in the centre of the room, racked with sobbing.

Gildroy put an arm around his shoulder. 'There, there. Gildroy's here now. Gildroy will make it better.'

The King wept uncontrollably in his brother's arms, then suddenly broke off and went to the window. Opening it, he looked up at the sky. 'It's not getting darker, is it? Do you think it's getting darker?' From far below came the screams of the dying and the strident howling of the mob. 'Come here, come here.' He motioned

Gildroy to join him. 'Listen! Listen to that! Do you see what I have
to put up with? Bloody noise every hour of the day and night.
Bastards! Bastards!' he yelled. Then, gripping his brother's shoulder
tight, he whispered urgently in his ear. 'They're not going to defeat
me, oh, no. They'll never break me – I'll smear this land with their
entrails from coast to coast before I give in. Do you hear that you
dogs?' he shouted out of the window. 'I'll bathe in your blood before
I yield to the likes of you!'

Turning back to Gildroy, he tapped the side of his own nose with
his finger. 'I've got a plan,' he whispered, an unnatural gleam in his
eye. 'Tick, tick, tick . . . eh? Eh, brother? If they don't like it they
can all go to hell!' The King dissolved in fits of giggles. 'Tick, tick,
tick!' Gildroy had always known that his brother was a little weak
in the head, but now it seemed that he'd completely lost his marbles.

The door opened. Gildroy turned as the Queen entered. A low
animal growl issued from Norval's throat and he advanced slowly
on her, a big smile on his stupid, sloppy mouth. The Queen was
transfixed with horror, like a deer staring into the eyes of a bear.
When Norval was almost upon her, the Wizard appeared as if from
nowhere and placed himself between them. Norval stopped short;
he wasn't sure of the Wizard. He dimly remembered the Wizard
doing something horrible to him many years ago.

'Well, well, well, you haven't changed a bit.' Gildroy extended
his hand and walked over to where the Wizard stood shielding the
trembling Queen.

'I was wondering when you'd turn up,' said the Wizard, ignoring
the proffered hand.

'And you, my dear, you look as lovely as ever. I think Norval's
taken rather a shine to you.' The Queen shuddered and, in her
confusion, involuntarily half-curtsied.

'Smeil!' called the Wizard. The little man came scurrying
through the door. 'It's time for the King's nap.' Smeil disappeared
momentarily, then reappeared with two burly stewards.

The men advanced on the King, who at once leapt onto the

windowsill. 'See, see brother? They're all against me! Well, they shan't take me alive!'

'Please, my dear, come down!' the Queen implored.

The King looked first at her, then out of the window at the long drop to the ground. He stroked his beard. 'Well, Queenie, you'd probably make a softer landing. Let's see if you can take my weight!' And with that he leapt at her. She sidestepped and the King fell into the arms of the two stewards, who led him off, raving.

'Go with him, your highness, see if you can calm him,' the Wizard instructed. The Queen took leave of her 'guests' and followed her distraught husband to his chambers. The Wizard turned back to the brothers. 'What do you want?'

Gildroy raised an eyebrow. 'Want? We want nothing, except to help our dear brother in his hour of need.'

'He needs no help from the likes of you.'

'Really? Forgive me, perhaps I've read the situation awry. It seems to me you have rather a problem on your hands: a population on the verge of revolt, a disaffected army, and what do you suppose the people will do when they find out their King is several archbishops short of a coronation?'

The Wizard went to the door and opened it. 'Leave now,' he commanded.

Gildroy clapped his hands together. 'Oh, I see. Of course, I understand now. The King is declared mad, but with the Prince too young to rule, you declare yourself Lord Protector and rule in his stead. Very good, very good. But there's one small detail you are overlooking, my dear Wizard. I am still alive and, as the nearest blood relation, the throne is rightly mine.'

'Perhaps you are forgetting that you were passed over and banished for treason.'

Gildroy's eyes were suddenly aflame. 'How could I forget the injustice done to me? It is all that has kept me alive these years – the thought that one day I would return and . . .'

The Wizard smiled. 'And what?' Gildroy's hand was on his dagger. One quick thrust and it would all be over. Gildroy swallowed hard. He had waited a long time for this; he couldn't afford to make a mistake. He wasn't going to jeopardize his plans by getting into a fight. After all, this was a wizard, and a powerful one at that. Gildroy took a deep breath and moved over to the window.

'Are you leaving, or shall I call the King's Guard?' enquired the Wizard.

Gildroy looked down at the grim soldiers overseeing the atrocities at the castle gates. 'Do you really think that they care about two old has-beens like us? They look to me like they've had enough.' Norval had been gradually manoeuvring himself behind the Wizard, and now stood ready to pounce. In an instant, the Wizard spun round and faced him. But in Norval's mind it was not the Wizard that he confronted, but a great dragon, its terrible mouth belching fire.

'Ah! No! Go 'way! Help!' Norval ran screaming to a corner of the room, and crouched there, terrified.

'Bravo! You must tell me how you do that,' Gildroy applauded.

The Wizard turned on him, narrowing his eyes. Gildroy had the strangest sensation that clawing fingers were forcing their way inside his head and sifting through his thoughts. But he quickly countered, and the Wizard's mind could find no purchase on Gildroy's mentally erected blank wall.

'Nice try,' said Gildroy. 'But I mastered parlour games like that years ago.'

'You may eat, feed your horse and bathe. Then if you are not out of the castle in one hour, I shall have you both executed,' said the Wizard coldly.

'Hospitable as ever. Just one request, Wiz. Before we go, we would like to pay our respects to the baby.'

All colour drained from the Wizard's face. 'You think I would let you near the Prince with the Blood Quest on his head?' Approaching Gildroy, he spoke quietly but forcefully. 'Go near the Prince and I swear I shall kill you myself.'

'I'll take that as a no, then.'

'I'll inform the servants you are leaving.' The Wizard slammed out of the room.

Gildroy turned to his brother, still moaning gently in the corner. 'It seems the Wiz has developed rather a soft spot for this Prince.' Gildroy stroked his brother's hump thoughtfully. 'There's more to this than meets the eye, Norval – much more. You know, for the first time in a long time I'm beginning to feel rather . . . light. Gay, even.' He began to leap from one stick leg to the other, slowly at first, then faster and faster. 'Look at me!' he cackled as he twirled, clapping his hands in time to some imagined devilish music. 'I'm dancing!'

Chapter 11

Malcom took a bite out of the doughnut and made a face. 'What's this, then?'

Beasely looked at the packet. 'Er, coffee vanilla.'

'Tastes like shit.' Malcom opened the window of the car and threw it out. 'What have *you* got?'

'Chocolate.'

'Give us it here.' Malcom seized the doughnut as it was halfway to Beasely's lips.

'Hey!' Beasely watched as the detective inspector devoured his breakfast in two bites.

'That's better,' said Malcom, covering the windscreen in moist crumbs. 'In future, get me chocolate. I hate coffee icing.' Beasely slumped, sulking in the passenger seat, listening to Malcom's slack-jawed chewing. 'How long's he been in there?' Malcom asked, picking his teeth with his little finger.

'We're just wasting our time.'

'How long's he been in there?' Malcom insisted.

Beasely sighed and looked at his watch. 'Hour and a half.' They were sitting across the street from the anonymous semi-detached house which served as Michael Daniels's office. A discreet brass plaque on the gatepost was the only evidence that this was the headquarters of Hilditch Leisure – the epicentre of Councillor Daniels's business empire. Daniels had arrived, as was his wont, at five a.m.

'What's he doing?'

'Running his business.'

Malcom turned in his seat and, leaning dangerously close, covered Beasely in a fog of chocolate-iced morning breath. 'I know he's running his business, prat. I was just wondering what's taking him all this time.' Beasely was on the verge of repeating his statement, but thought better of it. Malcom eased back in his seat and closed his eyes. 'So, go through all that business bollocks again. What's Daniels's scam?'

'It's not a scam,' Beasely sighed, 'it's perfectly legit. He owns Hilditch Leisure, which runs a casino and some of the leisure facilities on the pier, remember?' Malcom grunted. 'Right, well, he's just acquired a few more companies, that's all – Transcost Machines, Target Management and Coastway Excavations.'

'Target is into property management and Transcost is the one-armed bandit company, right?'

'Manufacturers of gambling machinery, yes.'

'And Coastway Excavations is an excavation company.'

'As its name implies.'

'Look pinhead, don't fuck around. This is a police investigation—'

'Unauthorized,' Beasely interrupted. He felt a tightening sensation in his groin and looked down to see Malcom's fist wrapped around his crotch.

'Let's get one thing straight, I don't give a fuck what you or anyone else thinks. I'm just making sure I've got all the facts, OK? Be nice to me and I just might let you keep one of your bollocks. Cross me and I'll have your tackle framed on my office wall.' Malcom released his hold and Beasely curled up in a ball of pain. While he got his breath back, Malcom lit a panatella. 'Now, Daniels got all this money to buy these companies from his wife, right?'

'Right,' squeaked Beasely.

'See, I am listening. Carry on.'

Beasely continued through small, painful gasps. 'His wife had all the real money; she was the daughter of Sir Scythius Greene, City bigwig. Personal fortune of ten million, and God knows how much in stocks and shares.'

Malcom snorted. 'Scythius. Stupid fucking name. And she died last year, leaving everything to young Daniels.'

'Yes. Daniels liquidized all her investments and started buying companies.'

'Why didn't he buy himself a decent car?'

'Not a priority – power is what he wants. He's been under his wife's thumb for most of his life, and now he's free, he's making the most of it.'

'But why an excavation company? Property management, fair enough, but what does he know about excavation?'

'Probably nothing. People buy all sorts of businesses all the time. It's usually just down to how much money they think they can make out of them.'

Malcom shook his head. 'Nah, there's something up, I know there is. I can feel it in my water. Speaking of which . . .' Malcom opened the door and, without getting up, opened his fly and relieved himself in the gutter, filling the car with steam. 'That's better.'

At that moment, the door of the small semi opened and Councillor Daniels appeared with a pink folder under his arm. Locking the door, he walked across to the pristine blue Rover parked in the drive. 'Here we go,' said Malcom, turning the key in the ignition. They followed the Rover as it drove down to the seafront and then turned left towards Brighton. Driving along the front, with the early morning sun turning everything butterscotch-yellow, they caught tantalizing glimpses of the sea – flat calm between rows of neat little beach huts.

At the Hove Street traffic lights, Councillor Daniels turned right for the King Alfred Centre car park. Malcom drove straight on and doubled back, parking in the adjacent seafront Texaco. The two policemen got out of the car and walked cautiously down to the sea. Peering round the corner of the swimming pool complex, they saw Councillor Daniels, pink folder still in hand, in conversation with another man. They were standing on the promenade, looking up at the Centre itself. Now and then, Daniels would point out a part of the structure and the other man would nod. Beasely felt a dig in the ribs.

'Here.' Malcom handed him a small camera.

'What's this for?'

'Holiday snaps, what do you think?'

'Why don't *you* use it?'

'I don't fucking know how to, that's why! Now take some fucking pictures!' Malcom hissed.

Reluctantly, Beasely took the camera and started snapping. After a few minutes, Daniels handed the man the pink folder, then they shook hands and went their separate ways.

In the car, trailing Daniels back along the seafront, Malcom scratched his cheek. 'What's he up to? Who was that other geezer at the King Alfred?'

'It's probably all perfectly innocent,' said Beasely. 'He might have been there in some sort of official capacity. The Centre is a Council building.'

'How many councillors do you know indulge in Council business at half-past six in the morning? Nah, there's something shifty about all this.'

The Rover turned right off the coast road and headed back up towards Daniels's office.

Malcom slammed on the brakes. 'Get out.'

'What?'

Malcom leaned across Beasely and opened his door. 'Get that film developed. I want to know who the other man is and what was in that pink folder.'

'How am I going to get back to the station?' Beasely moaned.

'You've got legs, haven't you?'

'But it's miles,' wailed the little man.

'Then get a bus.'

'Where are you going?'

'Important police business – I'm going to see a woman about a sausage. Now fuck off!'

Malcom pushed Beasely out of the car and screeched off down

the road. Malcom's police antennae were twitching, and when his investigative juices were flowing, other areas became stimulated. He was on his way to visit a certain lady, and was very eager to get there. Turning on the siren, he floored the accelerator of the police Vauxhall.

Chapter 12

Rex was floating in space, high above a vast and shimmering golden hoop. Slowly, slowly he floated closer and closer, until with a terrifying rush, he was engulfed in a kaleidoscopic whirlpool of images and sensations. It seemed that he was all the suffering in the world; in him a billion souls cried out in the unbelievable agony of their existence. The screams of men, women and children, ripped to shreds by the weapons of war, rang in his ears as he was drawn down, down into a sea of fire. Emerging, he found himself standing on a dark, windswept plain. Lightning split the sky and thunder rumbled over the land. In front of him stood a great misshapen castle, ages old. At the foot of the castle walls was a scene of devastation and death. The air was full of the sound of weeping and heavy with the sweet, sickly smell of burning flesh. There was a funeral in progress, but this was no neat and tidy occasion of floral tributes and smart black mourners listening patiently to a vicar's empty words. Here the grave was a slash in the ground, and while the dead were unceremoniously dumped into the long wound, all the epitaph the tumbled corpses could expect was the weeping of those they left behind.

Rex found himself at the edge of the mass grave, and looked down. Row upon row of grinning corpses stared back at him and as he watched, terrified, the cadavers raised their arms and pointed at him. 'Save us!' they chanted in their hollow voices. 'You are the Dawn! Save us!'

A movement caught his eye. On the castle battlements, a blood-smeared crown upon its head, danced a huge and hideous monster, mocking the sad scene below. Rex looked up into the creature's face, and the creature looked back. Then it was bounding across the plain towards him at incredible speed, whooping like a monstrous hyena. The last thing he saw were its blood-red eyes as it opened its terrible mouth to engulf him.

'Ahh!' Rex woke with a start. The dream was always the same. As a boy he'd often woken screaming in the middle of the night, and sought solace in the comfort of his parents' safe and cosy bed.

He looked at the clock – the illuminated dial read: 4:46. It was nearly time to get up and, anyway, the thought of closing his eyes and returning to that hideous place filled him with dread. Rex turned on the light and picked up his book off the bedside table. 'Let's see what Prince Nostrum's up to.' Sitting up, he adjusted his pillow and began to read . . .

Suddenly Orvis was aware of something yapping at his ankles. 'No! Go away!' He'd always hated dogs and, as Sparkie leapt and barked around him, in his confusion he let go of the bomb's remote control and it plunged over the side of the high plateau.

Prince Nostrum, far below, ran as fast as he could towards the small black object, tumbling rapidly earthwards. He had to catch it before it smashed into a million pieces on the rocks beneath – the future of the Earth depended on it. But he was too far away. He watched in growing agony as the remote control hurtled towards the hard rocks. Admittedly it wasn't his world, his home, but the people of this peculiar planet had always been good to him, and in return he had promised to do all in his power to protect them. 'Come on, Nostrum,' he urged himself, 'you made a promise.' The Prince dug deep inside himself, calling on every nerve, every muscle, every fibre of his being to make one last effort. 'For mankind!' he yelled and took off, covering the last ten metres in a single stride. In a desperate lunging dive, he caught the small box, centimetres from the ground. Safe!

When the dust had cleared, the Prince could hear Orvis's high, mocking laugh. 'Nice try, spaceman, but do you think I'd be stupid enough not to have used a fail-safe?' The Prince looked up at the manic cripple, high above him. 'It's on a timer: one hour and the world is history.' The Prince got up and strode immediately over to where the bomb lay, clicking and humming serenely, among the tree ferns. 'I wouldn't try anything if I were you!' called Orvis. 'It's tamper-proof. I've employed the latest quantum technology – you mess with it, or think of messing with it, or even look at it in a way that suggests that you might mess with it, and . . . boom! Checkmate, I believe.' Orvis opened the door of his time machine. 'Goodbye, Prince. And this time I really *mean* goodbye.' The door closed and, with an electric *kerrump*, the silver machine performed some advanced origami on a small piece of the space-time continuum, and was gone . . .

The beeping of Rex's alarm clock brought him abruptly back from the infant Earth. He looked at the clock: 5:00. With a groan, Rex closed the book and yawned. It was definitely time to get up.

Coming downstairs, he took in the newspapers that had been left on the doorstep and, after cutting open the bundles and stacking the shelves, relaxed with a cup of coffee. He savoured this time, taking a few quiet minutes before the morning madness to acquaint himself with the lead news story of the day, so that he would have something to talk about should any of his customers want to indulge in any social interaction other than the exchange of goods for cash. He picked up a copy of the *Guardian* and, under the headline 'Thrid Tremor in a Week', read one expert's theory on the cause of the mini-earthquakes that had been plaguing the south coast. The expert said that because of decades of plundering the Earth's resources – gouging out great chunks of the planet to turn into micro scooters and singing fish – the Earth had become unbalanced, causing a shift in its rotational axis and thus moving the Equator several degrees north. This, in turn, applied a whole new set of stresses and strains to the Earth's crust. What we were seeing in Brighton, the article went on, was the beginning of a redrawing of the boundaries of the tectonic plates. We were entering a whole new era in continental drift, and eventually southern England would break free from the rest of Britain, and join the Continent. 'That's going to upset the Eurosceptics,' thought Rex.

Putting the newspaper back on the pile, he looked around with satisfaction at the shelves gleaming with high-class glossies and, underneath them, the neatly stacked daily papers, still pristine. He knew that most of them would end up trampled into the floor of the seven forty-five to Victoria, but he didn't mind that. The transience of their usefulness only increased their allure. Rex didn't exactly love this job, but he was good at it. He prided himself on the fact that he could turn a *Telegraph* reader around in ten seconds flat, even if they hadn't come in with the right money.

He looked up at the photograph of his parents, thumbtacked to the side of the cigarette display. They stood smiling in front of the Cessna 152 in which they were about to embark on their last ever journey, that sunny morning seven years ago. 'Never even said goodbye,' he sighed. Although he still missed them, he took comfort from the fact that, were they ever to return, they would be proud of the efficiency with which he ran their shop.

The thought '*Daily Mail* and *Hello*' popped into his head. Seconds later the tinkling of the bell above the door announced the first of the commuter trade. The smart-suited businesswoman went straight to the shelves and picked out copies of the *Mail* and *Hello*.

The day wore predictably on. After the morning rush came the mid-morning lull, followed by lunchtime, when he usually did a brisk trade in glossies and chocolate bars. Then there was the school confectionery rush, followed by the return of the commuters, all wanting an *Evening Argus* to go home with.

As the last customer left, Rex locked the door. After cashing up, he picked up his book and trudged upstairs – the end of another day. But looking at the photograph of the author on the back cover, he felt an unaccustomed surge of tingling emotion, like he used to feel when playing truant from school. Tomorrow was going to be different. Tomorrow he was going to break the habit of a lifetime and close at twelve. Because tomorrow, at Brodders Books in Churchill Square, F. Don Wizzard was signing copies of his latest bestseller – and Rex was going to be there.

Chapter 13

In that inaccessible room in the west wing, the Wizard slumped hopelessly over a great circular table covered in strange symbols. Two large wrought-iron candlesticks held candles that illumined the gloom with a steady flame that could not be extinguished, and yet never burned down. 'What have I done? What have I done?' he moaned. 'How could I have been so naive? Oh, I am a wretched wizard!'

Dreadful sounds drifted in through the open window. Far below, the pitiful cries of the dying had now been replaced with the angry baying of the crowd. The King's Guard, unable to stomach any more killing, were now refusing to carry out the King's orders. They hadn't yet actually joined the mob, but it was only a matter of time. As word of the soldiers' mutiny spread, more and more people appeared out of the landscape to join the rebellious throng outside the castle. Their differences put into perspective by the enormity of the tragedy, Substantialists stood shoulder to shoulder with Conceptualists, as they defiantly chanted phrases from The Book.

Suddenly the Wizard looked up and sniffed. 'The madeleines!' he called out, and ran to the Aga in the corner. Hastily donning an oven glove, he yanked open the door and pulled out a baking tray full of small sponge cakes. Tipping them out onto the table, he inspected them closely. 'Caught them just in time.' Carefully picking one up between thumb and forefinger, he blew on it, then took a small bite. 'Hm, not bad. Not bad at all. Not as good as the fruit scones, of course. Bloody Doctor Perch.' The Wizard had lost his favourite recipe – for fruit scones – in the tunnels above the Salient Sea, and it was this text, discovered by Doctor Ohthyrhis Perch, that had unlocked the secrets of Franklin Gothic Lucida 2. Once decoded, it had languished deep in the archive of the University of Limbo, but now, of course, was lost for ever – burnt, along with everything else that had anything to do with The Book, or that was written in a suspiciously ancient language.

'Hurry, must hurry!' The Wizard placed the still-hot madeleines in a paper bag, then wandered about the room, picking up books and scraps of paper and arranging them in tall, unsteady piles on the great table. Going to a corner cupboard, he pulled out a large carpet-bag and placed it on the floor. 'Packing, how I hate packing,' he muttered. Taking hold of the edge of the table he up-ended it. Books, paper, candlesticks – everything – slid off the table and disappeared into the impossibly deep, dark depths of the carpet-bag. Then, grasping the table firmly in his hands, he gave it a sharp downwards jerk, and instantly the solid, unyielding wood was transformed into chiffon. Tying the flowing material around his neck with a flourish, he went to the window and opened it wide.

Tears pricked his eyes as he listened to the awful sounds far below. Blowing his nose on his scarf, he called down to the angry citizens, 'I'm sorry! It was all my fault! Believe me, it was never meant to be like this! I tried to undo the damage, I tried to make things better – I really did. I thought I could cheat fate but, of course, all I did was to make matters worse. Please forgive me!' He knew he couldn't be heard above the din, and it was a small enough gesture to atone for the gallons of blood that were on his head, but it made him feel a little better.

Closing the window he went over to a large oak chest and fingered the massive brass lock. 'Oh that I had locked up my thoughts as successfully,' he said. Then, guiltily turning the key, he opened it. It contained a first edition of a certain 47-volume work. As the Wizard opened the heavy lid of the chest, he remembered back to the time when, as a young wizard of just nine hundred summers, the idea had first come to him.

Limbo

Life in Limbo had been peaceful, uneventful; night followed day with monotonous regularity, and he'd been bored – it was as simple as that. He'd wanted something to happen, something extraordinary, and so was born the idea of 'The Book'. Of course, he being a wizard, and Limbo being Limbo, anything he wrote down had a habit of coming true, so he had written himself an adventure. But, oh the arrogance of youth, he had to involve the entire universe in his little escapade.

Almost immediately he had realized his mistake and tried to stop it. But once embarked upon, 'The Book' demanded to be finished. Worse, if left to its own devices, it would write itself. Passages dripping with blood would appear overnight, and any edits or rewrites the Wizard tried to make were immediately reversed the moment he lifted his pen.

So came the darkness – the night that would last for a thousand years. Even the Wizard's own hopeful passages about the coming of the dawn were marred by The Book's preoccupation with violence and gore – the Great Terror was entirely The Book's idea. The Wizard had even tried switching locations – moving the action to a 'far-off land' to try and reduce the damage to Limbo but, in so doing, had not only banished himself from his beloved homeland, but also put in jeopardy the whole of creation.

Reasoning that writing of its destruction would bring it about, the Wizard had introduced the story of Alcahoona and her family using The Book to fuel her cooking fire. But The Book had responded by bringing in that bloody doctor who'd ruined everything.

The Wizard had gazed far into the future and seen the gruesome outcome of his work, but was powerless to change it – he was at the mercy of his own creation. The word of The Book was law. *'What will be will be'* wasn't so much a whimsical invitation to resign oneself to the wishes of fate – it was a simple statement of fact. By the time he'd finished, so fed up had he become with the whole exercise that the last words – *'Well, thank goodness that's over'* – were straight from the heart.

The idea of violently expunging this work from collective

memory was a last desperate attempt to save the King's life and avert total disaster. The Wizard honestly believed that if somehow The Book could be removed from the nation's psyche, the future could be reclaimed. But, true to form, any interference with The Book's narrative only resulted in yet more bloodshed.

The Wizard glared into the trunk at this stack of books. He had tried, oh how he'd tried, to destroy them. Once he'd thrown the first volume into the flaming heart of the Aga. But the moment it had hit the flames, the book had screamed like a baby and he'd retrieved it, weeping, from the glowing embers. How could he watch it suffer? It was his creation. 'You have a lot to answer for,' he said, picking up one of the leather-bound volumes. 'I am very, very upset with you. You are coming with me to a place where you can do no more harm.' As he bent to gather more of the books in his arms, some of them darted out of the chest and flew around the room. 'Come back here immediately!' the Wizard yelled, while the books flapped around him. Some flew, teasingly, just out of reach above his head; others threw themselves at the closed window and fell to the floor like stunned birds. The Wizard chased after them, cursing, until eventually every last volume was rounded up and tucked safely into the carpet-bag.

After this unaccustomed exercise, the Wizard, breathing hard, ran his fingers through his hair and straightened his cravat. Then, walking over to a small bookcase, he pulled out a stubby, well-thumbed tome and opened it. A crystal as big as an egg gleamed up at him from inside the hollowed-out book. He picked it up and turned it this way and that in his long, elegant fingers. A shattered rainbow of light danced around the room. Gazing into the heart of the crystal, he could see, deep within, its peculiar and extraordinary flaw – a small, three-dimensional image of the castle, perfect in every detail, and underneath, the legend, 'Souvenir of Limbo'.

The Limbo Crystal had been created a micro-nanosecond after the Big Bang, and as such was the oldest thing in the universe. In the right hands, it was an immensely powerful tool: it was the key to the door between dimensions – between 'what is' and 'what could be'. With it, the Wizard had made many trips to the other side. Mainly to Knightsbridge and Harvey Nichols, where he had bought the Aga as well as numerous gifts for his friends at court.

'My old friend,' said the Wizard, his eyes brimming with tears, 'this leap we make shall be our last. I have committed an unpardonable sin and now I must atone. May the gods take pity on my sacrifice.' The Wizard put the glittering Crystal in his pocket and wiped his eyes. 'Now,' he said, 'only one, unutterably painful task left to perform.' Sighing, he picked up the carpet-bag and took a last look around the room. 'The madeleines! What have I done with the madeleines?' His eyes searched the empty shelves that lined the walls. Ah, there they were, resting on top of the Aga. 'For the journey,' he said, slipping the small, warm cakes into the carpet-bag.

The reason why nobody had ever been able to gain entry to this secret lair was due to the simple fact that there was no way in, nor indeed any way out. There was no door. None save a wizard could enter here.

'I shall miss you, I really shall,' said the Wizard sadly. 'This time, there is no way back.' And with that, he was gone.

Norval and Gildroy had bided their time. Camping on the edge of the woeful habitation, they had watched and waited.

They had watched the King's Guard lose heart, sicken and finally release the remaining prisoners. They had watched as the Guard had argued and torn itself in two, one faction joining the mob and the other retreating back inside the comparative safety of the castle walls. They had watched as the mob, their ranks now swollen with fighting men of rank and station, had grown ever more bold. Now the brothers knew the time was near. All that was needed was a gentle shove to turn righteous anger into dreadful, bloody revenge.

'Help me up, brother.' Norval gave Gildroy a leg up onto the massive black stallion and Gildroy settled himself in the saddle, shaking back his long, lank hair. Deep, dark clouds began to roll in over the beleaguered castle, and distant thunder rumbled over the plain.

'Showtime!' said Gildroy, urging the horse forward with his heels.

As the sinister threesome made their way through the howling mob towards the massive, three-sided gibbet, the crowd parted before them. Slowly, slowly, the angry chanting died away and Gildroy mounted the hanging stage in absolute silence.

'Brothers!' he intoned, throwing his arms wide like a great black crow. 'Nay, I have not earned the right to call you brothers; I have not suffered as you. For I know there is not one here untouched by the King's cruelty.' There was groaning assent from the crowd. 'None among you has not lost someone dear – husband, wife, daughter or son. And for what? To preserve the life of a feeble-minded, frightened man. What is to become of us? Can innocence ever be tempted to open its delicate flower again? Or do trust and the childlike dreams of morning lie defiled amidst the piles of rotting corpses? I say have faith. Have faith in the future and in our lord the Prince. Have we forgotten already the words of The Prophecy?

> ' " . . . and at that time, from his mother's womb,
> A son shall spring; a light, the one whom
> Every daughter and every son shall call The One,
> That brings from high great joy and eke
> Great happiness for almost everyone!" '

Hearing once again the forbidden words of their beloved Book, the crowd howled in anguish. In their minds The Prophecy had become synonymous with death and they had all but forgotten the birth of the Prince and the great joy promised by his coming.

Now Gildroy began to turn on the pressure. Raising the pitch of his voice a tone, he declaimed, 'Can we stand idly by and watch our still-green hopes be trampled in the entrails of our loved ones? The Prince yet lives within these castle walls, but can we trust this King, this brutal murderer, with our saviour?'

'No!' roared the crowd.

'Even so. Our lord is in great danger, for the King fears him. Every second the Prince remains within his grasp his life is in the balance. The Prince is ours, he belongs with us!'

During the chorus of 'Ayes!' Gildroy remounted his horse under the darkening sky.

'Follow me! Let us take up arms to preserve the fragile hope of morning promised by his coming.'

At that, the people began to look around for anything that might serve as a weapon – staves, stakes, long-tined forks. They even started dismantling the stage, ripping out jagged pieces of wood bristling with nails.

'Let us be avenged on him who has perpetrated this great injustice upon our land. The time has come to cry *enough*! To turn pain into anger, anger into vengeance!' With a splintering crash, a bolt of lightning slammed into one of the castle turrets. Gildroy smiled, the timing could not have been better. 'Behold!' he cried. 'The gods are on our side! The work we begin here today will reverberate down the ages, a thousand, nay a thousand, thousand years. Let tyrants beware! And let our cry be, *"All hail the Dawn!"*'

The citizens joined in the battle yell with satanic gusto, and in a violent frenzy hurled themselves against the castle gates. With a little help from Norval, the gates – only recently repaired – were off their hinges within minutes and the angry mob charging through the great stone arch.

The members of the Guard who had remained loyal to the King were quickly overwhelmed, and those that did not swiftly change allegiance were left in fast-spreading pools of their own blood.

The mob howled through the courtyard like a buzz-saw, killing everything in its wake. Housekeepers, kitchen maids, all the innocent servants of the castle were run down and impaled in horrifying agony on an assortment of makeshift weapons. Not even pets were spared the slaughter. The pathetic limp bodies of cats, dogs and canaries lay strewn across the cobbles among the corpses of their masters.

A small knot of soldiers loyal to the King fought a heroic

rear-guard action to allow the surviving servants to gain the sanctuary of the castle itself. Soon none was left alive, but they had served their purpose; the doors of the castle were now firmly locked and barred against the invaders.

Up on the battlements, crossbowmen appeared, raining steel upon the ad hoc army, killing many. But this proved only to rouse the mob to even greater efforts. Their bodies numb with battle frenzy, the screaming horde fell upon the heavy doors again and again, and soon, under this jarring onslaught, they too began to give way. With a despairing groan, the doors splintered in two, and with a yell the mob poured into the very castle itself, sealing the doom of nearly every man, woman and child contained within its walls.

As Gildroy clop-clopped sedately into the now deserted courtyard on his black stallion, Norval halted in his evisceration of one of the castle guards and smiled up at him with his blood-smeared face.

'Put him down, brother, you can finish him later.'

Norval let the limp body of the guard fall, and helped Gildroy out of the saddle.

'Now we have to go and rescue the Prince, but first you must learn the meaning of the word fratricide.' Gildroy walked casually over the castle doors, now lying in several jagged pieces on the ground, and entered the great maze of the ancient castle, with Norval shuffling behind him.

Smeil was distraught. The day had started reasonably well, with the King in good spirits. He had awoken shouting 'It's almost like being in Hove!' and had laughed solidly for twenty minutes. But now all Smeil's problems had come home to roost. It was bad enough losing his master to madness, but now he risked losing him to the mob. Since witnessing the defection of more than half the King's army outside the gates, Smeil had been trying to persuade his master to fly, but with little success – he'd been chasing him round the room for over an hour now. What made matters worse was that Smeil was on his own – all the King's body servants had either run off or joined the other side.

Having no idea of the danger he was in, the King was having the time of his life. He thought that he and Smeil were playing tag. Every now and again he'd stop running and yell 'It's almost like being in Hove!' and howl with laughter, tears streaming down his cheeks. He had no idea why this was funny; he only knew that it was.

At last came the moment that Smeil had dreaded. Down the corridors leading to the King's chambers came a terrible noise, as if a great rage were approaching. Suddenly it was right outside. There was a deafening clatter on the timbers of the door, like the sound of hail on a tile roof; the great oak staves creaked under the onslaught.

'The King, we seek the King!' roared the crowd.

The King had a strange feeling of déjà vu, although in his current state of mind, that's not exactly how he would have phrased it. 'Can't catch me!' he shouted back, and ran round the room giggling, looking for somewhere to hide.

'Sire, we must flee!'

'Come on Smeil, we'll give them a run for their money, eh?' He hadn't played hide-and-seek for ages, but dimly remembered that there were some terrific hiding places in this big, draughty old castle. Existing, as it did, on the very edge of fantasy, the castle only ever made sense to a child, so now all its secrets were laid bare to the childlike consciousness of the King. Pulling back a rug, a trapdoor was revealed. 'Yes!' he said and, throwing it wide, disappeared down the dusty, cobwebbed steps, followed in trepidation by the loyal Smeil.

The King knew exactly where he was going and, more importantly, how to get there. Coming to the bottom of the steps, he turned sharp left. While the noise of battle raged all around, he scampered, surefooted in the pitch-blackness, down the rediscovered passages of his youth. Smeil was soon left far behind, hopelessly lost in the maze of tunnels. On and on went the King, slowing here to negotiate a sharp bend, stooping there to avoid hitting his head on a low beam.

Pausing at a junction, he groped around in the darkness. 'Tick, tick, tick,' he chuckled. Finding what he was looking for, he felt his way up the side of one of the large barrels. His fingers eagerly explored the dry dustiness of its top, and came into contact with his old alarm clock. Picking it up, he checked the connections, and feeling the numerals with his fingertips, set the alarm for twelve o'clock.

'Boom,' he muttered, winding it up, 'Boom!' and ran off, giggling.

At last, squeezing himself up through a narrow grating, he emerged, immensely pleased with himself, right under the chapel altar. Peeking out from under the altar cloth, he made sure that the coast was clear, then scuttled across the flagstones and dived into the confessional. It had always been his favourite hiding place – but unfortunately for him, Gildroy and Norval had remembered it too.

There was a small crypt under the chapel, and many years ago the twins had made a hole in the ceiling, a small narrow slit right through the floor of the confessional, so that they could listen to their elders and betters as they unburdened their souls. In the dark, they had sat and listened intently to stories of adultery, cruelty and deep, deep shame. Blackmail had thus become a very successful way of supplementing their pocket money.

Gildroy and Norval waited there until they heard the shuffling of feet on the floor above. Faint mutterings came down to them through the narrow hole: 'It's almost like being in Hove. It's almost like being in Hove. It's almost like being in Hove,' over and over again, interspersed with bouts of manic laughter.

Gildroy looked at his brother and shook his head. 'I fear our brother is out of his wits. Let us put him out of his body.' Drawing his sword, he placed the tip of the blade against the hole, right under the confused King. 'With me, brother.' Norval wrapped his large, gnarled fingers around Gildroy's on the hilt of the sword.

There was something so familiar about the image, something so celebrated about the act, what was it? 'Ah yes,' Gildroy remembered:

' . . . *four hands grasp the sword as the point is driven home.*
The King meets his maker unshriven, alone.'

Gildroy turned to his lumpen brother, smiling darkly in the dim light of the crypt. 'Shall we?'

Above them the King, hearing something, paused in his demented mantra and, for a moment recovering his senses, wondered where he was and what he was doing there. 'It's almost like being in Hove? What does it mean?' were the last words he was to utter in this lifetime.

The four hands on the blade thrust upwards with such unworldly force that the floor of the confessional was split in two and the King impaled the length of his body, the tip of the sword emerging from the back of his skull. He let out a long, drawn-out sigh that had in it all the pointless dreariness of his life. And, while his soul sprang joyously free, his blood ran down the blade of his brothers' sword, staining their guilty hands crimson.

'I think it's fairly safe to say that the King is dead,' said Gildroy. 'Long live us!' He chuckled.

His brother joined in, and soon the crypt was echoing to their hideous, mocking laughter.

The clash of steel and the crying of the wounded, as the battle drew nearer, brought Gildroy back to the job in hand. Yanking the sword free from his late brother, who fell to the floor above them with a soft *whump*, he wiped the blade on his brother's tunic.

'Come, Norval, now your way to the Queen is clear. Shall we go and break the news to her highness?' At the mention of the Queen, Norval smoothed back his hair with a gory hand, plastering it to his skull with the dead King's blood, and smiled shyly up at his brother. 'Very natty,' added Gildroy. 'How could she resist?'

Letting young love lead the way, Gildroy followed his brother down corridors slippery with blood, Norval's burning lust and keen sense of smell leading him unerringly towards the Queen's chambers.

*

'Will I never see him again?' wept the Queen as she handed her baby over to the Wizard.

The Wizard took the sleeping child. His heart faltered as he looked into the Queen's beauty. 'You must face up to it, my dear,' he said.

'And you?' she said, stroking his face with tender fingers. 'Shall I never look into those eyes again?'

The Wizard swallowed hard and spoke quickly. 'If we weaken now, it is the end of hope, of dreams, of everything.' The Queen looked away, but the Wizard caught her chin and turned her head to face him. He looked deep into her eyes. 'I have done a terrible thing and I must make amends. That you must pay for my transgression pains me more than I can express. I am relying on you to be strong for me, my love. Those two black crows must believe that the Prince is the King's son. As long as he remains alive they dare not seize the throne, and there is hope for this land of ours.'

The Queen forced a smile. 'Let us hope that his exile is for a short time only.'

The Wizard smiled back. 'My dear, I leave this room and step into the unknown. God knows, given the choice I would rather take my chances here with you, and if you ask me to stay, I will. But if I do, it is the end of everything. My power is great, but even I cannot hold out indefinitely against the force of darkness that drives the ambition of those infernal twins. The Prince must survive – he is our only hope for the future.'

The Queen broke away and walked to the open window. The sun was setting and the sky growing visibly darker. 'And how shall I cope with the endless night?'

'Know that one day our son shall return, and with him the dawn that will last for an eternity.'

The Queen looked at him with big, moist eyes. 'And till then? Without you here to guide me, where shall I find the courage to face what must be?'

The Wizard smiled. 'I am right beside you always. Where you

go, I go. I am the other side of the veil. Look and you shall find me.'

Festrina, who was crouching with her ear to the door, suddenly sprang up.

'They're coming!' Down the corridor came the confident chink of spur-clad boots and also an indistinct shuffling sound. The Queen shuddered, but looking into the Wizard's serene, fathomless eyes, she found her strength there. Touching his cheek, she let her hand linger on his neat black beard, then looked down once more at the sleeping form of her child.

'Keep him safe,' she said, kissing the infant gently on the forehead.

There was a polite knock at the door. 'Can Queenie come out to play, please?' Gildroy called. 'There's a young man here who's longing to see her.' Norval's low growl set the room vibrating. Trembling, the Queen gripped the Wizard's arm. Looking into her eyes and seeing how helpless, how painfully alone he was leaving her, broke the Wizard's heart. But, sensing his faltering resolve, the Queen pulled herself together and replaced the vulnerability in her eyes with steel.

'Courage,' she smiled, picking up the carpet-bag and handing it to him. 'Go now,' she instructed.

The Wizard took a deep breath. 'Open!' he commanded the wall, and a doorway appeared, with a flight of steps leading down into darkness.

There was a mighty crash at the door. 'No manners, that's the trouble with people today,' Gildroy complained loudly from the other side.

The Wizard turned one last time to the Queen. 'My love, we shall be together,' he said, and marched swiftly down the steps, the young Prince in one arm. As the Wizard and the Prince disappeared through the doorway, it closed behind them.

The door gave way at the second crash, and Gildroy and Norval exploded into the Queen's apartments. Gildroy paced up and down, his small mean eyes searching the room.

'Where is he?' Neither Festrina nor her mistress spoke. 'I know he was here.' They remained impassive, eyes staring straight ahead. 'Look, I'm a man of limited patience. I'll ask you nicely only once more. Where is he?' But the two women remained dumb. 'Aargh!' Gildroy screamed in frustration and broke his sword against Festrina's skull. She fell to the floor like a rag doll. Gildroy then approached the trembling Queen. 'You see, my dear, I mean business.'

Sheathing his fractured sword, Gildroy turned back to his brother who was standing slack-mouthed in the centre of the room, eyes fixed on the Queen's bosom. 'Manners, Norval. You're drooling.'

Norval snapped his mouth shut with a wet *shlwup* and wiped his chin. 'Sorry, bro.'

Regaining her composure, the Queen drew herself up to her full height. 'How can I help you gentlemen?' she enquired.

Gildroy walked around her, eyeing her critically. 'She's not a bad catch, you know, brother. Got a few childbearing years left in her yet. Big hips too, that's good – you'll have lots of babies together.'

Norval smiled, looking at her with his big, uneven eyes.

The Queen shuddered. 'You would give me to that?' she said, pointing to the blood-caked mountain of gristle staring shyly at her. Norval was visibly stung, and looked sadly at the floor.

'Careful,' said Gildroy, 'you'll hurt his feelings.'

'You forget your place, sir,' said the Queen. 'Do you know to whom you speak?'

'The widowed Queen,' Gildroy replied.

'Widowed?' she asked faintly.

'Yes, he's down in the chapel. Blessed release, really. He was well gone in the cranial department.'

The Queen felt faint and almost collapsed against the wall. 'May I have a chair?' she whispered. In an instant, Norval was there with a heavy wing chair, carrying it as lightly as if it were a footstool.

Gildroy looked at her quizzically. 'I must say I'm a little surprised at your reaction. I rather thought that you'd transferred your affections to the Wiz. That you and he were – how shall I put it – engaged in an *affaire d'amour?'*

'How dare you, sir,' the Queen managed to squeeze out between small, sobbing breaths.

Gildroy perched on the arm of her chair. 'Now don't get your pigeon in a flutter, Queenie. I'm just getting my facts straight, that's all.' The Queen recoiled as he leaned closer – he smelled of death. 'Where is he?' he breathed.

'Thankfully he and the Prince are far from your clutches, and though I may never see him again, I console myself with the fact that one day he shall return and tear you to pieces.'

'Yes, that's always the fear, isn't it. That's why I need to know.'

'You shall never find him,' cried the Queen.

Gildroy drew an evil-looking stiletto from his boot and held it against the Queen's bosom. 'Now, you're not going to be difficult, are you?'

The Queen felt the shock of the cold steel against her skin. 'Don't get it out if you don't plan to use it,' she gasped. 'Or are you like most men, all talk and no action?'

Gildroy's eyes glowed red. The thrust was as quick as a viper's strike, but Norval was even quicker. Just as the point was about to pierce her skin, Gildroy felt the vicelike grip of his brother's hand tighten around his wrist. Furious, he turned on him but, looking into those great pitiless eyes which brooked no dialogue, Gildroy relaxed and removed the blade, its point leaving a small red mark in the milk-white flesh of the Queen's breast.

'You're right, brother,' he smiled. 'If we kill her now, we'll never know.' Placing the knife carefully back in his boot, Gildroy stood and addressed the Queen once more. 'Perhaps we'll leave further inquisition until the morning. I'm sure you'll think differently once Norval's had his way with you. Do you heal quickly? You'll need to – he tends to get rather carried away. He won't kill you – no, he likes you too much for that. But you will suffer; you'll suffer

horribly. And just when you think it can't get any worse, it will –
a lot worse.'

Norval smiled and nodded energetically.

'Enjoy!' said Gildroy, and turned on his heel. He was about to
leave the room when Norval rushed up and whispered something
in his ear. 'Of course, brother, how very remiss of me.'

Gildroy stood before the Queen. 'Stand up,' he commanded her.
She rose uncertainly to her feet. Taking her hand, Gildroy placed it
in Norval's. 'We are gathered here today . . .' Gildroy began. Norval
moaned and shook his head. 'Very well, I'll give you the edited
version. Do you take this woman?'

'*Hurgh!*' grunted Norval.

'Good, I now pronounce you man and wife.' Gildroy left them
standing side by side and made his way to the door, stepping over
the lifeless form of Festrina. Pausing in the doorway, he turned back
to the happy couple. 'I wish you great happiness and long life –
long, *long* life. I'll leave you in peace now – it's time for you to get
intimate. We'll talk again in the morning, Queenie.'

Norval, trembling with excitement, released the Queen's hand
to unbuckle his belt. Suddenly she was at the open window. Gildroy,
sensing the danger, ran back into the room – but too late. Before
either brother could stop her, she had jumped. They watched as she
fell, down, down, down, until her body disappeared in the gathering
gloom.

'Bravo,' said Gildroy. 'I never knew the old girl had it in her.'
Norval put his big misshapen head on his brother's shoulder and
wept his heart out. 'There, there,' said Gildroy. 'There, there.'

Chapter 14

Boarding on flight BA 2063 had taken place three hours later than scheduled because of a small technical problem – a drop in hydraulic fluid pressure in one of the undercarriage circuits – and now the delayed VC-10 had been sitting on the tarmac for nearly forty minutes. Iris Boggs, in seat 13A, was beginning to get a little worried. She turned to her husband Bernard, in the seat beside her. 'Is this quite right, Bernard? We should have left hours ago. Do you think it's safe, this aeroplane?'

'Well, I did see one of the wings drop off just as we got on.'

Iris's face was a picture. 'Really? Do you think we ought to tell someone?' Then, as Bernard cracked a broad grin, 'Ooh, you're terrible, you really are.' She hit him playfully on the shoulder.

The piped muzak dropped out and the captain's voice came over the PA. 'Good afternoon, ladies and gentlemen, Captain Thomas speaking. Sorry for the delay, but because of a minor problem with the aircraft we lost our take-off slot, so we're just waiting for air traffic control to give us another. Shouldn't be much longer now.'

Iris craned her neck to squint up at the steel-grey sky above. She still couldn't quite believe that soon, very soon – as long as they got their 'slot', whatever that was – she would be sailing high above those clouds in bright sunshine.

At last the captain announced that they had been given clearance, and the plane taxied down to the end of the runway. As the VC-10's mighty Rolls-Royce engines wound themselves up to full thrust, Iris no longer felt frightened. Apprehension was replaced by excitement as she felt the throbbing power of the bucking aeroplane straining to break free of the earth. Then the brakes were released and the VC-10 moved forward, slowly at first, wings wobbling slightly – gradually, gradually picking up speed. Through the window Iris looked down at the tarmac and watched the inset lights pass ever more quickly as the aircraft rumbled faster and faster along the runway. Pinned to her seat now, she watched the terminal building, parked aeroplanes, transit buses, all hurtle past in a confusing blur. The plane seemed to be travelling impossibly fast. Just how long was this runway? It seemed they'd been careering along it forever. Then, just when she thought it would never stop, a miracle happened. The bumpy unevenness of the ground was left behind, as one hundred and fifty tons of aircraft became weightless and soared majestically into the air.

'Ooooaaaaah!' chorused a number of seasoned and inebriated package-holidaymakers as they left the ground. Iris looked across at Bernard. He was sitting bolt upright, a big stupid grin on his face.

'Are you all right, Bernard?'

'That was great.' In the space of just over two thousand yards, Bernard had been transformed from flight virgin to flying enthusiast.

As the stiletto-shaped aircraft stabbed upwards through the sky, Iris looked down at oh-so-green England laid out like a living map beneath her. Toy cars moved along licorice-strap roads, and the white dots of sheep gambolled in patchwork-quilt fields. She was *flying* . . . like an angel. Thin wisps of cloud whipped past the window, obscuring the view, and soon it seemed they were enveloped in cotton wool. 'Oh,' she said sadly. Then, just as abruptly, the cotton wool thinned and streaks of sunlight pierced the gloom. The aeroplane rose spectacularly out of a great white-cloud sea and Iris found herself in . . . heaven. Lit by the golden rays of the sun, huge white thrones and alabaster columns took shape before her eyes. It was how she'd always imagined it – all that was missing were the reclining angels plucking harps.

'Ladies and gentlemen, Captain Thomas here again.' The dry

voice of the captain brought her back from visions of eternity. 'Could I have your indulgence for a few moments? Because we shall be flying over water, we are obliged to show you the life-jacket drill. I know you've all seen it a thousand times before, but I would ask you to pay attention to the demonstration by our cabin crew.'

One person who was paying attention – rapt attention – was Bernard Boggs. So caught up in the stewardess's performance did he become that, as she finished, he led the passengers in a round of applause.

'One final thing,' said the captain. 'To make up for any inconvenience caused by the delay, British Airways would like to offer you all a complimentary drink...' The rest of his words were drowned out by a chorus of *bongs* as almost every hand on the aircraft reached for the call button.

Some minutes later, and Bernard was happily clutching a gin and tonic. 'Cheers!' he said.

'Happy holiday!' said Iris as they chinked plastic cups.

It wasn't long before the soothing drone of the engines and the softly comforting view of the soul's eternal resting place outside the window, not to mention the brandy and complimentary gins, began to work their magic on Iris, and her eyelids grew heavy. At last she fell asleep, her head resting against the cold plastic of the window. Asking the stewardess for a pillow, Bernard gently settled her back and tucked the pillow under her head. The stewardess was touched by the care this man took of his wife, and watched, moved, as he placed her hands in her lap and kissed her gently on the forehead.

Chapter 15

Madame Frieda had been forced to open for business early that morning. Finding the large, pink-faced DI Collins, breathing hard through his oversized nostrils, on her doorstep, she had groaned inwardly. The small detached house in which her establishment was based was right in the middle of a respectable residential area overlooking Portslade docks. She was already under investigation by the Council because of complaints from her neighbours about 'noises after midnight', and had only escaped closure due to the fact that many of her regular clients were members of the vice squad. The last thing she needed was horny customers turning up in broad daylight, just when kids were going off to school – giving the curtain-twitchers even more ammunition in their ongoing fight to close her down. But, equally, she couldn't afford to alienate any member of the force. She sighed and stood aside as Malcom pushed past her and hurried upstairs.

From his vantage point behind the ample rear end of Sylvia, one of Madame Frieda's more popular employees, Malcom could just make out the proudly erect stack of Shoreham power station, which spurred him on to even greater efforts.

'Bulldog! Bulldog! Bulldog!' He shouted with each thrust.

Sylvia was used to the strange utterings of her clients. She'd once had a Japanese man who'd yelled 'Sashimi!' at the top of his voice during climax. She'd assumed it was some exotic Eastern love chant, until someone told her it meant raw fish.

'Oh, oh!' went Sylvia, desperate to get back to sleep. Luckily

Malcom was, as a rule, one of her shorter bookings, and when he got to the Bulldog stage, it usually meant the end was near.

'Bulldog!' Malcom thrust again, his great white belly wobbling like a lard jelly.

'Oh!' went Sylvia.

'Bulldog!'

'Oh!'

Gradually, through the softly mingling sounds of their love-making, each became aware of the shrill but unmistakable sound of the *William Tell* Overture. 'Bull . . . shit!' groaned Malcom and rolled off the bed to answer his mobile phone. 'Yes!' he barked.

'Hello, sir!' It was Beasely.

'This better be important, sergeant.'

'I thought I'd walk back to the town hall and get a bus from there . . .'

'Much as I'd love to hear your life story, I'm anxious to get back to what I was doing.'

'Well, on the way, I passed the King Alfred Centre and I saw Councillor Daniels's friend was still there. He had that pink folder open on the bonnet of his car – it looked like plans, blueprints, you know. He'd look down at the plans, then up at the Centre, and it seemed to me like he was trying to figure out how they related to the actual building, if you see what I mean . . . Are you still there sir?'

'Get to the fucking point!' Malcom yelled.

'Well, I did a trace on his numberplate, and guess what?'

'*What?*' said Malcom tersely.

'It's registered to Frederick John Davis, Director of Conservation in what used to be called the Borough Surveyor's office – now grandly entitled Environment and Housing Services.'

There was a pause as Malcom absorbed this information. 'Now that's very interesting.'

'How's that?'

Malcom allowed himself a smile. 'You're not thinking like a policeman, Beasely. You got to think lateral.'

'What's lateral about it? Daniels is on the Council and one of Davis's jobs is looking after Council buildings.'

'When you've been in the game as long as I have, you develop a nose for these things. Something's up, Beasely, you mark my words. Get that film developed, and don't show it to nobody. Good work, sergeant. You may even have won your bollock back.' Malcom turned off his phone and got back onto the bed.

'Oh, is this a double session, then?' asked Sylvia, stifling a yawn.

'You bet your life,' said Malcom. 'Now, where were we?'

Beasely sighed and put the phone back in his pocket. It wasn't that he minded playing the Sergeant Lewis role, he just wished that his Inspector Morse wasn't such a fat, brainless arsehole. He might, however, have revised his opinion of his boss had he known that along with the plans and blueprints in the pink folder there was enclosed an envelope containing £30,000 in used fifties.

Deep in thought, Beasely waited for his bus outside Hove town hall. In his mind he weaved an elaborate fantasy . . . He was leading Operation Status Quo – rounding up the arrogant criminals that poisoned his town by supplying the weak and feeble-minded with drugs, thus fuelling the plague of street crime. Oh, he'd had to overcome prejudice and ridicule to succeed – many of the drug barons had influential connections: powerful men who had attained high public office. But he wasn't going to be intimidated by threats, nor the unfounded rumours of his homosexuality – put about merely undermine his position. Nothing was going to make him deviate from his mission to rid Brighton once and for all of the pernicious drug menace.

His reverie was interrupted by the sound of a throbbing diesel engine and the swish of opening doors. As he raised his foot to step onto the platform, he felt – rather than heard – a low rumbling, as if somewhere deep underground a vast creature was grinding its teeth. He looked up at the bus-driver. 'What was that?'

'What was what?'

Limbo

Beasely looked around. The sun still shone, cars still moved along the street, people went about their business, unconcerned. Everywhere the world carried on as normal. Yet somehow, deep inside, he seemed to know that life, especially his own life, was about to change for ever.

'I can't wait here all day,' the bus-driver scowled.

'Yes, yes, sorry. I thought . . . Never mind. St James's Street, please.'

Chapter 16

The Wizard came to the end of the tunnel and looked out at the forbidding grey waters of the Salient Sea, far below him. He was tired now. Over the past few months he'd suffered enough anxiety, anguish and pain to last a lifetime – even his own two-thousand-year lifetime. 'I'm getting too old for this game,' he sighed. 'And it's not over yet.' He looked down at the form of the infant Prince, still fast asleep in his arms. 'Forgive me, little one. I'm as sorry to leave her as you are. You have to trust me that it is all for the best.'

A tear dropped onto the infant's cheek, and the child squirmed in his sleep.

'Silly old fool,' muttered the Wizard, wiping his eyes. 'There, there, sweetness,' he cooed, gently rocking his son. 'Back to sleep now.' The tiny hope for the future of Limbo gradually fell back into his rhythmically sighing sleep. 'Well,' said the Wizard, 'no time to hang about, we'd better be off.' He opened the carpet-bag and placed the Prince tenderly inside. 'You'll be safe in there.'

Then, searching with his fingers, he found an indentation in the smooth wall of the tunnel. He pushed hard with his thumb, and with a gentle hiss, a small door opened in the solid rock. Thrusting his hand inside, he touched a bundle of dry, ancient papyrus. 'Still there, thank goodness.' This was one example of Franklin Gothic Lucida 2 that Dr Ohthyrhis Perch hadn't found. 'Now then, how does it go again?' Kneeling, he unravelled the scroll and laid it out on the uneven rock floor of the tunnel.

Lips moving, he began to read.

*

'Hello?' sang Smeil to the pitch-blackness. 'My Lord? Are you there?' He stumbled blindly down the dark passages, feeling his way with his fingertips inch by slow inch, while all around him the castle exploded into violence. After what seemed like an age, he came to a junction. *Which way?* He felt a gentle breeze on his cheek. It could mean nothing, but it was the only hope he had. Turning towards it, slowly and painfully he worked his way along the cobwebbed passage. After a time it curved sharply and began to turn back on itself. Rounding a corner, the floor suddenly dropped away and he found himself running down a steep slope. Just as the floor began to level out, his head connected with a low beam. 'Ouch!'

As he sat on the cold floor of the tunnel, rubbing his head, a strange sound came out of the darkness. *Tick, tick, tick* . . . it went. Getting to his feet and groping his way around the walls, he collided with something hard and dry and solid. 'Ow!' It was a barrel . . . no, not just a barrel, but several barrels all roped together. And on top of them . . . Smeil explored with his fingertips . . . what's small and round and ticks? The King's alarm clock! What was it doing there?

Before he had time to ponder this problem further, he heard another sound – a sound that chilled his blood. It was like the braying laugh of the great Ass himself; a mocking, gurgling sound that had in it all the evil of the world. 'My Lord!' he breathed. With only one thought in his mind – the welfare of the King – he swallowed his fear and set off whence the awful noise had come.

Just as he was about to despair of ever finding his way out of this maze, far off in the distance he discerned a dim light. As he approached it, the tunnel grew brighter, and he strode out with growing confidence. Soon he was under the grating that lay beneath the chapel altar.

'Hello!' he called. No reply. Reaching up, he was delighted to find that the grating shifted. Pushing it aside, he heaved himself up and sat for a while, turning his head this way and that, listening for . . . he knew not what. Gingerly pushing aside the altar cloth, he peeped out. The chapel was empty.

'My Lord!' he called softly. 'Where are you?' He crept out

cautiously, the supple leather soles of his boots making no sound on the stone floor. He peered along every pew, snuffled like a dog the length of the choir stalls, even clambered into the pulpit. The King was nowhere to be seen. The little man was growing increasingly worried. The King was mad, there was an angry mob after his blood and Smeil had lost him: he could be anywhere. The mob might have captured him already. With rising panic Smeil began to imagine the horrors that his noble lord might be enduring at the hands of those uncouth savages. Oh, he was a worthless servant. 'Stupid! Stupid! Stupid!' he said, beating himself with the knotted cord of his belt. When he felt he'd punished himself sufficiently, he headed glumly for the door.

But passing the confessional, he noticed its curtains were drawn. This was puzzling because at the first sign of trouble the priests had all abandoned the castle and joined the other side. Yet if the curtains were shut it could only mean that the booth was occupied. But who, other than a madman, would enter a confessional when there was no priest to hear his confession? The little man smiled. 'My Lord, you are in a mischievous mood today,' he said, whipping the curtain aside.

The King lay on the floor, seemingly fast asleep, a contented smile on his face. 'Found you – you're *it*!' sang Smeil, dropping to his knees beside his lord. It was only then that he noticed the wet, sticky pool of burgundy-coloured blood that covered the stone flags. 'My lord!' He felt for a pulse and found there was none. Holding up his hand he gazed, half in horror, half in awe, at the King's regal blood. 'No, no!' Smeil grabbed the King by the shoulders and shook him violently. 'My lord! It is I, Smeil! Wake up!' Smeil released his grip and the King's body fell back upon the cold floor. 'You can't be . . . you can't be dead!' he wailed. 'Oh, Lord forgive me, it's all my fault! Why him and not me? Why him and not me?'

Feeling for the King's belt, he located his ceremonial dagger. Drawing it, he ripped open his own shirt to expose his breast, and raised the dagger high. 'I'm coming My Lord! I follow you!' He was determined to do it. He was going to plunge the blade into his heart, and then be with his master. His grip tightened around the jewel-encrusted hilt; he could feel the hard, unyielding gems biting into the flesh of his palm. His breathing became fast and shallow; every fibre of his being tensed. He would do it now . . . *now!* Then with a heart-rending sigh, he let go the dagger and it fell to the floor with a clatter. 'Oh I am worthless, worthless!' he cried, collapsing on the blood-soaked floor.

Cradling the beloved head of his dead master, he rocked back and forth, back and forth, while the chapel echoed to the sound of his broken heart.

With the unexpected death of the Queen, Gildroy decided it was unsafe to postpone the search for the Prince any longer. The castle was surrounded, so escape was impossible, but you could never tell with wizards; just when you thought you had them where you wanted them, they had a nasty habit of doing the unexpected. While Norval grieved for his bride, and his unrequited lust, Gildroy had the castle thoroughly searched. It was no straightforward task in such a fluid building. Rooms which had been searched in the west wing suddenly reappeared in the east; spiral staircases had a habit of going on forever, either up and up and up or down and down and down. One search party plunged to their death when the corridor they were following suddenly dropped away beneath their feet. Others simply stepped into rooms which promptly disappeared, and they were never seen again. Gildroy was becoming more and more frustrated.

Then he had an idea. He knew that the castle was riddled with secret passages – as a child he'd known them well, but the castle wasn't so easily read by the adult mind. Norval's mind, however, was a different matter entirely.

Taking the weeping bridegroom back into the apartment from which the Queen had made her final exit, Gildroy pointed to the wall. 'Brother, the wall.'

'What?'

'Make a hole in it.'

'But . . .'

Hastily improvising a story about what the Wizard had once done to the Queen with an aubergine and a quart of double cream, Gildroy soon had Norval in a foaming jealous rage. He slammed his fist into the wall. A thin hairline crack appeared. 'Did I mention the punnet of glacé cherries?' Gildroy taunted. Norval screamed and smacked the wall in vengeful fury. When the dust had settled, a hole was revealed, just big enough for the brothers to squeeze through.

They found themselves in a dusty passageway, confronted by a confusion of stairs leading up, down and around. Gildroy thought he caught a faint whiff of the sea and the far-off cries of seagulls. 'We're going to play hunt-the-Wizard,' he said, climbing upon his brother's back. Firmly grasping Norval's wide leather braces, he leaned down and whispered one word into his large cauliflower ear. 'Fetch!'

Norval sniffed the air for a moment, then suddenly turned and set off at a gallop, with Gildroy hanging on for dear life.

Unseen in the shadows, Smeil watched as the brothers headed off down the tunnel. Over the body of his dead master he had made a solemn oath – his murder would be avenged. His remorse overtaken by anger, Smeil had clambered back through the chapel altar grating and gone in search of the culprits. The little man fingered the jewelled hilt of the dagger in his belt, then scurried down the dark tunnel after the twins.

'Yes, yes, that all seems to make sense.' The Wizard, still on his knees, rolled up the scroll and tucked it into his belt. 'Now then.' He opened the carpet-bag to make sure that the Prince was still sleeping soundly, then reached into his pocket and pulled out the Crystal. Even in the dimness of the tunnel, the magnificent gem still managed to gather enough light to throw a peacock's tail of iridescence on the walls. Standing now, he was about to start the incantation when he thought he heard something. Something far off, like the snuffling of a great dog. 'Norval,' he breathed. 'Damn, I thought I had more time.'

From far below came the sound of surf breaking at the foot of the cliff. The sea breeze ruffled his hair and whipped his cloak around him as he stood at the very edge of the tunnel. *'Felix!'* he shouted to the wind. *'Felix qui potuit rerum cognoscere causas!'* He turned and listened. Norval was getting nearer; it was as if an earthquake were rumbling down the tunnel. He'd have to hurry. *'Ibant obscuri sola sub nocte!'* The sea began to boil and the wind to howl. *'Tempus edax rerum!'* he sang. The walls of the tunnel trembled as Norval grew ever nearer. Looking back, all the Wizard could see was an avalanche of darkness rolling towards him. Working quickly now, the Wizard held the Crystal aloft. It began to glow with a strange intensity, throwing a shower of sparks out over the brooding sea. *'Non omnia possumus omnes!'* he shouted, and with a hissing rush, the sea rose up in a glass wall before him.

Glowing white-hot, the Crystal fired a single beam of light into the transparency of the frozen wave, and a portal, like an eye, opened up in its centre.

Norval was nearly upon him; the Wizard could almost feel his hot breath on the back of his neck. This was it – it was now or never. Closing the carpet-bag on the sleeping Prince, the Wizard took a deep breath. *'Che sara, sara!'* he said, raising himself up on his toes.

But then he made a fatal mistake: he looked down. What was he going to? Where would he land? How could he leave his Queen at the mercy of such monsters? And his fear made him pause.

At that moment, deep in the subterranean maze of tunnels far beneath the castle, the hands on a certain alarm clock ticked round to twelve o'clock and made contact. The spark ignited the fuse, which in turn detonated a ton and a half of gunpowder. The explosion roared down the tunnel like a tidal wave. Smeil was the first to be caught up in it. Lifted off his feet, the little man was propelled like a bullet down the narrow passage. Norval, running flat out, looked up when he heard the explosion. Gildroy, in his slightly more elevated position, turned and saw the great cloud of fire and smoke bearing down on them. 'No!' he howled, but in an instant it was upon them, hurling them towards the exit in the cliff face.

Turning, the Wizard saw the brothers hurtling towards him with the speed of an artillery shell. Realizing his mistake, he tried to sidestep the human cannonball, but to no avail. With a smack that would have parted the spirit from the flesh of any mortal man, Norval and his brother slammed straight into him.

'No!' the Wizard screamed as the carpet-bag was jarred from his grasp. 'No!' he yelled as the Crystal flew out of his other hand. He watched in despair as the carpet-bag containing his son – the Dawn, the future's only hope – disappeared through the portal. He reached in vain to catch the Crystal as it soared up and up – and, describing a perfect parabola, fell down and down into Gildroy's outstretched hand.

The carpet-bag, the Prince, the Wizard, and the brothers all passed through the eye of the wave, and the moment they'd passed, it closed with a sound like all the doors in the world slamming at once . . .

In the darkness, the Great Hoop buckled and twisted. Plumes of energy billions of years long looped from its surface like the coils of the sun. Eternity passed in a single moment and, in that moment, time, space and imagination became one, and the unimaginable became reality.

Smeil was left hanging by his fingertips from the lip of the opening, far above the cruel rocks of the shoreline. For a few moments, the little man hung motionless, stunned by what he'd just witnessed. Then, slowly coming to his senses, he realized the perilous nature of his position. His feet scrabbled for purchase on the smooth rock of the cliff face.

'Help!' he screamed, then cursed his stupidity – who was there to hear his call?

'Don't look up.' The voice above him was strangely familiar. 'Whatever you do, don't look up.' Hands wrapped around his wrists and pulled him into the safety of the cave. He sat on the slimy rock floor breathing heavily, as the trembling subsided and the blood returned slowly to his limbs. After a little while, he looked up gratefully to see who it was that had saved his life.

He found himself staring into his own face.

'No . . . no!' he said.

'I told you not to look up.' The face smiled. Blackness ringed Smeil's vision, and with a small sigh, he passed out.

When he came to, he found himself sitting in the same position, but in his lap there was a book – embossed and leather-bound. On the cover, picked out in gold leaf was the legend *Limbo – The Final Chapter*. With trembling fingers, Smeil opened it.

On the flyleaf someone had written 'To my good friend Smeil. Thought this might interest you.'

Serena Kowalski scrambled up the ladder which sprouted from the curving wall of the hold, and threw herself onto the free-floating observation platform tethered to the top rung. She lay there for a while, breathing hard. Sneaking a look over the edge, she could see, far below, the great sea of garbage churning and boiling as the clams grew ever more active. Jesus, she was going to have to fix this thing soon or they were going to eat the ship, and her with it. She rolled onto her back and looked up. Far above, she could just make out the mangled remains of a Starcruiser, caught in the jaws of the giant pressure valve. 'Aw, shit!' Starcruisers were the earliest commercial spaceships, putting space travel within reach of the man in the street. They'd offered trips to the Moon, Mars, and later the dark side of Mercury. About as big as a twentieth century jumbo jet, it was nothing compared to the vast scale of the SS *St Francis Sinatra*, but big enough to give Serena a major headache. Somehow she was going to have to cut the thing free.

Cursing, she took the controls of the small platform and, unhooking the tether, piloted it up towards the valve. She was suddenly aware of a figure standing next to her. She turned to see a naked man holding a wrench. 'Hi, need a hand?'

'Aw, Jesus!'

'Aren't you hot in all those clothes? Why don't you take something off and—'

'Will you fuck off!' Serena screamed.

'I can take a hint,' the naked man said, as he and his wrench slowly faded. Because of this little distraction, Serena had failed to notice a burnt-out cable from one of the valve's motors hanging right in the path of the rising platform. The cable snagged the platform's small safety rail and tipped it up. Serena was thrown backwards and found herself hanging by her feet, staring into a writhing mass of garbage and clams about half a mile beneath her head.

Slowly and carefully she looked up. Her huge boots were trapped between the platform and the safety rail. Breathing deeply, she told herself not to panic. 'OK now, Serena, easy. Let's take this very, very easy.' She tried to reach up and grab the platform, but long hours spent hanging out in the virtual bar had left her stomach muscles soft and flabby – they ached with the effort. But she had another problem more serious than being out of shape. Any exertion loosened the rather tenuous grasp her feet had on the insides of the boots. Now she wished she'd taken the time to put on the thick crush-proof socks. She reckoned she had two options: she could either hang there until the clams ate the ship and herself out of existence, or try and swing up and grab the platform, and in so doing, fall out of her boots and into the waiting jaws of the little dears below. It wasn't much of a choice.

'OK,' she said. 'I'm going to swing. I know I don't have a rat's hope in hell, but I can't just hang around here all day.' She shook her head at the awfulness of the joke. 'Please, this is serious.'

Spreading her toes as wide as she could to try and wedge her feet more securely inside the boots, she began to swing like an acrobat on a trapeze. The first swing she got nowhere near ... at the second she was close ... and at the third she managed to get two fingers onto the safety rail. But that wasn't enough. Her feet had already slipped out of the boots, and she found herself falling ...

Meanwhile, the explosion in Limbo had sent a running fracture scything through the fabric of time, space and destiny – and at that moment it just happened to be passing through the hold of the SS *St Francis Sinatra*.

Serena dropped right into it.

'We shall shortly be commencing our final approach to Arrecife airport ...' The crackly tones of the PA dragged Iris back to consciousness. 'The temperature is a very pleasant twenty-three degrees ...' Iris eased the stiffness out of her neck. She'd had such a strange dream – about a little baby and a magician that were trying to get away from a horrible monster. She'd been rather disturbed by it, and reached instinctively for Bernard's comforting hand. But all she touched was the fabric of his empty seat. She looked round; he was nowhere to be seen.

'The local time is five o'clock in the afternoon,' the captain continued, 'and it's time for Iris to wake up.' Iris stiffened. She must be hearing things. 'Iris, time to wake up now.' There it was again – was she still dreaming? 'Wakey-wakey, Iris Boggs!' What was going on?

The moment she saw Bernard walking back down the aisle towards her, with a big grin on his face, she knew.

'It's not everyone who gets a personal call from the captain, you know,' he said as he sat down.

'Bernard, what *have* you been up to?'

'Well,' he said, retrieving the ends of his seatbelt and buckling himself in. 'I was having a long chat with the stewardess. I told her it was our first flight and I was enquiring about our route and ETA.'

'ETA?'

'Estimated time of arrival.'

'Oh.'

'And our cruising altitude . . .'

'Cruising altitude?'

'I suppose I started asking too many questions.'

'Never!'

'You know, how many foot-pounds of thrust the engines could produce – things like that.'

'Of course.'

'Anyway, off she goes, then comes back and asks if I'd like to visit the flight deck.'

'The what?'

'You know, where the pilot sits.'

'You've been with the pilot?'

'The captain, yes. He's a very nice man. I told him you were asleep and he said he'd keep it nice and steady for you. Then Lanzarote appeared and it looked so lovely I didn't want you to miss it, so I asked him if he could give you a wake-up call.'

'You're terrible.' Iris looked out of the window. The island lay beneath her – a jewel in an emerald sea. 'Oh, Bernard, it is beautiful.'

'Really nice bloke, the captain. He let me sit in his chair and everything.' Bernard held up his big hands. 'These hands actually held the controls.'

'Don't tell me you've been flying the aeroplane!'

'Only for a second. The first officer made sure I didn't do anything daft. Smoothness, he said – it's all about smooth, controlled movements. It was great, just for a moment, to hold all that power. Flying is . . . it's almost like magic, Iris. Did you know, the cost of getting your PPL is really quite reasonable these days?'

'Your what?'

'Private Pilot's Licence. And Shoreham's only just down the road, so why waste the opportunity? When we get back, I'm going to have flying lessons.'

Iris opened her mouth to speak, but no sound came. She tingled all over – it was the strangest sensation. Holding her hands up to her face she saw sparks crackling from the ends of her fingers. She turned back to Bernard and saw his big, concerned face was framed by electric fire. Little blue flames danced across his bald pate, and everything around him was becoming indistinct – like an out-of-focus picture.

The running fracture in time and space sliced precisely through seats 13A and B of flight no. BA 2063. Iris could no longer feel the seat beneath her and looking down at her feet could see, not the grey carpet of the aircraft floor, but the bottle green expanse of the Atlantic Ocean. Now she could feel the wind whipping around her and had the distinct impression that she was falling . . .

As the Wizard tumbled through eternity, he looked up and saw a terrible thing. Norval and Gildroy were melding; joining. Their agonized screams merged in the pain of their fusion, as bit by bit their individuality was wrested from them and they gave themselves up to the huge and frightening creature that would emerge from their union.

The Wizard watched this transformation in horrified astonishment. But something even stranger was happening to him. Feeling a touch on his hand, he turned and found himself looking into his own face. He could hear someone screaming and, just as he thought he could bear it no longer, he realized that it was him. Then there was blackness and a sudden quiet, like the closing of a book. Gradually the light returned and out of the silence came the sound of children's voices and the sighing of the sea.

In the unexpected silence, Bernard hardly dared open his eyes. Where was he? The plane must have exploded. A bomb! They'd been innocent bystanders caught up in the twisted ambitions of a crazed terrorist. So this is what it feels like to be dead, he thought. He had expected to feel lighter, more ethereal, like in those paintings of angels and cherubs he'd seen in Brighton Museum, but he felt very solid indeed, and appeared to be standing upright, not reclining on a cloud in an azure-blue sky. Cautiously opening an eye, he found himself looking at something light brown. It had letters on it. It took him a while, because he wasn't wearing his reading glasses, but eventually he was able to make out: 'Prichard's Paper Products – 3 dozen Festive Paper Bells – Store Upright'. If this was heaven, what were they doing stockpiling Christmas paper bells? Didn't they have enough of the real thing? Then he looked down to see a familiar brown block-pattern lino. He was in the storeroom at the back of his shop. Hearing an electronically tinny rendition of 'Happy Birthday to You' played, it seemed, on a hundred uncoordinated Stylophones, he turned round to see Iris perched untidily on top of a large box of novelty 'singing' birthday cards. Her weight had set them all off.

'That shouldn't have happened, should it, Bernard?'

'No, love. No, it shouldn't.' Then another noise cut across the out-of-time greetings chorus. It was slightly muffled, but unmistakable nevertheless: a baby was crying.

Iris and Bernard turned slowly towards the sound. At the other end of the room, smoking slightly and with small electric-blue flashes still playing around its handles, was a large carpet-bag.

Bernard took Iris's hand and together they approached. It took them a while to pluck up the courage but, with the child's voice becoming ever more insistent, they could delay no longer. Iris knelt down and clunked open the heavy brass clasp. Taking a breath, she opened the slightly stiff arms of the bag, to reveal a small, naked baby. For a moment the child's crying filled the room but, looking into Iris's softly smiling face, it stopped almost immediately and beamed happily up at her. Iris turned to Bernard with tears of joy streaming down her cheeks.

'It's a boy,' she said.

Part II

Chapter 17

The two men sat in their identical folding beach chairs, looking out at the flat calm sea. Identical thermos flasks nestled in the pebbles at their feet. One of the men was long and lean, his tanned face finely chiselled, the sharp line of his jaw emphasized by an obsessively trimmed black beard. The other was shorter and dumpier – his thin, grizzled ginger beard a poor attempt to disguise a double chin. The tall one wore a black bathing suit and had a chiffon scarf tied around his neck. The short one wore primrose yellow trunks, which clashed horribly with his chunky gold jewellery.

Although it was nowhere near its zenith, the two men could already feel the warmth of the sun on their skin and in the pebbles beneath their feet. The beach was deserted, it was too early for most people, but this was their special time of day.

The tall man unscrewed the lid of his thermos and poured himself a cup of coffee. The short one did likewise, pouring himself a cup of tea.

'A millpond,' said the short man.

'What?' snapped the taller one.

'The sea, it's like a millpond.'

'There you go again.'

'What did I say?'

'Interrupting, you're always interrupting. I am trying to think. The universe is about to be sucked into oblivion and you start babbling about bloody millponds!'

In the silence that followed, the short man put down his tea. 'I'm going for a swim,' he said. The tall man watched him crunch down the beach and remove his espadrilles at the water's edge. Hobbling over the short but painful distance to the water, he tentatively entered the sea and began to swim in a jerky breaststroke.

The tall man sighed; he hated being like this. He only had himself to blame, of course. How could he have lost the Prince? How could he have been so stupid? Even now, seven years after the event, the memory of that moment still tore at his heart. He had lost his Queen and the land he loved, and had thrown his son into the abyss – and for what?

The wizard sat on the beach and wept. A huge and terrifying creature now had in its possession the most powerful gem in creation. Thankfully it didn't know how to use it, but it was meanwhile banging aimlessly around eternity, tearing great holes in the fragile tissue of destiny. If this carried on, the fabric of the universe would begin to unravel. It would be the end of everything, and he was powerless to do anything about it.

'It's all my fault,' the tall wizard sobbed, burying his head in his hands.

'We'll find him.' The short man was kneeling at his feet now, dripping wet.

The wizard looked up. 'He could be anywhere. What if he fell into the sea? Or landed in the desert – or, worse, was devoured by wild beasts? I may have thrown him far into the future, or into the very depths of history. What do you suggest we do – put an ad in the *Argus*? "Prince lost, please return – substantial reward"?'

'It's worth a try.'

The wizard peered deep into the short, podgy man's eyes and found himself looking into his own – morning-blue, as deep and as placid as a mountain lake, with here and there a fleck of white, like swans taking flight. 'You know, sometimes I marvel at the fact that we are the same person. It's a revelation to me that I have a stupid side. Where have you been hiding all these years?'

The short man, long used to such abuse, ignored it. 'I think I left yesterday's paper in the beach hut, hang on.' He crunched up the beach, returning triumphantly a few moments later. 'Here we are,' he called, waving the local tabloid. Sitting back in his chair, he turned to the small ads section and dialled the number on his mobile phone. 'Hello, I'd like to insert an ad. Yes, of course ... ready? OK, here goes: "Wanted, large carpet-bag. Collector will pay best price." That'll go in tomorrow, will it?' After giving his credit card details, he switched off the phone and beamed smugly at his taller self. 'I don't know why we didn't think of it before.'

'Yes, all right,' the tall one glowered at him. 'It's a good idea. Desperate perhaps, but worth a shot. But what on Earth makes you think that he's *here* now?'

There was a rumbling, deep underground, like the sound of a huge creature grinding its teeth.

'Well, that's *one* reason,' said the short man. 'That's the fourth tremor this week. How often does Brighton suffer from earth-quakes? It must be nearly time.'

'Feminine intuition?' asked the tall wizard.

'Now don't take the piss. "*The skirted ones shall land and bow the knee ... on cobbles hard at Brighthelm by the Sea.*" Remember?'

'Unfortunately, yes.'

'Well, if that doesn't describe Brighton beach, I'm a Dutchman. Whatever's going to happen is going to happen *here*. And whatever is going to happen can't happen without the Prince. Don't worry, we're in the right place at the right time.' The tall wizard's other half – split from him by the great force of the impact that had propelled him into the portal – patted his counterpart tenderly on the knee, then poured himself another cup of tea.

'Yeurgh! It's curdled. That's strange. It was fine a minute ago.'

His other half looked up. 'It's started,' he said – and at that moment his chair collapsed.

Chapter 18

The tall, battle-hardened veteran and champion of the Philistines laughed when the boy began to advance, sling in hand. Now he knew the Israelites were defeated – in their desperation they were sending boys into battle. Out in the parched desert, the curly-haired youth, brimming with confidence, whirled the sling around his head and let loose his shot. As the stone left the sling and embarked upon its historic flight towards the big man's forehead, thunder rumbled across the desert and the ground began to tremble and shake. In the no man's land between David and Goliath, a shower of sparks fell from the sky and where once had been only sand, a great monster now stood, a gleaming Crystal in its hand.

The monster had all the ingredients that go to make up a man – two arms, a head, and the requisite number of legs – but its sheer size and the violence that oozed from it marked it out as something other than human. The monster caught the shot arcing towards it in its vast, gnarled fist. Turning the pebble over in its hand, the monster looked from it to the boy, his sling now hanging limply by his side. 'Little shit,' it growled. Dropping the pebble, it turned to Goliath and enquired politely if it could borrow his sword. Wrapping its great paw around the hilt, it began to draw the five-foot blade. When the big man protested, the creature head-butted him, laying him out cold. Turning from the prone Philistine, the creature lumbered towards the youth. 'You could have had my eye out,' it grumbled. 'Didn't your parents ever tell you not to throw stones?' Under the searing desert sun, the creature and the trembling youth faced each other. For a moment neither moved. Then the creature looked down at the sword in its hand . . .

The boy never stood a chance. As the great blade whistled down, its tip approached something near the speed of sound. When it reached the bottom of its travel there was a wet *tchac*! A groan went up from the Israeli army as the youth's head rolled in the sand.

The Great Hoop buckled and flexed . . .

Small blue lights began to play around the Crystal in the creature's fist. As it raised its hand to look at it, there was a clap of thunder like the end of the world, and the monster vanished as suddenly as it had appeared.

When Goliath opened his eyes, all that lay before him was the dead Jew – but he was soon overtaken by the cheering Philistine army and hoisted onto their shoulders.

Chapter 19

Malcom Collins leaned back in his chair and put his feet up on the desk. In his mind, the case against Daniels was coming together nicely, and although twenty-four hours had passed, his visit to Madame Frieda's still glowed warmly in memory. Beasely came in and headed straight for the kettle on top of the fridge.

'Good morning, sergeant. Sleep well?'

'Er, no, not really.' Beasely unplugged the kettle and went over to the sink.

'I thought you looked a little peaky.'

'Yeah, well . . .' Beasely trailed off. The truth was that he'd woken in terror in the middle of the night from a frighteningly real dream about a fire-breathing dragon that singed the flesh off people and then ate them. The image of a man on fire, screaming in agony, eyes bulging in disbelief, was still fresh in his mind. But it wasn't something he would have been comfortable sharing with DI Collins.

'My pictures ready yet?'

Beasely froze. 'Pictures?'

'You know what I mean – Daniels and the Borough Surveyor?'

'Oh, those pictures.' Beasely turned off the tap and tried to replace the lid of the kettle. It fell noisily into the sink.

'Are you all right?'

'I'm fine.' Beasely retrieved the lid and moved back to the fridge.

'Well?'

'Sorry?' Beasely plugged in the kettle and turned to face Malcom.

'You did get them developed, didn't you?'

'Well, I thought that now you knew who the other man was, you wouldn't need to see the pictures, so—'

Malcom sat up. 'Sorry, me old mate, I couldn't have made myself clear.' He was smiling but his eyes were dead. 'My pictures – you did get them developed, didn't you?'

'Um, er . . . yes, of course.' With a trembling hand, Beasely pulled a packet of photographs from his inside pocket. 'Your pictures,' he said, holding them up.

'Very good, very good,' said Malcom, relaxing back. 'Bring them over here.'

Beasely walked uncertainly over and placed them lightly on the desk. 'Is there anything you need,' he said, moving towards the door. 'Because I've just remembered, I've got to go down the shops.'

'Don't go just yet,' said Malcom, opening the packet. 'Make us a cup of tea, will you?' Beasely walked uneasily back into the room. 'Our Mr Borough Surveyor, what's his name again?'

'Er . . . Davis – Frederick Davis,' said Beasely, getting two mugs out of the small cupboard above the fridge.

'Davis,' Malcom said thoughtfully. He flipped open the wallet and withdrew the photographs. 'Has he got any form?'

'Any form? He works for the fucking Council; of course he hasn't got any form.'

'All right, all right, keep your hair on, I was only asking.' Although he had his back to him, Beasely could feel Malcom's growing frustration as he thumbed through the prints. 'What the fuck's this? I can't use this as evidence. It could be *anybody*. Why didn't you use the fucking zoom?'

'I couldn't figure out how it worked, until the end.'

'So you *have* got some close-ups then?'

'A close-up, yes . . .' said Beasely, carefully.

'One'll do.'

' . . . but not of them.'

Malcom came to the last picture. 'What's this? A fucking seagull?'

'Ah, you've found it,' said Beasely.

'That's it? I don't believe it. Thirty-five pictures of a couple of ants and one big fucking crystal-clear photograph of a fucking seagull! If I want to see seagulls I can look out of the fucking window!'

'I was just using up the film. I honestly thought I did have some good pictures of the two of them. But it was only when I was walking back to the Centre, after you'd dropped me off, that I realized I'd had the zoom on the wrong setting. I had one shot left, and there was this seagull, soaring over the sea. I thought it looked quite nice – white bird against blue sky.' Beasely smiled, trying desperately to sell the idea. He was never sure what to expect from the ticking bomb that was DI Collins – but it was usually something painful.

Malcom rose angrily, but the look of sheer terror on the face of the man cowering pathetically by the fridge awakened something in him. Not love – no, nothing so unmanly – nor compassion, nor pity. The look on Beasely's face bypassed his emotions and appealed directly to his latent paternal instincts – and his heart opened to the shabby little man. He wanted to get Daniels badly, and pictorial evidence of him and Davis together would be very valuable if he could prove a criminal connection. But there was no hurry – he'd get him. Softly, softly. It wasn't important enough meanwhile to upset his sergeant. After a pause that seemed like a week, Malcom smiled and looked down at the big close-up of the seagull. 'Yes, yes,' he said, 'very Japanese.'

Beasely breathed a sigh of relief.

Malcom sat back in his chair, hands behind his head. 'So then, my budding David Bailey, what else have you got for me today? Did you uncover any dirt on that shit Daniels?'

'No, but I have got something on the King Alfred Centre – and I'm afraid it blows your hypothesis out of the water.'

'Hypothesis, eh? My, my, have we swallowed a dictionary? So, what, my learned colleague, do we have on the aforementioned centre of leisure?'

'Marjorie Baines – one of the Labour councillors – is pushing to give the place listed status.'

Malcom let his feet drop to the floor with a crash. 'The King Alfred Centre? That horrible pile of bricks? Jesus, that's typical of the fucking socialists. If they had their way, every stinking urinal and tower block would be treated as a work of fucking art. The King Alfred Centre – has she had a good look at it?'

'Maybe not, but that must have been what Davis was doing – checking it out, making sure that the fabric of the building is sound. Nothing sinister and, as I always suspected, perfectly legitimate Council business.'

'You smug little git.' Malcom was on his feet and advancing on Beasely.

The sergeant, jammed between the fridge and the wall, had nowhere to go – he cowered in the steam rising from the boiling kettle. Malcom was so close he could smell his stale breath, the sourness of his three-day-old shirt, and his awful sweet, flowery aftershave. Beasely closed his eyes and waited for the sharp, jarring pain of fist connecting with bone. But instead felt a podgy hand on his cheek, and when he opened his eyes he was greeted by Malcom's face grinning from ear to ear. 'Well done, Beasely, good work,' he said, giving his subordinate's face a playful slap. 'But, not having the razor-sharp mind of a true detective, you have of course jumped to the wrong conclusion.' Malcom sauntered happily back to his chair. Beasely allowed himself to breathe again and straightened his tie. 'No, you see, the thing is,' Malcom continued, reassuming his position behind the desk, 'Daniels wants that building. I don't know why, but you mark my words, he wants it. So he pays his friend Davis to give it a dodgy survey. When the Council gets the report and sees how much it's going to cost to put it right, they panic. They decide to get rid of it quick, and Daniels buys it for a song. All this dyke Baines has done is to give Daniels the hurry-ups. He's got to get that building condemned before it becomes listed and as untouchable as the Queen's arse ... Just one sugar today, I'm on a diet.'

Beasely turned and threw a couple of tea bags in the mugs, then poured on boiling water. 'But what would Daniels want with the King Alfred Centre?' he said.

'How the fuck should I know? That's what we've got to find out. Maybe he wants to open a fucking ice-hockey rink.'

Beasely took a carton of milk from the fridge and poured it into the tea. 'Fucking hell!' he said as great lumps of white curd slopped into the mug.

'What's up?'

'Milk's off. I only bought it yesterday.'

'Must be your personality.' Malcom rose and went to the tall grey locker in the corner. 'Come on, I'll buy you a tea,' he said, handing Beasely a crash helmet.

'What's this for?'

'We're going for a little ride.'

Beasely hated bikes, and the thought of riding with the arrogantly feckless DI Collins filled him with dread. 'Shouldn't we take a car?'

'What? You really want to be cooped up in a smelly old car on a beautiful day like this? No, my pasty-faced little sergeant, you need to get out – get your face in the sun. You'll love it. Come on, see if it fits.' Reluctantly, Beasely tried the helmet on for size. 'Perfect – you're the dead spit of Peter Fonda in *Easy Rider.*'

Malcom opened the desk drawer and took out his Ray-Bans. As he put them on, the clear plastic nose-pads left a sticky slime-trail either side of his nose. 'What the fuck?' He thought at first that someone had smeared them with glue. But closer examination revealed that it was the small pads themselves that were melting. 'Fucking shitty sunglasses. They cost a fortune and all. Never mind, I can always charge it to expenses – glasses damaged in the line of duty.' Malcom smiled. Beasely cringed. He'd never seen his boss so happy – it was deeply disturbing.

'Now then,' Malcom said, 'on a bike there are two things you have to remember. *One*: lean when I lean – don't try and stay upright or you'll have us both off. And *two*: don't hold on to me, hold on to the rail at the back, I don't want people thinking we're poofs.'

Malcom opened the throttle wide, and the Harley shot out of the car park like a rocket. Beasely closed his eyes and clung, white-knuckled, to the sissy bar on the back of the seat. He had no idea where they were going or how quickly, and frankly he didn't care – he just wanted it to stop. It was a big relief when Malcom finally killed the engine and kicked out the side stand.

'Here we are.'

Beasely opened his eyes. They were in the motorcycle bay by the Palace Pier. The sun was shining and the pavement was crowded with people.

'What are we doing here?'

'Looking for clues. Maybe there's one of Mr Daniels's employees who's not entirely happy with the way his boss runs things. Maybe he can be persuaded to talk, spill the beans, shed some light on our man's nefarious business dealings.'

Beasely sighed. Sometimes working with this berk was embarrassing, it really was. It was bad enough having to go along with his weird fantasies, but even if Daniels was up to something, the last thing you would want to do was tackle his employees – they were bound to report straight back to their boss. No, all this visit was likely to do was to cause bad feeling and reinforce the view that the police were a bunch of knuckleheads.

With a sinking heart, Beasely followed Malcom through the summer crowds and onto the pier.

It would have depressed Beasely still further to learn that, somehow, Malcom had stumbled on something near the truth. Daniels *had* bribed Davis, and what's more he *did* want – he wanted very badly – the slightly decaying edifice that was The King Alfred Centre.

Chapter 20

They had set out from Gesoriacum at daybreak. One hundred liburnian warships sailing north towards the island beyond the edge of the world: the undiscovered country, land of myth and fable, that bore the name of Albion.

It was about noon when land was sighted. General Marcus Agrippa stood at the prow of his ship and looked out towards the chalk cliffs rising sheer out of the rippling blue sea. This was the campaign that, the gods willing, would etch his name in the annals of time. He had already secured Gaul for Octavius, and if he could pull off this invasion, he would have achieved what even Julius Caesar himself had failed to do – make Britain a Roman province. He'd return to Rome a hero. He could retire from these endless wanderings – the bloodshed, rape and pillage done in the name of 'civilization' – and stay at home. He stroked his chin. The feel of stubble did not please him, and he wished his slave had not dropped his master's entire shaving kit in the harbour that morning – he did so hate to go into battle unshaven. The slave had paid for his clumsiness – his head now bobbed in the harbour alongside the general's pumice stone.

Suddenly the general became unaccountably nervous. He was taking a gamble landing so far west. It meant a longer crossing, but the British would not be expecting an attack here – they'd be completely unprepared. He'd be able to form a bridgehead in relative calm, perhaps even bathe before marching north-east to take the main trading settlements by surprise. True, being out of sight of land so long, some of his men had needed strong persuasion that they were not going to fall off the edge of the world. But it wasn't the threat of mutiny that troubled him – no, it was hygiene. He always made a point of being smartly turned out at the start of a campaign, no matter what the circumstances. At the beginning of the Gallic wars, he'd found himself miles from fresh water and yet still managed to emerge from his tent, on the morning of the first battle, smooth-chinned and smelling of sweet oils, looking cool in his freshly laundered tunic. Other generals appeased the gods of slaughter by sacrificing chickens, sheep, even slaves. Not Marcus Agrippa – for him a shave and the feel of clean linen against his skin was paramount. It was tradition; the men expected it. The gods alone knew what would happen should he go to fight untrimmed. Then the general turned and looked back at the ships that stretched to the horizon, the armour of the legionaries that crammed their decks glinting in the sunlight, and his fears subsided. What did he have to worry about? He was at the head of a Roman army: an irresistible force that had hacked and sliced its way across the known world. Great civilizations that had stood for millennia had felt the shock of its power and bowed before it. And what lay ahead? A small island, poorly defended and populated by agriculturalists. What could possibly go wrong?

Chapter 21

The wizards had taken a small semi near the seafront in Hove. Of course, they'd argued about the location. The short one had wanted Kemptown, but the tall one said that it was too crowded, and the short one had had to console himself with the fact that at least here they had the beach on their doorstep.

The tall wizard stood in the kitchen scrutinizing his secateurs which had just fallen apart while he was pruning his roses. 'Look at that,' he said. 'Just like the beach chairs: the nylon plate anchoring the spring has completely disintegrated. It's as I feared: molecular cohesion is becoming unstable. It'll be alloys next, then base metals – it's very upsetting. What happens if the carbon atom begins to unravel? People are going to start exploding all over the place.' He sighed and shook his head. Opening the back door he threw the secateurs outside. They landed among the dustbins and the remains of their folding beach chairs with a loud metallic clatter. The short one, who was busy slicing tomatoes by the sink, tut-tutted under his breath. For a long moment the tall one looked daggers at his back, then stalked out of the kitchen.

It was clear that something peculiar was going on. Apart from a mass outbreak of curdled milk and a rash of collapsing beach chairs, the wizards' bidet had completely disappeared overnight. Gildroy and Norval – or, rather, the creature they had become – were doing untold damage to the fabric of destiny. They had to be stopped, but the wizards meanwhile could do nothing but wait: they were marooned in space and time. Fortunately, they still had the magic table, in the shape of the chiffon scarf that the tall one wore permanently around his neck, but none of the spells with which to operate it. Only with the Crystal could one move between dimensions, but with the table – as long as one knew the appropriate spell – one could enter the space between thoughts: the still point, the place of non-existence where one could gaze upon the face of creation. It was a sort of window on eternity. But the table was temperamental at the best of times, so they could get little out of it at the moment. The tall wizard had tried everything – all kinds of half-remembered spells and charms – but to no avail. It wasn't that he had a bad memory, it was just that at the moment this memory was split between two people. Together the wizards had a vast, magnificent mind, but separately their heads were like a couple of warehouses full of meaningless jumble.

After a cold lunch of tomato salad, chicken and new potatoes, the tall wizard rose from the kitchen table and undid the scarf from around his neck.

The short one looked up at him wearily. 'You're not going to try that thing again, are you?' he said.

'I thought I'd give it a go,' the tall one said, slightly sheepishly. 'Things are happening; destiny is changing shape – the time must be near.' The short man sighed and started clearing the table while his tall counterpart went into the front room and threw the scarf open like a tablecloth. '*Expedit esse deos, et, ut expedit* . . . er . . . *esse* . . . something!' he incanted. At once the scarf solidified into the round table that had once stood in the enchanted room in far-off Limbo Castle. 'Ah-ha!' the wizard yelled in triumph, then watched, dismayed, as the table slowly keeled over and the edge hit the floor with a crash – one of its legs was missing. 'Damn!' He looked at the lopsided table. 'Oh, well . . . erm, let's see, how does the next bit go? '*Deus et* . . . thing . . . *nihil, faci* . . . oojamabob . . . *frustra!*'

The wizard waved his arms and the strange symbols on the tabletop began to change shape and revolve. 'Well, something's happening.'

The symbols transformed themselves into long, wiggly black lines, some with strange humps or sharp spikes. Little black clouds took shape next to the word 'Low', and the word 'High' appeared alongside the symbol of a smiling sun. It was the short-range weather forecast for southern England.

The short wizard, busy at the sink in the kitchen, glanced up at the kitchen clock. 'Oh my God, look at the time.' Stacking the plates neatly on the draining board, he removed his yellow non-slip Marigolds and checked his hair in the stainless-steel door of the oven.

The tall wizard, hunched over the half-collapsed table in the middle of the room, looked up and watched as the short man bustled in and started realigning knick-knacks, wiping the odd speck of imagined dust off the mirror over the mantelpiece, all the while humming tunelessly to himself.

'What's going on?' the tall one said at last.

The short man turned, all innocence. 'What do you mean?'

'You're wearing too much cologne, you're buzzing about like a blue-arsed fly and you're humming selections from *Die Meistersinger*. You always do that when you're feeling guilty.'

The short man smiled and flushed slightly. 'Guilty? What have I got to be guilty about?' He turned and continued bustling. 'Any luck with the table?'

'A warm front will move westwards across the country, bringing rain to most parts by Thursday. And expect a shower of hail, or meteorites, I'm not sure which, this afternoon.'

'Well, that's very useful. I must remember to take my umbrella.'

The tall wizard glared at the short man. 'You still haven't answered my question.'

'I'm going out, that's all,' he said matter-of-factly.

'Where?'

'Never you mind where.'

The tall wizard eyed him suspiciously. 'You've been writing again.' The short wizard turned suddenly bright scarlet. 'Ah-ha! You traitor!' said the tall one, leaping up and down. 'You promised. You said, after the last one, that was it! Look how much trouble bloody books have got us into already!'

'But I like writing. It's something I can do for myself. It's not as if we're in Limbo any more. This is dull, grey, materialistic Earth. Besides, one of us has to earn something. How do you think we pay for this place? Not by messing around with knackered old magic tables.'

'And what's the subject of your latest oeuvre? Let me guess – there's probably a dwarf in it somewhere. There's usually a dwarf in it. What happens? Does he wrest the secret of eternal happiness from some evil queen and bestow it upon the grateful citizens of Earth? Oh no, I forgot, your hero is always that appallingly dull Prince Nostril . . .'

'Nostrum! You're just jealous that I'm a success and you're not!'

'That's not true and you know it! I've had several pamphlets published on the mathematics of meteorological prediction.'

'Oh, I see – so it's OK for *you* to write, is it? Well, what's sauce for the goose . . .'

'Those were scientific papers, not trashy science-fiction novels – there's a difference!'

The small man was almost beside himself with indignation. 'There is nothing trashy about my work. I'll have you know that I am a double Golden Talon award winner! The highest honour a writer in my field can achieve! And how many times do I have to tell you it's *fantasy*, not science fiction!' He picked up his small shoulder bag from the coffee table. 'I'm going to a book signing to mark the publication of my latest bestseller: *Beast on Top of the World*. The last time I went to such an event, there was a queue of people around the block, just hoping to catch a glimpse of me. Don't wait up, I may be late.' With that, the small man turned on his heel and strode haughtily out of the room.

Chapter 22

The battle had raged all day. The Norman soldiers had flung themselves at the wall of English shields ranged at the top of the hill time and time again, and time after time they had been repulsed. The English were exhausted. Barely recovered from a bloody battle with Harold Hardrada in York, they had endured the long forced march south only days before. Even so, Duke William was taking no chances. Harold held a strong position and his army was a seasoned fighting machine. William watched and waited.

As the day wore on, it became obvious that the English were beginning to flag; discipline in the ranks was breaking down. After every Norman attack, small sections of the English army broke out and pursued their own private battles with the Normans as they retreated down the hill.

William seized his chance. He ordered his cavalry to charge the English right flank. At the top of the hill, the cavalry feinted and, despite screamed orders to keep ranks, the entire flank chased the retreating Normans down the hill. Immediately the cavalry rode back and encircled them, and in a matter of minutes the English flank was reduced to lumps of bloody meat and guts. Harold was left badly exposed, and now the Normans began to smell victory.

Suddenly the sky grew dark and there was a clap of thunder like the end of the world. On the slope between the contending armies there appeared an appalling apparition – a huge edifice three times the height of a man, dressed all in black. A creature from the depths of the unconscious, a huge sword in its hand.

'Where the fuck are we *now*!' it bellowed, and its booming voice stilled the armies on both sides. One of the Norman archers, tensed ready to shoot before the monster appeared, looked up at the creature that had suddenly appeared before him. His trembling fingers lost their purchase on the bowstring and a single arrow cleaved the air, striking the creature in the ear. 'Ow!' The monster reached up and pulled it out. In its huge hands the arrow looked no bigger than a toothpick. 'There's always one, isn't there?' the monster growled, advancing on the Norman line. A hail of arrows went up, but to no avail – most of the archers were too terrified to aim with any accuracy, and those shafts that did find their mark seemed to make little difference. The monster looked down at the rapidly vacillating pikemen that made up the forward defence.

'Boo!' it said, and the line dissolved in screaming tatters. 'Who's in charge here?' the monster boomed.

The Norman commander urged his horse forward and bowed his head to the monster. '*Ce sont mes hommes! Je suis le Comte d'Orléans.*'

'Then you should keep them under better control. Somebody could get hurt.' The monster held up the arrow that had first pricked its ear. 'You'll probably be wanting this back,' it said, and hurled the arrow like a dart, straight at Orléans. It hit the Comte with such force it passed straight through his left eye and came clean out of the back of his head.

The Norman army looked on in disbelief as their beloved leader slid slowly off his horse and collapsed in the mud in a lifeless heap.

'Oh fuck.' The monster looked down at the Crystal that glittered in its fist. Little blue flames began to play around its gleaming facets, and then ran up the creature's arm. In a moment, the monster was surrounded by a crackling halo of electric fire. 'Here we go again,' it said and, with a sound like an inverted thunderclap, disappeared.

After a mystified pause, the English were the first to catch on to what had happened, and rushed down the hill to defeat the demoralized Normans. By the end of that October day in 1066, England was English still.

Chapter 23

Prince Nostrum had done it again. With only minutes to go before the atomic bomb reduced the infant Earth to rubble, he had travelled forwards in time and altered Oppenheimer and Bohr's calculations on the eve of the first atomic test at Alamogordo. The test was a damp squib, research funds were withdrawn – the bomb was never developed. Orvis's mother's DNA was never altered by radiation from the test; the foetus growing within her womb was born normal and grew up to be a leading light of the men's movement. Thus, not only did the Prince save the world in its earliest inception, he kept it free of the threat of nuclear warfare for ever.

Outside the United Nations building, Prince Nostrum paused to take his leave. Standing beside his time ship, he addressed the grateful citizens of Earth: 'Friends! For I think I have earned the right to call you friends. Live together in peace, support and nurture each other. Love your neighbour and your children, whatever they look like. Remember – all you have is each other.' The assembled citizens of Earth applauded and the Prince turned to Sparkie and said, 'Well, thank goodness that's over!'

'Ruff! Ruff!' barked Sparky happily, waving her paw. The Prince and the crowd laughed. Then, looking suddenly serious, the Prince stepped into his ship and took the controls. As the powerful motors began to hum, compressing the space-time continuum around the silver machine, his thoughts were with Aldariban, his home planet. How he'd missed its twin suns and limpid purple lakes. He was going home – home to Elthara, his beloved.

The assembled crowd watched the image of the ship falter and disappear. He was gone for now, but who knows when the citizens of Earth would next have need of Prince Nostrum?

Rex closed the book. 'Brilliant.'

It was a beautiful day, and arriving in Brighton early, Rex had slumped on the beach between the piers to finish off the book. He could barely contain his excitement; he was about to meet his hero. In just a few short minutes he would be standing face to face with F. Don Wizzard – the man who had given the world *The Singing Dragons of Phnell, Corridor to Doom,* and *Beside the Salient Sea.*

Deep in his reverie, he was only dimly aware of the figure that swayed uncertainly past him. But, suddenly brought to his senses by the loud clatter of something landing heavily on the pebbles, he looked up to see a man obviously in some distress. Rex heard a low moan and went over to him. Blood covered the front of his T-shirt and had soaked into his jeans. His face was a scarlet mess and his once-splendid walrus moustache was stiff with congealed blood. Rex knelt down beside him. 'Help me, please,' the man hissed damply through broken teeth, enveloping Rex in a fine red mist. Then his eyes closed and he slipped into unconsciousness. Rex froze, unable to comprehend what was happening – unable to move.

The man's injuries were horrific. His face was almost unrecognizable as human. Surely no fist could have done that? God, there were some maniacs around! As Rex looked down at the unconscious man, the world flickered and he could taste blood. Strong hands gripped him, and again and again the white tiles of the urinal dissolved in an explosion of stars. All he wanted was for it to stop. *This time he was going to die, this time he was going to die.* The same thought over and over again. *This time . . .*

'Are you his friend, sir?' Rex found himself staring into the kindly face of a paramedic.

'Sorry?'

'I need to know if he's on any medication.'

Slowly Rex came to. 'No, I er . . . I just found him here. I've no idea who he is. Is he going to be all right?'

'Don't worry sir, we'll take it from here.' The paramedic attended to the battered man, making him as comfortable as was possible. 'You can leave him with us now, sir.'

'Hmn? Oh, right, yes.' Rex got shakily to his feet and started walking. He wanted to get as far away as possible from this ugliness. Where was he going? Oh yes, the book signing. It seemed strangely distant now, and somehow small and unimportant.

Chapter 24

There was a small knot of pimply youths waiting inside the shop when F. Don Wizzard arrived. As he walked through the doors, they nudged each other and smiled inanely as their hero wandered into their midst.

'Is the manager anywhere about?' he enquired of the sales girl.

'Erm ... yes, he ... he's expecting you.' Her hesitation was inspired not so much by his celebrity, but more by his outfit – yellow dungarees, a loose black linen shirt, and gold flip-flops.

'So good to meet you,' the manager said, firmly pumping the wizard's hand and painfully rattling his visitor's heavy jewellery. 'We've put you upstairs, in the children's section. No reflection on your writing, of course,' he added hastily. 'It's just that there's more room there.' The manager laughed nervously.

'Of course there is,' replied the wizard.

As the manager and the famous author weaved their way through the crowded store, they drew fascinated glances from the customers, few of whom were aware that they were in the presence of a double Golden Talon Award winner. When they eventually reached the signing table in front of a large cardboard cut-out of Bob the Builder, F. Don Wizzard received a smattering of applause from the five or six people that were already forming an orderly queue. He held up his hands in a not very convincing show of humility.

Seating himself at the small table, draped with a slightly worn brown velvet cloth, he asked discreetly of the manager why he had not erected the promotional 3-D image of the monster – the 'Beast' of the title – had not the publisher sent it? The manager explained that, yes, the model had arrived and very good it was too – almost too good. In fact, so lifelike was it that it had sent several children into screaming fits. In the circumstances he'd decided to take it down. Mr Wizzard, of course, understood, but enquired if it was necessary for him to be seated in front of a representation of a popular figure from children's television, and wondered if it would be possible to move the cardboard figure of Bob the Builder to a place where people might not come to the erroneous conclusion that he was the lovable handyman's creator, flattering though that misapprehension might be.

With Bob now back in the under-fives section, F. Don Wizzard produced his fat gold fountain pen – the one with which he'd written all fifteen of his books. Looking up, he was surprised to find an elderly lady standing at the head of the queue. 'What's your name, dear?' he enquired.

'Ethel,' she said. F. Don Wizzard took a book off the pile at his elbow and opened it at the flyleaf. He wrote his usual inscription and signed it with a flourish. The old woman took the book and scrutinized the signature. 'What does it say?'

'To Ethel, the moon and stars are yours . . . F. Don Wizzard.'

The woman put down the book and looked at him long and hard. 'I thought you didn't look like Jeffrey Archer,' she said, and walked away shaking her head.

Next in line was a youth of about seventeen: beetroot red, with a mouthful of light grey teeth and an eruption of yellow pustules on his forehead. Hiding his grimace behind a smile, F. Don Wizzard focused on the boy's eyes; to look anywhere else would have been just too awful. 'And what's your name?' he asked.

The boy replied in a small, frightened yodel. The wizard repeated his question. Again the inaudible, cracked ejaculation. Against his better judgement, the wizard motioned the boy nearer. Immediately he was engulfed in a fug of teenage body odour as the boy inclined his head to speak into the proffered ear. The wizard cringed as the tip of the boy's nose brushed greasily against his temple and he felt hot, dank breath creep down his neck. 'Daniel,' the youth enunciated scratchily.

After half an hour of this demoralizing exercise, during which society's confused and inadequate paraded before him, he was ready to quit. It wasn't that he was a snob or even that he had any literary pretensions; he'd be the first to admit he was no intellectual. He just wished that his fans were normal, or at least took the trouble to wash now and then.

He sensed the next unfortunate standing in front of him. 'What's your name?' he said wearily, drawing another book from the slowly diminishing pile and opening it. With his pen poised over the crisp, virgin paper of the flyleaf, he looked up and his eyes met his own: morning-blue, as deep and as placid as a mountain lake, with here and there a fleck of white, like swans taking flight. 'Harmony,' the wizard breathed.

'Er, no. It's Rex, actually.'

The wizard stared at the young man standing before him, the son he had thrown into the abyss all those years ago. Apart from his eyes he was disappointingly unprepossessing. Large and ungainly, he stooped slightly, giving the impression that he wished he were smaller. His face seemed somehow unfinished; it had large, hamster-like cheeks, the eyes set too wide. And, as for his dress sense, well . . . But the saddest thing of all was that he was a *fan. At least he doesn't have spots*, the wizard thought.

'Rex?' he said. 'Well, that's appropriate.'

'Sorry?'

'Nothing, dear.' The wizard looked past him to ascertain the length of the queue. Behind Rex was a bloated, bald man sporting a long black beard and ancient, crusty denims, and behind him a small angry-looking girl with dyed black hair and metal spikes piercing every exposed part of her anatomy. 'Wait here a minute,' the wizard said to Rex, pulling two books out of the box at his feet. 'Here we are,' he said, handing one each to the man and the girl. 'On the house – they're already signed. Enjoy, enjoy.' He called the manager over. 'Look, I'm terribly sorry, but I've got to go. This young man has just informed me that my dog is seriously ill. I'm sure you understand.'

The manager eyed Rex suspiciously. 'Yes, I understand,' he said. 'Of course you must go.'

'I've signed the rest of the copies in the box, if there's anything else you need, please just let my publisher know,' the wizard said, ushering Rex past Bob the Builder and down the stairs. When they got outside and into the bustle of Churchill Square, a confused Rex turned to the wizard. 'I never got a book,' he said.

'A book? Do you know who I am? Silly question – you don't even know who *you* are. I've got something better than a book for you.' The wizard wrenched the bewildered newsagent through the crowded square towards the road, and hailed a taxi.

'Where are we going?' Rex asked as he was bundled into the back of the white and blue cab.

'Thirty-six Courtenay Gardens, please,' the wizard instructed the driver. Then, turning to Rex, 'I'm taking you home.'

Rex found himself in the grip of the complementary emotions of excitement and anxiety. Here he was, sharing a taxi with the greatest writer in the world, and actually on his way back to his house. But it had all happened so fast. 'Er . . . why are we going to your house?' he asked.

The short wizard caught Rex's anxious expression, and for the first time saw through his eyes the strangeness of the situation. 'Oh,' he said. 'Didn't I say?'

'No.'

'You've won.'

'Won what?'

'The prize, of course.'

'What prize?'

'The prize for being, er . . . my fiftieth customer today.'

'I didn't think there were that many people there.'

'Did I say today? I meant this week.'

'But today's the only day you've been there isn't it?'

'Now don't argue, dear. You've just won yourself a complete set of signed first editions. The entire Prince Nostrum collection – in hardback.'

'Wow!'

'Exactly, now just sit back and relax.'

But Rex couldn't relax. There was something odd about all this. He couldn't actually put his finger on it, but it just didn't feel right. By the time the taxi pulled up outside the wizards' pleasant three-bedroom semi, he had convinced himself that he'd been kidnapped, and was reluctant to get out of the cab.

Eventually persuaded to move at least as far as the pavement, Rex stood uncertainly outside the house, while the short wizard opened the door and called inside, 'You'll never guess who I've found!'

The tall wizard appeared almost immediately. 'What is it?' he demanded. The short one stepped aside, to reveal the diffident Rex, shuffling his feet in front of a lamp-post. The tall wizard squinted out into the sunlight and emotion seized him by the throat.

'Is it?' he said in a small voice. 'Can it really be?' The wizard stumbled, blinking, into the brightness of the day for a better look at his large and long-lost son. There was no mistaking those eyes. 'My boy,' is all he could say. 'My boy,' he repeated, tearfully.

Rex's first instinct was to run away as fast as possible. It was bad enough being kidnapped, but now he seemed to have stumbled into the final scene of an episode of *Little House on the Prairie*. The tall wizard came towards him, arms wide.

Rex seized the wizard's hand. 'How d'you do,' he muttered, pumping the wizard's arm in a manly fashion.

'Do you know,' the tall one said. 'The last time I saw you—'

'This is Rex,' interrupted the short one. 'He's won the prize.'

'Prize? What prize?' said the tall one. 'What are you babbling about?' The short one bobbed up and down behind Rex, pointing at him and shaking his head, his finger to his lips.

'What? Oh!' said the tall one, catching on at last. 'Of course, the prize! Congratulations, well done! Did you find the competition very difficult?' he said.

'No, I just had to queue up.'

'Well, now, queuing – that's an art in itself,' said the tall one.

The short one pushed in between them. 'Won't you come inside?' he said. Rex stayed where he was, eyeing the two men suspiciously. 'Come on,' the short one insisted. 'Have a quick cup of tea, collect your prize, then we'll send you on your way.'

'Well . . .' said Rex.

'We'll even call you a taxi,' said the tall one.

'It'll only take five minutes,' the short one beamed.

'All right,' Rex said at last, and reluctantly allowed himself to be ushered into the house.

'Please, won't you sit down,' the tall one said, indicating the white three-seat sofa in the bay window. 'Can we get you anything? Coffee?'

'Or tea?' the short one asked from the kitchen door.

'Tea would be nice,' said Rex. The short one smiled a self-satisfied smile and disappeared into the kitchen.

The tall one pulled up a leather pouffe and sat at Rex's feet, beaming up at him. Rex shifted uncomfortably on the sofa. He smiled back at the thin, eager man who seemed to be all bones and teeth. 'So, er . . .' the tall one said at last. 'Rex is it?'

'Yes.'

'Well, that's appropriate.'

'Sorry?'

'Nothing. What do you do, Rex?'

'I'm a newsagent.'

'A newsagent?' The tall one couldn't hide his disappointment. 'Oh,' he said flatly. 'Well, an honest profession at least.'

There was another awkward pause. 'I really can't stay long,' said Rex.

'No, of course you can't. We'll just give you your prize and then you'll be off. Exciting, eh? Winning a prize?'

'Hm,' said Rex. 'I didn't even know there was a competition.'

'Even better,' said the tall one. 'A surprise prize!' Rex nodded and smiled wanly. The tall one's chuckling laugh died away into silence.

At last the short one bustled in with the tea tray. 'Here we are.'

Rex was barricaded in behind a nesting side table, which was loaded with teacups and home-made walnut cake. When tea had been poured and cake passed round, the two wizards beamed expectantly at him over their steaming cups. There was something so familiar about their faces, what was it?

'Rex tells me that he's a newsagent,' said the tall one.

'Really? That must be interesting. I'll bet you've got a few stories.'

'He likes stories,' said the tall one, jerking his head in the short one's direction. 'He would – he's a writer,' he added sharply. 'Why don't you tell us your story?' he said to Rex. 'Did you have a happy childhood? Where did you go to school? What were your parents like?'

'You'll put the boy off,' said the short one. 'He'll tell us in his own time.' The tall one folded his arms and collapsed onto his knees. The short one turned back to Rex. 'You'll have to excuse him, he's a little overexcited.'

'No, that's all right,' said Rex. At the first available opportunity he was out of here.

'So you like my books?' said the short one after a pause.

'Oh yeah,' said Rex. The tall one scowled.

'What's your favourite?'

Rex didn't even have to think. '*The Singing Dragons of Phnell*,' he said.

'Oh please,' the tall one muttered.

The short one glanced frostily at him then turned back to his guest. 'What do you like about it?' he said. 'It's so rare I get an opportunity to talk to my fans and it's nice to know I'm giving them what they want.'

'Near the end, when the dragon's being freed from her earthly tomb – I love that bit,' said Rex. Screwing up his eyes slightly, he looked off into the middle distance. ' "Prince Nostrum's blade sliced through the ground as if it were butter. The earth heaved and split. A long gash appeared in the baked soil of the plain – a running wound that belched soot and fire. In a dreadful rush the dragon burst free of her prison and coiled hundreds of feet into the air . . ." Chapter eighteen – end of.' In the silence that followed, Rex tucked into his cake.

'Very dramatic,' said the tall wizard, flatly.

'I've read it quite a few times,' said Rex, his mouth full.

The short one smiled smugly at the tall one. 'And how's the cake?' he asked, turning triumphantly back to Rex.

'Very good,' he said, spraying crumbs over the carpet. 'Sorry.'

'Is your mother a good cook?' asked the tall one. The short one shot him an impatient glance.

'No – hopeless,' Rex replied.

'Really? What *is* she good at?' asked the tall one. The short one kicked him in the ankle. 'Ow!'

'She's dead.'

'Oh I am sorry,' said the short one, putting his hand on Rex's. 'Were you very close?'

'Yeah – but it was a long time ago now.'

'And your father?' asked the tall one, swivelling on the pouffe to take his ankles out of kicking range.

'He's dead too.' The short one bit his lip and squeezed Rex's hand. 'Well, we assume they're dead,' Rex continued, sliding his hand out from underneath the short wizard's.

'What do you mean?'

'They disappeared.' Rex took another bite of walnut cake and washed it down with a slurp of tea.

'Go on, dear.'

Rex shifted uneasily on the white, plumped cushions of the sofa. He hadn't told this story to anyone in years. 'No, it's . . . it's all in the past.'

'Please?' twinkled the short one. 'We'd love to hear what happened.'

Rex looked from the short wizard's eyes to those of the tall one.

They shone with an otherworldly intensity. There was something . . . What was it about them? He felt rather like a rabbit
caught in two sets of converging headlights. There was no way out.
Taking another slurp of tea, he began. 'My dad had caught the
flying bug. Mum said he'd always wanted to fly ever since I'd come
along. But with me to look after, as well as running the shop, there
was no time. Sometimes I'd catch him in the mornings, before we'd
opened the shop, browsing through all the flying magazines. Then,
when I was old enough to start helping out, I said to him that he
should *go* for it. Mum wasn't sure about it, but I said: oh go on, let
him have a little fun. So it was all my fault, really . . .' Rex broke
off. An unaccustomed tide of emotion was welling up inside him.
Fearing he might make a fool of himself, he knocked back the rest
of his tea and swallowed the feeling down. He smiled and looked
up at their concerned, expectant faces. 'You don't want to hear all
this.'

'Believe me, we do,' said the tall one with a gentle smile.

'Oh,' Rex sniffed, putting down his empty cup. 'Well, to cut a
long story short, he got his PPL.'

'PPL?'

'Private Pilot's Licence. Mum still wasn't sure – she never said,
but I got the feeling flying made her nervous. But she knew how
much it meant to him, so . . .' Rex shrugged. 'I'm not sure she ever
did enjoy going up with him, but she was like that – always supported him in everything he did . . .' Rex felt the tears pricking his
eyes and he broke off again. 'Sorry . . .'

'Would you like some more tea, dear?' asked the short one,
teapot raised.

'Thanks.' The wizards watched and waited as he drained his
second cup. Only the clatter of cup on saucer broke the silence.
Wiping his mouth with the back of his hand, Rex continued. 'It was
a sunny day with good visibility and virtually no wind. The aircraft
they'd hired had been regularly serviced – it was just going to be a
little jaunt down the coast to Bournemouth and back again. They
took off just after two o'clock into a blue sky, and were never seen

again . . . they just disappeared. They never found the bodies . . . I never even said goodbye . . .'

This time, Rex couldn't hold back the tears. The door to that dark place he had tried for so long to keep shut had been thrown open, and sunlight flooded in. He sobbed uncontrollably. The short wizard went and got a box of tissues from the sideboard. 'Thank you,' said Rex, taking a handful.

'It's all right dear, you let it all out.'

When the waves of emotion had begun to subside, Rex, embarrassed and confused, got up to leave, nearly knocking over the slender-legged occasional table. 'Sorry, I . . . look, if you can just give me my prize, then I'll be getting along.' Feeling a hand on his arm, he looked up into the unnervingly familiar eyes of the tall one. That was it! He had Rex's eyes!

'I'm afraid you've been brought here under false pretences.' Rex looked from the tall one to the short one. There they were again: they both had his eyes! 'There is no prize. But please, as you have been so good as to tell us your story, let us tell you ours.'

Rex, bewildered, weak with emotion, was too tired to argue, and obediently sat down.

'Did your parents ever mention a carpet-bag?'

Rex shook his head. 'Carpet-bag? No, I . . .' Then he remembered. 'Yes, I found one in the stock room when I was clearing it out after they died. But they never . . . wait a minute, was it you who put that ad in the *Argus*?'

'Guilty,' said the tall one. 'Seven years ago I stood at the edge of a distant sea and placed a beautiful baby boy in a large carpet-bag. Hurling him into the void, I thought I'd lost him for ever, but happily, now I see I was mistaken. But I'm getting ahead of myself. Let's start from the beginning.' The tall wizard cleared his throat. 'I . . .' The short one shot him a glance. 'Er . . . we,' the tall one corrected, 'are a great wizard . . .'

Rex listened in growing wonder as the tall, bony man unwound his tale of wizards and kings and evil deeds. A diabolical book spoke of shellfish falling from the sky, and people in skirts on Brighton beach, and all the while a monster, unstuck in time, clattered around the universe. The man was obviously barking.

When he'd finished, Rex looked at his watch, and with a 'My word, look at the time!' swiftly but politely took his leave.

At the door, the tall wizard handed Rex a business card. 'That's our number – give us a call, or just come round. Now you grasp the urgency of the situation, you'll understand why we have to get to work straight away.'

'Don't leave it too long, dear,' the short one shouted from the door as Rex hurried off down the street.

'No wonder his books are so lifelike,' thought Rex as he headed for the seafront. 'He thinks they're true.'

Chapter 25

Stalin was worried. Walking in the garden of his dacha outside Moscow, he brooded over the latest intelligence reports. He had been betrayed. It was his own fault, of course, and he cursed his stupidity. The innately suspicious Soviet leader had made the mistake of trusting Hitler, and now the German army was scything through the Ukraine. It would be only a matter of days before they were at the gates of Moscow.

Stalin pondered his next move. There was a train at Moscow station ready and waiting to evacuate him. He drew the small silver flask from his inside pocket and drank; the vodka was warmly comforting. And then, perhaps, a capsule of cyanide washed down with a slug of good Russian vodka wouldn't be such a bad way to go. But how would history remember him? As a gullible failure? A coward unable to face defeat? Just at that moment he looked up. A halo of shimmering blue light had appeared above his head, and through it he could hear a sound as if something was falling from a great height . . .

'Aaaarrrgh!'

The monster landed right on top of him, killing him instantly. 'Fucking hell, what am I sitting on?' The creature shifted on its great backside. 'You make a lousy cushion,' it said, pulling the remains of comrade Stalin out from underneath it. Almost immediately little blue flames began to play up and down the creature's arms. 'Oh bugger,' it said and, with a sound like an enormous plug being pulled from a bath, disappeared with a *ga-loop*!

When word got round the besieged capital that their beloved

leader was dead, the inhabitants of Moscow lost heart, the army deserted. The situation was hopeless – with Uncle Josef gone, what was there left to fight for?

On receiving the report that Moscow had fallen, Hitler was beside himself with joy. With the Soviet Union and all its resources under German control, the Führer was now poised to take over the world . . .

Chapter 26

'You shouldn't have done that, sir,' said Beasely, drawing on a cigarette as if his life depended on it. 'You could have killed him.'

Malcom and his sergeant were in The Sussex, an airy, Gothic-themed pub within shouting distance of the King Alfred Centre.

'I didn't know you smoked, sergeant,' said Malcom, turning back from the bar with two large whiskies.

'I don't. I gave up three years ago. It's working with you that's started me off again.'

Malcom smiled and handed Beasely one of the drinks. 'Drink up, it'll make you feel better.'

After they'd interrogated Michael Daniels's employees on the pier, one of them – as Beasely had predicted – had gone straight to his boss and alerted him. Daniels had complained and, true to his word, Superintendent Gerrold had immediately put Collins and Beasely on seafront lavatory watch. This entailed walking the length of the promenade between Brighton Pier and the King Alfred Centre, making sure that the lavatories were not being used for 'unnatural purposes'. Of all the shitty jobs in the panoply of horrible pastimes available to your average member of the force, it was the least favourite. It was bad enough having to hang around lavatories, and no policeman relished the idea of being mistaken for a homosexual. But on top of that, if you did make an arrest, you had to be very sure of your grounds so as not to upset the large and very vocal gay community. But Malcom was loving it. 'Perfect,' he'd said to Beasely outside the super's office after their carpeting. 'Now we can keep an eye on that bastard Daniels and if he makes a move, we'll know.'

DI Collins's mind – never a cosy place at the best of times – seemed to Beasely to be growing daily more unbalanced; and Beasely, long used to walking on eggshells around his superior officer, was now a nervous wreck. He never knew which way Malcom was likely to jump.

Malcom himself was on a hair trigger; he hadn't had a decent night's sleep for a week. Every time he closed his eyes came the dream, and with each repeat it grew more terrible, tearing his sleep-deprived senses to shreds. Horrifying visions of a laughing, blood-streaked monster would haunt his midnight hours. Sometimes he would find himself among piles of rotting corpses, and wake screaming and bathed in sweat. He had come to dread the night and the lonely, dark time.

He had only one way of dealing with his fear; one outlet for his sheer naked terror. Violence soothed him – it put him back in control.

Unpredictable was one way of describing the attack. Unpremeditated, unfounded, unprincipled and uncontrolled were other ways to describe the extreme violence Malcom had meted out to the man innocently having a pee in the seafront lavatory. It was nothing personal – it wasn't even really because he was gay. He just happened to be in the wrong place at the wrong time.

Checking the Gents by the pedestrian underpass to the Brighton Centre, they had come across a man, alone. Malcom had stood next to him at the urinal, and when the man had finished, he'd turned and slipped on the wet tiles. Throwing his hand out to steady himself, he'd happened to brush Malcom's shoulder. That was all.

What followed had shaken Beasely's belief in human nature to the core. He was still trembling. Never in all his years of policing had he witnessed anything so brutal, depraved or utterly pointless. He didn't think he'd ever be able to forget the image of DI Collins urinating on that poor man's head as he lay face-down in the trough, his blood mingling with the piss and fag ends.

'As soon as we get back to the station, I'm asking to be transferred – somewhere miles from here where I never have to come into contact with you again. You're a monster. You're a disgrace to the force. This time you've overstepped the mark, and I'm making a full report.'

Malcom smiled and sipped his whisky. 'No, you're not, my little ferret.'

'Oh yes I am. You're not getting away with this.'

'Oh, but I am. You see, there was another officer present at that little incident, one DS Beasely. And what was he doing? Holding the door shut. That makes him an accessory, and it blows any chances he might have of promotion right out of his arse. But that's not the real reason why he's going to keep his mouth shut. No, the real reason that he's not going to tell a soul is that if he breathes a word to anyone, I'm going to cut off his dick with a Stanley knife. Cheers!' Malcom downed his whisky. 'Your round,' he said, slamming his glass on the bar.

Beasely was in deep shock. This wasn't why he'd become a policeman. He'd wanted to help people, solve crimes, put villains behind bars, clear the streets of drug dealers – not protect bent coppers, but what could he do? Collins was mad, what he'd seen in the Gents today supported that. What chance did a little man like Beasely have against eighteen stone of pure, naked aggression? If he did report him, Beasley was sure Malcolm would kill him. He threw back the whisky and, struggling to keep the burning liquid down, called the bartender over. 'Two more large Bells,' he said, hoarsely, and nervously flipped open his packet of ten Silk Cut.

When they emerged into the bright afternoon, several large ones later, Beasely felt strangely detached from his body. He had the impression that he was looking down on himself from a great height: he was an insignificant dot on the pavement outside a Sussex pub. Around him were hundreds of other little dots. Once he'd had a dream – to make a difference in the world. Now he saw the reality of his position: he was just a dot amongst dots.

'Let's take a gentle stroll,' said Malcom, belching a sweet-smelling cloud of alcohol.

'Where to? Who are we going to beat up now?' asked Beasely, small and unsteady.

'Don't you worry, my little accomplice. I'm not going to hurt anyone. I'm feeling good. I'm feeling very good. I may even do someone a good turn. Come on.' Without looking, Malcom stepped off the pavement into the busy road. Beasely closed his eyes and winced. There was a terrifying sound of screeching tyres and the angry blare of horns. 'Come on, sergeant!'

Beasely cautiously opened his eyes to see Malcom standing in the middle of the road, one hand up to the oncoming traffic, the other waving him across. To the shouted abuse of the irate drivers, the beetroot-red DS Beasely walked timidly across the road. Once his sergeant had gained the sanctuary of the central reservation, Malcom saluted the frustrated motorists and followed him across. Beasely insisted they wait for a break in the traffic before attempting to cross the other carriageway.

Chapter 27

It was the insinuation that that strange stick insect of a man was his father which had really upset Rex. Did they really think that he'd buy their ridiculous story? Admittedly the coincidence of the carpet-bag was strange, but that's all it was – a coincidence. No, they were obviously just two sad old gays wanting to spice up their lives with a bit of fantasy role-playing. They had cast him as the handsome Prince and they were . . . what? The ugly sisters?

He was also cross with himself for telling them the story of his parents' disappearance. They'd drawn him into talking about something private and tender, and had then got off on his distress. He'd left the wizards' house angry and upset, determined to go straight home and clear his bookshelves of all Wizzard's titles. From now on he'd read true-life stories and try and live in the real world.

All in all, it had been a very unsettling experience, and although he rarely drank, he felt in need of a small tincture to steady his shattered nerves. Rex wasn't exactly sure when he entered that twilight world, but it must have been soon after he stepped into the seafront pub. He was used to having to wait to be served, but this was different. As he stood at the bar, it was the absolute silence that first drew his attention to it. Looking round he saw a strange frozen tableau. The midday drinkers sat or stood; caught, mouths agape, in grotesque poses of laughter, or mid-sentence – the expressions on their faces as motionless as if they'd been carved in stone. One man standing outside, wearing dirty jeans and a torn T-shirt, was pouring a pint of lager over his head. The golden liquid cascaded like a glass waterfall over his spiky hair and narrow, sinewy shoulders. Small droplets that had escaped the main flow hung motionless around him in an alcoholic halo, as his friends, their static faces contorted in a rictus of mirth, were held, motionless, in the act of turning away.

Rex backed slowly out of the bar. The promenade was crowded with similar statues. Some were frozen in the act of walking, defying all the laws of physics as they balanced preposterously on one leg. Was Rex having some sort of seizure? Perhaps he was dead and had been consigned to this limbo as a punishment for leading a boring life. Even the sea was still. Nothing moved. No, not *nothing*. Out of the corner of his eye he saw something flicker. In the doorway of a small arch under the esplanade, a rainbow-coloured bead curtain swayed in some imagined breeze. Rex approached with caution. Above the curtain was a sign which declared: 'Madame Huzinga – Palms read, destiny foretold'. On a board by the door was a frame crammed with the faded photographs of celebrities, many now dead, who had doubtless benefited from Madame H's advice and with whom she might still have been in contact. Rex peered through the narrow gaps in the gently swaying curtain and could make out a hunched figure sitting behind a small table, shuffling cards.

'Come in, dear. I've been expecting you.' The voice startled him and he stepped back into one of the people-statues on the promenade.

'Sorry,' he said to the immovable and unmoving young girl, her concentration fixed on the ice-cream cornet in her hand.

'She can't hear you, dear. Come in and sit down.'

Rex tentatively parted the softly clattering curtain and entered the small cubicle. The figure at the table appeared to be nothing more than a bundle of rags. She indicated the chair opposite her, without looking up. Rex sat and watched as the woman laid the cards out in a practised arc on the green baize.

She chuckled to herself in a chesty wheeze as she looked at the spread. 'You have a long way to go, my dear. You are full of contradictions. You were born on a Thursday in a place that has no need of such niceties as days of the week. Your father and mother loved you dearly, yet let you go when you were very small. Half in, half out of this world, you have been orphaned twice: once by sea and once by air. Now you have discovered your dream you are full of fear. Do not be afraid, all you have heard is true. Listen to your heart – you have a long way to go.'

The ancient creature looked up at him. Her complexion was as dark as weathered chestnut and had the texture of old shoe-leather. But her eyes twinkled like black diamonds.

'Give me your hands,' she ordered.

Rex laid his hands, palm side up, on the table. She studied them closely, tracing the lines with one stubby finger, knotted and twisted like a briar root. There was that wheezing chuckle again.

'You are more, much more than you believe yourself to be, but you are in great danger. It's time to wake up. The black lumpen thing, an emissary of hell, an evil beyond words, wants your blood and it will find you should you remain in slumber. You must believe. When the dragon turns in her sleep, you will know your destiny and you must act. You are the Light, and on your shoulders rests the future of all things. Bear it lightly. Follow the clue in your hand to reach your destination, you have far to go.'

Rex opened his mouth to speak, but the old woman shook her head and held a finger to her lips.

'There is someone here wants a word,' she said, and collapsed in her chair with a great sigh. She sat there, not breathing, for such a long time that Rex became a little concerned. He was just about to reach over and feel for a pulse when he heard a voice, a voice that was not hers, a gentle, soothing voice that seemed to come from far away.

'My son? I can't see . . . is it my son? Where am I? Harmony, is that really you? Oh, let it be you. I have so little time. I know that you are with your father and that gives me hope, but God knows how I miss you. You are your father's son and therefore will be strong and wise, and when you return you will bring balance again to our land that has grown so sad . . . This is not easy. You are fading – too fast, too fast! Know that I love you, I always will.

Tell your father I will wait for him. You must believe . . .' But her last words were drowned out by a roaring sound, like the rushing of a great wind.

Suddenly the old woman sat up. 'Did she come through?'

Rex nodded.

'Good, good. Go now and remember all.'

Rex put his hand in his pocket. 'No dear, this one's on the house.' The woman shook with mirth and, to the accompaniment of her wheezing chuckle, Rex walked out through the bead curtain onto the sun-drenched promenade.

It was a normal summer's day. People walked by eating ice cream, chatting happily to one another. He heard a wet spattering and looking round, saw a man pour a pint of lager over his head to the delighted whoops of his friends. Rex looked back at the doorway through which he had just passed. A rotting, graffiti-covered board now stood where the bead curtain of Madame Huzinga's had once been. He went cold. Uncertain that his legs would bear his weight for much longer, he lurched across the promenade, colliding with several of the suddenly animated strollers, and collapsed onto the warm pebbles.

What was going on? This had to take the biscuit for the strangest day of his life. Had it happened? Had *what* happened? Had time stopped? Or had he just lost his mind?

'*Your mother and father loved you dearly . . . half in, half out of this world, you have been orphaned twice . . . do not fear your destiny . . . all you have heard is true . . .*' The old woman's words echoed around his brain. What did it all mean? The '*great lumpen creature, an emissary of hell*' was uncomfortably close to the beast of his dream. He shuddered at the thought. And what was that at the end – the woman's disembodied voice? What had she called him – Harmony? Wasn't that what F. Don Wizzard had called him in the bookshop? Rex shivered. The simple explanation was that he was having delusions. But was the shock of his discovering that his favourite author was a sad old queen enough to flip him into some alternative fantasy existence?

As Rex pondered, the earth moved. Deep, deep underground he felt – rather than heard – a rumbling like some vast creature grinding its teeth. Another tremor. It was a strange experience, as if the ground beneath him, usually so comfortingly firm, so reliably concrete, had become fluid and treacherously unstable.

'When the dragon turns in her sleep . . . you must act . . .'

Rex felt very small and alone; he shoved his hands deep into the pockets of his jacket and felt the edge of the business card that the tall one had thrust into his hand as he was leaving. He pulled it out. 'Wizard & Wizzard,' he read. '36 Courtenay Gardens.'

What if they'd been telling the truth? What if he was heir to the throne of some faraway, lost land? Wouldn't that make sense of how he felt about the world, and his feelings of isolation?

Just then something thudded onto the promenade behind him, and the screaming started . . .

Chapter 28

In the drowsily warming summer sunshine, the two policemen plodding back down the promenade were soon overtaken by the urgent need to rest. Sitting down in one of the urine-fragranced shelters – by day utilized by venerable gentlefolk to rest their legs, and by night by the homeless as a hotel – Beasely passed out almost immediately and collapsed against Malcom, his head resting on his shoulder. Malcom looked down at the little man and smiled with drink-induced affection. 'Bless him,' he said, and closing his eyes too, fell asleep almost at once.

Deep in his ensuing terrible, blood-spattered dream of death, Malcom heard the screaming. He looked across the castle courtyard littered with corpses and saw, rolling towards him across the great plain, a tidal wave of human misery. It had no discernible features; it was just huge and dark and terrifying and threatened to engulf him in a sea of suffering. He looked up as the terrible tide was about to break over his head, and heard a thump.

He opened his eyes. Something had thudded onto the roof of the shelter. A string of white, slimy, foul-smelling goo dripped slowly from the eaves and onto his shoe. *Fucking big seagull*, he thought.

He closed his eyes again, but eventually the screaming penetrated his sleep and alcohol-befuddled senses and he realized it was coming not from the depths of his unconscious, but from outside – and quite close by. Forcing his brain to wakefulness, he looked around. A woman was standing on the promenade howling in horror. She was holding a dog's lead, the end of which seemed to disappear into a giant scallop.

'Strange pet,' Malcom said to himself. Still not one hundred per cent sure that this wasn't all part of his weird and disturbing nightmare, he heard another thud and watched in bleary disbelief as a giant clam bounced off the roof of the shelter and fell onto the promenade in front of him, its valves snapping angrily. In one ferocious bound, it leapt onto one of the shelter uprights and began devouring it. At last Malcom was stung into action. 'It's fucking real life Pac-Man!' he yelled, jumping up.

Beasely, having lost his human support, flopped over onto the bench and was startled suddenly awake just as a man in shorts and trainers ran past, trying to pull a giant clam off his head. Beasely had consumed three large whiskies and half a pint of lager – not enough to induce hallucinations, surely? Sitting up, he rubbed his eyes. Men, women and children seemed to be running everywhere, pursued by giant snapping molluscs. *No*, he reasoned – his brain finally getting into gear – against all the odds, *this was actually happening*. Families ran, screaming, from the beach as more and more of the clams fell from the sky. All at once they were everywhere, hungrily munching through railings, chomping through beach huts, leaping and jumping like monstrous demented fleas.

'Get on the blower, get some backup!' Malcom yelled as one of the clams slammed its shell closed on his foot. Malcom yelped in terror and kicked the animal against the side of the shelter. At the second attempt, the shell cracked and Malcom managed to pull his foot free. Then he jumped up and down on the wounded mollusc. 'Fucking hell! Fucking hell! Fucking hell!' he screamed. The resulting shower of soft, white flesh and shell fragments fell on Malcom, and his sergeant, in a malodorous rain.

'Giant clams on the promenade! Brunswick area!' Beasely shouted into the phone. 'They're eating everything! Need help!'

'Well?' Malcom asked, removing some clam roe from his left ear.

'They didn't believe me.'

'Give it here,' said Malcom, grabbing the phone. 'This is DI Collins and somebody better get their arse down here and help sort this out before there's a massacre.'

'Right sir,' came the reply. 'Straight away, sir. I'll send Sergeant Ivey with an extra-large bottle of Tabasco.' In the background Malcom could hear raucous laughter.

'Listen, Brighton's being invaded by fucking man-eating bivalve molluscs and we need some fucking support, you twat!'

There was a pause, then a familiar, well-modulated voice came down the line. 'This is Superintendent Gerrold. You'd better not be pissing about, Collins.'

'No sir, really sir, there are hundreds of them all over the place – just falling out of the sky, sir, never seen anything like it. Listen.' Malcom held the phone out at arm's length to catch the sounds of mayhem on the seafront.

'Very well, I'll get some men down to you immediately. But be clear about one thing Collins – if this is some half-arsed prank you're going to be out of the force so fast your feet won't touch the ground.'

'Yes sir, thank you sir.' Malcom handed the phone back to his sergeant. 'Beasely – over there!' he yelled, pointing to a small child and her mother, who were having a tug of war with one of the creatures over a pink tricycle. Gathering the wailing child under one arm, Beasely instructed the terrified mother to follow him as he ran towards the road, dodging the snapping shells. The traffic on Kingsway had come to a complete stop as the shellfish continued to pour out of the sky. Beasely opened the door of one of the stationary cars and piled the mother and child inside. 'Drive like hell!' he screamed, slamming the door and waving frantically at the other cars to keep moving.

Beasely did what he could to get people out of the area, but it was the height of the season, the beaches were crowded and the promenade was packed.

As Malcom tried to shelter from the murderous rain in one of the beach huts, it exploded and he found himself lying in its ruins, underneath someone dressed in what appeared to be a spacesuit. 'Jesus H. fucking Christ! Who the fuck are you?' Malcom said, pushing the spaceman off and painfully removing the remains of a deckchair from beneath him.

The figure lay on the ground, moaning softly. 'Cold water,' it groaned.

'You want water?'

The figure in the spacesuit shook its head. 'The clams – cold water kills them.'

'So you know all about them, do you?' said Malcom, reaching for his handcuffs. 'This is all your fault is it, you prick?'

'Please, hurry,' said the figure in the spacesuit. 'They'll eat everything.'

Malcom looked down at the name badge on the front of the spacesuit. 'S. Kowalski?' he read. Serena nodded. 'Well then, Mr Kowalski, I'm arresting you for failing to keep dangerous animals under control and destroying a beach hut.' He clunked the handcuffs firmly around Serena's wrists.

'No! You've got to do something,' she said, trying to get up. Malcom slammed a fist into her stomach.

'Having fun, Collins?' Gerrold was standing over him.

'He was resisting arrest, sir.'

'Who is he?'

'He's responsible, sir. He admitted it.'

Gerrold knelt down beside Serena who was doubled up in pain. 'Is there any way to stop them?' he asked.

'Helmet,' Serena gasped.

Gerrold leaned closer. 'Sorry?'

'Take the fucking helmet off!' Serena screamed. Gerrold fiddled ineffectually with the locking ring. 'Twist it! Twist it!' she yelled.

'Ah, right,' said Gerrold. 'I think I've got it now.'

The helmet came loose with a small hiss. 'Serena Kowalski, how do you do?' she said, the moment Gerrold had pulled it off.

'Oh fuck,' said Malcom. 'I didn't know it was a woman, sir.'

'Douse them with cold water,' Serena coughed. 'It kills them. I already told this idiot.'

'Did she, Collins?'

'I thought she was raving, sir.'

Gerrold stood up. 'Beasely!'

The small, shabby sergeant appeared, out of breath. 'Sir?'

'Apparently they don't like cold water. Grab whatever you can – buckets, cool bags – fill them up from the sea and douse the little bastards. For once we can be glad this is not the Caribbean.'

'Yes, sir.'

'Better get on to the fire brigade too, get a couple of their engines down here.'

'Right away, sir.' Beasely ran off.

'Get up,' the superintendent snapped. Malcom stood unsteadily to attention. Gerrold looked hard at the pig-faced detective. He detested the man. A bigoted ball of hate like Collins had no place in the modern police force. He was a dinosaur. 'You're a brainless arsehole, Collins, and you stink of whisky and old fish. Fuck off home.'

'But sir . . .'

'No buts, Collins. Go home, have a shower, sober up. You're back here on seafront patrol at twenty-two hundred hours.' Malcom looked blank. 'That's ten o'clock you imbecile!'

'Yes, sir. But what about my prisoner?' Malcom indicated Serena, still moaning softly on the ground.

Gerrold's fist tightened on the front of Malcom's shirt. 'We can do this two ways, Collins – the easy way or the hard way. The easy way involves you leaving now and reporting to my office at seven sharp tomorrow morning, where I may or may not cut off your balls with a rusty razor. But if you want to make things difficult for yourself, please, go ahead. Say one more thing and I promise you, I will personally insert your fat, ugly head up one of those clams' arses and watch it fart you to death.'

Malcom, unsure as to whether or not clams actually had arses, was about to voice his uncertainty, but the steel in Gerrold's eyes persuaded him otherwise, and he trudged unhappily away.

Beasely directed the police and members of the public into human chains to gather water from the sea and douse the clams. The plan worked brilliantly, and soon the promenade was littered with dead and dying bivalve molluscs. The fall seemed to have been limited to the Brunswick area and any stray clams were soon hunted down and hosed into submission by patrolling fire engines. In just under an hour, the Giant Clam Incident was over. Beasely received a commendation for his labours, and was given the rest of the day off by his grateful superintendent.

All that was left was the mystery of Serena Kowalski. Who was she? Where had she come from? Gerrold couldn't seem to get any sense out of her.

'Three people dead, scores injured and damage to property amounting to hundreds of thousands of pounds.'

'I'm sorry, I'm as bewildered as you are, believe me.'

'Let's go through it one more time.'

Serena looked at the superintendent across the desk. How many more times would she have to tell this story? 'OK,' she said with a sigh. 'One more time. The pressure's rising in the hold, I go down to see what's happening and find that the relief valve's jammed, so I go inside to see what I can do. It's hot in there, the clams are getting really excited and I realize I'm going to have to act fast. I climb on the observation platform to have a closer look – the thing tips up and tries to throw me off. There I am, hanging from my boots about half a mile above several billion tons of garbage. I try to climb back on, but I slip. I'm falling towards certain death. The next thing I know I'm lying on the ground being punched in the guts by your colleague. You people have a strange notion of welcome,' she said, gingerly stroking her bruised abdomen.

'I'm sorry, the officer in question has been reprimanded.'

'I know, I was there.'

'Look, I want to help, but I have to say that nothing you've said so far makes any sense.' Gerrold looked at his hastily scribbled notes. 'You say you are Serena Kowalski from Oregon, and that you are a garbage operative, third class, on the SS *St Francis Sinatra*.'

'Correct.'

'And that this is a huge ship which composts rubbish.'

'With the help of the clams, yeah.'

'But our helicopter was on shore patrol at the time in question, so we'd have spotted any large ships in the area.'

'Ah,' said Serena, the penny dropping. 'Did I say ship? I probably should have said spaceship.'

Gerrold thumped the desk in frustration. 'Look! Perhaps, where you come from, watching people being eaten alive by marauding shellfish is an amusing pastime, but here we take that sort of thing very seriously indeed. Do you have any idea of the damage you may have done to the tourist trade?'

'It's not my fault. Let me get on to my people, tell them what happened. Maybe they'll be able to help.'

'Very well.' Gerrold pushed the phone across the desk.

Serena looked at it. 'What's this?'

'A telephone.'

'Wow, I knew you people in England were behind the times, but this is a real museum piece.'

'Now, don't play games. If you want to phone somebody, go ahead.'

'OK. Global net, area 35267–99533/001.com,' Serena barked at the instrument. Nothing happened. 'Does this thing work?' Gerrold looked at her incredulously. 'Oh, I get it. I forgot the international dialling code.'

Gerrold exploded. 'That's it!' he said, standing and ripping the phone out of the socket.

'Careful, that's probably worth a fortune.'

Gerrold threw it across the room. It smashed against the wall. 'Now it's worthless!' he screamed. 'And if you don't start making sense very soon, I'm going to do the same to you!'

'You're dribbling.'

'Aaarrgh!'

'OK, OK, I'll tell you everything. Just calm down.'

The door opened and Sergeant Ivey popped his head into the room. 'Everything all right, sir?'

Gerrold looked up. 'Fine, everything's fine, thank you sergeant,' he said, breathing deeply.

'Can I get you a cup of tea?'

'Yes, that would be very nice, thank you.'

'And the, er . . . the lady?'

Serena craned round in her seat. 'Do you have maté?'

Sergeant Ivey looked blank. 'Er, it's Ty-phoo I think.'

'OK.'

Ivey lingered in the doorway. 'That will be all, thank you, sergeant.' Gerrold smiled a no-need-to-worry smile and sat back behind his desk.

'Oh, very good, sir.' The sergeant closed the door.

'I must apologize for my outburst,' said the superintendent, smoothing back his hair. 'It's been a bit of a day.'

'You're telling *me*.'

'Now, where were we? Ah yes, you were about to tell me everything.'

'Let me look in my journal.' Serena got out a small chrome object, about the size of a bullet, and laid it on the desk. 'OK, it was this morning when everything began to go wrong, so let's start there. Journal!' said Serena, addressing the small chrome object. 'August twenty-one, 2053 – a.m.' The small bullet started to spin. Above it appeared a holographic image of Serena entering the lift on the spaceship. Gerrold watched in astonishment as the commissionaire in the lift began removing his clothes. Serena coughed. 'Ah, yeah, we can probably fast-forward through this bit.' Then the image changed and there was Serena standing outside the hold, dressed in her pressure gear.

Gerrold looked across at Garbage Operative Kowalski. 'What date did you say?'

'August twenty-one.'

'Yes, yes, and the year?'

'2053, why?'

'One moment, please.' Smiling strangely, Gerrold got out of his chair and walked slowly and carefully to the door. 'I'll be back in just a second,' he quavered. 'Don't go away.'

Sergeant Ivey, tray in hand, was just about to knock on the superintendent's door when Gerrold came out. Ivey couldn't help noticing that the super had a strange look about him. 'Ah, Ivey,' he said. 'Good, good.'

'Are you all right, sir?'

Gerrold nodded slowly and thoughtfully. 'I'll take the tray now, thank you sergeant.'

'I thought I'd put a couple of Penguins and custard creams on a saucer – they like their cookies, Americans, don't they?'

'Very thoughtful. Would you do me a favour, sergeant? Get the Home Office on the phone, tell them I need to speak to them urgently.'

'Oh right, she's an illegal immigrant then, is she, sir?' Ivey prided himself on the quickness of his uptake.

'Something like that, yes.'

'Right, sir. Right away, sir.'

Ivey was already halfway down the corridor when Gerrold called him back. 'Ivey, don't tell a soul, OK?' he whispered hoarsely.

'Very good, sir, anything you say.' Ivey watched as the super, carefully balancing the tea tray on one arm and smiling inanely, backed slowly into his office.

Ivey put his hand on his hip and scratched his head in time-honoured 'confused policeman' fashion. Something was up, something was very definitely up. 'Strange times, Ivey, strange times,' he muttered to himself as he walked back up the corridor.

Chapter 29

Malcom looked at himself in the mirror. His eyes were bloodshot, and his hair was white with bits of pulverized clam. 'Fuck,' he said, succinctly summing up his feelings. He was pissed off. He was pissed off with that goody-goody hero Sergeant Beasely; pissed off with high and mighty Superintendent Gerrold; but most of all, pissed off with that bastard Daniels. It was all *his* fault. He climbed into the bath and turned on the shower. As the hot water rushed over his skin, and the Bubbleburst Lemon Zest Shower Foam cleansed his body of stringy bits of old shellfish and the stale smell of alcohol, he began to feel better. He even began to sing: a horribly mangled version of Eric Clapton's 'Wonderful Tonight' echoing around his small bathroom.

When he emerged, he was in a much better mood. He had been thinking of getting his head down for a couple of hours – he was in for a long night – but in the shower he had found a new resolve, an absolute determination to crush the hated Daniels once and for all. He would use the time to plan his next move. Pulling on a loose denim shirt, and his favourite Marlboro baseball cap, he went into the front room and picked up the packet of photographs that Beasely had taken on the promenade. Then he sat at the table and lit a panatella.

He laid the photographs out in a grid, six across and six deep, with Beasely's attempt at visual poetry – the seagull hanging in space – in the final place. 'White bird against a blue sky . . . I think I'll get that framed,' said Malcom, chewing the end of his cigar. He picked up the big magnifying glass his mum had given him for a joke when he'd first joined the police force, and methodically studied the distant images of the men in each picture. In the first two rows, both men had their backs to the camera, but there, right in the middle of the third row, was a tiny but absolutely crystal-clear image of the man with whom Daniels had shared the promenade that morning. Malcom stared at it long and hard. He knew he was looking at something important, but at first he didn't know what. There was something strangely familiar about the man. It gave him a tingle like he felt on seeing the long-forgotten face of someone he'd put behind bars. But this wasn't some petty criminal; this was the Borough Surveyor. Yet still there was that feeling, that unease – as if something long hidden deep in the silts of his memory was struggling to reach the surface.

He was just about to give up when it hit him. It was so unexpected, so shocking it made him gasp. Suddenly Malcom was back in that hideous place. He could feel the bitter cold; the touch of the scratchy woollen blankets on his naked skin as he tried to sleep, shivering, on that thin, damp mattress; and he could taste the fear, the fear that never left him, waking or sleeping. As Malcom looked at the photograph, he remembered. The face was a little older now, of course, and the sunken cheeks had become full and round from easy living, but there was no mistaking those high, arched eyebrows and those dead, dead eyes.

'Albie Morningside,' Malcom whispered, as if uttering an evil spell. 'My God, what's he doing here?'

Frederick John Davis, Director of Environment and Housing Services, (Conservation Dept.), was standing at his desk, poring over a set of plans for an extension to the Dome museum and art gallery – they said they needed more room, although why they couldn't have mentioned that before the recent multi-million-pound refurbishment, God alone knew. Several councillors had taken the opportunity to submit ideas as to how the new space should be utilized, and he was just wondering how popular Marjorie Baines's proposal for a gallery devoted solely to disabled lesbians in the textile industry would prove when the phone rang. He picked it up. 'Hello, Frederick Davis.'

'Hello, Mr Davis – or should I call you Albie?'

The Director, long practised in deceit, kept his voice level, but could do nothing to prevent his body from breaking out in a cold sweat. 'Who is this?' he articulated in an almost faultless Home Counties accent.

'We shared a room together once. A big room, sparsely furnished, with hot and cold running crap. What do you think Brighton and Hove Council would do if they knew their Borough Surveyor was an ex-Borstal boy, eh?' There was a sudden ringing in Davis's ears and stars appeared at the edge of his vision. 'You still there, Albie?'

'Yes,' Davis managed to gasp, sitting down and loosening his tie. 'Who are you, what do you want?'

'Oh, I'm nobody – just the little fat boy in the corner. You remember – the one you used to call Bucket. I've still got the bruises, Albie, but I'm all growed up now.'

'Bucket?' It was a name from the fringes of memory – from another time, another life. In Davis's mind's eye there appeared the image of a small, rotund, frightened bucket of lard that used to cry in his sleep and would pee his bed with monotonous regularity. What was his name? What was his name? 'Malcom? Oh Jesus!'

'Careful Albie, your accent is slipping. We don't want all your posh friends thinking you're not the proper article now, do we?'

'Look, it all happened a long time ago. I was young and confused. I'm sorry for what I did to you, but I'm straight now. I've got a responsible job, I keep my nose clean. I try and do good things, I—'

'What's Daniels got on you?'

Albie was brought up short. 'Eh?'

'He knows, doesn't he?'

Albie looked around the open-plan office. His colleagues were beginning to throw him curious glances. 'He's the only one. No one else has any idea,' he hissed down the phone. 'Please, please don't tell!'

'Steady on, Albie, no need to get upset. I'm on your side. Why don't we meet and have a little chat about old times? Now wouldn't that be cosy, eh?'

Chapter 30

Bernard wasn't sure where he was. He pushed the stick forward and dropped the nose of the two-seater Cessna to see if he could spot any familiar landmarks. After flying through that strange haze, the landscape looked completely different, and although it was only half-past two in the afternoon, it was growing darker by the second. All the instruments seemed to be working – apart from the GPS which was making no sense at all, and the radio, on which he could raise nothing but static.

'We're lost, aren't we, Bernard?' said Iris, matter-of-factly.

'No, love, not lost exactly. More . . . misplaced.'

'Lost,' repeated Iris.

'I've heard about things like this happening in the Bermuda Triangle, but never over Worthing.' He looked down at the strange, unfamiliar landscape. A dark grey sea lapped the shores of a vast, almost featureless plain stretching away to far distant snowcapped mountains, barely discernible through the gloom. The only thing that broke the monotony of that huge, flat expanse was what appeared to be a big lump of rock standing right in the middle of it. They'd been flying over this barren countryside for about twenty minutes now, looking for roads, railway lines, anything that would help them navigate back home, or at least tell them where they were. 'It's no good, Iris, we're lost.'

'I could have told you that. What do we do now? The plane's due back in an hour.'

'I know, I know, but these are exceptional circumstances, I'm sure they'll understand. We have two main concerns at the moment, one is the light – it seems to be getting dark awfully quickly – and the other is fuel. I've no idea where the nearest airfield is and whether we've got enough to get us there. If we don't see something we recognize soon, we're going to have to do an emergency landing.' He jerked his head at the great plain which lay beneath them. 'I'm going to make a low pass to see if there's anywhere suitable to set down.' Bernard eased forward again on the stick and the Cessna headed for the ground – with undue haste, Iris thought.

Bernard levelled off at about a thousand feet, and the big lump of rock grew turrets and buttresses. It was a great castle, or what remained of one. The walls still stood, but at its centre was an enormous hole – as if the heart had been ripped out of it. Gathered around this huge fortress, as if fearful of the forbidding expanse of the immense plain, clustered tiny houses, laid out without reference to any kind of formal arrangement that Bernard could discern – a town planner's nightmare.

As the strange machine passed over their heads, the inhabitants of the haphazard settlement looked up. Exhausted after their long ordeal, the population greeted this new development with hollow-eyed impassivity. What did this new thing portend? What did it matter? Dead to feeling, they waited only for events to unfold – good or ill, they didn't really care. Their own King had had them slaughtered, and their Light – the one in whom they had invested all hope for the future – had been cruelly snatched from them and was now probably lying at the bottom of the Salient Sea. The sweet flower of innocence had been cut down and now lay in the dust, broken and spattered with blood. Only one pair of eyes looked with anything like interest at this strange new machine. Smeil alone knew the significance of its arrival, for he had seen the future.

Bernard brought the Cessna down in a textbook three-point landing. 'My instructor would be proud of me.'

'Can I open my eyes now?' Iris asked nervously as the small plane jumped and bumped over the scrubby ground. Bernard brought the aircraft to a stop and cut the ignition. As the propeller slowed, then flicked to a juddering standstill, they were suddenly aware of the quiet. The shock of silence after the roar of the engine was always a surprise, but this was different – the stillness was total, all-embracing. Bernard opened the door. The wind soughed softly over the control surfaces of the light aircraft.

'Where are we, Bernard?' Iris looked into his eyes, and for the first time in their fifty-odd years together she saw fear.

Bernard looked away. 'Well, we can't sit here all day. Let's see if we can hail a friendly native.' He said it with a smile, but couldn't hide his true feelings from her. She reached out and took his hand. 'Don't you worry, love,' he said. 'We'll be all right.'

'I don't care what happens,' she replied. 'As long as we're together.'

Undoing his harness, Bernard leaned across and kissed her. 'I'm a very lucky man,' he said. 'Let's go exploring.'

Hardly had they stepped out of the plane than they were greeted by a breathless 'So sorry I wasn't here to meet you. Did you have a good trip?' Bernard and Iris looked at the small, smiling man, his grey-mouse hair plastered sweatily to his forehead. 'You must forgive my appearance, but I've run all the way – I wanted to be the first to welcome you. Have you come far?'

'Shoreham airport,' Bernard said.

'Of course, of course. Please follow me; we're a little short of space since the "incident", but I've had what remains of the southern apartments made ready. Do you have any baggage?'

Bernard turned to Iris. 'Only the wife!' he beamed.

'Ah, I can't tell you how nice it is to hear a joke – even one as old as that. Please, follow me,' and the little man hurried on ahead. Bernard and Iris followed in bewildered silence.

Chapter 31

'He's not going to show.' The tall wizard looked out of the bay window towards the sea, where hordes of seagulls were gorging themselves on an unexpected seafood banquet.

' "Expect a shower of hail or meteorites, I'm not sure which, this afternoon."'

The tall wizard turned. 'What?'

'Your weather forecast: a warm front followed by hail or meteorites, you couldn't say which.'

The tall wizard looked darkly at his shorter self. 'Go on, scoff all you like. You know perfectly well what that was – our famous shower of shellfish out of a clear blue sky. I only wish we knew what was going to happen next.'

'We do. Men in skirts are going to land on the beach.'

The tall wizard advanced furiously on him. 'This isn't a joke. We are heading into uncharted waters. Heaven knows the damage that hideous creature is doing. If all these predictions are coming true, it can only mean that things are coming to a head. We don't have the Crystal, the Book, the bag or the Prince. It's hardly a laughing matter.'

'Oh, don't be such a crosspatch,' said the short one, looking at his chunky gold watch. 'It's early yet, give him a chance.'

'Why should he come? Why should he believe such a fantastical story? He comes from a world obsessed with the here and now; a world that only believes in what it can see and touch. There's no magic here, only dull, grey materialism. Besides, he thinks we're gay.'

'Does he?'

'Of course he does. Look at yourself!'

The short wizard looked down at his yellow dungarees and fingered the hem of his black linen shirt. 'Doesn't this go with this?'

'It's not a question of whether it goes with it or not. It's the fact that you're wearing it in the first place!'

There was a ring at the door. For a split second the wizards froze, then both dived to answer it.

'Sorry I'm late.' Rex stood, framed by the doorway, the setting sun at his back crowning him with a golden halo. 'I've been . . . I was on the beach when it happened . . . and . . . well . . . there've been other things too,' he stammered.

Seeing him standing there, small and confused, the tall wizard was filled with compassion. 'My dear boy, it's so good to see you. Come in, come in. This must all be terribly perplexing for you. I'm just glad you're here. I'm very glad you're here.'

'We thought we'd lost you for ever . . . again.' The short one put an arm round Rex's shoulder and led him into the house.

Rex looked guiltily at them. 'I'm sorry, I thought you were just a couple of freaks. But when those clams started falling, I knew you must have been telling the truth. So when I got home, I dug this out.' Rex held up a carpet-bag, slightly worn and with what appeared to be charring to one corner.

The tall wizard seized it gratefully. He eyed him levelly. 'Have you opened it?'

Rex looked sheepishly at the floor. 'Yeah . . .'

'So now you know.'

'Yeah,' he said, keeping his eyes on the toe of his shoe. 'It took ages to get all the books back inside.'

The wizard opened it and thrust in his arm. Swiftly pulling out the two candlesticks – still burning – and a small paper bag, he snapped the heavy brass clasp shut. Teasing open the neck of the paper bag, he offered it to Rex. 'Care for a madeleine?'

Rex took one of the still-warm cakes and bit into it. 'Very nice,' he said.

'Not a patch on my fruit scones,' said the short one.

The tall one was about to reopen the carpet-bag, but the short one stopped him. 'Please, not in here.'

'But the spell – I need the spell.'

'I've spent all morning tidying. I'm not having that bloody book flying around making a mess.'

The tall one glared at him. 'Very well,' he said and, retrieving his long chiffon scarf from the coat rack in the hall, took Rex by the arm. 'Shall we go for a little walk?'

' . . . but if you've only been here seven years, then . . .' Rex shook his head. 'I don't get it. The three men strolled along the seafront in the softly fading evening light.

The tall wizard sighed. 'The explosion fractured time. Because we were not together, *we* ended up in one time – *you* in another.'

'Seven years! That was when my parents disappeared too.'

'That could well have been down to the same anomaly that first brought us into this dimension – a running tear in the fabric of time.'

Rex lapsed into silence. It was confusing, but it was incredibly exciting – he was actually in a Prince Nostrum adventure. 'So, who am I again?' he asked at last.

'You are Prince Harmony, uncrowned King of Limbo,' said the tall one.

'Prince Harmony, King of Limbo,' murmured Rex. 'King of Limbo,' he repeated, rolling it around his mouth. 'Limbo . . .'

'Landscape of the unconscious,' said the short one. 'At once far away yet as familiar as the smell of freshly laundered sheets. When you dream, you dream of Limbo.'

'And *you* are?'

'We're your father dear.'

Rex opened his mouth to speak, but the short one stopped him. 'Now, no more questions,' he said. 'Still your mind, try not to think.'

'Look at the sea,' said the tall one. 'Let it calm you.'

They'd stopped quite near a small beachside café called 'Mrs Bumble's'. The tall one produced a key and inserted it into the heavy-duty padlock on the door of a nearby beach hut – number 176. The lock popped open with a small *chink*, and the wizard drew back the flap. 'All will be revealed,' he said. 'Just give me a moment, will you?' Removing the chiffon scarf from around his neck and cradling the long-lost carpet-bag, he disappeared inside.

Rex turned to the short one. 'So . . . are you both wizards, then?'

'We are a Wizard, yes.'

Rex was trying to get to grips with all this 'we' and 'we're' stuff and failing miserably. 'There's something I don't really understand . . .'

'I'd be surprised if there wasn't.'

From inside the hut came a banging and fluttering, as if a huge flock of birds were trying to escape. 'Get back in here, right now!' the tall wizard screamed. 'I've had just about enough of you!' Gradually the sounds died away, to be replaced by a shuffling of paper and a muffled 'Where the bloody hell is it?' Then Rex and the short wizard were startled by a sudden cry – 'Ah-ha!' followed by the phrase *'Expedit esse deos, et, ut expedit, esse putemus!'* There was an unworldly whirring and a strange creaking and scuffling, followed by an ecstatic 'Yes, yes, yes!'

The short wizard smiled at Rex. 'Won't be long now.'

Accompanied by more banging and whirring came the incantation *'Deus et natura, nihil faciunt frustra!'* followed by a whoop of triumph and a yelled-out, 'Whenever you're ready!'

The short wizard took Rex's arm. 'Hold onto your hat,' he said, and ushered him inside. Rex walked through the door and found himself . . . nowhere. Void was the word that first came to mind, closely followed by vacuum. But vacuum suggested the *absence* of something, and Rex had the suspicion that there had never been anything here in the first place. All was blackness. No, not blackness, more nothingness. Yes, that was it. He felt as if he had been consumed by nothingness. Then gradually, with rising panic, he began to realize that he was a part of the nothingness.

'Where am I?' he tried to say, but no sound came.

'Strictly speaking,' came the reply, or rather the feeling – if, that is, it is possible for nothingness to have feeling – 'where we are at this moment doesn't actually exist – therefore neither do you.' If Rex had had a body it would have broken out in a cold sweat. 'It's a little odd at first, but once you get used to it, you'll find it's rather enjoyable. Just relax and look around.'

'Around?' Rex wanted to say. 'Where's around?'

But gradually, bit by bit, in small, thrilling rushes, he let himself go and began to come to terms with the giddy notion of being one with the void. It was a heady freedom.

Slowly, slowly out of the depths of the endless nothing there appeared a something. A something so heart-stoppingly beautiful that he would have been happy to gaze upon it for ever – an immense spinning hoop of molten gold, so unimaginably vast that it was beyond size, beyond time and space. Long loops and whorls of light leapt from its surface; and wrapped around it, like the braid on some cosmic pigtail, glittered a dazzling ribbon of sparkling silver. It was everything and nothing: the universal embodiment of eternity.

'Wow,' thought Rex, and immediately thought it rather inadequate.

'What you are experiencing,' came the feeling, 'is the Hoop of Destiny. It is the stream of cosmic consciousness; the river of perception; the distillation of awareness. It has. always been and, with a bit of luck, always will be.'

'It's beautiful,' thought Rex.

'It is everything. Wrapped around it, that dazzling silver ribbon you see – that is from whence you came. That is your kingdom. That is Limbo.'

'Wow!' thought Rex again.

'Please,' came the feeling out of the void.

Rex gradually became aware of small black shapes floating

around the Hoop in a great cloud. 'Those small black things, what are they?' he asked. 'Lost souls, trapped for eternity in the void between death and rebirth?'

'Socks,' came the reply.

'Sorry?'

'Socks, unfortunately, are just the right size and shape to slip through the narrow gaps between the strands of consciousness – especially when accelerated to 1,200 rpm in the spin cycle of a modern family washing machine. That is why your sock-drawer is always half full of partnerless socks.'

'I'd always wondered about that.'

'What else do you see?'

Rex looked across the vastness of eternity. Far, far off, he could just discern a thin black line running the width of the great Hoop, with ribbons of cosmic energy trailing from it.

'What's that?'

'The Hoop is fractured; destiny is unravelling.'

Now Rex was over the very lip of the fracture – a vast blemish on the face of perfection. Swirling clouds of energy, brighter than the sun, looped all around him and spilled out into the blackness of the void.

'A gap has opened up. A gap in comprehension; in time if you like. The cohesion of the circle has been destroyed, and those clouds you see are eternity spilling into nothingness. Unless we do something about it, the universe will be no more, it will simply dissolve – there will be nothing left. Already it may be too late – the gap may be too wide to bridge.'

'But how did it happen?'

'There is something very bad loose in eternity, unsettling its delicate balance.'

'How?'

'Altering things, changing history.'

'Oh, right. I've read about that. There's this story where a man travels back in time to hunt dinosaurs. Because they all became extinct, he reckons it's OK to kill them without it having any effect on the present. But once, when he travels back, he steps on a butterfly, and when he comes back home again everything's slightly different – he's changed time for ever.'

'Yes, a pretty story but not how it really works. Man always wants to put himself at the centre of things, in the driving seat; it's all part of his big ego trip. If he really knew how little effect he had on fate, he wouldn't feel quite so pleased with himself. Existence is a loop with no beginning and no end. Time, or destiny, is all of a piece; it's only man's limited perception that prevents him from seeing the whole picture. Pythagoras, Leonardo, Newton, Einstein – they all failed to grasp that fact. They all got hung up on the notion of time. And time – at least as they saw it, in linear terms – doesn't actually exist.'

'Time doesn't exist?'

'Man has created time by his insistence on separating past from future. Of course, it's easy to see why it happened. Existing in one single moment unfolding for eternity is going to be a little disconcerting for most people. Finding yourself coming back from the shops before you've even been, or being present simultaneously at your own birth and death is not something that many people are going to be comfortable with. Hence the development of the quaint but more easily comprehensible system of past, present and future. Which brings us neatly onto the subject of The Great Limbollian Paradox.'

'The Great Limbollian Paradox?'

'With the emergence of time appeared The Paradox. You can't have a new system without a law to govern it. The Paradox provided the framework within which time can operate. It goes something like this: *"Whatever you expect to happen will happen, unless something else happens instead."'*

'That about covers everything.'

'Yes, and it also works in retrospect – whatever you expected to happen has already happened, unless something else happened to happen in its place.'

'Nothing left to chance then.'

'Not quite – sometimes it's wrong.'

'How can it be wrong?'

'That's the paradox. Take liberties and you can end up with the kind of damage we're witnessing now.'

'I don't understand.'

'Just suppose that you could travel back in time, and that you did something to alter the outcome of the American War of Independence. Now, as far as Destiny is concerned, the English are meant to lose. If they win, it doesn't fit with expectation – no Coca-Cola, no Disney World, no *Frasier* repeats on cable, and so on – so Destiny will simply not allow it to happen.'

'But what if it already has happened?'

'It can't.'

'The Paradox?'

'Well done. Because time is an illusion, time travel is just like stepping through a door – as long as you have the key. But if you separate out past, present and future, then time travel becomes impossible. The Paradox created time, but no means of getting about in it. Therefore, according to The Paradox, time travel is beyond expectation and cannot exist – but it does.'

'The Paradox?'

'You know, you're brighter than you look.'

'Thank you.'

'So you see Destiny's problem. A monstrous creature has the key and is marauding through time. Destiny can't stop it, but at the same time, can't allow anything to change, and so it begins to tie itself in knots. All the contortions it has to go through just to maintain the status quo generate enormous tensions and, because of this, the Hoop is beginning to tear itself apart. The fabric of the universe – molecules, atoms, electrons – is beginning to break down. Was your milk curdled this morning?'

'Yes it was, as a matter of fact.'

'There you are then. Today milk – tomorrow perhaps Britain itself.'

'Britain's going to curdle?'

'Now don't be obtuse. You know what I'm talking about. The framework of the universe is coming apart. How many earthquakes did Brighton experience in the past week? Is that normal?'

'But what about parallel universes and all that?'

'You've been reading too much cheap science fiction.'

'Fantasy!' came another voice – or feeling – out of the void.

'Sorry?'

'Never mind. Where was I? Oh yes – any change is a wrong turning, a cul-de-sac.'

'But what if things *do* change?'

'Think of the universe as a five-dimensional Rubik's cube. If one little coloured square is in the wrong place, it will rearrange itself until everything is back in order. Imagine the confusion if one were to add one extra square of a completely different colour from all the rest. The universe would go through endless combinations trying to find the right one, when in actual fact it doesn't exist. The result? Chaos; breakdown; blackout. This monstrous creature, loose in eternity, is the one extra square of a different colour, and if left unchecked will tear destiny to shreds. It is so dense and so impossibly evil that it should not exist at all.'

'But it *does* exist and that's the paradox.'

'Bravo.'

The old woman's words came back to him, and he repeated them. ' "*The black lumpen thing, an emissary of hell, an evil beyond words . . .*"'

'Yes, that's rather a good description of it actually.'

If Rex had possessed a spine at that particular moment, a chill would have run the length of it. 'Oh my God, she was right.'

'Who was right?'

'The fortune-teller.'

'Oh, you shouldn't waste your money.'

'No, this one was different. She froze time.'

'Froze time? You haven't met Tumbril?'

'Tumbril?'

'A Lorelei – a sort of time-travelling agony aunt. One usually turns up in a crisis. It always makes me laugh – the Lorelei are supposed to be these beautiful, graceful creatures, when in fact they're grotty old hags to a woman. What's she calling herself these days, is it still Madame Huzinga – woman of mystery?'

'Yes, that's it. She said all sorts of stuff about the creature being after my blood, then she started talking in a strange voice, calling me her son and using the name . . . Harmony.'

'He's spoken to the Queen.'

From somewhere deep in the aching void of eternity came a sad sniff. 'How was she?'

'Sort of short and smelly and—'

'Not Tumbril, you idiot – the Queen!'

'Sorry. She said she didn't have much time and that I was with my father and that was all right because he was strong and wise and that I was going to return and put things right, or something like that . . . Then she said she loved me . . . and told me to tell you that she would wait for you.'

The void that has no beginning and no end answered with silence.

'You know,' Rex went on, slowly, 'something occurs to me. According to The Paradox, whatever happens is meant to happen – isn't that right?'

There was a slight pause. 'You're forgetting that sometimes The Paradox is wrong.'

'And that's the paradox?'

'Correct.'

'I'm beginning to understand.'

'Good.'

'So, shouldn't we do something about this horrible creature? Find it and destroy it, or something, before it does any more damage?'

'First we have to repair the harm it has done. Only then will it be safe to kill it. But we have no way of knowing where it is. The universe is a big place, so it could be anywhere.'

'Oh.'

Limbo

'There *is* one way of finding the beast.'

'No, no, he's not ready for that yet!'

'I know that, you idiot! Look, why don't we take a break?' said the void. 'I'm feeling a little peckish.'

Chapter 32

The old Shoreham lighthouse, a modest nineteenth-century erection whose reassuring beam once broadcast to fishermen out on the dark waters of the Channel that here was safe harbour, now stood in the shadow of the new Shoreham power station and brooded over the unromantic, automatic, twentieth-century light that had made it redundant. Malcom pulled up in the gravel car park alongside. The last explosive, throat-clearing roar of the Harley's engine echoed off the breakwater and died away, leaving the distant cawing of seagulls and the gentle slap of water against the green-streaked harbour walls. Kicking out the side stand, Malcom heaved his great backside out of the saddle and, taking off his helmet, stood beside his machine, easing the tension out of his back, as the setting sun slipped gracefully behind Worthing Pier.

'Beautiful. Beasely'd like that.' He pulled a panatella out of his boot and took the newly bought solid brass Zippo out of his shirt pocket. It was pleasingly heavy: smooth and chunky. But as he turned it over in his hand, he noticed that it was also a little damp – the assistant who'd filled it in the shop had overdone it a little. Malcom flipped back the lid and, as he had seen so many of his cinema heroes do, ran the wheel along his thigh. The lighter exploded in a ball of flame, leaving a trail of blue fire down his leg. 'Shit, shit, shit!' Malcom dropped his gleaming new purchase and leapt around, patting out his flaming trousers. 'Fucking thing!'

Once the fire was out, he picked up the lighter and examined it. Its once pristine surface now bore a scar – a small black nick in the soft metal of one of its corners. 'Bugger,' he sighed. He was about to put it back in his pocket when something else caught his eye, something he hadn't noticed before, and something he was sure was not the result of his throwing it on the ground: the wind shield was slightly warped. He ran his nail around the top of it, and a thin film of molten metal left a golden streak on the tip of his finger. It seemed to be melting. But it was a fucking lighter – it wasn't meant to melt. Just then there was the scrunching of tyres on gravel and a car pulled up alongside. Looking up through the dust raised by the red Mondeo's tyres, he watched as the door opened and Albie Morningside, ogre of his adolescence, got out.

Malcom would not have admitted to anything as effeminate as apprehension at this meeting with his erstwhile persecutor, but he hadn't really been looking forward to it either. The last time he and Albie had come face to face was the day of Malcom's release. It was just after breakfast when Albie and his lieutenants had jumped him in the lavatories. As Albie had lit a cigarette, the other boys had held down the overweight, struggling boy and ripped off his shirt.

'Something to remember me by,' Albie had said, and ground the cigarette out on Malcom's chest. But somehow, Malcom couldn't equate that nasty, crop-haired adolescent with the man that now stood before him. He was smaller than he remembered, less assured, and it gave him particular satisfaction to note that he looked very, very frightened. Malcom closed the lighter and put it back in his pocket. 'Hello Albie. How's the surveying business?' Malcom extended his hand. A manilla envelope was thrust into it.

'There's ten thousand in there. Now stay away from me and keep your mouth shut.'

Malcom looked at the envelope, weighing it in his hand. 'Did you know that bribing a police officer is a very serious offence?'

Albie leaned back against the door of his car, all the breath seemed to have been knocked out of him. 'Look, I'm really sorry for what I did. I did a lot of things in those days that I regret, but I'm a changed man now. I've got a life, a family, a good job. You wouldn't destroy all that, would you?'

Malcom laid the envelope carefully on the petrol tank of the

Harley. 'There's no need to get upset, Albie.' He reached into his pocket for his lighter, then thought better of it. 'Have you got a light?'

'No – no, I don't smoke.'

'Given up? You used to smoke. You used to smoke all the time. You once even used me as an ashtray.' Malcom opened the top two buttons of his shirt to reveal a small, round, puckered scar. ' "Something to remember me by," you said.' Albie's jaw was moving, but no sound came. He stood, eyes like saucers, mouthing like a fish. Malcom threw him his Zippo. 'Here, see if you can make this work.'

Albie caught the lighter and looked at it. 'It's been overfilled.' Leaning into the car, he opened the glove compartment and pulled a Kleenex out of a small pocket pack. 'I used to have one. Put too much petrol in them, and either they don't work at all or they burst into flames.' After wiping the excess fluid off the exterior and the inside of the lid, Albie struck the wheel with his thumb. The wick obediently took flame and burned steadily and civilly.

Scowling, Malcom put the panatella between his teeth and, grabbing Albie's wrist, pulled the lighter towards him. When he was happy that the cigar was burning evenly, he leaned back, wreathed in smoke.

'You're shaking,' he said with a smile. Albie pulled his hand free and snicked the lighter shut. Malcom took it from him. 'You've got me all wrong, Albie. I'm not after revenge. I don't want to shop you. I just want some information.'

'Oh sweet Jesus,' Albie breathed, putting his hand to his chest. He walked the length of the car and back again. Coming to rest in front of Malcom, he mopped his brow with the Kleenex.

'Steady on. Like I said, all I want is information.'

'Do you mind if I sit down?' Albie asked.

'Be my guest.'

'Thank you.' Albie collapsed gratefully into the driver's seat of the car. 'Information?' he said weakly.

'What I'd like to know is, what could a geriatric multimillionaire possibly want with the King Alfred Centre? Take your time.'

The colour drained from Albie's face. 'I don't know what you're talking about.'

Malcom crouched down beside him. 'You can do better than that,' he smiled.

'No, no, really, I don't know what he wants with it.'

Malcom took a deep draw on his panatella and exhaled a noxious plume of blue smoke into Albie's face. 'I'm torn, really I am. Torn between wanting to help my old friend Albie, and my duty as a guardian of the law. You see, if Daniels is putting the squeeze on you, I may be able to help – that's what friends are for. If, on the other hand, you refuse to assist me with my enquiries, I shall have no alternative but to report your attempt to bribe an officer in the course of his duties. You see my problem?'

Albie was sweating profusely and shaking so much that the car was beginning to vibrate. 'I . . . I . . . all I know is that he wants it. He asked me to give it a dodgy survey so he could get it at a good price. But that's all I know, I swear.'

Malcom looked up at the crucifix dangling from the Mondeo's rear-view mirror. 'Final answer?' Albie nodded.

Malcom sighed and stood up. 'Fair enough,' he said. He took the cigar out of his mouth and dropped it on the ground, grinding it out with his boot. Then in a sudden, terrifying lunge, he pulled Albie out of the car and slammed his head against the roof. Wrapping Albie's tie around his left hand, he pulled it tight, driving his knuckles into the man's Adam's apple. 'Why don't I believe you?' he said. Then he yanked him round to the rear of the car.

He was about to throw him onto the boot when something caught his eye. 'What's that?' he said, pointing to the representation of a fish on the boot lid.

'You're strangling me.'

'I asked you a question.'

'Ichthys,' Albie hissed.

'What?'

'Ichthys. It's Greek for fish.'

'What the fuck are you doing with a Greek fish on the boot of your car?'

'Please, I can't breathe.'

Malcom pulled tighter on Albie's tie.

'All right, all right,' the man said hoarsely. 'It stands for Jesus Christ, Son of God the Saviour.'

'Since when did you get God-happy?'

'After you left ... something happened ... my fault ... really, I'm going to faint.'

Malcom let go of his tie and threw him face-down onto the boot. 'Hands behind your back!'

'Please ...'

'Hands behind your fucking back!' Albie did as he was told. Pulling out his handcuffs, Malcom snapped them on. 'Carry on, you were telling me the story of how you got Jesus.'

'A boy killed himself ... I pushed him too far. It taught me a lesson.'

Malcom rolled him over. 'Oh yeah? And what was that?'

'We're all in this together. We have a responsibility to each other.'

'Doesn't Jesus have something to say about people who don't tell the truth?' Malcom grabbed hold of Albie's tie again and dragged him back around the car towards his motorbike. 'Isn't there something in the Bible that says that people who tell porkies shall be punished?' he said, forcing his prisoner to kneel beside the big Harley. Albie could feel the heat from the engine on his cheek.

'This is my bike.'

'It's very nice,' Albie said huskily.

'I've just ridden it here at seventy miles an hour so, as you can imagine, it's pretty hot. What do you think a chrome exhaust pipe, heated to 500 degrees, would do to human flesh, eh?'

Albie looked up at him with frightened eyes. 'You wouldn't ...'

'When we were together in that stinking shit-hole you taught me something very important, Albie – never make an empty threat.

That's the lesson *I* learned from reform school.' Malcom grabbed the back of Albie's shirt collar. 'Now then, we'll try again, shall we? What does Daniels want with the King Alfred Centre?'

'I can't . . . he said he'd kill me . . .' Albie whimpered.

Malcom tightened his grip on his collar. 'Sorry, that's the wrong answer. You are the weakest link – you leave with nothing but nasty facial burns.' He pushed Albie's head towards the searingly hot exhaust pipe.

'No! No! Please! He said he'd hurt my family!' Albie screamed, writhing in terror. But Malcom held him fast. Albie managed to uncoil one of his legs and stick it out in front of him, but the heel of his shoe scrabbled over the loose ground. Wrenching his head to one side, Albie could feel the skin on his right cheek beginning to blister as the smoking-hot metal came ever nearer. 'AHH! NO!' His face touched the engine and began to burn. 'STOP! I'LL TELL!' There was a sizzling and the smell of burning flesh. 'PLEEEASE!' Malcom let go and Albie fell on the ground in a sobbing heap. 'You hurt me, you hurt me, you cunt!'

Malcom crouched beside him. 'Language,' he chided. 'That's the trouble with bullies,' he said softly. 'They can dish it out, but they can't take it.' Pulling another panatella from his boot, he took out the Zippo and studied it carefully. After wiping it on Albie's jacket to remove the excess fuel, he flipped it open and flicked the wheel with his thumb. As the wick leapt into flame, Malcom smiled and lit his cigar. 'Now then,' he said, exhaling a blue cloud. 'The little matter of the president of the Brighton and Hove Bowls Association and the King Alfred Centre.'

'Oil,' sobbed Albie.

'Oil?'

'There's oil underneath the Centre.'

Malcom sighed. 'You know, Albie, I can't tell if you're very stupid or very brave.' He yanked him upright by the scruff of the neck.

'No, really, it's true. When all these tremors started, cracks started appearing in the Centre. He called in an excavation company to do some investigatory drilling . . . check the foundations.'

Malcom loosened his grip on Albie's collar. 'Coastway Excavations.'

'That's right. They struck oil – and not very deep down.'

Malcom inhaled thoughtfully on his panatella. 'Go on.'

'He bought the company at well over its market value, just to keep them quiet. And me . . . although I was a lot cheaper.'

'Oil? In fucking Brighton?'

'I know. It shouldn't be there. It doesn't make any sense, but the whole geology of the area has completely changed. It's weird.'

'He's going to start drilling for oil in the middle of a conservation area?'

'No, he hasn't got the money or the expertise. But if he can get his hands on the site, all he has to do is sell it to BP, or Shell, or whatever. If it's a big field he could make a fortune.'

'They'll never get planning permission.'

'We're talking fucking oil, and oil is power. If they found oil under Buckingham Palace, they'd get permission.'

'Well, well, well. Michael Daniels, oil tycoon.'

'You won't tell him I told you, will you?'

'Don't you worry, my little cellmate. He's not going to do you any harm. You can now consider yourself under police protection.' Malcom retrieved the bulky manilla envelope from its resting place on the Harley's tank, and tucked it into his shirt. 'I'm holding this as evidence. Just in case Jesus tempts you to repent or something fucking stupid like that.'

'I wouldn't dream of it,' Albie said, shaking his head.

'I believe you,' said Malcom, throwing his leg over the bike. 'Nice to see you again. Let's not leave it so long next time, eh?' The bike roared into life. He clunked the machine into gear and heaved it hard around. The back tyre, scrabbling for grip, threw dust and gravel into Albie's face. The man turned his head away as the bike roared off towards Brighton, down the Shoreham Road.

Soon a certain detached house in Portslade would be reverberating with the word 'Bulldog!'

Albie was left kneeling in the dirt – burned, bruised and very frightened. He felt small and vulnerable and wanted to cry. The bastard hadn't even taken the handcuffs off. How was he going to get home? Great, wet, self-pitying tears began to roll down his cheeks as he staggered to his feet. Looking at his face in the wing mirror of the Mondeo, he could see an angry red weal running from the cheekbone to the ear. The skin was beginning to tighten up. 'Jesus,' he said, then, 'Forgive me Lord.' Backing carefully into the car, he slumped in the driver's seat. 'Dear Lord forgive me . . .' Slowly at first, then with more speed and vigour, he began to bang his head against the rim of the steering wheel, over and over again . . .

Chapter 33

'I hope you'll be comfortable here.' Smeil led Bernard and Iris into one of the castle's brighter rooms. 'What little light there is, this room gets it.' He indicated the large French windows opening onto a generously proportioned patio. 'This window is fairly well behaved, but please check that the patio is there before stepping out. We've lost so many guests that way.' Bernard glanced sideways at Iris, as Smeil continued, 'I took the liberty of giving you a double bed, I hope that's all right. It can get rather cold – it's an awfully draughty old castle.'

'You need double glazing,' said Bernard. Iris elbowed him gently in the ribs.

'I haven't the faintest idea what you're talking about, but I'm sure that's a wonderful idea,' said Smeil. 'You see, you're having ideas about refurbishment already. I knew you'd be right for the job.' The little man fussed busily around the large suite, patting cushions, smoothing the bedspread, and talking the while. 'The usual offices are in here,' he said, opening the door to the en suite bathroom, 'and there's plenty of cupboard space.' He waved a hand airily around the room. 'Well, I'll leave you to settle in now. If there's anything you need, just ring. The bell pull's over in the corner, by the bed. Of course it sometimes works its way over to behind the door, but if you can't find it, just yell, someone will hear.' He paused in the doorway and beamed at the couple. 'I can't tell you how nice it is to see you at last. Ah!' he said, throwing his hands in the air. 'I see good things, good things!' And then he was gone.

Iris and Bernard were left alone, marooned in the middle of the room. Iris was the first to speak. 'Where are we, Bernard?'

'What did he mean, he knew I'd be right for the job?'

'It's a lovely room, I hope it's not too expensive.' Iris pulled back the bedclothes and ran her hand over the sheet. 'Egyptian cotton, Bernard. This is very high class.'

'I didn't like to ask him about the tariff. I didn't want to offend him.' Bernard wandered over to the French windows.

'Careful!' called Iris. 'Remember what he said about checking that the patio's there.'

'Bloody ridiculous,' Bernard muttered, throwing open the big glass doors. 'Come here, petal, it's a beautiful view.' Iris joined him. Off in the distance were the lowering peaks of the South Range, rising sheer out of the perfect flatness of the Great Plain, and to the west the Salient Sea sparkled dimly through the murk.

'It's lovely,' Iris breathed, 'but it's a bit chilly.' She snuggled up to him and together they gazed out over the broad plain. 'I hope Rex is all right,' she said suddenly.

'He'll be fine,' said Bernard. 'He's a responsible lad.'

'But he'll be wondering where we are.'

'We'll give him a call a bit later to let him know we're OK.'

Just then, the canopy of grey clouds parted, and revealed, on the far-off horizon, the endlessly setting sun. For an instant, a single shaft of sunlight pierced the gloom and shone like a heavenly spotlight on the Boggses. They were wrapped in a wonderful warm glow that seemed to say, 'Everything is as it should be.' Bernard thought he could hear a distant heavenly choir, although it may just have been the wind roaring through the flying buttresses. Then the clouds closed and the temperature dropped.

'Brrr,' Iris shivered. 'Shall we go back inside?'

Stepping back into their suite they noticed immediately that something was different. The room seemed even bigger, and an arch had miraculously appeared in the wall to the right of the bed. Taking Iris's hand, Bernard led her through into an exquisite galleried dining hall, the tables laid for dinner. 'Well, this is the funniest hotel I've ever been in,' said Iris.

'I think it likes us,' said Bernard with a smile. 'Would madam care for a spot of dinner?'

'Yes, madam's ravenous.'

'Well, then, let's get stuck in.' Bernard pulled out a chair and Iris sat. The moment Bernard was seated a small band struck up in the minstrel gallery, and Smeil appeared as if by magic.

'Settling in all right?'

Bernard jumped. 'Oh, hello. Er . . . yes, it's very nice.' Iris kicked him under the table and nodded her head in Smeil's direction. 'Eh?'

Iris kicked him again, and this time Bernard got the message. 'Oh yes, Mr . . . ?'

'Smeil – just call me Smeil.'

'Mr Smeil.' Bernard dropped his voice to a whisper, although he and Iris were the only guests in the dining hall. 'The matter of the bill . . . ?'

Smeil laughed. 'Let me stop you right there. No, no, no. Don't worry about a thing, we are honoured to have you. Please, treat the place as your home. But you must be hungry. I'll send someone to take your order. Can I get you a drink while you wait?'

'Gin and tonic,' said Iris, without having to be asked a second time.

'I'll have a . . . I'll have a whisky,' said Bernard, beginning to relax.

'That's the spirit,' and Smeil was gone as abruptly as he'd appeared.

A moment later a young waiter arrived with the drinks, closely followed by the sober-suited maître d'hôtel, pen poised. 'Are you ready to order, sir, madam?'

'We haven't seen the menu yet,' said Iris.

'What would you like?' the man asked.

'What would we like?'

'Yes, what would you like?' He smiled at them.

'Anything?' said Bernard.

'Anything at all,' The man still smiled.

'Well,' said Iris, taking a sip of her ice-cold, lemon-zested gin and tonic. Settling back in her chair, she fixed her eyes on the ceiling. 'I'll have prawn cocktail to start, followed by grilled Dover sole with those cheesy, oniony potatoes, and baby carrots. And, for pudding, floating islands. Oh, and those water ices between courses – you know?'

'Refreshing sorbets to cleanse the palate – certainly, madam. And you, sir?'

'Anything, you say?' said Bernard thoughtfully. He sipped his whisky. 'I think I'll have some paté to start – a good strong one.'

'Game?' offered the waiter.

'Very good. With that curly toast.'

'Melba toast, yes, sir.'

Bernard closed his eyes. 'Then fillet steak, bloody,' he said, warming to his task. 'With chips . . . no, not chips, French fries, lots of them, and English mustard. And, for afters, hot apple pie, with clotted cream.'

The maître d'hôtel finished writing on his small pad. 'Would you like some wine with that?'

Bernard and Iris looked at each other. 'Champagne,' they said together.

'An excellent choice. Thank you for giving me the pleasure of serving you.' The maître d' bowed briefly, and left.

'I could get used to this,' said Bernard.

'Cheers!' said Iris, raising her glass.

'To the most beautiful woman in the world,' Bernard replied, then added, *sotto voce*, 'That's a very big bed they've given us.'

Iris flushed. 'Bernard, stop it.'

'I feel like we're on honeymoon all over again. All that's missing is the band playing "Volare".'

'Where are we, Bernard? What is this place?'

He reached across the table and took her hand. 'I don't know and I don't care. We may even have died and gone to heaven. All I know is, if this is paradise, I'm happy to spend eternity with you.'

'And I with you,' Iris said, her eyes brimming with tears. She raised his hand to her lips.

'Ahem.'

Looking up, they saw they were surrounded by a small army of liveried servants. With the maître d' conducting proceedings, silver platters covered with silver domes were placed in front of them, and an ice bucket located at Bernard's elbow. The maître d' himself proudly presented the bottle of champagne, and then tackled the serious business of removing the cork. When their glasses were full of golden froth, the domes were removed. 'Prawn Cocktail Castle Creek and Game Paté au Limbo. Bon appétit!' The maître d' bowed again and shooed away the coterie of servants, as the band struck up 'Volare'.

The 'honeymoon couple' exchanged misty-eyed glances over their starters, then tucked in.

Chapter 34

Malcom was feeling fine. He hummed a little tune to himself as he patrolled the promenade in the fast-failing light. Puffing contentedly on a panatella, he smiled as he remembered the look of horror on Councillor Daniels's face when he'd turned up on his doorstep. Malcom had not been greedy; he'd only asked for a third share in the profits from the oil well. He didn't see the point in having three times as much money as you could spend in a lifetime; but then Malcom was not a businessman. He was an ordinary mortal, basking in the certain knowledge that he was about to become a millionaire.

'A millionaire,' he said to himself, and was immediately suffused with a cosy, warm inner glow. 'Millionaire,' he said again. 'Malcom Collins, millionaire. Thank you my man, here are the keys to my Bentley, don't scratch it or you'll be wearing your tackle as a necktie,' he chuckled contentedly.

It had been so easy, but then, what choice did Daniels have? Malcom had agreed to Daniels's only condition – that he stay in the police force for the time being, so as not to arouse suspicion. Why not? It was in both their interests. The fewer people who knew about this the better. In any case, with luck, Gerrold would give him the push tomorrow morning. For once, the timing couldn't have been better.

He began to sing, 'Who Wants to be a Millionaire?' swinging his American-issue telescopic truncheon in time. All he needed to complete his happiness was to catch some worthless-scum homo in the act. He'd just checked the Gents by the bowling green, and was on his way back towards the King Alfred Centre. As he watched the brick and concrete edifice loom up out of the darkness, swathed in the orange glow of the streetlamps, he thought it the most beautiful building he'd ever seen. He paused by Mrs Bumble's tea shop to admire the view. Suddenly, in front of him the door of a beach hut creaked open, and he watched as three people came out. Two older men were helping a younger one to stay upright.

'Well, that's one of the weirdest experiences I've ever had,' said Rex, holding on to the short wizard. 'My legs have turned to jelly.'

'It's always a bit strange the first time,' said the short wizard.

'You filthy perverts!'

They looked up to see a large fat man, his oversize nostrils quivering with indignation.

'Can we help you?' asked the tall wizard.

'Police. And I'm arresting you for gross indecency.'

There was something vaguely familiar about the policeman's face, but Rex couldn't quite work out what. 'Haven't we met before, officer?' Rex smiled dreamily at him.

'You've drugged him, you bastards. People like you make me sick.'

'No, no, it's not what you think – really,' said the tall wizard. 'He's my son.'

Malcom exploded, making a noise that went something like 'Yoopervifuckibastaaaard!' His telescopic truncheon was out of his waistband in an instant. Raising it above his head, he ran full pelt at the tall wizard. But instead of feeling the satisfying crunch of rubber-sheathed metal on scalp, Malcom found himself lying on his back, looking up at the stars.

'Wow,' said Rex. 'You're even better than Jean-Claude Van Damme.'

'That was "Falling Pig" – a move taught me by Prince Shotoku back in 604,' explained the tall wizard.

Malcom got to his feet, a big smile on his face. He loved it when they resisted arrest – it allowed him carte blanche on the 'reasonable force' front. As he prepared to run in again, the tall one held up his hand. 'I think I should warn you,' he said. 'I'm a Yoko-Hano, fifth dan. I don't want to hurt you.'

'You don't want to hurt me? That's very magnanimous of you. I, on the other hand, want to hurt you – I want to hurt you very badly.' Malcom came in again, whirling his truncheon around his head. 'Yaaarrrgh!' he screamed. He wasn't sure what happened next – it was all a blur – but somehow Malcom's eighteen stone had become weightless, and he found himself flying through the air. Unfortunately his excursion into space was all too short-lived. 'Oof!' he said, landing heavily on his back.

Rex applauded.

'That was "Water Buffalo Shows Udders to Stars",' said the tall one.

'Enjoying yourself?' said the short one.

Malcom heaved himself to his feet. 'You're in serious trouble, sunshine – gross indecency and assaulting a police officer, not to mention the matter of inhabiting a beach hut after sundown.'

'I think it's monstrous that we pay our rates to be abused by those who should be protecting us,' said the short one.

'If I had my way I'd lock you all up. You're a menace to society.' Malcom raised his truncheon again, but looking into the implacable eyes of the tall wizard, thought better of it. Instead he pulled out his mobile phone. 'This is DI Collins – King Alfred Centre – seafront. Officer under attack – send a meat wagon, now!' Malcom knew that this request would immediately attract a vanload of eager policemen, ready to jump into the fray to protect a fellow officer – even this officer.

'Come on,' said the tall wizard to his companions. 'One idiot I can just about deal with. A truckload may prove more difficult.' He and the short wizard marched briskly off down the promenade. They'd gone nearly fifty yards before they realized that Rex was no longer with them. 'Come on,' the tall one shouted back. 'We've no time to lose.' But Rex didn't hear, he was staring hard at Malcom. What was it about his big, porcine face? He'd see it somewhere before, but couldn't for the life of him remember where.

'We can't afford to get arrested, dear,' the short one yelled. 'We've got to save the universe, remember?' But Rex didn't budge.

The tall one ran back. 'Rex, come on!' In the distance they could hear the siren of an approaching police car. 'We have to leave, now!' The wizard grabbed his arm and hustled him away from the nervously sweating policeman.

Rex and the two wizards set off at a run. They had reached Grand Avenue before they saw the headlights coming towards them along the promenade. They turned left onto Kingsway but as they were about to cross the road, a cruising police car screeched to a halt in front of them. Turning back towards the sea, they retraced their steps to the King Alfred Centre, but were cornered in the car park as more police cars and vans arrived. Soon the seafront was swarming with adrenaline-rich policemen, all deeply disappointed that the promised fracas had failed to materialize.

Rex and the two wizards were handcuffed and jostled into one of the waiting vans, then driven at high speed back to the station.

'Can't you just . . . you know, vanish – pouf!' said Rex, holding on for dear life in the back of the bouncing van.

'Can't we just what?'

'Wizard us out of here.'

'Oh,' said the short one.

'No,' said the tall one.

'Why not? You are wizards, aren't you?'

'It's not that simple,' said the tall one. 'We are not one. We are disparate; disassociated . . .'

'We are two when we should be one . . .'

'Together we are a great Wizard. But apart . . .'

'We've no power,' the short one finished the sentence.

'Anyway,' the tall one continued, 'this world is too materialistic. People's minds are so full of facts and statistics there's no longer any room for wonder.'

'Can't you do *anything*?' said Rex.

'We can predict the weather,' said the tall one.

'With varying degrees of accuracy,' added the short one. 'We used to be able to mind-read, but all that stopped ages ago.'

The police van lurched suddenly, throwing the tall wizard to the floor. 'Do you mind!' he yelled. 'Bloody police drivers!'

'Hang on a minute!' exclaimed Rex. 'That's it! He's the one who beat that man up.'

'You've lost me,' said the tall one, clambering unsteadily back onto his perch.

'Our fat policeman. There was this man on the beach who was in a really bad way. I meant to tell you about it. It was as if I knew what he was thinking; I saw in my mind what had happened to him. It was like I *was* him.'

'How long have you been able to read people's minds?' asked the tall one, leaning forward.

'Well, I've always been able to tell what newspaper someone wants the moment they come in the shop.'

'No. I'm talking about being inside someone's head; knowing their every thought. Has anything like that happened before?'

'Er, no, not really.'

'The Awakening,' said the short one.

'Sorry?'

'You have a wizard's genes, and they're trying to get out,' said the tall one. 'This is excellent – the timing couldn't be more perfect. You'll need careful tutoring, of course, if you're going to become as great a wizard as your father.' The short wizard rolled his eyes heavenward. 'Now, we should turn our attention to the more pressing problem of saving the unravelling universe.'

'Um, didn't something like this happen in *Time Is a Ribbon*?' asked Rex. 'Remember, where Prince Nostrum discovers a gap in the space-time continuum? With the universe about to fall into the void and be lost for ever, he travels forward in time to find Anthony Avatar. Because he's from the future, his brain patterns contain the missing information needed to fill in the gap. Anthony gets into Prince Nostrum's time machine, and together they drive off the edge of time and into the gap . . . it's very exciting.'

'Oh, please,' groaned the tall one. The short one shot him a look. 'No, but really – you used this in one of your books?'

'I didn't know it was actually going to happen.'

'That's what you said last time, and look at all the trouble that got us into.'

'What *I* said? Oh, I see, it's all *my* fault now, is it?'

'I told you not to write any more of your bloody nonsense. I knew it would only end in tears.'

'Oh, yes, you know it all now, Mr High and Mighty, Wise-after-the-Fact. I'll have you know, over half a million people bought my last load of "bloody nonsense".'

'It's not my fault the world is full of idiots!'

'Sometimes I don't know why I put up with you, I really don't!'

'Because you don't have a choice, you daft bat! Neither of us does! If you weren't my other half, do you think I'd still be here? Do you think I enjoy seeing you flouncing around the house in your leopard-print underpants?'

'How could you!' The short one was in tears now.

'Um, look . . .' Rex began.

'Don't worry about him,' said the tall one. 'He only does it for effect.'

'You brute!' sobbed the short one, pulling a hanky out of his sleeve.

'It seems to me,' Rex continued in his measured way, 'that we should be putting our heads together to try and solve this problem, not arguing about it.' The tall one glared at the floor; the short one took Rex's hand and squeezed it tight.

'The boy's right,' said the short one, blowing his nose.

'You said there was a way of getting to the monster,' said Rex.

The wizards looked at each other. 'The Blood Quest,' said the tall one after a pause.

'What's the Blood Quest?'

'Suits me, sunshine!'

'Suits me—?'

'Not yet!' yelled the tall one. 'Please. It is imperative you do not utter that phrase until I tell you to, for this it is that will discover the Beast. But it will only work for one person.'

Rex looked from wizard to wizard. 'Who?'

'You,' said the short one, still dabbing his eyes.

'Me?'

'It was issued against the King, but never taken up, and so passes to his descendant. Utter it and you will find yourself face to face with the hideous creature.'

Rex swallowed hard.

'I'd advise against it at the moment,' said the tall one. 'You have much to learn. Face the monster now and it will most surely kill you.'

'Oh, right,' said Rex. It was one thing reading about Prince Nostrum; it was another thing entirely actually being him. Then something began to dawn. 'Hang on, if you . . . er . . .' – he looked from wizard to wizard – 'and you, are my father, then how can I be the King's heir? And if I'm not, then none of this is really my responsibility.'

The tall one sighed. 'I am the first King of Limbo. I founded the dynasty two thousand years ago.'

'Oh.'

'I soon wearied of Kingship. I'm a wizard, not a politician. Whenever I was called to resolve a dispute between my subjects, I inevitably made matters worse. And all those formal engage-ments . . . I never was one for dressing up.'

'Shame,' interjected the short one.

'So I abdicated in favour of my first son,' the tall one continued, 'and spent the next nine hundred years wandering the desert, per-fecting the art of wizardry. Then, later on, came the Book fiasco and, after the hash I'd made of things, I thought I'd better offer my services to the then King – my great-grandson to the power of twenty-seven – to see if I could help put matters right. I couldn't of course.'

'As *our* son,' said the short one, 'if you don't have a right to the throne, then I don't know who has. So you see, whether you like it or not, you really are King of Limbo and I'm afraid no one else can do what you have to do.'

'It is your destiny. On your shoulders rests the future of life, the universe . . .'

' . . . and everything,' Rex finished with a sigh. The three wizards slumped into thoughtful silence as the police van continued on its bone-jarring way.

'What about the *Time Is a Ribbon* idea?' said the short one at last.

'Brilliant!' said the tall one. 'OK, let's shoot off into the future, kidnap someone who has the next hundred years imprinted on his brain, and wire him up to the Hoop! Terrific idea! Except for one small but fatal flaw. We can't travel through bloody time!' he screamed.

'Please! Can't you at least try and be nice, just for a moment?' said the short one. 'Don't worry, dear' – he turned to Rex – 'he's all puff and no go.' But Rex was no longer listening. He wasn't actually there at all. He was in a spaceship floating far above the Earth, with Vivaldi's *Four Seasons* playing tinnily on a small speaker.

The police van lurched to a halt, and Rex came suddenly back to himself. 'Kowalski,' he said quietly.

'What? What did you say?' asked the tall one.

The door of the van was yanked open. 'Come on you perverts!' someone was shouting. 'Get your sore arses out here now!'

'Serena Kowalski,' said Rex. 'I think we've found our time-traveller.'

Chapter 35

'Miss Kowalski, there's something in your story that doesn't quite add up.' The man in the dark grey suit and wraparound sunglasses stopped pacing and sat down opposite Serena. 'Do you think you could go through it one more time?' he said, folding his hands on the desk.

Serena groaned. She was tired now. After speaking to Gerrold that morning, she thought everything had been cleared up and that soon she was going to be put on a flight home. But after lunch these two suits had turned up and she'd had to go through the whole thing again – in triplicate. She'd been questioned continually since one o'clock and, although the gloomy basement interview room had no window, she was sure that by now it must be getting dark. Serena looked up into the shaded eyes of her inquisitor. 'Can you see anything?'

'Sorry?'

'Through those glasses – can you see anything? I mean it's not as if the sun's burning your eyes out down here.'

The man looked towards the door where his taciturn accomplice stood. The silent man nodded. 'Would you be more comfortable if I removed them?'

Serena jerked her thumb towards the man at the door. 'You have to ask him for permission?'

'It's better if we coordinate our actions.'

'What happens if one of you needs to take a shit?'

'Please, Miss Kowalski, just answer the question.'

'Which one?'

'Would you like me to remove my sunglasses?'

'Yes.'

The man in the dark grey suit obliged.

'Green eyes,' she said. 'You've got green eyes. Where are you from?'

'I am not at liberty to divulge that information.'

'Jesus. You could at least give me a name – it doesn't even have to be a real one.'

'My name is Jim.'

'Now we're getting somewhere. How's it hanging, Jim?' Serena extended her hand. Jim looked at it. 'Come on, shake my hand.'

'No physical contact allowed, I'm afraid, Miss Kowalski.'

'Of course not.' Serena let her arm drop onto the desk, rattling the tray of used tea things.

Jim swivelled his eyes towards the door and the silent man nodded once again. Jim leaned forwards on the desk. 'OK, Serena, it's like this: we don't know who you are or where you're from. You suddenly appear on the beach amid a shower of clams, saying that you have fallen from a spaceship in the year 2053.'

Serena spread her hands in a 'search me' gesture. 'That's right – I'm as confused as you are, believe me.'

'Firstly – there are not, and never have been, any spaceships like the one you described orbiting the Earth. Secondly – the clams with which you arrived are of a species unknown to science. And third – the year is 2006. So you see why we're a little uneasy about you.' Serena's eyes widened. Jim continued, 'This is either a very elaborate hoax or I'm looking at a spacewoman from the future.'

'Name?' asked Sergeant Ivey.

'F. Don Wizzard.'

'Could you spell that for me, sir?'

The short wizard sighed. 'W-I-Z-Z-A-R-D.'

Sergeant Ivey filled in the relevant box on the charge sheet. 'Occupation?'

'Author: A-U-T . . .'

'That won't be necessary, sir, thank you.' Ivey gave the short wizard a long, hard look before laboriously filling in the appropriate section. There was an audible crack and the sergeant's ballpoint oozed a big, sticky pool of ink onto the sheet. 'Oh dear.' Ivey looked closely at the end of his pen. Where the metal ball should have been was just a hole – the ball itself had completely disappeared. 'Oh well,' he said cheerily, 'I'll just pop out and get another pen, then it looks like we're going to have to start all over again.'

Downstairs, things were not going much better. Malcom eyed the tall wizard across the desk. 'Not feeling so brave now, eh? Now the odds are more in my favour.' He indicated the two burly constables drafted in to help subdue the prisoner if he tried anything. 'So, where shall we start? How about what you were doing in that beach hut with two other men after sundown?'

'You wouldn't understand if I told you.'

'Come on, you can't shock me – I'm a man of the world.'

The tall wizard closed his eyes and breathed deeply, trying to remain calm. 'You have no idea how urgent it is that I am not detained here a minute longer.'

'I'm terribly sorry, but I'm afraid you're going to be enjoying the legendary hospitality of the Sussex Police Force for a little while yet.' Malcom bent down and picked the carpet-bag up off the floor, thumping it down on the desk. 'What's this?'

'Please, don't open it,' said the wizard.

'What's in here then?' said Malcom, raising an eyebrow.

'You open that, and I will not be responsible for the consequences.'

This only fuelled Malcom's curiosity. 'Ooh, must be something important. I'll bet it's full of your little games accessories, eh? What are you into then? Whips? Leather? Or is it rubber truncheons? Let's have a look-see.' Malcom clicked open the heavy brass clasp.

'Please! You have no idea what you're doing!' the wizard yelled.

'Oh yes I do, sunshine, I'm about to uncover some very valuable evidence.' Malcom yanked open the bag. 'See, that wasn't so painful, was it?' At first, as he peered into the depths of the bag, nothing happened. 'Funny, it looks bigger on the insi—' At that moment a torrent of books spewed out of the bag like molten magma from an erupting volcano. Malcom was knocked to the floor and stared up in amazement as all forty-seven volumes of The Book poured out of the bag and began to fly around the room. Some flew into the walls, bringing down charts, knocking plants from shelves and toppling carefully stacked files onto the floor. Others dive-bombed the constables, who made a panicked rush for the door over the prone form of DI Collins, who was, for once, reduced to stunned silence. Until, that is, one of the books took a fancy to him and landed on his head, opening and closing its cover like the wings of a resting butterfly. 'Ah! Ahh!' he screamed, jumping up and running from the room.

The tall wizard stood and looked up at the circling books. 'Do you know, in all these years, this is the first time you lot have ever done anything useful,' he smiled.

In another interview room close by, Beasely was attempting to take a statement from Rex. It was a small room and Rex had the only chair, so Beasely had to perch uncomfortably on the desk. His discomfort wasn't helped by Rex's refusal to cooperate; he hadn't said a word for over a minute now. 'So, you say you're a newsagent?' enquired the sergeant for the third time. Rex's gaze remained fixed on the shabby sergeant's face. Those extraordinary blue eyes seemed to be able to see right through to Beasely's very soul – it was an unnerving experience. 'Ahem,' he coughed politely to try and bring Rex's attention back to the matter in hand. 'Shall I put "newsagent"?'

'That's it!' Rex said suddenly, clapping his hands. The shock nearly sent Beasely flying off the desk. 'You're the other man!'

'Sorry? What? What other man?'

'The man in the loo. The other one, the one that looks like a pig – he did the beating up, and you held the door shut.'

Beasely leaped off the desk and closed the door. 'Who put you up to this?' he whispered, feeling in his pocket for his cigarettes.

'Don't worry, I know that you didn't want to do it. You're just frightened of him.'

'I don't know what the fuck you're talking about.'

'Do you know what happened to that man? Is he all right?'

'I bloody well hope so . . . shit!' Beasely dropped the packet of cigarettes on the floor. Trembling, he knelt to pick them up.

'It's all right, I'm not going to tell anyone.'

'Look,' said Beasely on his knees, 'I don't want any trouble. Did that bastard Collins put you up to this? Just tell him I'm a man of my word – I'm not going to blab.' Beasely tried to put the spilt cigarettes back in the packet with his shaking hands, but only succeeded in breaking most of them. 'Shit!'

Rex put a hand on his shoulder. 'You really don't have to worry. I think you should put in for that transfer.'

Beasely stood up suddenly. 'What transfer? How did you know?' He put one of the less badly broken cigarettes in his mouth and felt for his lighter. 'I think,' he said, backing towards the door, 'I should get someone else to conduct this interview.' He opened the door just as two screaming constables ran past, followed by a flying book. He shook his head. 'Get a grip, Beasely,' he muttered to himself.

Standing in the corridor, he struck the wheel of the disposable lighter with his thumb. A yard-long jet of flame shot out, singeing his eyebrows. 'Jesus!' Beasely immediately released his thumb, but the lighter refused to shut down. With trembling fingers he tried to adjust the flame, but the top of the lighter disintegrated in his hand and he was left holding a blowtorch. Wondering what he should do next, he became vaguely aware of something flying down the corridor towards him, and looked up in time to see the book on its return journey.

Beasely watched in disbelief as the book fluttered closer. It seemed to be drawn, mothlike, to the lighter, and hovered for a moment in the flame. Then, as the pages took fire and began to curl, the book screamed in pain and hurtled down the corridor, throwing itself against either wall in an effort to put out the flames.

At the end of the corridor Gerrold's door opened. 'What's all the bloody racket?' But seeing a flaming book, screaming in agony, flying towards him, suddenly he realized he didn't want to know. He was on the point of closing his door and pretending it wasn't happening when Malcom came howling into the corridor with a book firmly clamped to his head. Other books rapidly followed, gushing out of Malcom's office, their paper wings crackling like locusts'.

'What's that noise?' said Jim when the screaming started. He pulled out his gun and ran to the door. For a moment, the two grey-suited men stood there and listened, then Jim turned to Serena. 'OK, how many of you are there?'

'2006?' muttered Serena, deep in thought.

'How many?' Jim repeated.

'What?' said Serena.

'These are obviously your people come to rescue you. How many can we expect?'

'I don't know what you're talking about,' said Serena.

'I'm going outside,' said the other, silent one.

'Well, what do you know – it talks!' said Serena.

The man went to open the door, but the metal handle bent in his hand, leaving grey slime on his palm. 'The door handle – it's melting.'

'Let me see.' Jim inspected the handle – then looked over at Serena. 'How did you do that?'

'How did I do what?'

'Can melt metal,' Jim murmured into a small microphone on his wrist. 'We've got to get her out of here,' he said to his accomplice. 'Cuff her. No, on second thoughts use the plastic ties.' He turned back to Serena. 'Or can you melt those too?' The silent man took a black plastic strap out of his pocket and, pulling Serena's arms behind her, tied it around her wrists. It stretched like chewing gum.

'Hey, look at this.'

Jim ran over. 'How do you do that?'

'How do I do what?' said Serena.

'Use something else,' Jim instructed.

'What?'

'I don't know – anything! Use your tie!'

'Would it be OK if I just promised to be good?' Holding her with one hand, the man removed his tie and wrapped it tightly around her wrists. 'Are you trying to cut off my circulation?' The big man yanked Serena to her feet and dragged her to the door. 'Ooh, you're strong, big boy. What's your name?' The man remained silent. 'Look, I'd love to help you guys, I really would, but I've got as much of a grip on what's going on here as you have. Is this really 2006? How can it be 2006?'

'Shut up!' the man yelled suddenly, listening at the door. Distant screams echoed down the corridor.

'Jesus, what was that?' said Serena.

'Why can't you be fucking quiet?'

'Because if I stop talking, I may start thinking about the facts of the situation here, and if I did that I might just lose it completely. So, humour me: you never told me your name.'

'What?'

'What's your name?'

'Tell her your fucking name,' said Jim.

'Trevor – my name's Trevor.'

'Hi, Trev, nice to meet you.'

'How are we going to get out?' said Trevor. 'We can't open the door.'

'Shoot the lock.' Trevor needed no second prompting. BLAM! BLAM!

The door creaked open. 'Just like in the movies,' said Serena.

Jim went first. Running across the empty corridor he threw himself flat against the wall and looked left and right. Satisfied that the coast was clear, he waved to Trevor, who dragged Serena out. As the three of them started down the corridor, a book came flying towards them. Without thinking, Trevor blasted it – BLAM! The book screamed and fell to the floor, writhing in agony. Trevor stood over it and put two more slugs into it to put it out of its misery.

'Accomplices disguised as flying books,' Jim muttered into his wrist microphone. He turned to Serena. 'How many more?'

'Did you see that? It was a flying book! This place is crazy!'

'We're evacuating the premises, client in tow,' Trevor murmured into his lapel.

'So, I'm a client, huh? That makes me sound kind of special,' said Serena.

'As far as I'm concerned, you're a useless piece of shit that's ruining my day,' said Jim.

'Aw, and I thought we were friends.'

Upstairs things were going from bad to worse; the books had infiltrated every corner of the building. The flaming book was starting little fires wherever it touched, and the corridors were beginning to fill with smoke, triggering fire alarms throughout the station. Policemen and women ran around in growing confusion. Gerrold still stood uncertainly in his office. Spacewomen and man-eating clams he could just about cope with, but flying books were another matter entirely.

Rex, left alone in the small room, was becoming aware of another problem. He could sense that Serena Kowalski, the only hope for the future of the universe, was being taken away. He had to contact the wizards – but how? 'Come on, you're a wizard, too,' he told himself. Closing his eyes, Rex broadcast with his mind a tentative *Hello!* He felt a little foolish but, after all, the future of the universe was at stake.

To his surprise he got an immediate response. *Hello? Bloody hello? Is that the best you can do?*

Sorry, thought Rex. *But they're taking her away.*

Be specific – who's taking who away?

Persons unknown are taking Serena Kowalski away. We've got to stop them.

Sorry, dear, what was that? came another voice.

Oh, pay attention!

I wasn't talking to you!

It was rather unsettling having the two wizards arguing in his head. *Please, this is serious,* thought Rex.

Sorry.

Sorry, dear, carry on.

Now, thought Rex, *they're taking Serena out the back way – we've got to stop them. Can you both get out?*

Yes, came one voice.

What's going on? came the other. *My policeman's gone a bit loopy – he's barricaded us both in and is raving about flying books . . . Oh you big lummox! You didn't open the bag?*

I didn't – they did!

Now don't start, please, thought Rex. *Where are you both? I'm in a room off the corridor leading up from the front desk.*

So am I.

Good.

And I'm on the second floor.

Typical!

Well, it wasn't as if I could choose my own room.

Look, Rex aimed his thoughts at the tall wizard. *I'll meet you in the corridor, and then together we'll see if we can get up to the second floor.*

Rex stepped through the door. A policewoman ran past, chased by a flapping book. The smoke was getting denser now and, as Rex looked around for the tall wizard, the sprinkler system spluttered damply to life.

The tall wizard stepped out of an office a little further up the corridor, carpet-bag in hand. 'Bloody country,' he grumbled. 'Only in England could it rain indoors.'

Rex and the tall wizard made their way upstairs through the

drizzle, past sad little piles of soggy books, their pages flapping hopelessly like butterflies on a pond.

'Of course,' said the wizard, bending down and picking one up. The book whimpered pathetically. 'Why didn't I think of it before? Water! Books hate water.' The cover came away in his hand and the pages fell apart under his fingers. But as he watched the loose leaves float away and cascade down the waterfall that was now the stairs, he couldn't help feeling a little touch of sadness: a small catch in the throat at the death of his 'child'. It had caused unimaginable chaos and brought the universe to the brink of destruction – even now it might be too late to undo the damage it had done – but it was his creation, how could he not feel remorse at its passing?

'Um, I don't think we should hang about.' Rex was meanwhile waiting for him at the head of the staircase, water dripping from the end of his nose.

'Of course – we have work to do.' Taking one last look at his drowning opus, the wizard sniffed, then, setting his jaw, sprang into action. 'You look very wet,' he said, his long legs taking the stairs three at a time.

Rex looked down the long, door-lined corridor. *Where are you?* he thought.

Third on the left, dear, came the reply.

Rex turned to the tall wizard. 'Did you hear that?'

The tall wizard nodded. 'I suppose we'll have to rescue it.'

Finding the door, Rex tried the handle but it came off in his hand. The tall wizard took it and examined it closely. 'Molecular degeneration is accelerating,' he said. 'We have to move fast.'

'How do we get in?'

'Brute force, we'll have to run at it. Come on, Rex, with me.' Rex and the tall wizard backed to the opposite side of the corridor. 'Ready?' Rex nodded. 'On a count of three. One-two-three!'

Rex and the wizard slammed into the door. It didn't give an inch.

'I think I've damaged my shoulder,' said Rex.

Very James Bond, I'm sure, came the thought. *But you'll never*

get in like that. There's a filing cabinet and about three years'
worth of crime files stacked behind that door.

'That information would have been more useful thirty seconds
ago!' the tall one yelled at the closed door.

'What do we do now?' said Rex.

The tall wizard thought for a moment, then smiled. 'Over to
you, son. Think of this as your first test.'

'Eh?'

'You're a wizard – use your powers.'

'Oh.' Rex looked at the door, solidly barricaded – there was no
way in there. Then he noticed something about the wall. Where the
water was hitting it, it was beginning to warp. That could only
mean one thing – it was a partition wall. Plasterboard! One good
thump and he'd be through. Rex made a fist and drew back his arm.

The tall wizard winced. 'No, no, please . . . I didn't mean . . .' He
closed his eyes as Rex's knuckles made contact with the wall. But
to his surprise there came no anguished cry. Opening first one eye,
then the other, he watched as his son attacked the seemingly solid
wall, tearing it to pieces. In a few moments there was a hole big
enough to step through. The tall wizard's eyes brimmed with pride.
'I'm impressed, I'm really impressed,' he said, patting Rex on the
shoulder.

'Shall we?' said Rex, and led the way inside. They found the
short wizard seated in the middle of the room, and a bewildered
sergeant, on his knees in the water, muttering the Lord's Prayer.

'I think he's religious,' said the short wizard.

'Did you see that?' said the tall wizard. 'Walked straight through
a solid wall. Oh, he's his father's son all right.'

The short wizard looked long-sufferingly at Rex. Then turned
back to his other half, standing proudly in the middle of the room.
'Well, are we going? I thought we were in a hurry.'

'Wait a minute!' said Rex suddenly, closing his eyes. 'They're
taking her outside. They've got a car waiting!'

The short wizard took his leave of Sergeant Ivey. 'It's been a pleasure dear, but I really must dash.' The three of them then slipped and slid their way out of the office and back downstairs.

'They told me England was damp, but this is ridiculous,' said Serena.

'One more funny remark and I'm going to break your time-travelling neck,' said Jim.

'I'm only trying to lighten the mood. You guys are sooo serious.'

They were now at the police station's back entrance. Trevor spoke rapidly into his lapel microphone. 'Operative zero-one-five. Code Red, repeat, Code Red. We are at the rear of the building about to attempt rendezvous with the vehicle – do you copy?'

'Why can't you just say, Bring the car round back?' said Serena. 'Where are we going, anyway? Hell, who cares? At least it'll be nice and dry outside.'

Jim pressed the muzzle of his gun to Serena's temple. 'Will you shut your fucking mouth!'

'I'm cool,' said Serena.

Trevor looked through the small wire-reinforced window in the top of the door. The driver of the anonymous black limo saw him and flashed his lights.

'Vehicle standing by,' said Trevor.

Jim put his shoulder to the door. 'Let's go,' he said.

'Attempting egress,' Trevor said to his lapel.

'Attempting egress?' said Serena. Jim turned angrily on her. 'Sorry.'

Jim crashed through the door and, pointing his gun left and right, took station midway between the car and the door. 'Clear!' he shouted back. Trevor took a firm grip on Serena and pushed her through. They ran full pelt for the car, and Serena was bundled into the back seat. Trevor followed her in.

'Go! Go! Go!' Trevor yelled at the driver. The tyres screeched on the tarmac. Jim hurled himself into the moving car just as it swung out of the car park.

Rex and the wizards ran out through the back door in time to see its rear lights disappearing up the road.

'Bugger!' said Rex.

'Now what?' said the short one.

The tall one turned on him. 'You're the writer, *you* tell us.'

'You can't let it be, can you?'

'No, come on, you're supposed to be good with plots – what happens next?'

While the wizards argued, Rex searched the car park for inspiration. He was in a real-life adventure. It was hard to believe, but at this moment the safety of the entire universe was in the hands of Rex Boggs. But that was an awful lot of responsibility for a Lancing newsagent. 'Mustn't panic,' he said to himself. 'What would Prince Nostrum do?' That was easy, Prince Nostrum would simply leap into his time machine and go after them. But, not having a time machine . . . 'Improvise.' That was the strength of the hero: the ability to make the best of a bad situation. *We haven't got a time machine but we are standing in a car park,* he thought. Rex had never stolen a car before, but these were exceptional circumstances – Serena had to be rescued, that was all that mattered.

Rex eyed the rows of police cars – no, too obvious. After the rescue there was the getaway to consider, and a police car would stick out like a sore thumb. There were private cars too, but nothing that looked as if it could hold its own in a chase. Then he saw it. Over in the corner, all on its own, gleaming dully in the glow of the street lights – a big Harley-Davidson. 'Yes!' he said.

It was very big and smelt intimidatingly of oil and petrol, but there was no time for petty fear – he had a universe to save. He threw his leg awkwardly over the machine. 'So far so good. Now how do you start this thing?' He looked down at the gleaming chrome of the headlamp nacelle – the ignition slot was empty. 'Bugger.' He was about to give up the whole idea when a thought occurred to him. 'You're a wizard,' he told himself. 'Think like one.' He closed his eyes and concentrated . . .

The first the wizards realized that Rex was no longer with them was when they heard the big motorbike roar into life. They stopped in the middle of their argument to watch as Rex weaved unsteadily out of the car park and off down the road.

'Can he ride a bike?' asked the short one.

'He's about to find out,' replied the tall one.

From inside the relative safety of cell no. 6, Malcom could hear something familiar. His quickening heartbeat told him it meant something important. But what? His body was way ahead of his brain – it was already feeling the sense of loss that the theft of his beloved Harley would inflict. 'No,' he said, the penny dropping. 'No! Not my bike!' He pushed the heavy door open and ran down the wet corridor. The sprinklers had stopped, but the corridors were still slippery. Slithering round a corner at a desperate canter, he found Superintendent Gerrold standing in his way.

'Collins, I'll see you in my office, *now*!'

'Fuck off,' said Malcom, running him over. Gerrold was left in a spluttering heap among a pile of dead and dying books. Malcom crashed through the back door and into the car park. His eyes went immediately to his parking spot over in the corner. Empty. He looked around in disbelief. For a moment, against all logic, he thought that perhaps he'd parked it somewhere else. But in his heart, he knew he'd left it as he always did, over in the corner in the space marked 'Solo M/C's'.

'Bastards!' he yelled at no one in particular. 'Fucking, cunting, bollocking bastards!' he screamed, jumping up and down, his great belly wobbling perilously.

The two wizards, standing to one side of the back door, watched as Malcom raged. 'No prizes for guessing whose bike that was,' said the short one.

Rex hadn't ridden a bike since his sixteenth birthday, when his friend Julian Tuft had let him have a go on his Yamaha 150. But that little over-revving moped was a totally different experience from the two litres of raw power that currently throbbed beneath him. The Harley was big and heavy and, although not the fastest thing on the road, was by far the most powerful machine he'd ever piloted. He opened the throttle and the bike leapt eagerly forwards, the blare of its twin exhausts turning heads a hundred yards away. 'Gently,' he said to himself.

He could see the car up ahead. It made a left turn into Kingswood Street and left again onto Grand Parade. Then the driver put his foot down. Diving across two lanes, he swung right round Victoria Gardens, crossing the traffic coming up past the Royal Pavilion, and ignoring the indignant blare of horns from drivers who'd been waiting patiently at the traffic lights. Rex followed unsteadily as the car headed up Marlborough Place. The car was fast, but the Harley was faster. However, Rex was on a steep learning curve. Gradually, he began to remember bits of what Julian had said to him that bright summer's morning all those years ago: 'Don't steer, lean . . . in fast corners, steer in the opposite direction . . . whatever you do, never, *ever* let the power off in a corner . . . and don't bend it, mum'll go mad.'

Rex opened the throttle – the sudden surge of power threw him backwards and he nearly let go of the handlebars. Immediately he slammed the throttle shut and slid painfully forwards onto the petrol tank. 'Get it together, Rex.'

The big black limo ran all the red lights to Preston Circus, then took a squealing left up New England Road. Under the railway bridge, the car went through another red light, and took the right fork down the Old Shoreham Road.

Rex would have loved to know where the car was going, but it was hard enough just staying on the bike without the complication of trying to probe their minds. 'Don't steer . . .' he murmured to himself. 'On fast corners, steer in the opposite direction . . .' He tried it while turning left up New England Road and was pleasantly surprised to find that it worked; steering away from the corner tightened the bike's trajectory round it. Immensely pleased with his new-found riding skills, he allowed himself a small whoop of triumph, but this momentary lapse sent him swerving into the path of an oncoming truck.

'Concentrate!' he said to himself, yanking the heavy bike back across the road.

The Old Shoreham Road was pretty straight, and at this time of night fairly quiet, so all he had to do was to hang on and hope for the best. Even so he felt desperately out of his depth. 'What am I doing?' he said to himself. 'I'm a newsagent, I'm not Prince bloody Nostrum.' But something inside urged him on. This was his chance to be like his hero – to live his dream. If he didn't grab it with both hands, he might never have the opportunity again. Rex gritted his teeth as he followed the speeding car down the wrong side of the road and through yet another red light.

Eventually they reached the dual carriageway. The driver floored the accelerator, but Rex managed to stay with him. Then, all too soon, the Holmbush roundabout came into view. The car went round it sideways and then took a left onto the Shoreham Bypass. Rex followed onto the roundabout, and immediately realized he was going too fast. He cranked the bike right over so that the foot peg was scraping the road. 'Steer in the opposite direction . . .' he reminded himself. The tarmac, speeding swiftly beneath him, was growing closer all the time, and he could feel the back tyre searching for grip – it could let go at any moment. His instinctive reaction was to close the throttle, but Julian's warning echoed around his brain: 'Never, *ever* let the power off in a corner . . . and don't bend it, mum'll go mad.' But in the present circumstances he could probably ignore the last part of that sentence.

Then, suddenly, there in front of him was the exit for the bypass. Hauling desperately on the handlebars, he managed to keel the heavy bike over and change direction. Leaning almost off the bike, his left knee scraping the road, he roared down the slip road. 'Don't bend it . . . don't bend it . . . don't bend it . . .' he repeated over and over again. The crash barrier came closer and closer as he fought the bike round the long, looping left-hander. He was sure he was going to die. At some point he must have closed his eyes, because when he opened them again, he was still in one piece and haring down the Shoreham Bypass, the black limo within sight.

'Yee-hah!' he shouted into the wind. 'Prince Nostrum rides again!'

Malcom stood, angry and out of breath, in the middle of the car park. Something had to be done. Somebody had stolen his bike and they were going to pay. He strode purposefully towards the nearest police car. Getting inside, he clicked on the radio. 'This is DI Collins. I want to report a stolen vehicle. Put out an APB – find and detain rider of a Har—' The microphone was taken from his hand.

'I don't think we want to do that, now do we?' said the tall wizard from the seat next to him.

'Ah! Don't hit me!' said Malcom, shielding his face with his hands.

'We aren't going to hurt you,' said the short one from the back. 'We'd like you to take us for a little drive, that's all.'

'Yes, somewhere quiet,' said the tall one. 'With a sea view.'

'I'm not taking you nowhere,' said Malcom defiantly.

'Now that's not the attitude is it?' said the tall one, finding the pressure point underneath Malcom's left ear and squeezing with his thumb. Suddenly Malcom couldn't breathe. The pain was excruciating; he wanted to scream, but he was paralysed. As he was about to pass out, the tall wizard released his grip.

'Ow! That hurt!' Malcom sobbed.

'Let's start again, shall we?' said the tall one. 'You're going to take us for a little drive.'

Malcom obediently started the engine.

'Unbelievable,' said Serena in the back of the careering car. She was looking out into the blackness on either side of the Shoreham Bypass. 'Are they really fields?'

'Yes,' said Trevor, tersely.

'Wow. Where I come from there are buildings everywhere. They've even built over the desert. The only place you can walk is down the street. You know, people grow grass in their window boxes just so they can touch it from time to time.' She looked out into the darkness once again. 'There's really nothing out there but fields?'

'There's nothing out there,' said Jim.

'Wow,' said Serena, a big smile on her face. 'What it must be like, to walk on grass. Sure, I've walked on virtual grass before, but you just know it's not the real thing. Do you think we could stop and—'

'No we could not stop and do anything!' said Jim. 'Do you think you could stop talking just for a minute?'

'I think we need to discuss our client – bodyguard relationship,' said Serena.

Jim turned round and grabbed Serena by the front of her suit. 'Let's get one thing straight – I am not your fucking bodyguard!'

'He's still behind us,' said the driver, looking in his rear-view mirror.

'Shit!' said Jim, letting Serena go.

'Slow down,' said Trevor, pulling out his gun.

'No,' said Serena, 'you can't do that.'

'We can do what the fuck we like, thanks to you.'

'What do you mean, thanks to me?'

'Our instructions,' said Jim, 'were first to ascertain whether you were telling the truth – of which I think we have ample evidence. Then to transport you to headquarters using any means necessary to ensure your safety. *Any means necessary.*'

'Slow down and pull over into the left-hand lane,' said Trevor, winding down the window.

'You can't kill someone just because they're following you – that's murder.'

'When you work for the government it's called necessary force.'

The single headlight in the driver's mirror grew larger. Soon they could hear the throbbing of the big Harley's engine.

Rex had seen the car slow and pull over. A minute ago they'd been bowling along at over a hundred, overtaking everything else in sight. Now their speed had dropped to just on sixty and they were travelling in the slow lane. What was going on? It might just be that they felt safe now they were on the open road. Or it might be that they were waiting for him to catch up. Whatever the reason, he reckoned he'd better be careful. What would Prince Nostrum do here?

The big motorbike was right behind. Trevor waited for it to draw level. 'Slower! Slower!' he shouted. The driver eased off and watched the bike's headlamp move across the mirror as it pulled out to overtake. Now it was almost up to the rear bumper. Trevor's finger tightened on the trigger. As the Harley's front wheel drew level with the back door, Rex killed the throttle, weaved back behind the car and dived up the inside.

'Shit!' When Rex appeared in the nearside window, Trevor opened fire across Serena. Two crazed impact circles appeared in the bulletproof glass.

Rex twisted the throttle forwards and let the bike drop back. Now he knew: if he approached they would try to kill him. What should he do? Something told him to wait – to follow and wait.

Inside the car there was pandemonium. 'You idiot!' yelled Jim. 'You should have let me take him.'

'I forgot about the glass,' muttered Trevor.

'Prat! If you'd just waited, I could have taken him easily.'

'I thought you were supposed to take me in *alive*!' said Serena. 'You could have killed me then. And do you know how much damage you can do to your eardrums by letting one of those things off in a confined space?'

'Shut up!' yelled Jim. 'Where's he gone?'

Trevor craned round to look out of the rear window. 'He's dropped back – there are two cars between us now.'

'Terrific. Put your foot down and take the next left,' Jim said to the driver.

The black limo pulled out and accelerated away. Rex followed at a discreet distance and watched as the car turned left at the Lancing College traffic lights. *That's the way to the airport. Are they going to fly her out?* wondered Rex, suddenly panicking. He tried to tune in to the occupants of the car, but it was no good, he couldn't ride the bike and mind-read at the same time. 'Think, think!' he said to himself. Where would you take a woman from the future? London? No, London was full of prying eyes and newspaper men, and you'd want to keep her a secret, at least for the moment. Secret? Of course! You'd take her to your most secret base – Porton Down. Once there, Serena would be almost impossible to get to. And if they had a helicopter standing by, they could be in the air in minutes. Rex had to do something *now*. He opened the throttle wide and the bike shot forwards.

He needn't have worried. 'Where the fuck are we?' said Jim.

'I don't know,' said the driver. 'You said turn left, so I turned left.'

'Bloody great!' said Jim.

'It's an airport,' said Trevor.

'Wow, look at all those little planes,' said Serena looking at the array of assorted small aircraft. 'They're so cute, they ought to be in a museum.' The car lurched over an unseen speed ramp.

'Jesus! Careful!' snarled Jim.

'Sorry,' said the driver, 'I didn't see it.' A single headlamp appeared in his rear-view mirror. 'Oh bugger,' he said, 'he's back.'

Jim and Trevor swivelled round to look out of the rear window. 'Stop the car,' said Jim, unbuckling his seatbelt. The car hit another speed ramp and his head hit the roof. 'Stop the fucking car!'

'All right! All right!' said the driver. He slammed on the brakes and the car slewed sideways and came to a slithering halt. Jim and Trevor both got out and trained their guns on the approaching headlight.

Serena couldn't stand it. Hands still tied behind her back, she wriggled across the seat and fell out of Trevor's open door. 'They've got guns! They're going to kill you!' she yelled.

'Get her back in the car,' barked Jim.

Trevor manhandled the protesting Serena into the car while Jim took careful aim with his automatic. The sound of the motorbike grew louder. Jim focused on a spot just above the bike's headlamp. He curled his finger round the trigger and squeezed.

BANG! The gun exploded in Jim's hand. The top flew off and hit him square between the eyes, knocking him cold.

'How did you do that?' gasped Trevor, still wrestling with Serena. Releasing her, he pulled out his pistol and took aim. The motorbike was getting nearer, its headlight illuminating the unconscious Jim, lying flat out on the tarmac. Trevor was beginning to have second thoughts now. He looked at Jim, then at his own gun, then at the approaching motorbike, then back to Serena. If she could do it once, she could do it again. 'Oh shit!' he said, throwing the gun away and raising his hands in surrender.

The driver moved his hand towards his breast pocket. 'Don't even think about it,' said Trevor. 'If these people can disguise themselves as flying books, who knows what else they're capable of?' The driver raised his hands too.

Rex, hearing the report from Jim's gun, was lying flat on the petrol tank to provide a smaller target, but to his surprise and great relief, no further shots were fired. As he approached, he was even more surprised to see one man lying on the ground and the other two standing with their hands raised. He brought the bike to a standstill about twenty feet from the vehicle, and called out, 'Serena! Serena Kowalski!'

Serena stuck her head out of the rear door. 'That's me. Who are you?'

'I'm here to help you.'

'Oh yeah?'

'You'll have to trust me. Get on the bike, we haven't much time.'

'How do I know you're not going to experiment on my brain or something?'

'No – that's what these guys were going to do. I won't hurt you, believe me. We need you as much as you need us.'

Serena ran up. 'Can you explain how I got here?'

'You fell through a running fracture in time.'

Serena looked into Rex's big, honest face. It was as good an explanation as any. 'OK,' she said. 'They think we're aliens with magic powers,' she whispered, clambering onto the seat behind Rex.

'Really?' said Rex with a smile. He cleared his throat and addressed the men. 'Resistance is futile!' he said. 'You will remain here until my people arrive, at which time you will be assimilated.' Rex turned back to Serena. 'I've always wanted to say that. Think they bought it?'

'I wouldn't be at all surprised,' Serena smiled. 'We're not talking rocket scientists here.'

Rex kicked the Harley into gear. 'Hold on,' he said and turned the bike around. He looked back at the men still standing obediently with their hands in the air. 'Klaatu, Barada, Nikto!' he shouted and, opening the throttle wide, roared off down the airport perimeter road.

'Beautiful isn't it?' said the short wizard looking out at the moon-dappled sea.

'What was your expression? Millpond?' said the tall one.

The short one looked back up the beach towards Malcom, now handcuffed to the promenade railings. 'What are we going to do with him?'

'We'll let Rex decide, he seems to have a firm grip on the situation. He's a very bright boy.'

'That's not what you said when you first met him.'

'That was before I'd got to know him,' said the tall wizard. 'I think he takes after his father,' he said proudly.

'Do you really think he's up to it?'

'We can only hope. It doesn't seem fair . . . to find him only to have to throw him back into the void.'

'Is there any other way?'

'No,' said the tall wizard sadly. For a moment the two wizards sat in silence.

'Wiz,' said the short one, suddenly thoughtful. 'What's going to happen when we go back to Limbo?'

'If we can't heal the Hoop we won't have a Limbo to go back to.'

'I know, but assuming everything works out . . .' The short wizard left the sentence hanging in the air.

'We may not be able to go back,' said the tall one. 'After what we did there, it may not accept us back.'

'No,' said the short one, looking coyly down at the pebbles. 'That's not what I meant. I'm talking about us, you know, being together – not being separate any more.'

'Oh that. Yes, it will be strange.'

'I'm going to miss you,' said the short one, tentatively letting his head fall onto the tall one's shoulder.

'I shall miss you too,' said the tall one, putting his arm around him. Side by side and silently, the two wizards sat on the beach and stared out to sea, as the moon, the stars, and the velvet mantle of the night slowly dissolved in the warm, red rays of the rising sun.

The Hoop flexed . . .

Suddenly the wizards found themselves enveloped in thick fog. 'Now what?' said the tall one.

Chapter 36

Up on Devil's Dyke, a part of the South Downs with views across the Weald in one direction and the sea in the other, Rex watched mystified as Serena rolled, laughing, in the long grass. 'You have no idea how amazing this is. Where I come from we have coast-to-coast concrete.'

'Yeah,' said Rex. 'Um, look. I don't want to hurry you, but I think we'd better get a move on.' The sky to the east was already beginning to turn a deep red.

'Can we just watch the sun come up, huh? It's been so long since I've seen it from ground level.'

'Oh, well, I suppose so.' Rex sighed and sat down on the grass next to Serena. 'What's it like then?' he said after a pause. 'In the future?'

'It stinks. That's why I chose the garbage job.'

'Yeah, but I bet it's exciting – space travel and all that sort of thing.'

'Space travel is overrated. Anyway there's nothing out there – just rocks, space, and more rocks.'

'But what about, you know, advances in medicine?'

Serena sighed. 'We've had a cure for cancer for over a decade, but nobody can afford it.'

'Oh.'

Serena tugged at a piece of grass and, putting it in her mouth, chewed the sweet, succulent end. 'You really want to know what it's like?' she said.

'Yeah,' said Rex enthusiastically.

'OK. Imagine an enormous city that stretches from pole to pole—'

'Can I stop you there?' Rex interrupted, involuntarily putting a hand on her knee. 'Would you mind if I . . .'

Serena looked at him levelly. 'Would I mind if you what?'

He swiftly removed his hand. 'No, no, I didn't mean . . . I wasn't . . . Look, I know it sounds silly, but I can read minds. At least I'm supposed to be able to read minds. Do you think I could read yours?'

Serena stared at him. This had been a crazy day – time travel, flying books, and now mind-reading. 'Is there any touching involved?'

Rex blushed. 'No, no touching – absolutely no touching whatsoever.'

'Shame,' Serena sighed. 'OK, why not?'

'Thank you. Now just relax.'

Serena lay down and looked up at the sky. 'This OK?'

Rex nodded and closed his eyes. At first nothing happened: all he could see was blackness. Then gradually a picture began to take shape. To start with it was hazy – as if he were seeing through a cloud. But then the mist cleared and, with a rush, a torrent of images spilled into his brain. He saw a world covered with people. A twenty-four-hour world where nothing stops, nobody sleeps. Food so full of chemicals that it never rots. Genetically modified farm animals so densely packed with meat they can't stand up. The polar ice caps are melting: Asia, Europe, and the eastern seaboard of the United States are drowning in the sludge-brown sea. The poor and the destitute live among the garbage on the endless streets. Everywhere there is the sound of gunfire. But you're not even safe when barricaded into your home – accidentally download a virus onto your biogenic computer, and it might just kill you. Even space is full of shit. The only way out is death – home suicide kits are on sale in every pharmacy.

Rex had seen enough. 'Aaah!' he screamed, opening his eyes. 'Oh my God, oh my God.'

Serena sat up and looked at the moon just beginning to pale in the dawn light. 'You know,' she said calmly, 'they even use the moon for advertising.'

'The moon?'

'Yeah.'

'It's a bloody nightmare!'

'Now you'll understand my overexuberance at seeing so much unadulterated nature.'

Rex lay back, breathing heavily. It was hard to reconcile the terrifying vision he'd just had with the quintessentially English countryside scene that was spread out before him. Serena lay down beside him. 'Will you hold me?' she asked. Rex suddenly looked anxious. 'It's OK,' she said. 'It's just that I haven't been held by a friendly human for such a long time. Just hold me. Please?'

Rex rolled onto his side and put his arm around her; she pulled him tight and they dissolved in each other's warmth. Together they lay as the sun rose slowly over the Weald, turning the small neat fields first ruby, then orange, then bright, bright gold, while the symphony of the dawn chorus built gradually to its glorious climax.

'I'd never realized how beautiful it is,' Rex said.

'Make the most of it,' said Serena. 'It's all going to disappear. In fifty years' time all this'll be concrete.'

'Not necessarily,' said Rex thoughtfully. 'Come on, we really have to go.'

'OK.' She kissed him on the cheek. 'Thanks.'

'Thank you, too.' Rex blushed.

Getting up, they turned their backs on the splendours of daybreak over Sussex, and as they walked back to the Harley parked outside the Devil's Dyke Inn, there was another tremor and the world seemed to flicker, like a fluorescent light being switched on. Just for a moment there, on the sea far below, Rex thought he saw an armada of ships stretching to the horizon. Then suddenly they were gone, and the coast was shrouded in mist.

'That was weird,' said Serena.

'That sort of thing's been happening a lot recently,' said Rex.

They climbed onto the bike. Rex pressed the starter button and the engine burst into life but, almost immediately, the normally regular throb of its exhaust became uneven, and a violent banging and the harsh sound of metal on metal emanated from the crankcase. Rex killed the engine.

'Sounds like the big end,' said Serena.

'Eh?' said Rex.

'I know bikes. My dad used to have one of these. I lost count of the times I saw him pull it apart and put it back together again.'

Rex got off, and squatting down, looked hard at the engine. Serena joined him. 'Believe me,' she said. 'This is one dead bike. We're going to have to walk.'

'I'm just going to try something,' said Rex.

'OK, but you're wasting your time.'

Rex put his hands on the crankcase. In his mind's eye he could see the soft, twisted metal of the crankshaft and the overstretched gudgeon pins. It was a mess far beyond the abilities of any emergency call-out service. But something inside told him it *would* work for him, if he asked it nicely.

Rex got back on the bike. 'What are you doing?' asked Serena. Rex pressed the starter button and the engine roared sweetly into life. Serena was amazed. 'You know, Rex, I like you – you're a really weird guy.'

Rex smiled. 'Thank you, Serena. That's the nicest thing anyone's ever said to me.' Serena climbed aboard and wrapped her arms around him – which felt nice. 'Hold on tight,' he smiled, and soon the South Downs were echoing to the obscene blare of the Harley's twin exhausts.

Marcus Agrippa peered into the mist which had fallen like a blanket. A moment ago they had been sailing towards the shore in bright sunshine under a cloudless sky. But suddenly the wind had dropped and they had been engulfed in a thick fog. The helmsman called out to the other ships but received no answer. There was no sound save the muffled slap of the oars. Marcus Agrippa was worried; he'd heard things about this island. They said it was enchanted; peopled with witches and sorcerers who played tricks on the unwary. Was this weather a wizard's trick? No, Marcus Agrippa had no time for superstition. It was more likely that the gods were punishing him for entering on a campaign with a stubbly chin. He scratched it nervously. 'Helmsman!' he called. 'Take a sounding.'

The lead weight splashed into the sea. 'Twelve feet, general!'

'All stop!' the general commanded. The water dripping from the raised oars was the only sound to break the absolute stillness. Marcus Agrippa strained his ears into the enveloping mist. Nothing – not a murmur. No rustle of wind through trees. No cawing seagulls. Nothing to suggest that they were anywhere near land. All was eerily quiet. Then there came a harsh grinding as the keel began to touch bottom. At last the ship lurched forwards, as its bows struck the shore and stuck fast.

Marcus Agrippa looked across at his helmsman, who had paled visibly. 'Well, we've arrived. But where?' Marching to the prow of the ship, the general drew his sword and jumped down. His boots clattered onto the pebbles and he was relieved to find himself on relatively stable ground. 'I, Marcus Vipsanius Agrippa, claim this island in the name of Rome!' he announced to the silence. He was just about to call his men to follow him when from far off came a sound like nothing he'd ever heard. It was as if the sky were alive with the roar of giant wings, and the sound was coming his way.

Suddenly, as if someone had turned on a light, the fog lifted. On the promenade in front of the King Alfred Centre, the early-morning joggers and dog walkers were amazed to see a Roman warship, filled with soldiers, beached on the shore. Marcus Agrippa looked around at the strange buildings, at the people in their bizarre attire, and up at the Sussex Police helicopter puttering towards them along the shoreline.

'What place is this?' he wondered aloud. A fearful groan went up from his men. Some of them, believing the helicopter to be a harpy, screamed in terror and threw themselves into the sea; others manned the deck-mounted ballista and started firing bolts at the flying beast. Marcus Agrippa realized he would have to find shelter, and quickly.

Looking around, his eyes lit upon the perfect place – large and seemingly undefended. He urged his men to disembark. Adopting the Roman 'turtle' formation – shields interlocked above their heads – they made their way up the beach, away from the infernal monster that fluttered above them, and towards the refuge of the King Alfred Centre. People ran in all directions as the soldiers clattered up the steps and onto the promenade. Marcus Agrippa looked through one of the windows in the wall of the swimming-pool complex. 'The gods be praised – a public baths! On men, on! For the glory of Rome!'

'You're not going to believe this,' the helicopter pilot said into his radio. 'But we've got a full-scale Roman invasion going on in front of the King Alfred.' A ballista bolt then penetrated the floor of the cockpit and lodged in the helicopter's roof. 'Jesus! Golf-Sierra-Uniform-Sierra-X-Ray under attack – withdrawing out of range.' The helicopter swooped away and rapidly gained altitude.

The wizards, seated a little way off, witnessed the Romans' arrival. '*Skirted ones*,' said the short one, matter-of-factly.

'Yes, I was wondering when they'd turn up,' said the tall one.

'What do we do now?'

'Make ourselves scarce – rather brutal, the Romans.'

The two wizards marched up the beach towards the slumbering form of DI Collins. His handcuffs had fallen apart in the night and he lay flat on his back, snoring soundly. The tall one picked up one of the pieces of handcuff and eyed it critically. 'This is either British workmanship or things are really beginning to come apart at the seams.' He put his hand on the promenade railings. The metal was like putty under his fingers. 'Serious ferrous degeneration. I wouldn't be surprised if we had a rather nasty collapse pretty soon,' he said, looking up at the blocks of flats along the seafront.

'Wakey-wakey!' said the short one.

Malcom spluttered awake and opened his eyes. 'Please don't hurt me!'

'You're free to go,' the tall one smiled. 'If you don't want to end up as a Roman kebab, I'd run like hell.'

Malcom stumbled to his feet. The sight that met his eyes didn't make any sense. Men in fancy dress were running all over the place. Was this rag week? No, these weren't skinny, pasty-faced students, they were trained, muscular fighting men and the swords they were carrying looked lethally real. In fact they were terrifying. There was no time to question the evidence of his own eyes – he took the wizard's advice and belted down the promenade in the direction of Portslade.

The janitor never stood a chance. There to open up for the early-morning 'body-conditioning' class with 'Sheryl', he was standing outside the back door enjoying a quiet fag in the sunshine when suddenly he was confronted by a wall of ancient Roman aggression, bristling with steel. 'No, no, no, you can't come in here, the complex doesn't open for another—' A Roman sword cut him short. The invading army piled through the door over his skewered body.

The body-conditioning class, for 'the mature woman who's not yet ready to spread', was coming to an end in the big downstairs room. To the booming sound of a dance track, heavy with bass and drum machine, Sheryl led her 'ladies' through the final part of the routine. 'Four on the left! One-and-two-and-three-and-four! Now the right! One-and-two-and-three-and-four!' The women moved as one, back and forth across the floor like a well-drilled school of killer whales. 'Good, keep it up – nearly there!' Sheryl exhorted. Suddenly the door was thrown violently open and Roman soldiers poured into the room.

'Excuse me!' Sheryl called out. 'We've got this room for another five minutes yet.'

'Women!' smiled one of the men, leering at the sorry array of sagging, Lycra-clad flesh.

'I've got a standing booking!' said Sheryl, trying to keep her class going. All the while the room was filling up with horny Roman soldiery. The women, sensing anything but gentlemanly intentions from the invaders, ceased their gyrations and began backing away.

Kerchunggg! A Roman short sword sliced right through Sheryl's Panasonic music centre with extra-bass button and dubbing functions.

'How dare you!' she squealed in the sudden silence. 'That was a present from my nan!'

'Bar the doors!' shouted one of the men, and the women found themselves encircled by a slavering bunch of sex-starved ancient Romans, for whom rape was one of the essential perks of warfare.

'Excuse me! Are you gentlemen deaf? I said . . . Get your hands off me!' Sheryl screamed.

'Leave the women alone!' boomed the voice of Marcus Agrippa. The men immediately fell back as their general marched into the centre of the room. 'You can indulge yourselves later. First we make this building secure. Centurion!' An officer was immediately by his side. 'I want the building cleared and all exits secured. Post a lookout on the roof – the rest of the fleet must be out there somewhere. Get a ballista up there too; we must be prepared for any eventuality. And get these women out of sight. I don't want the men distracted.'

'Sir!'

The centurion had the women rounded up and placed under guard in a small anteroom. Then, assembling the soldiers, he led them out into the rest of the building.

After a few minutes, the centurion reported back to his general. 'Clear and secure, sir.'

'Good, now let's have a look at the baths.' The centurion led the general down corridors decorated with brightly painted jungle scenes, where lions and tigers and elephants played innocently together, and brought him out into the lobby which overlooked the pool. Looking through the windows at the water-fun slide and plastic-palm-tree-fringed beach, Marcus Agrippa was amazed. 'It's like no baths I've ever seen – but no matter. This speaks of some sophistication, and I thought the people who inhabited this island were savages. We must be wary, centurion. But first we must bathe!'

Chapter 37

Malcom hammered on the door of Hilditch Leisure – Councillor Daniels's operations headquarters. 'We've got a problem,' he blurted out as soon as Daniels opened it.

'Come in, come in,' Daniels said impatiently, pulling the overweight policeman inside and looking nervously up and down the street. 'My God, have you been sleeping rough?' he said, hurriedly closing the door.

'I spent the night on the beach.'

'What the bloody hell were you doing on the beach?'

'It's a long story. Look, forget about where I was last night. We've got a problem at the King Alfred.'

Daniels suddenly went very pale. 'Problem?' he said faintly. He knew that involving this idiot would cause trouble, but what choice did he have? Morningside he could control, but this bucket of guts was immune to threats. He should have got rid of the oaf as soon as the man had found out, but he couldn't risk the police mounting a full-scale murder inquiry and unsettling things, at least not before he'd secured tenure of the Centre. 'What sort of problem?' said Daniels, sitting down.

'Romans.'

'Romans?'

'They've overrun the place. What are we going to do?'

Daniels gazed up at the sweaty, red-faced blimp of a man and cursed the fate that had brought them together. 'I wouldn't worry,' he said. 'They're probably just foreign language students.'

'No! Romans – you know, with little skirts and swords.'

'Roman soldiers?'

'Yeah, that's it.'

'Are you feeling quite well, Malcom? Would you like a glass of water?'

'I'm serious! There are hundreds of them. They arrived in a big fucking boat and ran up the beach straight into the King Alfred Centre.'

Daniels tried to get his head round the idea of an ancient Roman army invading his Centre. What could it mean? Did someone else know? Was this an elaborate stunt by a competitor to blow the whistle on his plan? 'Who have you told?' he barked.

'What?'

Daniels got up and advanced on Malcom. 'Who have you blabbed your stupid mouth off to?'

'No one, honest.'

'Well, someone knows. That's what this little stunt is all about.'

'I haven't said a word.'

'You'd better be telling the truth, Collins. If I find out that you've been talking, I'll have your tongue cut out.' In Daniels's clipped upper-class accent it sounded like a line from *Mutiny on the Bounty*. Daniels wasn't a big man – he barely came up to Malcom's shoulder – but looking into his cold, grey eyes, Malcom felt a shiver run down his spine, and knew that Daniels wasn't joking.

Chapter 38

This wasn't Gerrold's week. He stood with a group of his officers, bleary-eyed and still damp from the sprinklers, on the pebbles beside the beached Roman ship. 'Anyone in there?' he said, nodding towards the King Alfred Centre.

'What – apart from the Romans?' said Sergeant Ivey.

'Of course apart from the Romans,' Gerrold snapped.

'A group of women taking a body-conditioning class, and the janitor, now deceased,' said Beasely, sorting through his soaked packet of cigarettes in the hope that there would be one dry enough to light.

'Bloody animals,' said Gerrold. 'Who are they?' Ivey was on the point of asking who he meant by 'who', but thought better of it.

'No idea, sir,' said Beasely. 'According to eyewitnesses, they just appeared out of the mist.'

'Have they made any demands?'

'None as yet, sir.'

'Let's see if they want to parley.' Gerrold picked up the loud-hailer resting on the pebbles at his feet, and started up the beach. 'This is the police!' Gerrold's amplified, distorted voice and accompanying feedback echoed off the brickwork. A gleaming helmet appeared on the roof of the swimming-pool complex. 'Release the women and we'll talk.' A ballista bolt struck the loud-hailer a glancing blow, knocking it out of his hand. 'Jesus! Take cover!' Gerrold ran for the shelter of the sea wall. His men dived over the nearest groyne. 'Beasely!' Gerrold yelled.

A head appeared over the top of the groyne. 'Yes, sir?'

'Get on the blower – get the firearms unit up here.'

'Yes, sir!'

Marcus Agrippa was floating on his back in the middle of the pool. This was a bizarre place – no tepidarium, no caldarium, just this massive pool. The people who had built this complex obviously didn't have a clue, he thought, feeling rather more superior than he had for some time. He was just beginning to relax, allowing the tensions of the sea voyage to seep gradually away, when there began a commotion outside. Someone seemed to be shouting with the tongues of a hundred men. What now? He swam to the side of the pool and got out. As he was drying himself, a centurion clattered into the room.

'Sir!'

'Report, centurion,' said Marcus Agrippa.

'We are surrounded by a force of men in blue. One of them had a strange device which issued forth a booming and terrible sound.'

'Yes, I heard it. How many of them?'

'No more than a hundred, sir.'

'Assemble the men.' The centurion saluted and left. Marcus Agrippa sighed. He hadn't expected resistance so soon. It was especially worrying as he had only a small fraction of his army. The odds were on his side, it was true; a hundred men would be no match for his well-drilled, battle-trained force, had he only half their number. No, his concerns centred on the enemy's strange weapons – machines that could fly and this . . . noise-maker. What other outlandish devices might they have? He pondered upon this as he donned clean linen.

Beyond the police cordon, a small crowd was gathering. Sheltering behind Mrs Bumble's, the wizards stood and watched as armed police officers were deployed around the Centre. 'That seems rather unfair – guns against catapults,' said the tall one.

A big motorcycle came rumbling along the promenade. It was Rex. Killing the engine, he kicked out the Harley's side stand and went over to join them.

'What's going on?' he said.

'My boy, good to see you. Did you get her?'

'Yes, she's at your place.'

'She'll be safe there for the time being. I think the police have enough on their plate without troubling themselves about a missing spacewoman.'

'What happens now? How do we introduce Serena to the Hoop?' asked Rex. Just then, one of the bricks in the side of Mrs Bumble's exploded in a shower of red dust.

'Molecular cohesion is becoming very unstable,' said the tall wizard. 'There's no time to lose. Rex, listen to me very carefully.' The wizard fixed the newsagent with his remarkable morning-blue eyes. 'Before we bring Serena in, there is something you must do – something extremely dangerous. Unschooled as you are in the art and craft of wizardry, you must . . .' The wizard looked into the earnest, trusting face of his son. 'Oh, but it's impossible. We need more time.' He searched the heavens for inspiration. Across Kingsway, the portico of the Princes Marina Hotel suddenly collapsed. Grabbing Rex by the shoulders, he tried again. 'You must . . .'

'Kill the beast,' Rex said. 'I know.'

'He's such a brave boy,' said the short one.

'Are you ready to face such a task, alone?'

'Look, I've been thinking,' said Rex. 'Apart, you two are powerless, right?'

'Well, that's not *quite* how I'd put it,' said the tall one.

'But what if we link minds? Remember *Guardians of the Gates of Doom*, when Prince Nostrum joins minds with the twin gatekeepers, Antaris and Andromeda?'

The tall wizard glared down at the short one. 'I'll speak to you later.'

'What do you think?' asked Rex. 'If you were both joined together in me, then it would be like you're one person again, with all your old powers.'

'He means a connecting,' said the short one.

'He's too inexperienced,' said the tall one.

'Perhaps, but it's worth a shot.'

'He would have our power, but not the skill to use it – his mind is weak. Do I have to remind you it took us nearly a millennium to perfect our art?'

'Look,' said the short one. 'We are sending him off naked to fight a creature powerful enough to tear the universe apart, so the least we can do is give him the benefit of our experience.'

The tall one looked long and hard at his other half. 'Very well, if you think he's up to it. Let us join hands.'

The three men held hands. They stood in a circle, stock-still, eyes closed, as if playing a static game of ring-a-ring-a-roses. To all outward appearances, nothing much was happening, but in Rex's brain a violent storm was raging, whipping up whirlpools in the fabric of his mind and unleashing an almost overwhelming surge of images. His being was flooded with pain, despair, terror, anger and grief; with joy and sadness and unbearable happiness. In a matter of minutes Rex experienced every taste, every touch, every anguished thought of the Wizard's long, long life. It was too much – he pulled his hands free and opened his eyes. 'AH!'

'Now you know all,' said the short one.

'Ye-es.' Rex was stunned. His brain was so stuffed with information, it no longer felt like his own. Searching through the unfamiliar territory of his mind, full of strange new impressions and ideas, he came across a shrine. 'My mother was very beautiful,' he said.

'Yes,' said the tall one, his eyes misting over. 'Very beautiful.'

'And you loved her deeply.'

The short one turned to him and nodded silently. Rex squeezed both their hands. 'And me,' he said. The wizards nodded, then suddenly seized him in their arms and held him tight.

'My son, my son,' the tall one sobbed. 'I've only just found you. How can I throw you back into the void?'

Rex hugged his twin fathers, then broke away. 'But you're coming with me' – Rex tapped his head – 'in here.' He looked into their red-rimmed eyes. 'How can I fail with you to look after me?' The short one dabbed at his tear-stained face with a handkerchief. 'We must hurry. Give me the table,' Rex urged.

The tall wizard removed the scarf from around his neck and handed it to Rex. 'The power is yours,' he said.

Rex headed towards the beach hut. At its door, he turned back to them. 'The Book was a really stupid idea,' he said.

'We know,' said the short one, 'we know.'

Entering the beach hut, and without really knowing what he was doing, Rex spread the chiffon scarf on the ground and stood in the middle of it. Without a moment's hesitation, he intoned,'*Expedit esse deos, et, ut expedit, esse putemus*!' The scarf was immediately transformed into the large circular table. 'Whoah!' he said, his head hitting the roof. 'What now?' He tried to think, but his mind felt dense and heavy – a bit like fruitcake. At the same time, he received the impression that his new amalgamated brain wanted something from him. A region deep in the consciousness of the Wizard was calling out to him; asking for . . . what? Thinking about it just gave Rex a headache. He decided the best way to deal with it was not to think, but simply to do the first thing that occurred to him and hopefully the Wizard's brain patterns would guide him.

The first thing that did occur was to say, '*Deus et natura, nihil faciunt frustra*!' Now things really began to get wild. The walls of the beach hut expanded rapidly outwards, and he was standing on a table that stretched to infinity in all directions. Then, looking down, he saw that the table was dissolving, becoming smaller as the edges disappeared into the encroaching nothingness. Suddenly he was floating, then he too began to dissolve.

But just before he merged completely with the void, he yelled at the top of his voice, 'Suits me, sunshine!' And in an instant he was gone.

'What's going on, Frank?'

Gerrold turned to see Councillor Daniels. 'Hello, Mike. Place is full of bloody Romans.'

The leader of the firearms unit ran up. 'My lads are all in position now.'

'Thanks, Geoff. Keep them standing by.'

'Looks serious, what are you going to do?' Daniels asked.

'I don't know. They've got fourteen women in there, so I don't want to do anything hasty.'

'When you say Romans . . .'

'Ancient Romans, you know, with skirts and swords.'

'Yes, but they can't be *real* Romans, can they?'

'They sliced the janitor in two – how real do you want?'

'My God!'

'Exactly. And they've got a bloody great catapult up on the roof. They even fired a bolt at me.'

'What do they want?'

'Can't get any sense out of them. They don't seem to speak English.'

'Excuse me, but I may be able to help.' Gerrold and Daniels turned to see a tall, lean man with a neatly trimmed beard. 'I speak a little Latin.'

'Latin?'

'These men have become misplaced in time. Judging by their uniform they're from around the first century BC, well before English, as we know it, came into being.'

'Don't be ridiculous,' said Daniels. 'Frank, get rid of this madman. Frank?'

But Frank couldn't answer. He'd had no sleep, been bombarded with giant clams and time-travelling garbage operatives, his station had been set on fire by flying books and he'd been soaked to the skin by an over-efficient sprinkler system. An invasion by Romans from the first century BC was the final straw. Something had just clicked off in his brain, and he stood, mouth open, staring off into the far distance.

'Frank? Frank?' Daniels looked into his eyes: all systems were down. 'What's happened to him?'

The tall wizard smiled sympathetically. 'It's been a long day. He needs to rest. Officer!'

Sergeant Ivey spun round. 'Yes sir.' Looking into the wizard's face he could have sworn there was something familiar about it. He looked sideways at the wizard with that expression all policemen must cultivate – the look that says, 'If I know your face, you must be a villain.'

'Haven't I seen . . .?' Ivey began.

'The superintendent needs to lie down. Can you take him somewhere and make him comfy?' The wizard twirled the superintendent round and dropped him into Ivey's arms. He was as stiff as a board. Looking at his vacant expression, Ivey knew right away that something was up with him. Something was most definitely up.

'Oh, yes sir, certainly sir. I'll see to it right away.' Ivey dragged the cataleptic policeman away, the super's heels leaving small parallel furrows in the grass.

'Are you saying that these are Roman soldiers from the time of the invasion?' asked Daniels.

The tall wizard laughed. 'Good Lord, no.'

'Thank heavens for that.'

'About a hundred years before the invasion actually.'

'That's impossible.'

'Is it?' Councillor Daniels looked into the remarkable blue eyes of the wizard, which seemed to go on for ever. There was a small *plink!* and suddenly the tiny Smeil was standing between them.

'Hello, Smeil, what are you doing here?'

'It's very urgent I talk to you, sir.'

Daniels saw it but didn't believe it. A man couldn't just appear out of thin air – even a man as small as this. A thousand questions simultaneously flooded his brain but, try as he might, he couldn't articulate one of them.

'Would you excuse me, Councillor? Perhaps you could help the superintendent,' the tall wizard said, pointing in the direction that Ivey had dragged Gerrold.

'Yes, yes, of course,' said Daniels, backing away, glad of the excuse to leave.

The tall wizard turned back to Smeil. 'Now then, what is it?'

'There's no time to explain, sir,' the little man said. 'You must do exactly as I ask.'

Chapter 39

In the parched desert, the curly-haired youth, brimming with confidence, faced the tall, battle-hardened veteran and champion of the Philistines. Whirling the sling around his head, he let loose his shot. As the stone embarked upon its historic flight, thunder rumbled across the desert and the ground began to tremble and shake. In the no man's land between David and Goliath, a shower of sparks and mismatched socks fell from the sky, and where once had been only sand, a great monster and a man now stood.

Rex looked up at the huge malevolent creature. 'Wow!' It was the beast from his dream. But there was no time to be frightened – he was here for a purpose. Where the hell was he? Quickly taking in the situation, he summed up: 'Boy with sling; big man; horrible, nightmare creature.' What did it mean? The boy with the sling rang a distant bell . . . now what was it? Dennis the Menace? No . . . David and Goliath! But there was only one giant in the biblical story – he didn't remember any mansion-block-size monsters.

Think, boy, think! said a voice in his head.

Rex looked back to where David stood, and saw the stone zipping towards him. Now he understood. He spun round and addressed the monster. 'Your shoelace is undone!' he yelled. As the lumbering creature bent down, the shot whistled over the top of its head and struck Goliath square between the eyes. With a groan, the big man buckled at the knees and fell in a crumpled heap on the hot sand.

'Wait a minute,' said the monster, looking up from its elastic-sided boots. 'I haven't got shoelaces.'

'Got you!' shouted Rex.

'I hate practical jokes,' grumbled the monster and, reaching down, drew Goliath's massive sword. 'Joke your way out of this,' it said, raising the sword above its head. Rex, undefended save by a two-thousand-year-old intellect, cowered in the sand. In the final analysis, a large brain is little protection against five feet of razor-sharp steel in the hands of unblinking antagonism. But as the sword began its downward trajectory, blue flames played around its tip and, in a moment, both monster and man had disappeared as if they'd never been there.

David, stunned and shaken by what he'd just witnessed, but never one to let the grass grow under his feet, ran over to the prone giant and started hacking off his head.

The battle had raged all day, with neither side gaining any significant advantage. The English were exhausted, but had the superior position. The Normans were attacking uphill, under a constant hail of English arrows. But then, at last, Duke William had the break-through that he needed. With discipline breaking down among the weary English, his cavalry managed to draw out Harold's right flank and demolish it. Harold was left badly exposed, and now the Normans began to smell victory.

Suddenly the sky grew dark, and there was a clap of thunder like the end of the world. On the slope between the contending armies there appeared an appalling apparition – a huge edifice, three times the height of a man, dressed in black. A creature from the depths of the unconscious, a huge sword in its hand.

'Where the fuck are we now!' it bellowed, and its booming voice stilled the armies on both sides.

With a small *pop*, a man tumbled out of the ether and landed at the monster's feet. *Now what?* thought Rex. *Don't tell me, let's see . . . a hill, two armies, lots of bloodshed – could be anywhere.* One of the Norman archers, already tensed to shoot before the monster appeared, looked up at the creature that had suddenly appeared out of thin air, and his bladder and trembling fingers simultaneously lost their grip. *Ptwang*! A single arrow cleaved the air.

Rex watched the arrow sail up into the sky, and for some inexplicable reason the word Bayeux popped into his head. *Bayeux, Bayeux ... that's France isn't it? Why Bayeux? Bayeux ... Bayeux ... tapestry! Bayeux tapestry ... yes! Harold – 1066!* The arrow was heading straight for the monster's left ear. Rex looked around – the ground was covered with the spilled guts of dead men. 'Look!' Rex screamed, pointing at the monster's right foot. 'I think you've stepped in someone!'

The monster looked down and the arrow passed harmlessly over the creature's shoulder. Well, harmlessly for the monster, but Harold wasn't so lucky – the arrow went straight through his left eye and exploded out of the back of his head. The English king fell dead in the mud, surrounded by his loyal, exhausted and now terminally depressed housecarls.

'There's nothing on my foot,' boomed the monster.

'Got you again!' said Rex.

Little blue flames began to play around the monster's head. The air was full of crackling static electricity. 'I'm getting fed up with this,' it said and, with a sound like an inverted thunderclap, monster and man disappeared.

After a mystified pause, the Normans were the first to catch on to what had happened, and rushed up the hill to defeat the demoralized English. By the end of that October day in 1066, England was Norman property.

Chapter 40

It was most unsatisfactory; Marcus Agrippa was surrounded. From his quarters in the small centre café overlooking the pool, he pondered his next move. True, the cordon surrounding the building was only one man deep, all the entrances to the fortress were narrow and easily defendable, and they had limitless water. But without food it was doubtful they'd survive a long siege. They'd have to break out, and the sooner the better, before hunger had a chance to weaken the men.

The enemy's main force and reserves were drawn up on a small patch of ground to the west of the Centre. The obvious tactic was for Marcus Agrippa to divide his force in two, break through the cordon on the east, then circle back to trap them in a pincer movement. But to be sure of success he needed to get as many men out as possible in one surge. However, the eastern exit was only wide enough to allow two men abreast – they would become easy targets for the spears and bolts of the 'men in blue'. But there was no other way. The first men out would simply have to shield those emerging behind, with the ballista on the roof providing cover until those outside were up to strength. Then and only then should they try and break through the encircling troops.

After outlining his plan to the senior centurion, Marcus Agrippa wandered idly around the small café. Behind the counter, he found a stack of small, square boxes. He picked one up. 'Fruit Pie,' he read. 'I wonder what is Fruit Pie?' On the cover of the box was a picture of an apple, some grapes and a pear. He opened it and slid the shrunken offering out onto his hand. He sniffed it suspiciously. It smelled like food even if it didn't look like it. Cautiously he took a bite. The puréed filling was nastily tart, and the pastry, from long contact with its contents, disgustingly soggy. 'Ach, yeuch!' He spat it out on the floor. 'I was wrong,' he muttered, 'it is obviously not for consumption.'

A soldier hurried into his presence. 'General!'

'Yes?'

'We have had a request to release the women.'

'From whom?'

'A man.'

'Well, obviously a man, but which man?' the general snapped.

'I . . . don't know sir. He wishes to speak with you.'

Pushing the soldier aside, Marcus Agrippa stalked out of the café wiping his mouth.

The tall wizard saluted as the general's head appeared over the edge of the roof above him. '*Ave*, general. I trust you had a good crossing.'

'What do you want?'

'Very well, I'll get straight to the point. Unless you release the women you will all die.'

The general laughed. 'Ha! Who dares oppose the might of Rome?'

'You are new to this island. You will not before have come across the all-powerful beings who stride these shores.' And with that, the wizard turned and pulled out the top bar of one of the sets of ornate railings that ran along the promenade. Holding it up to the general, he proceeded to tie the metal pole in a knot. 'You see,' he said, casually casting it aside, 'your puny force is no match for the mighty men of Hove.'

The man on the ballista gasped and, although he would never have admitted it, a chill gripped Marcus Agrippa's heart. The general stroked his chin. Damn this stubble, he thought. 'That's nothing more than a trick,' he said.

'No, general. Not only do we command the earth, we also hold dominion over sea and sky. Watch!' The wizard pointed out to sea.

Marcus Agrippa followed the strange man's long, bony finger. At first he wasn't sure what he was supposed to be looking at, but as he watched, he saw the narrow line of the horizon begin to widen. It was as if sea and sky were being wrenched apart. The general gaped in wonder at the power of this man: that he could command the very elements! 'We wish you no harm, general. We simply ask for the release of the women. Think it over.' The wizard turned and headed back towards the police ranks.

Marcus Agrippa was torn. The conquest of this island meant glory, power and wealth; the adulation of a people whose heroes' stature was measured in land conquered and enemy blood shed. Failure was not an option. Marcus Agrippa looked at the horizon – the gap was still widening. On the other hand, he thought, what did the fat, complacent people of Rome, safe in their luxury, know about the realities of a foreign campaign? Who need know what had happened here? Who had seen it save his small band of men?

'Wait!' he called. The wizard stopped. 'Stay there!' The general disappeared from the roof. A few moments later, the women from Sheryl's early-morning class ran screaming around the side of the building, followed by Marcus Agrippa at the head of his force. 'Very well,' he said, kneeling before the wizard on the hard stones. 'I yield.' He drew his sword and offered it to the wizard. 'We are no match for your powers.'

'Very sensible, general. I've always admired Roman logic.' The wizard took the sword and invited Marcus Agrippa to follow him. 'If you'd all care to walk this way,' the wizard announced to the men. The demoralized troops followed in a limp crocodile.

The cordon of police moved cautiously forward as the Roman soldiers appeared. 'There'll be no trouble, gentlemen,' the wizard told the anxious policemen. 'So there'll be no need to use force.' The Romans' shields and swords clattered noisily onto the promenade as they divested themselves of their weaponry.

Sheryl went straight up to the first policeman she saw, which, unhappily for him, was DS Beasely. 'I'd like to make a complaint. I've got an agreement that plainly states I have that room from eight o'clock to nine,' Sheryl whined. 'I paid three months in advance. I've even got receipts. This is typical of the Council. It's not the first time this has happened, you know – I've had trouble with them before. You can never trust anybody these days . . .'

Sheryl wittered on, but Beasely was no longer listening. He was looking out to sea, watching the horizon unzip itself like a gigantic fly. But that wasn't all: in the gradually widening gap between sea and sky, there was . . . nothing. An absolute, mind-scrambling blank. The wizard and Marcus Agrippa strolled past.

'Are you listening to me?' asked Sheryl.

'Sorry, love, be back in a second.' Beasely left the fuming fitness instructor and ran after the wizard. 'Excuse me!' he said, grabbing the wizard's arm. 'What is that?' he asked, pointing towards where the horizon should have been.

'That,' said the wizard with a wan smile, 'is the end of the universe, and it's heading this way.'

Beasely reached instinctively for his cigarettes. There was just one that had escaped the ravages of the police-station sprinkler system. He put it to his lips and immediately it began to sprout green tendrils. In a few seconds, Beasely had a young and vigorous tobacco plant in his mouth.

'Fascinating,' said the wizard. 'Reversion. I had no idea this would happen. By the way, sergeant, have you met . . . I'm terribly sorry, I don't know your name.'

'Marcus Agrippa,' replied the defeated Roman general, eyes fixed on the rapidly growing plant in Beasely's mouth.

'Sergeant Beasely, Marcus Agrippa,' said the wizard, introducing them.

'Pleased to meet you,' said Beasely vaguely, as they shook hands.

The short wizard hurried up. 'We'd better get a move on.'

'Ah, there you are,' said the tall one. 'Look,' he said, pointing to Beasely's sprouting cigarette. 'Not only do we have molecular degeneration, we also have reversion to type.'

Beasely's cigarette wasn't the only thing that was listening to its DNA memory. The blue serge uniforms of the police were also feeling the irresistible urge to return to their natural state. The constabulary, already under considerable strain, watched in disbelief as the fabric of their uniforms regressed to the fleece whence it was teased. With their tunics and trousers translated into little woollen vests and shorts, the frenzied officers of the Sussex police force resembled nothing more than a troupe of prancing satyrs.

Beasely was beyond smoking now. He took the tobacco plant out of his mouth and threw it onto the beach. It immediately took root and burst into flower. He wouldn't have been surprised if it had run down the promenade giggling.

'Come on,' said the short one. 'Smeil said it's nearly time.'

'Yes, of course.' The tall one turned to the small, shabby, and deeply, deeply disturbed detective sergeant. 'Would you mind clearing a space for us on that little patch of grass? It's rather important.'

Beasely looked at the tall man. Why not? At that moment, if he'd been asked to pretend to be Hermann Goering and whistle 'I've Got a Lovely Bunch of Coconuts' in waltz time, he would probably have done it.

Chapter 41

Smeil rushed into Bernard and Iris Boggs's room. 'It's time! It's time!' the little man shouted, jumping up and down. 'Time for what?' was on the tip of Iris's tongue, but she didn't want to appear rude. 'We must hurry. Come on, come on!' Smeil stood by the door, urging them out.

'Now, let me see if I've got this straight,' said Bernard, slowly. 'Would I be right in thinking, Mr Smeil, that you are desirous of our company?' He winked at Iris.

Smeil was hopping with impatience. 'Now is not the time for levity, Mr Boggs. You must come immediately, it is of the utmost importance. Destiny hangs in the balance.'

Bernard raised his eyebrows at Iris. 'All right, Mr Smeil, we're coming.'

'It's Smeil – just Smeil!' the little man yelled irritably as he ran off down the corridor.

Outside the castle gates was a largish, roughly circular area, marked out with small white flags.

'Cricket? Who's playing?' asked Bernard. 'Is this a local match?'

'Please take a seat,' Smeil said breathlessly, indicating two chairs by the boundary. A few of the hollow-eyed citizens of Limbo stood listlessly about, indifferent to the scene that was unfolding.

Bernard and Iris sat in the two deckchairs. 'I always forget how comfy a good deckchair is,' said Bernard.

Superintendent Gerrold, flat out in the back of a police van, was stirring. 'What the bloody hell are you doing?' he demanded of

Ivey, who was trying to stuff his rolled-up jumper under the super's head.

'Oh, you're awake, sir,' said the sergeant. 'Are you feeling better? I was a little worried about you.'

'Thank you, but I'm perfectly fine now.' Gerrold hastily buttoned up his tunic and clambered out of the back of the van. Just then, the fragile mechanism that held past separate from future, long stretched beyond its limit, broke down under the strain. Time collapsed, snapping shut like a telescope, and the entire history of the universe was reduced to one single unfolding moment. Superintendent Gerrold watched as a herd of brachiosaurs lumbered along the tree-fern-fringed shore, scattering a mêlée of Regency dandies and Stone Age tribesmen before them.

Ivey, who'd been putting on his jumper in the van, joined the super out on the grass. 'Anything I can get you, sir?' he asked. 'Do you know, for a minute there you lost all your colour – you were as white as a sheet.' Ivey looked into the blank face of his superior officer. 'A bit like you look now, sir. Sir?' Gerrold slid slowly back into Ivey's arms.

With the collapse of time, the destiny of Limbo and Hove seafront, fused together by the shock that had catapulted Gildroy and Norval and the Wizard through the portal, now became apparent – they existed simultaneously in the same space. The police, the Romans and the promenading Edwardians gasped as Worthing disappeared under the massive Southern Range, and they found themselves standing on the broad expanse of the Great Plain. Similarly, the citizens of Limbo were amazed to see a herd of Jurassic monsters and a big, square building appear just outside the castle gates. Marcus Agrippa looked around at the transformation. 'What men are these?' he whispered.

The tall wizard, who had just materialized next to Bernard and Iris, introduced himself. 'Mr and Mrs Boggs, I presume,' he said, shaking hands. 'Please call me Wiz. You've done a really wonderful job – truly wonderful. You must be very proud of him.'

'So glad you could make it,' said the short one, appearing on their other side. 'We're Rex's father,' he added, by way of explanation.

'Hello! Serena Kowalski!'

Rex had told Serena to open the door to no one but him, but it was hard to ignore the incessant hammering. She pulled aside the curtain in the bay window and peeped out. There was a very small man with mouse-grey hair banging on the door and shouting through the letterbox.

'Serena Kowalski!' Smeil looked up and saw the face in the window. 'Ah, Miss Kowalski. You must come with me!'

'That's all anyone ever says to me these days,' Serena shouted back through the glass.

'Please open the door, time is short.'

'How do I know you're not from the cops or the government, or something?'

'I've got a message for you!' said Smeil, 'from Rex. It goes like this: "Klaatu, Barada Nikto – and you're a lousy motorbike mechanic."' Smeil smiled hopefully at her. 'OK?'

'OK,' Serena smiled back, and went to open the door.

Pushing her way through the Late Cretaceous forest that had sprung up just outside the door, Serena followed Smeil down the street. Arriving at Kingsway, they stopped to watch a hansom cab go by. The driver raised his hat as he clip-clopped past. Down on the front there was more weirdness. An ancient ship lay stranded on the shore; a group of hairy men in animal skins, and women with parasols, ran screaming from a pack of dinosaurs; and a cluster of policemen were running around in woolly underclothes.

'I can't go down there,' said Serena. 'I'll be arrested.'

'You're quite safe, I assure you,' said Smeil. 'You have to trust me.' Taking her hand, Smeil led her down to the promenade.

A cordon of Roman soldiers guarded the roughly circular arena that Beasely had cleared to the west of the Centre, or outside the gates of Castle Limbo, depending on how you looked at it. The difference between Roman discipline and that of the modern-day police force was instantly apparent. While the policemen, who laboured only under the threat of dismissal, ran around in futile panic, the Roman army, under pain of death, remained focused and under the control of their officers.

'It's very important nobody interferes – it could upset everything,' the tall wizard was explaining to Marcus Agrippa. But the Roman general wasn't really listening, he was watching the fabric of time unravel. Above the warm, shallow ocean, lush with great clumps of bacteria, flocks of pterosaurs squawked in terror as the Luftwaffe thundered through them on their way to drop death on London.

'Just one more thing to do,' said the wizard, and squeezing through the circle of Roman soldiers, he thrust Marcus Agrippa's short sword into the ground in the centre of the arena. 'There,' he said. 'Now all we have to do is pray.'

Walking in the garden of his dacha outside Moscow, Stalin was brooding over the latest intelligence reports. The German army would be at the gates of Moscow in days. Stalin pondered his next move. Drawing a small silver flask from his inside pocket, he drank. Maybe a capsule of cyanide washed down with a slug of good Russian vodka wouldn't be such a bad way to go. But how could he let history remember him as a coward? At that moment he looked up and saw a halo of shimmering blue light which had appeared above his head. Suddenly a man appeared out of thin air and landed in a heap at his feet.

'Oh dear . . .' Rex groaned. He felt as if he'd been through the no-crease programme of a tumble drier. Looking up he noticed the fat man with the moustache who was staring at him with eyes as big as saucers. He looked vaguely familiar. Joe somebody, wasn't it? Joe . . . Joe . . . oh what was it? Stalin! Stalin? He was Russian wasn't he? What was Rex doing in Russia? But there was no time to think about that now. He had to prevent the monster from doing any more damage. Speaking of which, where was it?

Above them came a whistling, roaring sound, as if something was falling from a great height. Now Rex understood. He looked up at the leader of the Soviet Union. 'I may be wrong, but I seem to remember that you weren't a very nice man. However, any moment now a ton and a half of pure nastiness is going to land on your head, and I've got to save your life. I just want you to know that it's nothing personal.' So saying, Rex shoved the Soviet leader out of the way. The monster landed with a shuddering thud right where Stalin had been standing.

'Oh fuck!' said the nightmare creature. Then, looking over at Rex, 'You again!'

'We really must stop meeting like this,' said Rex. Almost immediately little blue flames began to play up and down the creature's arms. 'Bugger,' it said and, with a sound like the seal being broken on an enormous Kilner jar, both it and Rex disappeared.

Stalin was left shivering in the thin October sunshine. He looked down at the silver flask in his hand, then deliberately poured its contents onto the ground. 'Get a grip, Josef,' he muttered. 'Get a grip.'

Somewhere at once nearby and very far away, Rex and the monster that was the distillation of his distant cousins drifted through the rapidly unravelling weave of destiny. Bound together by ancient blood ties and the power of fate, Rex could feel the dark madness in the monster's soul, and sense its hatred of things in general and him in particular. At the same time, he got the impression that it was searching his mind; probing for weaknesses, trying to fathom Rex's strategy for the contest that must come. But as Rex had no strategy, he wasn't too bothered about this intrusion.

*

In the middle of the patch of grass alongside the King Alfred Centre, something was happening. Little blue flames began to play around the hilt of Marcus Agrippa's embedded sword. A crackle of static electricity filled the air and a shower of sparks fell from the sky. With a sudden *whump*! two figures appeared in the centre of the arena.

A gasp went up from the crowd. In that moment, the classical world, the Regency *beau monde* and the drab twenty-first century were united in horror at the sight before them. A young man faced what could only be the model for all monsters that dwelt in nightmares past and yet to come – a hideous, malformed edifice, with a head the size of a boulder that rested on shoulders as broad as a building.

'Fucking hell!' it boomed, silencing the watching crowd. 'What now?'

Rex recovered slowly. Time travel didn't agree with him. It was a bit like seasickness, only in four dimensions. 'Bleaugh!' he said, sitting on the ground and shaking his head. Coming to himself, he rapidly assessed the situation – big hideous creature (again), Roman army, King Alfred Centre, frolicking satyrs, mountains, dinosaurs, mum and dad – yes, well that all seems . . . Wait a minute, wait a minute. Mum and dad? King Alfred Centre? What was he doing in Hove? Was he in Hove? If so, then why were there mountains where Worthing ought to be? *Well, that's no great loss*, he thought. But if this really was Hove, what was the Roman army doing here? And dinosaurs?

He went through it all again. No, no, he was right the first time. It was all a jumbled mess of times past, and something else – he couldn't quite work out what. Why not times to come? Rex looked at the horizon and the ever-widening gap between sea and sky. Of course, there were no times to come – the future was dissolving. That was one part of the mystery solved; but times past and . . . what else? It was all vaguely familiar but as soon as he concentrated on it, it evaporated.

The big monster's sword sliced a three-foot divot out of the ground, missing Rex's left thigh by a whisker. 'Ooh!' went the crowd. Rex stood up and grasped the hilt of the Roman short sword standing in the middle of the arena. While the monster struggled to pull its sword free from the clinging earth, Rex jabbed the creature in the toe.

'Ow!' went the monster.

'Aah!' went the crowd.

Iris gripped Bernard's hand so tightly she nearly dislocated a finger. 'Steady on, love,' he said.

The monster's sword came free in a shower of earth. 'Wanker!' it rumbled, and again the blade whistled earthwards. Rex sidestepped and the creature's sword plunged harmlessly into the earth once more.

Parry – he's supposed to parry, the monster's thoughts came loud and clear into Rex's consciousness. *I've been looking forward to this fight for several millennia and what do I get – a wimp with a matchstick? Why doesn't he parry? This isn't sword fighting – it's pig-sticking. Fuck, where's he gone?*

Rex had danced round behind the great creature and was poised to plunge his sword into its massive thigh. But he'd figured without the monster's lightning reflexes. This creature might be big but it was no slouch. As Rex leaned on the hilt to drive home the point, the monster spun and parried the thrust with such force, his opponent was sent spinning into the encircling ring of Roman soldiers.

'Oooh!' went the crowd.

'See! That's what you're supposed to do – parry! Parry!'

'I get the picture,' Rex responded feebly, picking himself up.

'I can't watch this!' said Iris. 'Why did you bring me here?' she asked Bernard, her eyes full of hurt and confusion. For once the big man was speechless. After all, this was his fault, wasn't it? Had he brought her here to see the apple of her eye cut down in a brutal, one-sided contest? Bloody flying! If ever they got out of this alive, he swore he'd give up flying for good.

Malcom, watching from the road, was thoroughly enjoying

himself. His only regret was that he didn't have a camcorder. He could have made a bomb flogging this fight to the lads in vice.

What is it about this place? Rex was still thinking. Something about the scenery gnawed at the back of his mind.

The monster's sword came whistling around at head height, and Rex ducked. *Don't think – fight* came the thought.

'Got it! Limbo – this is Limbo! I'm in Limbo! Happy that at least now he knew where he was – relatively speaking – Rex flung himself wholeheartedly into the fray. When a giant shin appeared before him, Rex slashed at it. A great howl went up from the creature and, as it crouched to hug its smarting leg, it dropped something – something glittery about the size of an egg. The Crystal! Rex dived on it and rolled out of the monster's range. Tucking the magnificent gem safely in his pocket, he was about to go for the monster's other shin but, seeing him coming, it turned and swatted him like a fly with the flat of its sword.

Rex flew over the circle of soldiers, and landed in a heap in front of Bernard and Iris. 'Hello mum,' he said. Iris reached tearfully out to him, but as she did so, a monstrous hand descended and picked him up by his belt.

'No!' she screamed as her precious baby was hoisted aloft. 'Somebody do something! Why doesn't somebody *do* something?' She looked around, but all eyes guiltily avoided her gaze. The monster looked impassively at her and deliberately dropped her son from shoulder height onto the hard ground in the centre of the arena. Rex landed with a bone-jarring thud.

'Ooh!' went the crowd.

'Leave him alone!' screamed Iris.

'Do you want some, too, granny?' the monster growled. This was too much for Bernard; he got up angrily, but on realizing that his usually imposing six foot four inches came no higher than the hellish creature's thigh, his resolve deserted him and he sat down again, feeling rather foolish.

Rex – winded, dizzy, sore – needed time to think. Above him there was the flash of steel, and he rolled to avoid the giant blade as it whistled down in a deadly arc. *Like I said – don't think!* came the thought.

Of course – that was his mistake. He wasn't trusting his wizard's brain. Although blessed with a Vauxhall Astra cranium, he had a Rolls-Royce of a mind shoehorned into it. All he had to do was to let go and allow it to take over. But that would take courage and Rex's reserves were rapidly running out. As the monster bent to free its sword from the earth yet again, Rex limped around behind it, buying himself a few seconds. *There's no other way*, he thought. *OK, here we go – what will be, will be.*

Instead of desperately trying to figure out what to do next, he allowed himself to be – just be. In an instant his mind was a limpid pool – clear, lucent and vast. *The Singing Dragons of Phnell – chapter eighteen, end of,* was what, rather confusingly popped into it. What did it mean? *Don't think, don't think!* he told himself as he felt the clawing fingers of panic begin to cloud his vision. *Let go!*

As the monster wrenched its sword free, showering the breathless audience with great clods of earth, Rex dissolved into the Wizard's ageless wisdom. Now he understood everything. He no longer existed – he was simply an observer of his own being. With detached amusement, he felt his grip tighten around the hilt of his sword, and wielding it aloft, heard himself declare, 'I call forth the sleeping Dragon of Phnell!' and with a force far beyond his own, plunged the sword hilt-deep into the earth. The monster looked round, concern registering on its face for the first time.

Rex stood back, a beatific smile on his face. While the universe continued unlacing itself, and the aching void came galloping towards the shore, the dark heavens boiled with foreboding and distant thunder rumbled across the great plain. Then out of the lowering sky a thunderbolt slammed into the half-buried sword, opening up a fissure in the ground.

The Romans, fear overcoming even their long-practised subjugation to authority, fled in disarray as the earth split and buckled beneath them. The gash ran the length of the arena, but it didn't stop there. All eyes were fixed on the running fracture as it headed straight towards the King Alfred Centre. As the ground underneath it opened up and smoke and boiling fire began to spurt from the ever-widening chasm, the building was torn in two and collapsed with a sigh into the steaming fissure.

Then with a terrible rush, in an explosion of steam and molten lava, a huge beast, dreadful to behold, rose out of the centre of the ruins, its wings on fire, the wound in its neck gushing greasy-black blood. Spitting brimstone and snorting scalding clouds of sulphurous vapour, it broke out of its tomb – a gargantuan, malevolent worm. The Great Dragon of Phnell was free!

There was pandemonium, and Malcom grabbed at the ashen-faced Michael Daniels. 'You didn't strike oil, you berk – you struck dragon!'

The monster knew its fate. It looked up at the evil serpent coiling hundreds of feet above its head, and saw its own death. Rex reached into his pocket and took out the Crystal: the oldest thing in the universe, key to time and space. Holding it in his hands, he looked deep into its core. It glowed with a fierce intensity, and Rex seemed to be suffused with light; an electric-blue halo flickered around his being. Then, looking up at the creature, he smiled and threw his arms wide.

Before all terrible events there is a pause, allowing the witnesses to feel guilty for years to come as, in the absolute clarity of hindsight, they replay the scene and see what they could have done to avert the tragedy. This was such a moment.

Bernard and Iris, the wizards, Serena and Detective Sergeant Beasely all held their breath, watching, waiting. The monster smiled back at Rex, and raised its sword in what seemed to be tribute – the chivalrous act of the vanquished in defeat. But this was no hero – it was the distillation of all pettiness and evil thought.

As the dragon swooped, its jaws flickering tongues of fire, the monster roared, 'If I can't have Limbo, then neither will you!' and plunged its great sword into Rex's breast. Then the dragon snapped its terrible jaws shut and the monster roared no more.

Rex crumpled and fell to his knees. 'You cannot kill me,' he said, 'for I am already dead!' The saviour of the universe collapsed in the arena, blood gushing from his mortal wound. The dragon unfurled its leathery wings and, with the monster's twitching legs still protruding from its vast mouth, took off and flew into the nothing that was beginning to gnaw at the beach.

In the shocked silence that followed, wizard reached for wizard's hand, Bernard cursed his cowardliness, and Iris, blinking in disbelief, stared at the pathetic figure of her pride and joy, her only one, her little Rexie, lying on the unforgiving earth, the smile still on his lips.

Romans, Regency dandies, Edwardians, and the Stone Age peoples of the South of England were united in sadness, and approached the awful scene with reverence. As Iris entered the blood-soaked arena, a great pall of doom fell over the land. It was the end of everything. There was no hope – no future. There would soon be no past. It would be as if nothing had ever existed. Iris knelt to caress her fallen boy's head, then, looking into his face, she cried out in alarm. 'But he's old!'

'Let me . . .' began the tall wizard, but his voice was drowned out by the noise of five hundred tons of shingle beach slipping slowly into oblivion.

The Roman army groaned in despair as they saw their ship, upon which they had pinned any hope of ever leaving these terrible shores, slide over the lip of destiny into the great emptiness beyond.

As the terrace outside Mrs Bumble's disappeared into the endless void, a Harley-Davidson, parked on the edge of the promenade, teetered perilously close to the edge of the abyss. 'My bike!' yelled Malcom, dashing towards it.

'Collins, you idiot!' screamed Daniels, as the policeman leapt into the saddle. Searching frantically for the keys, he managed to start it, he even managed to find first gear, but the rear wheel spun uselessly in the void. With the engine screaming at full revs, the detective inspector and his gleaming machine slid slowly backwards into emptiness.

'Serena!' Over the sound of the disappearing beach came a familiar voice. 'Serena, I need you now!'

Iris turned at the sound and watched, unbelieving, as Rex stepped out of a certain beach hut. 'Rex! Rex!' she called, running to him. Rex caught her in his arms. 'Oh, Rex, love, I thought you were dead!'

'It's a long story, mum.'

'What have you done?' yelled the tall wizard.

'No time now!' bawled Rex. 'Serena! Smeil! Where are you?'

Smeil hurried Serena Kowalski through the crowd to stand at Rex's side. 'Boy am I glad to see you,' she smiled. 'What's happening?'

'Trust me,' said Rex, pulling the Crystal out of his pocket. 'Just hold this in your mind: Your future is a blank page; make of it what you will.'

'You can't do that,' said the tall wizard. 'What about The Paradox?'

'I rewrote The Paradox.'

'You rewrote The Paradox?'

'I'm not saving the universe just so we can make the same mistakes all over again, and end up in Serena's nightmare future. So I rewrote The Paradox. Now it goes: "Whatever you expect to happen will happen, unless you want something else badly enough to happen instead." Don't you see? The future has dissolved. This is a golden opportunity to start again; to make tomorrow something to be looked forward to – not to be feared.'

The tall wizard looked at him aghast. 'But The Paradox is a universal law. It cannot be changed.'

'I changed it.'

'And that's the paradox,' said the short one.

'You've got it,' said Rex.

Slowly something dawned on the tall wizard. A great, warm, beautiful sun rose in the sky of his understanding. 'But that means . . .'

'Yes,' said the short wizard, smiling up at him. 'We can create our own future.'

The two wizards joined hands. The short one gazed up at the tall one with moist eyes. The tall wizard looked down and was overwhelmed by affection for his small self. He threw his arms around him and held him tight. 'Are you thinking what I'm thinking?' he said. The short wizard nodded tearfully.

Rex took Serena's hand, at the edge of the abyss. 'Ready?' he asked.

Serena looked into the indescribable nothing in front of her. 'Whatever it is, I'm not sure if I'm up to it,' she said.

'Yes, you are,' said Rex. 'Remember, your future is whatever you want it to be. Live your dream.'

Serena looked into those remarkable morning-blue eyes, then suddenly pulled him to her and kissed him full on the mouth. After a long, lingering moment, she broke away. 'Ready,' she breathed.

'OK,' said Rex, happily bewildered and slightly flushed. 'Here we go.' Taking a deep breath, he spun the Crystal as hard as he could. It floated slowly upwards, showering the scene with rainbows.

As Rex and Serena stepped off the promenade into infinity, there was a sound like all the drains in the world gurgling at once. The Crystal, spinning rapidly, rose, incandescent, into the sky. In a moment, all of creation was engulfed in a painfully bright white light . . .

The Great Hoop, reduced to an ailing crescent, shuddered and shook. Like an invalid, tired of living, it stopped and hung breathless in the forever. Soon it would be no more. Nothing would ever have been – no spark, no light in the endless darkness to illumine the gloom. Then it happened: a vast, cosmic detonation. In an instant, a pure white light – a great, boiling, churning heat – filled the dark recesses of the universe. When the light subsided, there in the endless nothing was a heart-stoppingly beautiful vision – a Great Golden Hoop hanging in the darkness, spinning silently. The impassive river of destiny flowed forever on, forever moving, forever staying the same. And all the while the glittering, laughing strand of fantasy danced and weaved playfully around it.

Beasely waited for his bus outside Hove town hall. Deep in thought, he pondered with a sinking heart his future as DI Collins's sergeant. What the fuck was he going to do? His reverie was interrupted by the sound of a throbbing diesel engine and the swish of opening doors. As he raised his foot to step onto the platform, he felt, rather than heard, a low rumbling, as if somewhere deep underground a vast creature was grinding its teeth.

There was a blinding flash of light, and for a split second he could have sworn he was falling. His ears were full of a sound like all the drains in the world gurgling at once, and he was tumbling through a whirlpool of images – monsters, dinosaurs, huge dragons . . . Coming to himself, he gazed up at the bus driver. 'What was that?'

'What was what?'

Beasely looked around. The sun still shone, cars still moved along the street, people went unconcerned about their business. Everywhere he saw the world carry on as normal. Yet somehow, deep inside, he seemed to know that life, especially his own life, had changed for ever, and probably for the better.

'I can't wait here all day,' the bus-driver scowled.

'Yes, yes, sorry, I thought . . . never mind. St James's Street, please.' Detective Inspector Beasely had to get back to HQ. Today, the Sussex Chief Constable, Sir Frank Gerrold, was presenting him with an award for the success of his brainchild – Operation Status Quo. He'd put a lot of the drug barons supplying the Brighton scene behind bars. Of course, the war against drugs was never-ending, but he'd won a vital battle.

Marcus Agrippa, about to embark on his mission to conquer Albion, watched as his servant slipped on the gangplank and dropped his shaving kit into the murky waters of the harbour. The servant, trembling with fear, fell to his knees before his master and begged forgiveness. But to pardon this slave would only show weakness in front of his men. Pulling out his dagger, Marcus Agrippa grabbed the man's hair and held the blade to his throat. But as he was about to sever the man's carotid artery, a cloud passed across the sun. It was an omen. Without his shaving kit he could not shave – and going into battle with a stubbly chin was against all his principles. The gods were trying to tell him something, warning him against this risky enterprise.

Marcus Agrippa smiled down at his quivering servant. 'You are a messenger from the gods,' he said to him. 'Go in peace, for you have saved my life.' The expedition was called off. Soon after, Marcus Vipsanius Agrippa would find fame at the battle of Actium, and later see his friend Octavian become Emperor Augustus.

It would be almost another hundred years before Britain would come under Roman control.

Councillor Daniels did manage to buy the King Alfred Centre for a song, but after BP had made an exploratory survey of the area and found nothing, he was left with a rotting hulk on his hands which he couldn't sell on and refused to refurbish. Eventually the Council repossessed the building and the councillor lost his seat and the presidency of the Hove Lawns Bowls Association at a stroke. Over the next ten years he sunk most of his fortune into a detailed and desperate geological exploration of the south coast, buying several mining companies in the process. He found nothing out of the ordinary. Now he spends his days polishing his classic Rover and dreaming about what might have been.

The King Alfred Centre, revamped with the help of Lottery funding, is now a modern leisure complex bristling with bars and restaurants, with an annual turnover of two million.

*

On a small island somewhere in the limpid Pacific, World Government Senator Serena Kowalski – author of several 'green' bills which had prevented huge tracts of the Earth's surface disappearing under billions of tons of concrete, and most notably, architect of the garbage non-proliferation treaty, signed by all nations in 2030 – opened her eyes and looked out over the crystal-clear waters of the sea lapping gently against the warm, white-sand beach. The smell of barbecued fish told her lunch would soon be ready. Maybe she'd have a dip before she ate. Or maybe she'd play frisbee with her kids. Or maybe she'd just roll over and get her face in the sun. Whatever, it was the weekend – she had nothing to do and plenty of time to do it in.

She smiled at the sound of her children laughing and talking excitedly as they laid the table in the cool shade of a palm tree. Life was good. Things hadn't turned out quite how she'd dreamt. No – they were much, much better.

On flight BA 2063 to Lanzarote, the stewardess, checking that all seatbelts were fastened for landing, was just passing the sweet couple in seats nos 13A and B when time seemed to slow down. There was a roaring, a gurgling in her ears; blue flames flickered around the man's bald head, and beneath her feet she could have sworn she could see the bottle-green expanse of the Atlantic. Then, all of a sudden, everything returned to normal. Or did it?

'Could I give you this?' The man in seat 13B handed her a pillow. 'I don't think we need it any more.' Now he had a full head of hair – glossy and thick – and a thin, immaculately trimmed beard. And the woman was beautiful – young, with fine pale skin and a mane of curly black locks.

'But, surely . . .?' the stewardess began, then stopped, puzzled. What was it? She tried to hold the thought, but it was like a dream, a mist that evaporated the moment she tried to catch it.

'Yes?' The man smiled up at her with his extraordinary eyes –

blue like the morning sky, as deep and as placid as a mountain lake, with here and there a fleck of white, like swans taking flight.

The stewardess shook her head and took the pillow. 'Nothing, I . . . I'll just stow this for you,' she said, opening the overhead locker.

The Wizard took the Queen's hand and placed it to his lips. 'I hope you like birds,' he said. 'I believe where we're going has a fine nature reserve.'

The Queen looked up at him, her eyes full of wonder. 'My love,' she said, and kissed him – oh how he'd missed the tender caress of those lips. 'I thought I'd never see you again.'

'I was with you always – in the next room; behind the veil.'

'What of our son?' she said.

'A fine boy. Our dreams are safe in his hands.'

'He must be a great, great wizard.'

'He takes after his father,' the Wizard smiled proudly.

'And us? Can we really be together now?'

'Not together, but one – now and for ever.' The Wizard looked into the Queen's soft brown eyes and great wet tears of joy ran down his cheeks.

The transformation was almost unbelievable. Sad, hopeless, despairing Limbo had overnight become a land of smiles and laughter. Many wounds had been healed, but there was no way of turning back the clock on the Great Terror. Some things, some really terrible things have to stand as lessons so that future generations might hopefully learn tolerance and understanding from the mistakes of the past. But with King Bernard and Queen Iris on the throne, this was the dawn of a new era of hope and compassion.

The castle, repaired with what remained of the King Alfred Centre, now boasted a swimming pool and indoor bowls arena, and fine dining in the banqueting hall on the third floor, open to all. Well, it was usually on the third floor. Actually it was anywhere Bernard and Iris wanted it to be. The castle and the land so loved them that they were desperate to please. When Iris took her afternoon nap, not only did the castle remove the windows in her room, the sky put blinds on the sun. They were the only clouds in the sky of the citizens of Limbo.

Smeil, too, had never been happier. Given the job of running the mezzanine café-bookshop, he bustled about taking orders, making coffees and generally feeling immensely pleased with life.

As for Malcom, he didn't fit into anybody's future. He didn't really fit into anybody's past either; and those whose lives he had impinged on wished he hadn't. He just didn't belong. There was only one place for him now. Always travelling, never arriving, he rode his bike around and around the Great Hoop of Destiny, like a fairground rider on the Wall of Death.

If you listen closely on a still night, you may just be able to hear, over the distant sound of a large V twin, someone shouting, 'Bloody socks!'

The man opening the door to Boggs's Newsagent's, which always smelt of baking, could have no idea that he was entering anything other than a small corner shop in Lancing. But this was no ordinary shop. It had a secret – a secret so secret that only one man knew about it. As the bell over the door tinkled, it summoned Rex Boggs, Wizard to the court of Limbo. 'Yes?' said the Wizard, appearing through the bead curtain behind the counter. 'How can I help you?'

Having supplied the customer with the latest copy of *Double Glazing Professional's Gazette,* and 50 grams of pear drops, Rex walked back through the curtain and straight into the small, inaccessible room somewhere among the towers and turrets of Castle Limbo. The shop was a link with his past that Rex couldn't quite let go. He knew he was only being sentimental, and every day promised himself that soon, very soon, he would get rid of it. But in his heart of hearts he knew he never would.

Placing the Crystal back on the shelf, Rex looked down at the book that lay open on the great circular table, the book that was at last nearing completion. Through the half-open window came the smell of new-mown grass and the sound of children laughing. It was ironic that the happy, carefree life going on outside was all thanks to a book that had yet to be finished.

'Hah!' he chuckled to himself.

This time there would be no mistakes, no Great Terrors. This was not an adventure story, it was a book of dreams – a fairy tale ending to a catalogue of horrors. Soon Rex would summon his loyal servant Smeil to travel back in time and place the book in his own hands in the tunnel in the cliffs above the Salient Sea.

Rex wasn't Prince Nostrum, no, but he had no desire to be a hero. Besides, it was all very well for fictional characters to belt around all over time and space. The reality, as Rex had discovered, was rather sick-making. True, he still had one final leap to make – to change places with his young self in the arena on Hove Lawns and intercept that mortal blow from the monster. But wizards were long-lived, and it would be a good few years yet before he had to face that challenge. It is given to few people to know the exact time and manner of their death, and he took comfort from the fact that his would be whenever he wanted it to be. One day when he was old, and his powers were running out, he would step through the portal for the last time. Besides, he wasn't afraid of death. In that glorious moment in the arena, standing before the monster, the veil of illusion had been whipped aside and he had seen everything. What was death but the opening of a door?

With Limbo flourishing under Bernard and Iris, Rex saw no reason to assert his right to the throne. Ruling was a people thing, and Rex . . . well, Rex was more at home among his books. He still saw his parents every day; in fact it would soon be time for him to go and join King Bernard and Queen Iris for lunch in the Great Banqueting Hall, now known affectionately to all as 'Boggs's Brasserie'. They did a very good linguine ala vongole of which Rex was particularly fond.

Limbo

Now there was only one thing left to do. Picking up his pen and wiping excess ink from the nib on the lip of the inkwell, with a flourish he wrote the closing line of his great work, *Limbo – The Final Chapter*:

'Well, thank goodness that's over . . . and now for lunch.'